For my late parents

Jack and Margaret

&

Bob and Maureen

How to Keep Well in Wartime

'Dead living' means *asleep*, but can also be translated as *alone*. The Edaben tell me that the end of life can happen long before a person stops breathing.

Vanessa Barton,
Religion and Ritual in the Edaben of the Lowlands

Tolstoy was wrong. Every family is a unique mixture of joy and misery, happy and unhappy in its own way. Neither aspect can exist without the other.

Sir Richard Vine,
The Sociology of the Family

Ghosts. 1993. Emily's story

The rasp of his breathing tube fills the room. A relentless sound, like tide-strewn gravel, scraping out and in. It's all that matters. Thin green blankets reveal the outline of his bones, and his skin is paper pale against them. Does he look like Dad? Like me? A mask screens most of his face and I wonder how the doctor really knows that he can't hear us. Even if he wanted to move, the equipment would weigh him down.

'He's a fighter,' says the paramedic, pressing my arm lightly as she leaves.

I hope she's right, because I need him to explain. When I try to imagine the accident, all I can see is Carrie. Did he step right out without checking, like her? Did the driver swerve? A shock of red, then a screech of brakes, a pause, the soft sickening thud as his body slammed the bonnet.

My great-grandfather is a stranger, run through with tubing, pinned to a narrow bed. They've taken his bloodied pyjamas and dressed him in a backless gown. Half tucked under the bed are old-fashioned slippers with real carpet uppers and thick rubber soles, neatly paired as though he could just reach over, slip his feet inside and walk away.

This ward hasn't changed, though it's years since I said goodbye to Carrie here. Cardboard dishes on lockers. Low humming machines. The cloying scent of disinfectant and the smell of what it tries to mask. Clear tubes taped across face and hands; bruises around the ports where they attach. I remember the blanket being pulled up over her head and the sharp metal taste of blood as I bit my lips silent.

Condensation builds on the window, blurring lights from the car-park. We need some privacy. As I reach to pull down the blinds I start at my ghostly reflection, knocking over a full jug of water with an ill-fitting lid. It clatters to the floor, and I scrabble for paper towels. Nurse flies in and glares at the gathering puddle.

'You should go home, dear.' She bustles about, saving her equipment with rolls of absorbent material. With a look of disapproval, she drops the sopping mess into a yellow bin. 'You've been here hours. If his condition changes, we can contact you again. Lucky we could reach you.'

Lucky? Certainly not for him, yet this is how we found each other. At least we will have, if he wakes. All those years I spent wishing for family and suddenly here's my great-grandfather. Not just a relative but an ancestor, filled with possibility, secretly living near our family home. Who else might there be? According to the doctor he lived alone. It's unbearably sad.

'There must be something I can do?'

She finishes cleaning, tests a couple of switches, takes his observations in her brisk, professional manner. I sit on the oversized chair while she perches against the bed rail and puts a hand on my arm. Nurse Evans—I notice the badge—is wearing a ring on a chain around her neck. Hygiene compliance, perhaps, preventing a wedding ring's contamination. She has tired eyes, hair wired through with grey strands.

'I'll let you know if his condition changes.'

She doesn't need anyone else to worry about and I'm in the way. 'It's easier to get me on this number.' I pull out a couple of thick, cream-coloured business cards, a gift from the printers used by my publishing company. Usually there's a thrill of pleasure in my title, *Emily Green, Commissioning Editor, Social Sciences and Anthropology*, but it's unimportant tonight. Nurse Evans' face is impassive as she scans the cards and slips them into the pocket of her blue cotton top.

The tube is closed, and it would cost a fortune to get back to the flat at this time of night. Ian will understand why I give the cabbie my parents' address instead, it's only five minutes away. There's no point in phoning so late to tell him because he'll be fast asleep, ready for another early start.

The empty house is different than when I was here this afternoon, silent and creepy, and the porch light's sudden glare makes me fumble with the key. Anna hated that light. When she tried to sneak home after curfew it caught her every time. She still tried. She was always braver than me. Our parents' rules weren't something she worried about; I was never prepared to upset them. As I open the door, I half expect Dad to be sitting in his chair by the TV. All is dark and quiet.

They've already decamped to their villa, like they do every winter. They've gone for longer this year, experimenting with a permanent retirement move. Every few days they're asking me to find something they can't live without and ship it to them. Steak knives it was this time, as if you couldn't buy them in Spain. But if they hadn't sent me here, I wouldn't have answered the phone this afternoon, would never have known I had an elderly relative at all. What if Dad had been here instead? Would he have told anyone? Something's being hidden.

The phone's shrill bell had startled me, catching me with my hands in a box of old photographs, looking at Carrie and wondering what she would look like now, momentarily unsure where I was. I thought it must be one of their friends, not realising they'd left. But it was Queen Mary's hospital. 'I

11

think you'd better call your father, let him know what's happened. If the details we found are correct he's the next of kin, his grandson.' I'd mumbled thanks, asked for details. 'His name is Jim,' said the voice. 'Tell your father it's Jim.'

It's late, too late to check the time, and I need a drink. I reach up to the small pot on top of the dresser to see if the key to the cupboard is still kept inside. It falls into my hand. I find dark rum, pour a glass and drink it slowly, soothed by its sweet rough taste. Tomorrow I'll get some bread and milk, a few staples, so I can stay near to the hospital.

The steak knives. I'll get them while I'm here. One by one I open the sideboard drawers until I spot the box, floppy with age, the knives polished and replaced in their half-moons of elastic. I should probably repack them, but it would upset Mum and Dad if they weren't exactly the same. They never like anything to be out of routine. Anna, always resentful, says it's all that keeps them alive. When they first went to Spain, I'd imagined them living a colourful life at last, learning a language, eating exotic foods. But they chose a gated ex-pat community, recreated the kitchen of their London townhouse and started shipping things out as they spent more time there, retreating further into familiar comfort as they grow old. I see worrying elements of fastidiousness in Ian too: the way he folds his napkin, the teacups saved for 'best', his drawer of paired, rolled socks. He also dislikes surprise. I'll have to find the right way to tell him this news.

I pad around, trying one chair after another in the beige expanse of the lounge. I might as well have stayed at the hospital. There's nothing to read, no food, nothing to distract me. A tidy, neutral house, even when me and Anna lived here. We never wanted friends over, always finding an excuse because we didn't want our parents to come home from work and serve us silent dinners then sit upstairs to avoid us. Were they always the same, before Carrie, or did losing her make them that way? It's hard to remember much of before because my twin was my entire world. Her absence is a wound, made fresh tonight, and worsened by the continual pretence that it's healed: the silence of my parents, the distance of Anna and the ignorance of those I meet now, for whom Carrie never existed at all.

We were eleven when she died, the week before secondary school. Everyone said she was the dominant twin, the stronger one; the leader. All I knew was that I was safe when she was there. I wasn't worried about the new school, even though we'd been told we'd have separate classrooms. We would feel each other, Carrie said, and I believed her because it was sometimes hard to tell where she stopped and I started, despite how different we looked. People often said we didn't look like twins, but we felt it.

We'd been out to buy school shoes with Mum and Anna. Carrie chose ours, neat black t-bars with silver buckles and tip-tap heels, so shiny we could see our faces in them. Carrie loved those shoes, insisted we kept them on, so Mum put our old ones in a bag, to keep for playing out, and all the way home we danced and tip-tapped, oblivious to anything except our feet. We didn't see the car as it pulled out to overtake the parked bus while we crossed. It hit us both, though Carrie, being first, took the impact. I remember the colour red, a thud, a roaring sound. A tearing shock that left a hole the size of the moon. No-one ever answered my questions. And all the things I wanted to say, I just learned to keep them to myself.

Heartsongs. 1915. Jim's story

A dusty white veil covered the table and chairbacks and for a moment Jim thought they'd been bombed. Zeppelins had reached as far as Yarmouth already and Ma said they'd be next in line. A neat row of pies on the windowsill reminded him it was Saturday, baking day. Ma wiped her hands with a cloth and carefully brushed the spilled flour back into its tin. Wastefulness loses wars: Pa had said that often enough. Jim remembered the argument the pair of them had the day before he joined the Navy, so furious she'd used a precious egg to glaze the pastry that he'd refused to eat the pie at all, sitting in rod-backed righteousness in front of his empty plate while the rest of them finished their meal. Jim eased himself into a chair and pulled off his boots.

'Want me to get you a soak?'

'Don't fuss, Ma.' When would she ever leave him alone? He might be the youngest, but he was still eighteen. Man of the house now that Charlie had a family of his own.

'I'm allowed to look after you.'

'I've only done a half day.'

'I'll make you some tea then, nice and strong, might be able to find a bit of sugar for it too.'

Jim nodded. With Pa and Charlie gone they were alone together in the house, and her love would suffocate him if he let it. Last night he caught her standing in the doorway of the bedroom he no longer shared, watching him while she thought he slept.

'Charlie here yet?'

'He went out again this morning. It was calm as a millpond earlier, at last, thank goodness.'

'I could help him. He can't manage Pa's boat with just Tom.'

'Your cousin's a good lad.'

Jim bit his lip and stood up to carry his boots to the back door for an airing. Surely Charlie needed help. Tom was fourteen! Nice enough boy, but weak, and so quiet he must be no company at sea. He stood by the back door, watching for sight of the *Annie-May*. Though the waves were calm and pale it was frightening how quickly they could turn, slamming relentlessly into the shingled walls and taking the cliff's edge inch by inch. Waiting for a chance to turn against the boats. Every family in Winterton had lost men to the water; fathers, sons, his own uncle as he tried to help another boat in trouble in the great storm tide. Ma could barely bring herself to look when the tides were rough. Why couldn't he help Charlie with Pa gone? It drove him mad that she wouldn't even discuss it. Why insist he worked Kearsy's farm for less money and longer hours? He was sick of being treated like a child. In high summer she walked to his cows with jars of her lemonade and sat with him while he drank it. When the snow brought chilblains she lined his socks with cotton pads and soaked them off with spirits, wrapping his feet in a soft shawl. What kind of love was that? He was grown now, he was always going to grow; he shouldn't have to feel guilty that it broke her heart.

He sighed and walked back into the kitchen. Ma was leaning heavily against the stove, looking older and more careworn. A thick line of flour streaked her cheek and, as he leaned forward to brush it away, she caught hold of his hand and kissed it, standing for a few moments with it pressed to her face.

'You all right, Ma?'

'What would I have to worry about?'

'I don't know, you just looked… I wondered if you were missing Pa, or something.'

'Don't be silly. Can't go thinking of ourselves when there's a war on. Navy needs him more than we do.'

Jim nodded, unconvinced.

'I just wanted to have all this done before you got home, that's all. You're back early today.'

'Kearsey sent us home, don't know why.'

Annie frowned. 'Don't want anyone accusing you of getting favourite treatment, that won't look well.'

'Not just me, Ma, everyone, I think he was taking his missus out in that new car of his. What would it matter anyway?' Ma worried too much about what people might think but he knew exactly what she meant: Lilly.

The only daughter of Sam Bramwell, the head of Kearsey's dairy, Lilly was socially elevated enough to consider farm workers beneath her station and Jim was still confused by their relationship. They met a few years earlier, when that summer's relentless heat threatened the crops and every available pair of hands was conscripted into bringing in the hay. Lilly had been stationed with Jim. Unused to hard work, she'd complained bitterly about the rough chaff on her sore hands and Jim, barely fifteen years old, had brought her Ma's lanolin poultice, pressing it into her palms with his own, catching her fancy with the same kindness he showed everyone. She chose him then and he was still struggling to work out what it meant.

'Doesn't take long to get the tongues wagging round here. I don't know what we'd do if you didn't have that job.'

Jim was about to answer that he could fish with his brother, like he wanted, but he bit his tongue.

'Just a few hours off, don't fuss.'

'I'm not fussing,' said Ma in the calm, deliberate voice that meant she wanted to talk. She poured more tea into blue and white striped cups and set a plate of scones on the table. It was hard to eat when he had the feeling that something was coming. Jim waited.

'I cleaned your bedroom today,' she paused, tucking a stray hair behind her ear. 'I didn't mean to pry but I was sweeping under the bed and I knocked over that old tin. Why do you have that photograph?'

Jim felt his cheeks burn, angry with himself for chasing dreams and with Ma, who couldn't leave him alone. How many men his age had to put up with that? People poking and prying into their lives? She cleaned his room a bit too often.

'What photograph? It's full of photographs.'

'You know the one I mean. Where'd you get it?'

She levelled her gaze at him and he shrugged. What did she want him to say?

'She's Bert's sweetheart, Jim.'

'I know.'

'They'll be getting married soon.'

'They haven't said.'

'You know it.'

'I don't know that it'll be soon. Bert's only a year into his apprenticeship.'

Nothing got past Ma. She stood by that kitchen window half the day, staring out at everything that happened in the fields, every walker on the coastal road. Strips of deep blue paint peeled from its wooden frame and he knew she was still waiting for him to fix the left shutter, but the panes sparkled from their weekly clean with lemon juice and newspaper. They were clean enough to show the bubbles in the corners of the glass. Yesterday she'd emptied the dregs and he was surprised how much it annoyed her that she couldn't get another. Upset over a bottle of lemon juice, when her husband, his pa, was fighting for his life somewhere at sea.

Were they ever close? They didn't act like Lilly's parents, holding hands and patting each other in public, gossiping in the kitchen. Ma talked mostly to her sons; Pa rarely talked of anything. Every Friday Pa took coins from the stone jar in the pantry and slipped them into his pocket before walking along the cliff road to The Jolly Sailor. It was hard not to feel relief when the door closed behind him. There was never much in the jar to take because most of the profit Ma earned from her eggs and the vegetable patches was hidden under Jim's bed, a secret that skulked between them. When Pa volunteered for naval service it seemed, in the feel of his handshake, that he'd known all along. He took the shilling with two of his friends and left the same day, handing over the boat to Charlie and walking to the station with barely a backward glance. It felt empty without another man in the house, but Ma didn't seem to miss him. She'd turned over all the photographs: 'We can do without worrying he'll die at sea.' It was hard for Jim to shake the feeling that, if Pa didn't return, the pair of them might be to blame.

Settling down. 1993. Emily's story

'What are you having?' Ian asks, eyes fixed on the menu. He's alternating gulps of his whiskey sour with handfuls of salted nuts. 'I'm starving.'

'You'll spoil your appetite.' I move the bowl away and he gestures for the waitress.

'Another of those. And some olives. Do you want anything, Em?'

I lift my glass to show him that it's still almost full and shake my head.

'Looks like you had a better day than me. Six weeks we've been working on the new programme and now Keith says the specifications were 'misinterpreted', which roughly translates as he's briefed us wrongly but he's not prepared to admit it.'

He looks like a sulky child in his oversized jacket. All those late office nights have made him thinner, and his hair has grown in soft curls.

'How's things? New series going well? Got those final manuscripts in?'

'I'm beginning to wonder whether we shouldn't have used more experienced authors and...'

'I warned you about that,' he cuts in. 'Working with hippies.'

'Anthropologists. They're always a bit erratic with deadlines. Most of them live miles away from anywhere they could even post a manuscript.'

'Hippies. How's... the office?'

I've been there seven years. He doesn't know the name of anyone I work with.

'I haven't really been in much this week.'

Ian glances up. 'You feeling OK?'

I sip my wine. I probably look awful; definitely tired. I'm getting too old to skip sleep. The night in A&E and the shock of sudden family have kept me up for days. Why didn't I know about Jim? Dad swore he didn't know about him either, but it was hard to gauge his reaction on the phone and I don't know what to believe. I've been drawn to Jim's bedside several times since, sitting quietly with the ghosts he's woken.

'I'm fine, don't worry.' He hasn't even asked how Jim is doing.

'How long are you planning to stay at the 'rents place?'

'Not sure. It's easier to be closer to the hospital, for now. There hasn't been much change, but I want to be there when he wakes up.'

'He's a *really* old man. He's probably not going to wake up. What's the doctor said?'

'I only had about ten minutes with her. I think she was trying to prepare us for the worst. It's not as easy as that though. He's family.' And you should know how important that is to me.

'It's hardly like he's close family.' Ian's voice becomes loud and a couple of the waiting staff glance over in our direction, anxious about the ambience. He drains his glass and stares at the menu again, shaking his curls.

'You haven't even visited him yet.'

'Why would *I* go to see him?' He wears an exaggerated expression of disbelief. 'He wouldn't even know I was there.'

But I would know. I'd know you wanted to share this with me, I'd feel safer with you there in the hospital dusk.

'When he wakes up, I'd like you to come and see him.'

'Sure, if he wakes up.' He nods. 'We should order. I'm having the crab, then the pork belly, how about you?'

The menu is scrolled around a rolling pin, making it hard to read. 'The risotto, I'm not that hungry. And I'm going into the office next week, whatever happens, I've got a meeting with Sir Richard on Tuesday.' That isn't exactly true, I'm trying to set one up though and Ian likes Sir Richard Vine because he has a title and once had a short TV series on the two years he spent living with a Brazilian rainforest tribe at the time when a major Hollywood film on the subject meant knowing about Brazilian rainforest tribes was fashionable.

'I saw Sarah today, out with the baby, it must be three months now. Should try to get out with Andy, wet its head and all that.'

All of Ian's friends are settling down. It makes me nervous. It's easier to go out in a bigger group with people you don't know all that well, and the prospect of visiting rotas, in homes with children, is daunting.

'You should.'

Ian stops rolling his fork around the table and looks straight at me. His amber eyes are faintly flecked with red. 'Did you ask them?'

'Ask them what? You look tired.'

'About the date. I thought you wanted her as your... I don't know what you call them. Bridesmaid? Sounds wrong.'

'I was waiting until I could see her.' I don't want to tell him it slipped my mind. Proposing was such a big thing for him; carried out in his usual perfect style, under a sky of stars at Greenwich Observatory. After all these years together, I didn't even consider saying no, but I think I was happier as we were.

'You're not having second thoughts?'

'Don't be silly. What have I done now?'

'Nothing, that's the point. We haven't even found

anywhere for the reception. These places get booked up way in advance.' He reaches down and pulls a plastic wallet from his bag, opens it and hands me a neat wad of paper.

'It looks complicated.' I leaf through stapled pages. The thought of this many extra things to do is overwhelming. More than anything I'd like to talk about Jim.

'It's not really. My PA got it from some wedding planner. It's the one she used for hers.'

Who's his PA? I can't picture her; they seem to get moved around the company frequently. Maybe they don't like working for him; he's quite a perfectionist. The last one I met was disconcertingly similar to me, tallish and slim with shoulder-length light-brown hair, the sort of skin that always looks slightly tanned. When I mentioned it, Ian laughed, reminding me that she was barely out of college as though I was trying to flatter myself.

'Great. It looks great.'

'You might find a little more enthusiasm, Em.'

'I will, but it's just empty lines. When we start choosing everything it'll seem real.'

'It's going to be a big event, this will make sure nothing goes wrong. You've been working with hippies too long.'

Why does he keep saying that? It's not funny. Rather my eccentric colleagues than the city boys he works with.

'How big?'

'What?'

'A big event. How big?'

'I've got about a hundred and fifty on the list so, I don't know, maybe a couple of hundred in total?'

Most of the places I'd thought of wouldn't cope with such a crowd. I nod in a manner I hope looks thoughtful and concentrate on spreading butter onto rock hard bread.

There'll be time to talk about things properly before we make any decisions. Ian pours a glass of wine. I hold it up a little too long as I consider his face, handsomely bathed in its rosy light, and imagine how marriage will change us.

Two medals. 1915. Jim's story

Grace tossed her chestnut hair and Jim tried hard not to stare at the elegant line of her neck.

'Don't be boring, Bertie! Tell them about Kearsey's car.' Her fingertips brushed his arm, burning his skin. 'You're going to love this.'

Jim stole a glance at Ma, expecting disapproval, but she was playing with Charlie's daughter, Ruby, by the wall.

'Not much to tell.' Bert smoothed his mop of hair with oil-stained fingers, pulling a frown that momentarily darkened his handsome face. 'He got stuck. Me and the wax boy couldn't pull him out between us.'

Peals of laughter broke the gentle summer hum and Bert leaned in with a serious expression. He offered a cigarette that Jim refused, embarrassed, conscious that smoking was the first thing they hadn't done together since they were children.

'He wasn't even in for his car, Jim. Said he was looking for a machine to pull ploughs. Couldn't afford it, but you can tell he wants one badly, he was in with Butler for hours talking about them. You want to watch that. If he gets his machines what happens to you lot? When are you going to let me teach you to drive?'

Jim smiled at Bert's constant prophesies. At that moment, stretched lazily in late afternoon, with Grace close enough for him to smell the sun on her skin, nothing seemed quite so irrelevant as the future.

Lilly stood up slowly and brushed the dry grass from her dress, lips pursed. 'I can't sit here while you talk about Father's employer like that, James. He's never been anything but good to you. Perhaps you could cycle me home. If it's not too much trouble?'

'Stay, sit down… ignore Bert,' Jim soothed. 'He's spending too much time in the bright lights of the big town, it's gone to his head.' He cuffed his friend gently on the shoulder and Bert rolled his eyes.

'You want to think a bit more about bright lights and a little less about what's not happening in Winterton. The world is ours! And it's bigger than these flat fields,' Bert exclaimed.

'James! I said I would like to go now. I'm tired in this heat; I don't know how you can all sit out in it,' Lilly rubbed her thin forearm as if she was burned, though she never seemed to catch the sun. She was light as a cloud with blue-white skin and huge blue eyes. Jim nodded and rose to attention.

'I'll see you all at the dance next Saturday. Grace, I'll probably wear my blue, with the rose print, I was rather hoping you would not wear *your* rose dress, maybe your green? It suits you so well.' Lilly beamed as though it was settled, ignoring Grace's muttered, 'Yes, m'lady.' Pulling on her gloves, she waited as Jim went to fetch her bicycle and wheel it back to her, dusting down its seat before going off to find his own.

The Bramwells were good people, well meaning. It wouldn't be so bad to have them as in-laws and Lilly was sure to be happier once they were married. By the time they'd stopped bringing out tea and let him leave it had grown dark. A clear web of stars stretched down over the sea and it was too beautiful to hurry home.

Jim slowed and wheeled around the little church by the sea wall, half tempted to visit his painting: an image of the

Virgin, rendered in deep jewel tones. During Father Hubert's sermons he followed the line and colour of her skin, the blue folds of her dress, the light in her eyes as she gazed at the bundle in her arms. Grace's similarity to the woman in the painting made his head swim. When Bert first introduced them at the Cromer Dances he'd had to go straight outside to pull himself together in the cold salt air. Clearly Grace was too good for him. In a funny way that made things easier to bear, though it hurt sometimes to see her with Bert; those obvious looks they shared. If only they'd hurry up and marry so he could stop worrying they might be found out. She'd be ruined.

He jumped off his bike. Should he go inside? Not now. If Father Hubert was there, he'd only face a telling off for his absence all these weeks. He'd go to the service on Sunday instead. Ma would be pleased and, right now, it seemed important for everyone to keep their side of the bargain, to make sure He answered their prayers when they needed Him. People tried not to talk about it much, but it was clear that prayers would be needed before long.

He leaned over the railings by the slipway and the sharp salt sprayed his cheeks. Shards of light sparked the horizon. What must the dark ocean feel like? He imagined the solitude and the raw clean air every time his boat, the *Annie-May*, lurched from the harbour. Pa would be out there, somewhere, but it was hard to picture him on a ship full of other men.

A dark human-looking shape at the edge of the shoreline caught his eye and, fighting the fear of what he might find, Jim leaned his bike against the handrail at the top of the steps and walked onto the beach. Drawing closer he saw it was a dead seal, washed up on the beach alone; a huge grey bull lying on a ring of rust-coloured sand, shards of metal embedded in its side.

Jim crouched beside it, flinching at the wet film on its skin. Pieces of boat hull lay scattered around. Were there other bodies too? Men thrown from the sides of the wrecked ship as it blew? Nothing lay nearby. Cold sweat ran along his spine, and he shivered in the evening chill. This was what war would look like. It was how he'd imagined it, silent and terrible, slick with blood. He'd have to stop Ma walking this way in the morning, she'd call it a sign and maybe she'd be right. The thought made him want to run to his bike, cycle home as fast as he could, bolt the gate behind him. But he made himself stare; he owed it that. Poor creature. It must be the biggest he'd ever seen, so awkward and out of place on land; like Pa and Charlie it was happiest in water. Had it lived a full life, raised families, travelled oceans? It was too heavy to move. He pulled up the largest piece of boat and placed it over the seal's head as some protection from the claws of seabirds. Life should be marked, especially life given in honour. Jim walked to the line of stones that ringed the shore, once, twice, three times. By the time he'd finished a neat round pile of pebbles stood next to the body, topped with a makeshift cross of driftwood sticks.

From Ma's favourite position at the kitchen window, it was easy to spot the man striding down the cliff path. Despite the loose, uneven surface he walked stiffly upright. Jim took in his gold-edged hat, the neatly braided baton folded under one arm, boots shining like mirrors. No good news could come from a visitor dressed like that. Jim called to his niece, who was cutting biscuits on the kitchen table.

'Want to go and play outside, Ruby? Tell Granny there's a visitor.'

'Not done.' She carried on, pressing out each circle with the rim of a tea-cup before placing it on the baking tray, careful to not let it touch the others.

'Almost finished?'

Another shake of the head as Ruby pushed a stray currant into the mixture.

'Me and Granny need to talk to someone who's coming to visit, it might be a bit boring for you, Ruby.'

'Auntie Violet?'

'Someone who works with Grampy, on the ships.' Jim could hear the man's footsteps now, heavy boots crunching on shingles.

'Grampy's home?' Ruby stretched out her arms, asking to be lifted to the window. Jim brushed the flour from her cheek, pulled her loose curls back into their ribbon.

'He'll be home soon. Why don't you feed the chickens while I get Granny?' Once Ruby was coaxed outside, she'd forget about everything else and stay there until she got hungry, or the light faded, whichever came first.

'Not ready yet.' Ruby gave him an anxious look.

'Chickens don't eat biscuits, Ruby. Can you open the shed door yourself, like a big girl and get the feed out? All by yourself?' Ruby nodded. 'Good girl, remember to put your boots on.'

Ruby ran to get her boots and stamped her feet into them as she called down the garden. The boots had new laces, but they'd been his once. Ma kept all their childhood things, hoping Pearl would have a boy this time so she'd get more use from the box of clothes. Charlie had already decided to call him Alfie.

Sweeping and clearing in her brisk, efficient way, Ma bustled into the kitchen. By the time the man had reached the door she was sitting by the stove in a clean pinafore with freshly pinned hair, with every muscle braced, waiting for the kettle to boil. Three firm knocks on the front door and Ma rose slowly, taking her time to move the shoes and crates from behind it. No-one ever came to this side of the house because the back door was always open and regular visitors knew it.

'Mrs Avery? Wife of James Avery?'

The age of the boy was shocking, barely older than Charlie. Ma nodded.

'Able-Seaman Alfred Barbour, ma'am, King's Navy.'

They eyed each other across the porch.

'You'd better come in, don't worry about your boots.'

Ma pushed him towards the one good chair, then stood awkwardly, while Jim busied himself with milk and cups. They had to let the boy take his time. No doubt he'd been practising his words on the walk from the station. Alfred Barbour had thin, straw-coloured hair and raw patches of razor scrape under his chin. They glared red against his pale skin.

'I'm here to tell you that your husband died in service, ma'am.'

Jim bit his upper lip to stem his tears, he wouldn't make things any harder for Ma. Bad enough that it seemed like the first assignment for this sailor. Maybe every time was like the first time. Some things don't get any easier the more you do them.

Ma closed her eyes and leaned hard on her elbows, pressing her hands over her mouth. 'How did it happen?'

Why did she want to know?

'You should be proud of him.'

Jim hovered with the tea cups, wanting, and not wanting, to know more.

'He sent the rest of the crew to lifeboat, while he manned the boilers that saved her from sinking. If it wasn't for his actions, many more of the crew would have died.'

How were they supposed to respond? Jim knew barely anything about Pa and now, just when he really wanted to picture him, he found that his brain refused to recall his face. Evidently Ma felt the same. Slowly she walked to the lintel, picked up the frame that was lying face down and stared into the eyes of her dead husband.

Barbour reached inside his bag and brought out a length of thin rope, frayed at both ends.

'Mr Avery used this rope to learn knots. He said if his rope held out, he knew he'd get back, that he...'

'What?' said Ma, her voice sharp.

'That he hoped to put things right.'

Smoke curled through the door of the oven and with a little cry Ma ran over to grab the tray of charred shapes in a tea-towel. 'What a waste!'

Ruby burst into the room holding a bunch of leaves. The little girl stood still for a minute, looking from one to the other as though trying to work out why the grown-ups were unhappy.

'Don't cry, Granny, it's just biscuits,' she said, but her own wide eyes began to fill with tears.

Chance meetings. 1993. Emily's story

Nurse Evans started her shift a while ago and it's comforting to have her here. We understand each other a little and she no longer makes me feel I shouldn't be here. She seems to find me amusing, making comments on my trouser suits and high heels whenever I visit after work. She appears in the short corridor bearing two cups of tea, one of which she hands to me. 'Here you go, Milady. Since you're obviously too important to look after yourself.' I take it gratefully, warming my hands on the mug.

'He's come back, just now. The driver,' she says in her direct manner. 'Come to check if Jim's OK.'

So the other cup is for him. I suppose he needs someone to tell him it wasn't his fault. 'Do I have to talk to him?'

'I think it'll probably help.' She meets my gaze, calm and steady, arms folded and head tilted slightly to one side. 'Don't you want to see him?'

'Not particularly.'

'He says he knows him. And he does seem upset. His name's Daniel.'

In the tiny side-room a man is standing like someone used to waiting: still, with his legs wide apart and his hands clasped behind his back. He's big, easily over six feet tall, and with the muscular build of a swimmer or runner, wide chest and long legs.

Daniel: it's an old-fashioned name, I was expecting someone middle-aged at least. But the guy who takes the tea from Nurse Evans must surely be younger than me. Not handsome in Ian's classic, well-groomed style but not bad looking. He has deep grey-blue eyes and a fringe of dirty

31

blonde hair. Something about him makes me think of the sea. He gives me such a frank look of appraisal that I am momentarily alarmed to have been caught without proper make-up and my fingers move to my face, trying to blend the inevitable dark mascara smudges.

'I'm sorry.' He grips my hand in a firm, almost painful, shake. I nod, unsure where to start.

'Thank you for coming. I appreciate it. Shall we sit down?' I sound like Ian's mother, what's wrong with me? I'm used to running meetings with all kinds of people I neither know nor like, bringing them to difficult contracts and agreements. Why do I feel so awkward? I don't need anything from this man.

'Thanks.' Daniel's voice has the trace of an accent I can't quite place. Before we sit, he eyes the plastic chair as though he doesn't trust it to take his weight. He rubs at the back of his neck like it's sore.

'I'm so sorry. I don't know where to start.'

His concern seems genuine, his eyes sad. I want so much to talk to anyone who knows Jim, anyone who can tell me about his life. Mum and Dad were apparently as shocked as I was to hear that Jim is alive and had been living so close to us all these years, though it's hard to tell from a phone call if they're hiding something, and Nan's not here to ask. She had plenty of her own secrets, things I'm only just beginning to understand. She tried to tell me once about Dad's father, then seemed to think better of it, leaving me guessing at the truth and unable to ask Dad in case I upset things.

'Nurse Evans says you know Jim?'

'Only by sight, to nod to, in the corner shop or wherever. He lives at the other end of Hall Road to my mum.'

Close to my parents too. Life is such a game of chance

meetings and missed friendship; we barely speak to the people who are right under our noses.

'My parents live on Ryland Road, just off the High. I did too. On and off until a few years ago. I don't remember seeing you before.'

'I don't live there, I go to see Mum a lot though, and I'm spending a couple of weeks there so I can be near my daughter.' He spreads out his hands as if he's said too much already and I nod, letting him know this isn't about him, that I won't ask any questions. I'm surprised he has a daughter. I wonder how old she is.

'It must be awful for you to see him like this.' He looks anxious.

Whatever I say will sound bad. May as well be honest. I take a deep breath. 'I never met him before. We lived so near all our lives, and I didn't even know he was there. He had my Nan down as next of kin, but she's gone so Dad was the next on the list, and if I hadn't taken the call...' Daniel looks puzzled and I'm ashamed for my family, the way we've crumbled. No doubt his own family is close knit and inseparable, Sunday lunches, barbecues in summer, tears on shoulders. 'Believe me that's not how I would have chosen ...' I haven't the energy to explain.

Daniel looks at me kindly, with his sea-coloured eyes. 'You'll get the chance to know him, I'm sure of it,' he says. 'But I can tell you what I know, if that helps?'

I nod, sip my tea to cover my embarrassment and listen.

'He's always polite but not overly friendly. He's a private man I think, possibly lives on his own. Mum always tries to have a chat with him, she loves a chat, gets a bit annoyed when other people don't want to. I don't know his name other than Jim, neither does she, but we always say hello to each other. You can tell he was a serviceman. Not just his age, that bearing, that's a long-term military bearing, all upright and purposeful. I'd say he was a career military man. He's always well turned out, with a hat and overcoat, old-fashioned smart. The last time I saw him I noticed his turn-ups were pressed. Funny thing. You don't see that often.'

No, you don't. I like this image of Jim, it makes me think he must look after himself, or have someone to care for him, even if they aren't family. Daniel rubs at his neck again.

'Is it sore? Your neck?'

'A bit. Whiplash. They say it takes a while to… I've never been in an accident before. You'd think I'd be tougher.' He reaches inside his t-shirt and pulls out a dog tag.

'Oh.' That would explain his physique. I've never met a soldier before, and I feel suddenly shy. His life must be so different to mine. A married father, a fighter, we have nothing in common. I mumble, 'So that's how you figured out Jim was in the army?' He nods.

'I shouldn't have braked like that. If there'd been a car behind me… but you don't think about that, you just… you don't want to hit them. You think only of that. I didn't want to hit him,' he pauses, rubbing his eyes.

He's a nice person. Someone I could see as a friend.

'He came straight into the road. By the time I saw him it was too late for me to do anything but slam on my brakes. He was so upright, so quick. When my car finally came to a stop and I ran back I thought… at first I thought I'd hit two people.'

Nurse Evans arrives at the right time, gently prising the empty cups from our hands and saving me from descriptions of the crash. She's seen it all before here, probably daily. People using her bright-lit side-room for life-changing conversations.

We exchange numbers. But Daniel needs nothing from me he can't check with the ward and I won't contact him. What would be the point? He's told me everything he knows about Jim already. On the way out, I take the bouquet he brought for Jim to Nurse Evans, because I know they don't allow them in intensive care. She rewards me with a tired smile, and I wonder when she last was given flowers.

Even when you've known someone for years it's still possible to convince yourself there's a part of them that's better than all the small disappointments. 'Thinking the best of people,' Nan used to say. Despite everything, I thought Anna might want to know about Jim but I've left four messages now.

Long distance buzzing as the number dials and rings, crackled waiting time before Anna's clipped voice message. Her accent has become deliberately English in the four years she's lived in the US. I can't be bothered to leave yet another message with the same information. Suddenly the recording cuts out.

'Yes?' A gunshot answer. Her and Mum both answer the phone the same way.

'Hi. It's me. Sorry.'

'It's five in the morning here for Christ's sake.'

'I thought you were always up early. I wanted to catch you before you went to the gym.' She goes every day, aerobics or step or whatever New Yorkers do to exercise. She's always struggled to keep her weight down, hating her naturally broad back and wide thighs. A good walk or a swim has always been more my thing but then I've never had to diet. Compared with Anna's spectacular curves I look like an adolescent boy. 'I've had trouble getting hold of you.'

'I was going to call you, but the new brand is launching this week and I have been *really* up against it; I've been meaning to get back to you.'

'For two weeks,' I reply, then kick myself. Anna on the defensive isn't going to help, I'm just going to hear about how busy she is.

'I didn't realise it was that long, actually, but the kinds of hours I've been working...' For a while I listen to her tales of the city. I haven't seen her since she moved but, whenever we talk, which isn't often, it's the same lament on the food, the hard-work, the lack of holidays, the impossibility of settling down with just one guy. She never asks about my life, I don't think she has any idea what I do for a job. I wait patiently for her to finish.

'You've heard what's happened?' Anna is silent for a moment. Of course she knows. She talks to Mum and Dad pretty regularly, probably more than I do, though she doesn't seem to like them much. There's a resentment about their distance that can be surprising in its bitterness.

'You mean our long-lost great grandfather?'

'Has Mum said anything to you? Or Dad?'

'About what?'

'About Jim!' Is she hiding something?

'Mum told me, yeah.'

'Did she say anything else? Like how come he lived so close?' Mum's bound to have told her more than me.

'Just that Dad always assumed he was dead. Nan never mentioned him. Apparently she used to talk about her mother sometimes, say she was 'troubled', which probably means she couldn't handle men or drink or whatever.'

'Is there anyone else to ask? Can't you remember anyone from when you were little?'

'Hey, I'm not that much older than you!' She's thirty-three, five years older, though it may as well be twenty; she still talks to me like I'm a kid.

'But you spent more time with Mum. Just think. You might remember something.' I pause to give her time to remember. She'd probably rather be telling me about her amazing social life. She was always outgoing and self-sufficient, at after-school clubs every day, either playing in a tournament or training. I often pretended I had a different sister, someone sensitive and academic. But perfect imaginary sisters are hard to keep up and, besides, I had Carrie for that.

'I can't remember anyone coming to the house except Aunty Jean and Mrs Matthews. They were there all the time.'

Aunty Jean is just Mum's old school friend. Mrs Matthews, only Mum's age but for some reason always more formal than her other friends, used to live next door. I could probably find their numbers, but could I talk to either of them? If Mum and Dad are really hiding something, would they know? Mrs Matthews was terribly house-proud. She always smelled of something odd, something I used to think was cleaning fluid, but which I now know to be the smell of strong drink.

'What is all this anyway, Emily? You're very keen on our family tree all of sudden.'

'You should see him, Anna, he's so fragile. I can't get over the fact that he lived so close to us.' He could have seen us cycle to school from his house. You up front with Tilly and the rest of your gang, trying to look like you weren't racing to catch up with the older boys, me dawdling behind and holding one-sided conversations with Carrie. 'When he wakes up, I think you should come over for a visit. You haven't been back yet.' Absence makes a sibling fonder. If she came over to see Jim, it might bring us closer. Is that why he's appeared? To sort our family out? She'd probably hate staying at Mum and Dad's with me and she doesn't seem to like Ian. He doesn't like her either.

'Doesn't sound like he's going to last long. Do you think he knew about us?'

'I sort of hope he didn't. If anything changes, I'll let you know, leave a message or whatever. The doctor said he's stable, for now.'

There's a long pause before she speaks. 'I wouldn't keep going to see him. It's not like he'll know you're there and it'll only make you low again, you know it doesn't take much... Oh and Emily?'

'Yes?' She's going to send a nice message to him, or maybe tell me things are going to be OK, that I'm OK.

'Aren't you going to wish me luck with the new brand?'

New boots. 1916. Jim's story

Jim walked around the cottage turning back the photographs; no need for superstitions now. Pa was almost handsome in his naval uniform. Hard to remember the last time they'd actually looked at each other. Now he'd never have the chance. Ma insisted he took the medals, though really Charlie should have them. They were beautiful, nestled in their velvet cases on maroon and purple grosgrain ribbons. They sat safely in his tin with the photographs and the length of frayed white rope.

Charlie hadn't said a word since he'd arrived with Pearl to collect Ruby. Whereas Auntie Violet hadn't stopped asking questions. She'd flown round as soon as she'd heard, wanting the details. He could feel her watching him, storing it all up to share in the village. Aunt Hilda wouldn't know yet, living in London she was the last to hear family news, but she should know. When he got a chance, he'd remind Ma to write. He moved closer to the fire and worried the logs with the poker until they caught again.

'I've told you everything I remember.' Ma looked wiped out. 'The boy said he saved everyone, the whole crew, with his life. That's what he said.'

'We should have asked for details,' said Jim. When Barbour left, he'd scrubbed himself clean under the cold pump in the yard, put on his best shirt. There wouldn't be a funeral, would there? Charlie seemed to be taking it hard. After all, he'd had a father to miss; all those hours on the sea together, they would have shared the closeness of men who must trust each other to survive.

'Nice to think he was a hero,' said Aunt Violet, stretching

her feet out to warm them. 'Who'd have thought it? James being a hero? I'm happy to tell people, if you don't feel up to it. Shall I start later? Or I could go into the village tomorrow and see a few people for you?'

'Do you want some help, Ma?' asked Jim as he watched her counting plates.

'It's good for her to have something to do, she needs it don't you, Annie?' Aunt Violet was enjoying herself, letting Ma wait on everyone as usual. Her two youngest were perched on the arms of her chair, cramming sandwiches into their mouths with fierce intent.

'Granny burned her hand. And the biscuits,' said Ruby.

The side of Ma's index finger and thumb were blistered and weeping from the heat of blackened tin through damp cloth. She stared down at it, face white.

'Sit down, Ma, let us look after you for a change.' Jim couldn't bear it. Charlie looked almost as bad. Was it going to be down to him to lead the family now? In the fireplace the logs hissed and spat like curses.

'You haven't been yourself for a while, Annie,' said Aunt Violet. 'If you ask me, it was a strange thing to do with the photographs. It was like you knew he wasn't coming back. I wonder if you're getting the sight?'

Aunt Violet never could hold her tongue. She couldn't be more different to her sisters. He'd never heard Ma gossip about anyone and quiet Aunt Hilda, who'd lost her son, wouldn't enjoy the news like this. She'd be looking after Ma. He should write to her, before Violet did. He'd sit down with Ma in the morning and work out who else needed to know.

'Nobody did ask you, Violet, nobody ever asks you. In fact, why don't you just take your opinions and shove off back to your own kitchen?' Charlie's knuckles whitened on the table edge. Their cousins stopped eating and looked at him with solemn faces.

Ma put her hand on his shoulder. 'Don't, Charlie, you need your family now.'

'I need to do something about this bloody war.' He banged his fists down hard on the table. Pearl shrank back and placed a protective arm over her swollen belly.

'Don't get angry about your pa.' Violet pulled her cardigan around her and smoothed it down over her lap. 'You want to go and make a difference, Charlie. We're never going to win this war without young men stepping up.'

Jim stared at her in horror. She couldn't mean it.

'My Billy reckons you might not get a choice soon, they're bringing in conscription, course he wouldn't be able to go, not with his flat feet…'

'And his lazy arse,' muttered Charlie under his breath before adding, 'It's true Ma, they'll be making us join up soon so why don't we go for it now and get a better deal out of it? The navy would have us, he could be proud of us then.'

Pa was already proud of Charlie, wasn't he? He must have been. Charlie was a good fisherman, sturdy sea-legs, strong with the boat. It was Jim who had to prove himself. There was no way he'd let his brother sign up alone.

'He *was* proud of you, *both* of you.' Ma looked fierce. 'Don't you ever forget that.'

'Of course he was.' Violet smiled and helped herself to another sandwich. 'Billy says they're doing the rounds of the villages next Saturday, you could do it then.'

'Don't talk like that, think of the baby, think of Ruby.' Pearl looked stricken and Charlie seized Ruby in a smothering hug.

'Think of what I'll say when they ask me what I did in the war! I'm not going to wait until they come and take me.'

Any worries Jim had about proving his age were dispersed as they shuffled forward in the queue. Plenty of boys looked younger than him; as far as he could see from here not one of them was being turned away or asked to show a birth certificate. Percy Mann wasn't that long out of short trousers, and he was near the front with his older brothers, all of whom played cricket for Winterton, all wearing their good coats, laughing like they were off to the Pleasure Beach for the afternoon.

The thin line of men and boys stretched back from the doors of the church. Every single one of them was smiling. Jim already felt a distance between himself and the others. He watched Bert enviously as he joked and jostled with Freddie Warner's brothers, shaking hands as they laid bets on how soon they'd all be back. This summer there'd be no team at all; the thought of the empty cricket green left him numb, pushed sudden tears to his eyes. Why should he cry when Charlie must be thinking of Pearl, of the baby he might never get to meet?

Ma had insisted on old clothes, worried that they wouldn't get them back when the uniforms were handed out. She'd watched them walk all the way down the road until they were out of sight. This time she wouldn't turn over photographs, instead she'd been searching for more, taking all the pictures she had of her sons and sticking them to the walls until Jim felt dozens of pairs of eyes watching his every move.

When they got to the front of the line Bert stepped back to let Charlie go first.

'Charles Alfred Avery enlisting for duty, sir.'

'Like the sound of that do you, son? What size boots?' The sign-up officer barely lifted his head from the desk.

'Size 10, sir, if you have them, sir. I was, well we were, hoping to be put down, for navy sir, for the navy, sir, if that's possible, at all,' Charlie's voice crackled.

The man raised his head, revealing a luxuriant moustache and a low, thick set of eyebrows that glowered over his florid face. He put on a falsetto voice: *'Please sir, if it's not too much trouble, I'd like to sign up so I can do whatever I please, sir.* This isn't the fourpenny ticket booth, you know. Who do you think you are?'

'I just thought, my father was navy, sir, a sailor, he always said you struggled with navy recruits.'

Did he? Jim had never heard him say that.

The officer looked slowly from Charlie to Jim to Bert and back again, sizing them up. 'Stay here.'

Jim half-hoped that the man would refuse. For ten minutes the three of them stood in silence, watching the enlisters deep in conversation over a huge sheaf of papers at the back of the booth and then two other moustachioed officers accompanied the original back to the desk.

'You all take after your father then? You?' He prodded Jim with his baton until he dropped his eyes to the floor. 'You a good sailing man?'

Jim shook his head, still looking down. 'No. sir. Charlie is. I never went to sea. But only because Ma wouldn't let me.' A roar of laughter burst from the men behind him. He felt his ears redden. 'I was keen, sir, but after my uncle went under they didn't really want me to. I worked the farm.'

'And you?' He prodded at Bert in disgust as though he was something on the bottom of his shoe. 'No doubt you had better things to do as well?'

'As a matter of fact, yes.' Bert offered a cheerful hand. 'Albert Baxter, engineer and mechanic at your service.'

The officer ignored the proffered hand and reached under the desk, bringing up two kitbags and two pairs of boots, one new, stiff and shiny and the other cracked and worn. 'Royal Norfolk Regiment you two, stand over there on the left. And you,' he gestured to Charlie. 'They'll need you in the navy, see the man in the white hat at the end there.'

Was that it? They were supposed to be together, weren't they? Now they faced each other awkwardly. Surely Charlie felt the same need to hug his brother, just this once. Jim ought to be strong. It would be worse for Charlie, leaving Pearl and the kids. Little Ruby would miss her dad. He was a good one too and who knew where that came from? Instinct, it must be but, as Ma always said, you could never tell how people would turn out once children arrived. Charlie ought to know how much his brother loved him. But their arms were full; they were being watched. The tears he'd been fighting all day filled Jim's throat and blocked his words.

Charlie clapped him on the shoulder and held his hand there. 'Chin up, old man.'

'Oi.' The enlistment officer rapped on the desk, breaking the spell. 'What are you waiting for? Your mother's permission?'

Jim's tin. 1993. Emily's story

Jim's eyes are open wide enough to show they're a pale lilac-blue that must have been striking once, before their colour faded. 'Jim,' I whisper, then louder, 'Jim. How're you feeling?' but he doesn't move his head or register my touch on his hand. Is he awake? Just when I need her, Nurse Evans isn't here. Another nurse sits at the desk; a young man with deep-pitted acne marks and gelled hair. Two yellow stripes are sewn across the tops of his uniform pockets, whatever that means. I go out to ask his help.

'It happens.' He shrugs. 'Sometimes means things are getting better, sometimes means things are worse.' He scratches at a pink plaster stretched across his left eyebrow.

'I'd like to talk with the doctor,' I insist. Returning to Jim's room, I sit with my chair facing the door, looking pointedly at the nurses' station in case he tries to slope off without calling one. Doctors don't seem to be around much. Don't they realise that patients aren't the only people on wards needing attention? I've spoken to Dr Melrose twice, for around ten minutes, and she was only interested in asking questions about Dad's medical history, trying to uncover any underlying conditions.

Doctor Iqbal, when he finally arrives, looks like the kind of man who always works a full double shift. His eyes are heavy-lidded, tired, knowing. After we shake hands, exchange names, he goes straight to Jim's bedside and performs an elaborate medical check. It's entirely for my benefit, nevertheless his attention to detail is reassuring. When he shines his penlight directly into Jim's pale eyes they don't flicker.

'Why's he like this?'

'Eyes open? Or in a coma?'

'Yes. Both.' Like anyone talking to a doctor, I just want to know if there's hope. That's all we ever want but we never ask outright, partly because we like to pretend we know exactly what they mean and partly because we know they're not really allowed to tell us if there's reason to hope. In case they're wrong. In case we try to sue them for their empathy. Instead, we read between their words and reach our own conclusions.

'Coma means that the patient is in a state of unconsciousness. He will not respond to normal stimuli, even if he appears to be awake.'

'But his eyes weren't open before. Doesn't that mean something's changed?'

'As you can see, Jim is still failing to respond to stimuli. One tiny impulse may have caused his eyelids to open. Some comatose patients can move limbs or make sounds, but if no normal responses occur they are still unconscious.' He gives me a thin smile. 'The brain is a complex organ, Miss Green. Coma is always the result of damage to the brain stem and the cerebrum. We do not know what else is happening with those injuries precisely because the person is unconscious.'

'He doesn't have a head injury.' I've stared at his face enough, it's unmarked by anything other than age.

'Anyone as old as Jim would have a slowing down of brain function. But brain injury, the kind of damage that might induce a comatose state, can be caused by other trauma to the body, a heart attack, perhaps. Or a disease, like diabetes, or a stroke.'

I look at Jim. Bright white hairs are sprouting from his chin. They're surprisingly long. I hadn't thought your hair kept growing like that when you were old. Jim isn't bald either, he has a professorial shock of white, fluffy hair.

'Has he any of those things?'

'No.' Dr Iqbal looks down at his notes. 'We don't think so. But he *has* suffered a lot of internal bleeding. His body has undergone quite a trauma. The coma could be the result of haemorrhage or simply the shock.'

'If it's shock, will it just be a temporary thing?'

'We must not assume that.' His tone becomes firmer, more confident, he doesn't want the relatives of his patients misled by false hope. 'Shock is a serious thing, especially for a man of his age. After a severe shock it is not unusual for the brain to simply wish to shut down. It can be a decision that the brain makes for itself.'

From the kerbside the house looks friendly, with a sweeping red brick porch smothered in a climbing rose. They've given me his keys; I may as well use them. I had, after all, promised to go there if Jim woke. According to Dr Iqbal he's not awake, even though his eyes are open, but I must hope he'll improve soon. I may as well get some of his own things to make him more comfortable when he does.

Glazed tiles cover the bottom third of the outside wall and the path is paved in black and white, edged with twists of terracotta. An imposing house, wide and open, and surrounded on all sides by garden. The kind of house that hasn't been built since the turn of the last century. Many of the houses around here are of similar age, though newer buildings have sprung up in the holes left by bomb damage. In the 1960s, half our street was in-filled with tall townhouse-style properties, like the one I grew up in. They seem flimsy next to houses like this.

Stepping into the hallway I see piles of junk mail,

suspended cobwebs, layers of dust. A pair of leather shoes and a small suitcase sit expectantly by the door, so clouded in a mist of greenish mould that it's impossible to tell what colour they once were. It looks as though the owner died years ago. Is this how old people live: in dust and shadows? Daniel said he always looked smart. A front for the world, perhaps, because keeping going is easier than stopping. I can empathise with that. When thoughts close in, and others move on, there's nothing left to interact with. You just put one foot in front of the other and try to keep breathing.

Most of the internal doors are closed and I worry about what I might find behind them. Carrie wouldn't hesitate, she'd go straight in to explore. The thought makes me braver, and I walk along the hallway. It drops three steps at the end, another short corridor opens into the kitchen with more natural light and a large window. French doors lead into the garden. Dampness mingles with dust, mould stains the tattered linoleum. The pantry is full with newspapers from floor to ceiling, neatly folded and pristine, unread.

There's an odd kind of charm here. It would look so nice if it was cleaned. Would Jim take offence? It could be a surprise for his return. I must stay positive, imagine him coming round. He's alive, even if his brain's shut down. I think of Carrie's tiny body under that blanket, of the days she spent fighting to survive. Did *her* brain choose to shut down in the end? Did mine?

An old-fashioned fridge in a brown cabinet contains nothing but an open tin of Spam, half an apple, some yellowing milk. Out of date tins sit on the shelves above. Where were social services? And Daniel's mum? His other neighbours? How could you live near someone for years, know them by sight, notice what they wore even, and not know this about them? Impulsively I called Daniel on the way here, but he didn't answer and I didn't leave a message. Now I feel like calling again, to tell him what this is like. I'm angry he never checked, angry he knew Jim and I didn't. I would have checked.

Lying on the floor beneath the kitchen table, half open as though it's been thrown, is a photograph album—there's a note tucked inside the cover: 'For both of you, it's time, let me know when we can visit. Love M.' All the photographs seem to be of one child, beautiful black and white prints set on windswept beaches. Norfolk perhaps? That's where Dad was raised but I don't recognise these. They stop when the boy looks to be around 12 years old. It could be Dad, though he's smiling a lot in these, and very thin.

I close the book carefully, set it down on the table, remembering the last conversations with Nan and the hints about Dad's father. Conversations I never repeated with my own parents because where would I start? All us kids knew was that Nan lived alone, we never asked about a grandad. If Dad had wanted me to know what Nan had hinted to me before, that he was born in scandal, he would have told me. That's the kind of man he is.

Scant facts about Jim that I know to be true: he served in the war—one, both? He was married, Nan was his daughter. Nothing else magically unfolded when I unlocked the door. I'm about to leave the sitting room in darkness again when something on the table catches my eye. A tin, unusually shaped, like a blunted shield. Rust has pitted and discoloured the lid, clouding the original pattern, but I can still make out the wording: *Mackintosh's de luxe favourites*. The pattern is easier to see on the tin's high sides, a stylized vine from which hang ripe fruits painted red against the dark blue background. The old metal grates and scrapes as I lever off the lid. Its underside is still shiny.

The tin is filled with photographs and papers; orders of service from weddings and funerals; an Old Testament with tiny print and wafer-thin pages, inscribed with love; several news clippings; an empty ring-box from Bravington's in Ludgate Hill; a set of medals, tangled with a frayed length of white rope. But mostly the tin is filled with photographs. Someone has lined it protectively with greaseproof paper, now spotted with mildew, but still many of the photographs have faded beyond recognition. Some have been coloured by hand, in garish blues and pinks.

A thick cream envelope holds a dozen or so neatly folded newspaper clippings. 'Open Verdict Returned: Mystery of Barnes man's death not solved'. A small, hard-backed funeral script, an Order for the Burial of the Dead, lettered in perfect handset type by Sanders of Richmond, is dedicated in 'Loving Memory' to the same man, known to his family as Bert. Heartbreakingly formal for one so young. Many more orders of service are stacked in the tin. Might it be possible to piece this together? The same faces appear again and again. I wonder how someone with all those faces in a tin can end up alone. Is it that easy for people to drop out of your life, one by one? Is this how I will be?

As I spread the contents of the tin across the floor dozens of eyes stare out from the serious sepia faces of my unknown relatives. In other cultures, people believe that we are always being guarded by the spirits of our ancestors; the Ibo give these watchful spirits the first mouthful of every single meal, casting it to the floor in offering, to appease them. A custom that has always made perfect sense to me. Now I think the people trapped in this tin must need appeasement too. They need their stories to be heard.

A meeting. 1916. Jim's story

Jim kept his bundle of post at the bottom of his kitbag. Some from Lilly, or Ma, one from Charlie and dozens of messages from Ruby, the little girl's letters made with such effort he could picture the set of her face as she carved words into paper. If he closed his eyes he could see her in Ma's kitchen twisting a curl around her fingers while she was thinking what to write, swinging her legs back and forth on the chair and distracted by the chickens that wandered in to peck the rugs, climbing down to tell them off every five minutes. Dear letters, childishly innocent: he'd read and re-read them so many times that the pencil marks were almost worn away, but if he pressed them to his face he could still smell home. Fourteen months of letters. Long months in which Charlie's second child had been born, weaned, started walking and learned to live with only women around him. How old would Alfie be before Jim saw his face?

He replied in brief paragraphs, telling them about the villages, the old farmers in their little wooden dog carts. No point in sharing the worst, they didn't need to know. To survive he had to imagine Winterton just as it had been when he left. The memory of Grace was like a siren's song, pulling him home. Clearly not a song that Bert could hear above the nightly raids along the line. Nearby, beyond the burned and roofless farms, was a tiny French village they used for supplies and Bert had wasted no time in charming the young widow who lived in the furthest cottage with her elderly mother and two small children. Jim disapproved silently but Bert had plenty of other willing listeners. The war hadn't changed him; it had increased him, made him more intensely male. Duties didn't wear him down; he seemed to take his energy from the charged air around him, revelling in the camaraderie. Little things still mattered to Bert—jokes, songs, people's stories, personal grooming. He still teased his curls forward, managing to make the short haircut suit him, using his water rations to wash and clean it properly instead of simply rubbing off the mud like everyone else.

Jim, crouching in the dust on the floor of the cow barn, watched him as he walked over, whistling as though he hadn't a care. Bert was a great whistler. Could barely speak a word of French but he could whistle the *Marseilles* beautifully and he would use it to charm the locals, all of them, especially the women who would wave and salute as he whistled his way past.

'Still fiddling with these girls?' Bert grinned and jerked his head towards the cows. 'His nibs is at it early today for some reason, wants his cuppa sharpish, sent me to find you.'

'Had to warm my hands properly or Daisy would have given me another kicking.' Jim rolled his sleeve to show the livid bruise on his left forearm from the previous day's milking. Once they'd appropriated some painfully thin cows with their calves, two horses and a goat from the farms, Jim had quickly fallen into the role of company herdsman. It was funny but a lot of the men, even the ones who played it big, were frightened of farm animals. He'd been slightly nervous of the horses himself, but they'd submitted quickly to the low authority of his voice as he brushed mud from their legs. He was happy here with the animals, less homesick, glad of the excuse to find the solitude he craved.

'I'm not sure how much these poor girls have left in them. The hay's all gone, and this grass is more mud than food for them. Feels cruel to make them work.'

'They're playing up, having a bit of fun with you, typical girls. You know they love it really.' Bert laughed as he patted the behind of the pale cream cow. 'They're lucky no-one's getting over friendly with them. I've heard some terrible stories, especially down the line with the Suffolks. Desperate times, old son, you want to keep an eye on these ones.' He laughed again and lit a cigarette, sparking his lighter loudly, startling the cow into jerking her head on the tether, giving a sharp kick with her back foot.

Jim narrowed his eyes against the sun to look up at his friend. Bert never did like the farm, couldn't wait to get away from 'all the muck and fur'. He rolled up both his sleeves and settled back onto the low milking stool, talking softly to the cow under his breath, starting with gentle strokes to calm her down before squeezing firmly, sending a thin spray of foamy milk into the waiting bucket. Bert finished his cigarette.

'Bowler reckons there's a colonel up the line who's so fond of his cow he's keeping her in the actual trenches.' The idea of it made Jim give him a smile that Bert pretended to mistake for disbelief. 'Straight up! Been there for five months apparently… he's got a grass rota for the boys, sends them off to fetch the stuff for her, says she's too valuable to leave behind.'

'Wouldn't fancy being downwind of her in a dug out, smells bad enough out here!' Jim steadied the bucket against the stamps of the cow, agitated by the noise.

'Depends where you put her. I'd imagine some of those fine country scents would improve the air around Potts.'

Jim laughed; Bert was right in a way, at least this was a fresh, honest smell. There was something evil about the smell of decay in the line that no amount of fresh mud could mask.

Every time he went back it took hours for his senses to readjust.

'How come the colonel's cow lasted so long at the front?'

'Divine intervention? Innocent beast of the field. Can't imagine a cow'd be much good with a gun.'

It was part of Bert's charm that he could always find something to laugh about. He was like a king here, no longer Jim's best friend but everyone's, because friends could be made so quickly through shared exhaustion and knowledge they were all charging headlong towards death. Sometimes Bert and his easy jokes were the only relief. Everyone sought him out for nightwatch duty; something about his manner made them less uneasy in the dark.

'What's up with his nibs then?' asked Jim, handing over the bucket and untethering the cow, giving her flanks an encouraging pat to move her away.

'How should I know? I'm only ever the messenger. No one tells me what's going on. He wants me to take something into town for him this morning, urgent, though he's got time for his tea first.'

Several miles to the north of their headquarters was a market town, large enough for a few of the men to have heard of it before leaving England, although only Bert had actually seen it since they had arrived. Having quickly made himself indispensable, as both mechanic and driver, he was the battalion's despatch rider, trusted with the battered Douglas motorbike, known as The General, that he tended and sheltered as lovingly as Jim looked after his stock. It was a model he knew well, several of his customers from the Yarmouth shop had owned them and, like most drivers, were nervous of carrying out their own repairs. Almost as thin as a bicycle, with a rigid leather seat and an elongated wedge-shaped tank, it was a thing of rare beauty to Bert, who relished both his duty and the freedom it gave him to explore.

'You want to watch it, talking about him like that. You know he's waiting for you to slip up and there's plenty who'd take your place.' Bert's assignment was much against the better judgement of 'his nibs', Captain Henry Nissington, who'd been there since the start of the campaign, watching his stock of good men dwindle and increasingly feeling he had to take what he could get. The only one who hadn't succumbed to Bert's charms, he was nevertheless impressed by his ability to strip, repair and rebuild a bike or a gun in a matter of hours and he trusted him with machines in a way he'd never trust him with the men.

'He'll still be waxing his bloody moustache. There's some meeting today at the tea rooms in the main square. Talking about deployment probably. Second thoughts, you better forget I said that. Anyway, I've got to drop a box of documents and wait around to bring another one home, easier than tying them to pigeons, I suppose. But they won't be wanting me all day, so I'll be at leisure until I'm needed to bring the stuff back.' Bert grinned broadly and folded his arms across his chest, apparently well satisfied with this outlook.

'What are you going to do with yourself then?' Jim felt a stab of envy that he tried to hide, turning his face towards the wooden fence and shuffling his stool along to the side of the tethered goat. Even his war was charmed. They were supposed to be out here together, fighting for freedom, but hadn't Bert had that all along? His sense of freedom was, perhaps, what others craved from him.

'I daresay I'll start with a little visit to the hospital, see what shift Mathilde is on then we might go for a walk along the river for a while or wander through the town or she might take me back to her parents' house again.'

'Who the hell is Mathilde?' Jim let go of his pail with a start of surprise and the nearby goat saw her chance to give it a good kick, sending it halfway across the barn in a trail of wasted milk. 'Shit, now look what you've done,' he grumbled, jumping up to fetch it. Half of it was gone and he'd have to work hard to get much more.

'No need for the green eyes, Jimmy boy. If you ask nicely, I'll see if she's got a friend for you.'

'I don't think Lilly would like that. Or Grace, remember her?'

'These are dark days, Jimmy! Everyone needs a cuddle. Even you. And if I know Grace, she'll be having plenty herself. There's a war on, in case you haven't noticed, that means wartime rules.'

Bert was still standing with his arms folded, an easy grin on his handsome, open face but his eyes quickly darted away, and Jim could see why women went to such lengths to hold his gaze. He fell silent, torn between loyalty and love for both Bert and Grace and he realised with sudden clarity that whatever happened in this war they couldn't survive it unchanged.

'Look lively, here comes his nibs, how long've I been here gassing? Quick get some more in that bucket.'

Captain Nissington was a tall, upright man, possessed of a fierce set of moustaches and his own clear light, a presence and bearing which meant he had no need to stand close to Bert to be forceful. Nobody seemed to know much about him; like most of the officers he followed the standard advice that the less the men knew about you the better for you and for them, because they needed authority too and they didn't want that authority to have a particularly human face. He wasn't the first officer to take a dislike to Bert. Jim suspected that men in such positions feared him. They must sense that his popularity could bring trouble to the ranks.

'On my way to find you, sir,' beamed Bert, grabbing the pail and holding it up. 'Been a bit of a mission this morning I'm afraid, what with Daisy escaping. Good job we were both here to get her back, she's a pretty lively one.'

'Really,' said Nissington, sniffing the air slowly and deliberately, 'and I suppose you had to offer her a smoke too?'

'Ha ha, can't get much past you, sir. That was of course for *my* nerves, not Jim's here, he's all too used to these beasts, but I prefer my beasts made of iron, as you know.'

'I do indeed, Private Baxter, and your defence of your non-smoking friend is heart-warming, if unnecessary.' Bert continued to beam at his officer, despite the stern glare. 'If you've quite finished, perhaps you may have time to give The General the once-over before you leave?'

'Spent my free hour on her yesterday, sir. She's oiled and shined and ready to ride in style.' Bert knew well that his passengers dreaded breaking down en route, in sniper-filled woodland, and he was proud that The General had never let him down. He was the only person with enough skill to fashion a spare part from debris to get the bike working again and the only one foolish enough to run the gauntlet along the tracks behind both trench lines to get messages through.

'Very good,' Nissington replied, nodding at Jim. 'And how are the animals bearing up?'

'As well as could be expected really, sir,' he replied. 'I'm not sure how much longer they'll be here though. The calves aren't growing and their diet is pretty poor.'

'Not as poor as ours would be without them. Keep at it,

man, you're doing a grand job. Spend as much time with them as you need, that's an order.' He turned sharply on his heel and indicated Bert to follow him.

'Shaping up to be a lovely day for a walk, sir.' Bert turned to wink slyly at Jim as they disappeared, the milk pail swinging carelessly from his fingers.

Jim sat back on his stool and watched until they were two specks of dust on the hazy skyline. Was Grace waiting for Bert? Would she forgive him, as everyone seemed to? If only he could write to her without causing suspicion. His letters to Ma and Lilly focused on things they'd find familiar, updates on men they knew if the news was good, though they must guess when something happened and he stopped mentioning them. Bert's exploits on The General usually took several paragraphs, more to make Lilly laugh than anything. Perhaps she would share them with Grace, so the poor girl would at least know he was alive. It was hard to think of going back to Lilly. But since Grace was spoken for there seemed little point in worrying about who could take her place; it may as well be Lilly. Marriage and children had worked for Charlie, and he'd make them work for him too.

As usual Bert got his own way, persuading Nissington that Jim should join him. 'It's safer with two, sir.' Jim didn't feel safe, perched on the tiny back seat with his arms behind him, spattered with black mud. He tried to brush down his uniform as they waited for Mathilde and her friend to finish their shift, Bert leaning into the wall as he smoked. Where did he get all his smokes? He looked like Valentino. The stiff collar of his greatcoat was turned up against the mist and the sloping line of the khaki wool emphasised his cheekbones as he smiled to himself at the ordinary business of the street.

Bert's smile widened when a pretty young nurse appeared in the doorway. She raced down the steps towards them, reaching up to take his face in her hands and kiss him. A window flew open and a woman in a black dress shouted down in French, liberally peppered with obscenities—the only words Jim understood. The nurse waved up at her, blowing kisses, until the scowling woman retreated inside with a loud, indignant banging of the wooden shutter.

'Where's your friend?' asked Bert. 'This is Jim. I've brought him specially to meet her.'

'Francine is tired. She has worked for many hours without stopping. The men they brought in yesterday were bad. So she is sleeping in the hospital. I have to go now to her maman's house to let her know.' Her English was halting and formal.

Bert started to apologise but Jim was glad. How could he talk to a young nurse? Even the town frightened him, with all the heaps of rubble where buildings once stood. It looked as though the world was being rubbed out before their eyes.

'We'll walk you there then. Walk with us for a bit, Jim, no need to rush off.'

Jim shuffled along behind them as they linked arms and began to stroll towards the river. The less he saw of this the better, or he'd never be able to look Grace in the eye. He'd give it ten minutes, for form's sake, then make his excuses and leave.

'It was easy for you to come here?' The top of Mathilde's head only reached to Bert's shoulder; she leaned into him as they walked.

'Not at all.' Bert adopted a mock serious look. 'We had to fight off dozens of the enemy to get to the bike today, then we had to...'

Mathilde nudged him playfully. Did she understand what he was saying or know from his tone he was teasing?

'We've got a few free hours.' Bert smoothed a loose strand of dark hair away from her forehead, offered her a cigarette. 'Are you tired?'

She nodded, inhaled deeply, sighed as she blew out a curling ribbon of smoke. Jim had heard enough stories from the hospital. How far could a dozen inexperienced nurses stretch across hundreds of shattered men? Enough to patch them up and put them back on the conveyor belt.

'There were medals today,' she said, shaking her head, 'for if you have given a leg or an arm for the war. We had to stop the things we were doing, to watch. Why are men all so happy to have these things?'

'Not everyone, I bet.' Jim had seen plenty of friends sent here for patching up, sometimes with injuries so severe that only their eyes reminded you they were men.

'One of them had nothing. He was wounded. But they took him today because they said he had not been brave. They were going to shoot him?'

Jim knew what she meant, the boys had been talking last night. Private Wainwright, nervous and jumpy, was due to be court-martialled for cowardice. Everyone knew he'd tried to shoot his own foot with his rifle, but he'd stumbled and shot himself in the chest as well. He'd almost died. But he'd been nursed for six weeks until he was well enough to face trial. Poor girls, watching their patients so carefully until they were strong enough to be sent back out to die.

They walked in silence, tracing the curving path of the wide grey river. Along the steps to the towpath were pots of geraniums, shocking splashes of red against the grey streets. Two children in wooden shoes were sailing paper boats by the inlet. They reached over a plank bridge to guide the boats away from the bank with long sticks, giving orders to each other in high, excited voices. They would have been around Ruby's age. What would she look like now? Time in her world would be different to his. Jim set his jaw, folded his arms.

'They've got those things all wrong.' He indicated the children trying to rescue a capsized boat from the water. 'You two carry on, I'm going down to show them how it's done.'

Institutions. 1993. Emily's story

A spring-bright bunch of flowers sits in a bag of water on my in-tray, next to a packet of lavender shortbread. A touching gesture. I've barely been out of the office for two weeks, but time passes slowly in the hush of academic publishing, and my excuses were vague. They'll be thinking the worst. I'm not looking forward to explaining, but I'm happy to be back, in control and with something useful to do.

Two cover designs in plastic wallets need sign-off. I slide them onto the desk, propping them up against the divider that separates me from Shona, commissioning lead for our business studies list. The first cover is a standard number in our *Modern Living* series, the same Mondrian-style design and blocky typeface with a new square of colour on the spine, to differentiate them on library shelves. With a pica rule I measure the exact spine width and check it against the number of pages I have in the final manuscript, a job that's already been carried out by the production team but which I always check. Mistakes are better rectified earlier, when the entire batch won't need rebinding. I turn my chair to look at the other spines on the high shelf behind me, check that yellow hasn't already been used for the square and then tick all the boxes on the form, replacing it with the cover inside its plastic slip. It's a neat process, one I enjoy. If only everything in life was as easy as making books.

The second cover is for a small ethnography, a three-month study of traditional societies in the far north of Japan, and shows a detailed close-up photograph of an elderly man. He wears a wide ceremonial hat, thickly embellished with gold thread and glass beads, and a snow-white beard that reaches below the edge of the image. Around his sunken eyes the skin is wrinkled so deeply that it resembles folded fabric and I realise he must be almost as old as Jim, surely an anomaly for such a harsh climate, even in Japan.

Members of traditional societies, especially if they are nomadic, rarely live beyond 50. They'll often die much younger. So those that do survive until old age tend to be revered as living gods. They've had the same environment, exposure to illness and accident and the same struggles of life, yet they have somehow survived a lifetime longer. It makes them special. People ask them questions, want their guidance. Warriors and initiates have a vested interest in caring for elderly relatives because if parents or grandparents survive to extreme old age it reflects well on the whole family and means they're treated with respect. Such elders enjoy ceremonial positions and carry out rituals; daughters from that family might be chosen to be among the wives of the chief and his brothers.

It's a powerful photograph, projecting this strength perfectly; just right for the book. It's been taken by the author too, so it's copyright-free; even better if the book ever reaches reprint. I tick the boxes on this form too, signing and returning the slips, then leaf through the rest of the documents. There are two brown envelopes, battered at the edges, both from Vanessa Barton, one of my ethnographers who's living with a tribe in Peru. Her writing is lyrical, strong; the scenes she creates make you feel as though you have lived them with her. One of the chapters is half hand-written. In a scribbled note she explains that electricity is too scarce after recent storms and she's waiting for charge, but she didn't want to miss the deadline for delivery. If only all my authors were the same. Apparently she's due back in the UK soon and wants to visit. We've never met, but we get on well in letters and calls and I've offered her a place to stay, not really expecting her to accept. Turning over the envelope I can't see a postal date and, in any case, it could have taken weeks to get here.

'Hello, stranger, we thought you'd run off to live with some of your natives.' Shona peers over the divider and I stand up with an awkward flap of my hands. My instinct was to hug her.

'Thank you for the flowers. I'm guessing that was you?' We walk down the aisle towards the small kitchen at the side of the room, screened from the desks by a series of huge architectural pot plants. There are only two chairs, high stools in white plastic and chrome, and Shona perches on one, throwing me concerned looks as I make the tea.

'How are you then, Emily? Marcus said you'd had some sort of family thing going on. You know I'm always here?'

'Yeah, I know.' People say that, they don't usually want to listen though. I hand her the tea in a mug that reads *Have you carp'd your diem today?* and she rolls her eyes.

'Thanks. Did you pick this one specially for me? I've been industrious while you've been away.'

'I'm sure you have.' I smile. Shona is a slightly plump and eminently sensible person, the type that makes you feel safer when she enters the room. She wears her black hair closely cropped, her shoes flat and all her suits grey, the overall severe look usually offset by impossible earrings that show her fun side, the one she likes to hide from her authors. I've missed her.

'It's not your parents, is it? Is everything OK? I know it's hard when they're so far away.'

I shake my head. 'They're fine. It's my great-grandfather,

he's in a coma, in Queen Mary's. I've been staying at my parents' house so I could be near in case anything changed. But it hasn't. So, they're just going to contact me if it does.' It sounds natural when I say it like that, without the admission that he's a stranger to me and I barely know my family at all.

I've missed talking. Conversation with Jim is a sad, one-sided monologue that gives me too much time to think. I want to share everything with Shona, about Jim, my parents, about Carrie. For a moment it would feel good. I could lay my head on her sensible shoulder and cry without stopping and she would comfort me, I know she would. But what then? Where would we be? It would change things, make the office less safe and calm.

'Anyway it's OK, it's been a bit of a shock and obviously there's just me, with Anna in New York and my parents away.'

'Upsetting to see a loved one like that. Did he have pneumonia or something?'

'No-one's sure to be honest. He lived on his own and there was no-one to tell the paramedics so...' Something in my tired face seems to warn her not to ask any more questions.

'Let me know if there's anything I can do.'

She can't listen if I won't talk to her. 'We'd better get back to work.'

'I guess so.' Shona steps down from the chair and begins to fill a glass with water. 'On a happier note, how are the wedding plans going?'

'You don't want to hear about all that,' I bluff. 'Tell me what's happening in Shona Towers. Any thrilling conferences last weekend? Rotherham? Leicester? Somewhere else exotic?'

'Morecombe actually,' she laughs.

'Ah, I was right. And did the facilities live up to your usual standards?'

Shona is breaking into an hilarious impersonation of a seaside landlady when her editor comes to find her for a meeting. 'You know where I am,' she repeats as she leaves.

Mum always says I'm not a 'people person'. By which I think she means that I'm awkward and uncomfortable at parties and gatherings, whereas Anna is a master of the art of room-working and small talk. My choice to study anthropology baffled my parents, who were equally surprised and delighted that it would qualify me for any kind of a job. I was bookish and careful with research. When I graduated from my second-rate polytechnic it seemed natural that I should start work at a publishing house and Whittaker's University Press certainly carried some prestige, even if the starting post was menial. Seven years later, with the slow and steady promotion that rewards those who simply stick around, I have a good life, a nice flat, the job I wanted. My closet is full of clothes from the upper end of the High Street. The maisonette I share with my nice-looking, solvent boyfriend is the top half of a quiet townhouse in Fulham, surrounded by restaurants and cafés that we visit often. When I'm trying to feel fulfilled, I itemise my blessings in this way.

Work affords an escape of sorts, though there's no fiction and little romance involved. My authors write books about hospitals, asylums, factory floors; trying to find meaning in human behaviour by judging how we react to these makeshift prisons. There's no mystery as far as I can see, we react as any animal would; if you take away its need to think and give it regular food it will become docile and passive. However wearying I find them, these textbooks are Whittaker's bread and butter, top sellers in our undergraduate series, *Modern Living*; a lucrative stream of work for the company.

I prefer to commission old-fashioned tribal ethnographies—thin poetic tracts on the rituals of hidden cultures. These authors spend their lives immersed in research, developing malaria, tick-borne disease, frostbite, malnutrition and worse, hoping for three or four of these pamphlets at best as their whole life's work. I rarely meet them. They go back to the US intermittently and post me their chapters, get paid their meagre royalties. I'm sure they'd be more interesting than the slick lecturers that contribute to my *Modern Living* series. There isn't much you can tell them, well-paid sociologists being generally self-satisfied with their superior understanding of people and culture. I've grown to resent the time I spend with them on lunches as much as I resent the money it wastes. I could feed several of my ethnographers for a month on the cost of a lunch. At least my daily trips to hospital are helping me to understand their fascination with institutions.

'You don't need to come if you don't want to.' Ian is tight-lipped. 'But you *did* agree. And you know how Mother is. She'll have been planning it for months.'

'I know. I'm sorry. And it's not that I don't want to, really, it's just that after Jim and everything I feel like I need to see Mum and Dad, face to face, to find out.' He thinks I don't like his parents but I'm fine with them. They're formal, and his mother dotes on Ian in a way that can make me feel uncomfortable, but they're hard to dislike. 'We spent Christmas there last year.'

'We're talking about New Year.'

'But if I get this flight then I won't get back from Spain

until the 30th'

'They're only in Oxford.'

'It's not that.' He knows I won't want to spend too long not visiting Jim. He's trying to make me say it, but it will only end in an argument. I've tried so many times to get him to understand. It's hard enough being back at the flat, the journey across town is over an hour on a good day. 'Who else have they invited?'

'I'm not sure, Andy and Sarah, I think, so they won't be happy if we don't go. It'll be hard for them anyway at that time of year with a new baby.'

Ian's an only child, his friends have always been a big part of family life and Andy used to go on holiday with them every summer. Easier to choose your own company than put up with a sibling you'll never be close to understanding. Easier for his parents, too, to have a polite additional part-time child.

'Did you meet up with him in the end?'

'Tuesday. He had two beers and then cried off.' He pulls a sulky face.

'He's probably exhausted.'

'Not a good advert for it.'

'Sheldon's only a few months old; it'll get easier. Just make sure you keep asking him out.' This is better, a safer topic. Tonight is supposed to be special for us after these weeks of upset and I've tried hard with the food, I don't want it ruined.

'Andy was asking about a date.'

'For dinner? Be nice to see them.'

Ian stares at me as though I've said something stupid. 'For the wedding.'

Of course; he's going to think I'm getting cold feet. I know he's keen to do it soon but now, with everything that's going on, it seems too much to think about it. 'We said next year.'

'That could be a few months.'

'I was thinking autumn.'

'We still need to book somewhere. Let people know.'

I don't have anyone to invite. Mum, Dad and Anna will come if it suits them, if it doesn't, then it won't matter how much warning they have. I start to clear the plates. Ian's gratin is virtually untouched.

'You didn't like it then?'

'Bit wholefood for me.'

He smiles and I wish he'd do that more often. It changes his face. In an instant I feel as though marriage is not such a stupid idea. 'September. A September wedding. Maybe late in the month. It'll be warmish without the wasps.'

'Sounds good. Shall we have a think about venues tonight?' He reaches across for his plastic wallet and I put my hand on his.

'I wanted to show you something.' The tin is still in my shopping bag. I fetch it, pulling it out carefully before placing it on the table. He pulls a face.

'Doesn't look particularly hygienic.'

I should have cleaned it up. The lid sticks as I prise it off and a few photos fall onto the surface.

'I found it in Jim's house.'

He stares silently at the images.

Look at them, all those people that I never knew. Tell me you want to help me find my family.

'When did you go there?' he asks finally.

'Monday. I wanted to find out about him. I want to know him. It's why I need to visit Mum and Dad and I don't want to be away too long.'

'You'd rather be with someone you don't know, who's out

cold, than visit my parents who are throwing a party because we're supposed to be there. It doesn't make any sense. How many years will we have left with them?'

'That's ridiculous! They're only in their sixties.'

'Anything can happen.'

'Yes. And it does. What if he wakes up?'

'And what if he doesn't?'

Hospital life is all silence and waiting. The people who work here adapt to institutions, starved of sleep and natural light. They develop dark humour. Night and day are the same, there's no hot or cold weather, the heating is always boiling. There's a pervading atmosphere of imminent death that makes every moment feel stolen. Almost anything could happen, but generally never does. It leaves long-term visitors like me simultaneously pent-up, cheated and relieved. A curious, chemical, edgy rush that my sociologists thrive on.

I straighten Jim's covers, two cotton blankets with open weave like those for babies, so they can breathe through the holes instead of suffocating when they cover their faces in the night. Sarah is probably covering Sheldon in the same way. It's not the sort of thing we'll ever be able to talk about. Sarah is Andy's wife, Ian's friend first and foremost. Perhaps I'll be a mother too, and then we might have things in common. It isn't something that's been discussed. The wedding comes first because things must be in the right order; it's how Ian likes to do things. My life is being measured out in teaspoons.

Would I be different if Carrie had survived? She was always stronger. I'd have followed her anywhere when we were small. She chose our games, our clothes, our friends. There's a part of me that still feels lost without her. I wish I could ask her what I should do. 'It is not unusual for the brain

71

simply to wish to shut down', the phrase spirals inside my head. How appealing it sounds. To be able to close the ability to think.

Dieu, notre seule espoir. 1917. Jim's story

Jim stared down at the face of the young boy in pale grey uniform. How had he come to be here? He was barely past puberty. Oversized uniform made him look younger still. Fine, blonde hair so pale it was almost white where it fell over the red gash on his forehead and reached the black braiding on his collar. Eyes of the palest blue gazed beyond the blackened horizon, emphasised by the unnatural position of his slender neck. He looked cold lying there in the mud. Purple-blue veins ran threadlines across hands that still clutched something precious.

When the line was cleared, they'd been told to check all the bodies for anything useful, before they pushed on. Jim swallowed, nudged the boy's rigid fingers with the toe of his boot. It felt wrong to disturb him. Someone should be covering his face, saying some words for his bravery. What would Bert do? Bert would want to know what he was holding, thinking of reward. But as he knelt down, knees sinking into mud, Jim realised it wasn't a document but a large, curled photograph. An old couple, standing in front of a low wooden cabin, stared solemnly out of the picture. Their house looked pretty, nestled with others in the dip of a hill, not unlike home. Ma and the rest of them once, in their own flint cottage. Nausea rose painfully in his empty stomach. The boy had been young enough to die clutching a picture of his parents.

'What you got there, Jim?' Bert sauntered over, his hands full of weapons, a new pair of boots swinging from his arm by their laces. He had no business whistling today. In six solid months it was the first ceasefire, eerily quiet without the noise of the guns.

'Nothing.' The boy's fingers were too stiff to take the photo back. Jim folded it, slipped it into his pocket. It wouldn't help to hear what Bert thought.

'Need any socks? Got some good ones here. I was going to swap them for rum rations but since it's you.'

That smile. No wonder he did as he pleased. You could love him even while you hated his words. Jim shook his head. If he took off his own boots and socks he'd never get them on again. Blisters wept into the wool, sticking them to his ankles, protecting his raw skin from the filthy mud. He didn't want to end up like Alf, one of the few Winterton men left, who'd gone to the bench to have his left foot amputated over a blister, crying like a baby with the wasteful shame. Trench life was marked with incidents that made the others feel lucky.

'I'm fine for socks. Thanks. You've done alright.'

'Pity your horses have gone, could've used one to get this lot back.'

They had been ridden straight over the top into no-man's-land on a raid for wireless equipment in the dead of night, months ago. A suicide mission that ended in coils of wire and piercing screams. The feisty little goat had run off soon after, the starved cows served in stew Jim couldn't eat. Without his animals he was just another private. Another thing he'd never share with Bert.

'Give us a hand with this lot, then.' Bert threw his haul to the ground next to the dead boy and held up his boots. 'What size is Fritz? Too small. You know what they say about small feet.'

It wasn't funny.

'What's up with you? Not enjoying the peace and quiet? We won this round, Jim boy. Listen: not a sound. It's what we're here for.'

'He's so young.'

'So are ours. I didn't get all this from the other side you know. Toughen up, mate, or it'll be you that gets it. Think of Charlie, your Ma.'

'I do. Least he won't have any mud at sea.' Perhaps he was even at home, with Ma and his own little family. Married men were always given leave priority.

'Or bodies. They stitch them up in bags and throw them overboard, don't they? Disease risk keeping them on ship.'

Jim shuddered at the sudden image. He scooped up half the spoils and helped Bert to carry them along the empty lines to the rest of the company.

The new stretch of trench was stronger than the ones they'd dug themselves, made on stable soil, with sand-bagged avenues that afforded some shelter and comfort. It felt good to have dry socks and trousers, to sit sheltered from the bitter wind. Enough boarded dug-outs to occupy without the need for digging. Chalk dust covered the dugouts like a veil of flour.

Jim finished his tea and sat with the warm mug on his knees, surveying the mayhem of their hasty camp and wondering how long it would take them to set it all right again. It was hard to know where to start. Most of the men had gone further down the boarded tunnel to his right to explore and test for weakness in the wall, but he'd volunteered to start the clean up here with the officers, in no hurry to throw himself underground again.

Further along the skyline something caught his eye, a

wicked flash of green against the lowering dusk. It was starting already. Staccato noise rose and he felt a stab of anger that his brief respite was over. Any hatred for the enemy, so strenuously fostered in training, had faded, replaced with pity: for the dead, for the injured, for himself. Swift came the survival instinct as the lights swept towards their section and Jim jumped to his feet, grabbed his helmet, bumping into Nissington as he shouted for men.

'Where the blazes has everyone gone, Avery?'

'Below, sir, scouting for supplies.' They both dropped to their knees and shouted down the entrance to the tunnel. In return came a faint response; it seemed the tunnels went on for much further than assumed.

'Get. Back. Up. Top,' barked Nissington. 'You're needed for a raid and that's an order.' He and Jim glanced at each other, knowing how long it took to crawl along the narrow holes.

'What are you dithering for, Avery? Leave them, they'll be up soon enough. Take this.' He thrust a rifle and a cartridge belt roughly into Jim's arms. 'And put yourself at the top of the ridge. Potts and Fletcher are already there. We need another ten minutes to re-bolt the guns. Go!'

Jim hadn't seen who'd gone in through the airshaft, but there were quite a few, possibly Bert too.. He had to make sure they came out, before the shelling buried them alive.

'Need I remind you of the consequences of ignoring orders, Avery?'

A blinding flash of lightning threw Jim to the floor and collapsed the entrance to the tunnel behind him in a spectacular spray of earth and mud. He'd once heard someone say that the shell which was meant for you always went about it quietly but of course there was no-one alive to confirm the truth. He'd lost his helmet. Before Jim could lift up his gun, the sandbag in front of his face ripped open and he was blinded and half choked with the spray of its insides. Something hard stung his head and he slumped forward, feeling a flash of guilty relief that it might all be over.

Pain in his throat roused Jim's senses before he woke. His head was on fire. Sweat poured from the bandage round his scalp. At first his vision was blurred but gradually the ward swam into view and he struggled to pull himself up. Movement made his head pound and he slumped back, frail and weakened. Men in beds next to him were sleeping and he stared curiously at their bandages, the reddened skin of their wounds. He tried to feel his face, to check for signs of damage, but he couldn't move his right hand any higher than his elbow without a searing hot pain in his chest that made him bite his lip for fear of crying out. The left seemed better. He reached up with his fingers, exploring the skin of his face, feeling a dried crust of blood but no obvious wounds. As his fingers touched the tail of a bandage he remembered a stinging feeling, the sandbag, the shells. No-one had rescued Pa. Why did *he* deserve it? He hadn't managed to save anyone. How would he explain that to Ma, to Charlie? Lilly wouldn't want to look after a damaged man, she needed farm life, strong arms. No use thinking of Grace at all. And then there was Bert, the tunnel, the sickening sound of collapse. Surely none of them could have survived it.

Raging thirst tore Jim's throat, through the pain in his chest and the top of his head. If only he could sit upright, he might get some attention. Slowly he inched himself up on bolsters as solid as sandbags, focusing on the illuminated script of the framed sign on the opposite wall, *Dieu, notre seul espoir*, trying to make out its meaning, though he only understood the first word. He didn't notice the nurse until she touched his arm, helped him sit and gave him a cracked cup full of water that he wanted to gulp but found himself only able to sip.

'You are hard to kill, monsieur. Even a bullet in your head has not killed you.'

He recognised her voice. It was Mathilde, looking careworn. Below her eyes were shadows like bruises, rimmed with a deep, dark red.

'What happened?' he croaked.

'I do not know what happened to you in the field. You were brought in with two other men, many days ago, you were covered in dust. A bullet, it travelled along under your scalp. There was much blood but the doctors say it is not so serious. A little miracle.'

Mathilde smiled again and Jim saw how pretty she still was. A little miracle. For the first time in his life he felt interesting, almost glamorous.

'Why does my chest hurt so much? I can hardly breathe.'

'You were near a shell, right behind the blast, it has hit you with bits of wood. The doctors took many bits of wood from your arm and from your chest.'

She held up his jacket with the round burned holes in the cloth and he turned it over in his hands, marvelling at its history. He couldn't wait to show it to Ruby and little Alfie. And Charlie. Charlie would be proud of him now and no mistake.

'The tunnel...' he whispered, and all his excitement vanished, leaving him the guilt of not dying after all.

'Sorry? I don't hear?'

'There was a lot of wood,' he said. 'The tunnel, it was boarded inside. We all thought it meant that we would be safe when we saw it.'

Mathilde shook her head as though unsure of his meaning.

'You are not well, Monsieur Jim, even yet, and you must rest for as long as you can.'

'Who… were the others, the ones I came with?'

'Neither of them is still here,' she said briskly and he didn't have the strength to ask why. 'But they did not wear this.' She indicated the regimental badge of the Royal Norfolk on his jacket, which she'd hung on a small wooden chair by the side of his bed. 'This is your *régiment?*'

Jim nodded. Mathilde repeatedly stroked the small round of her belly in a way that made him feel uncomfortable. A tattered photograph stuck out from the deep pocket of her apron. They stared at each other for a while.

'What does it say?' Jim asked eventually, 'the sign?' He indicated the wall opposite.

'It is our motto, monsieur, it means 'In God Our Only Hope'.'

Of course. That was where he'd seen it before, in the little church at Winterton with the painting of Grace. After all this, after everything he'd seen, it was strange how small the world was.

'Bert was also with your *régiment?*' Mathilde seemed to choose her words with care. 'I would like to see him.' She drew the photograph from her pocket, smoothing the edges before handing it to him.

Bert was captured perfectly, standing beside The General with one hand on her seat, laughing for the camera as though he hadn't any cares. Hot tears welled up in Jim's eyes, threatening to spill if he moved his head and he held the image until his knuckles turned white. Mathilde sat down heavily on the coat, its rough wool still caked with dust and grit, and covered her face with her hands.

It never crossed Jim's mind that it wasn't the honourable thing to do, not when she sat like that, when he watched the silent torture of her thin spine heaving over sobs that had run dry. He couldn't let the poor child live without a father's name. Even in these strange days it wasn't hard to see what that would do to its chances. Once Mathilde had explained that a father must be physically present to register the birth he didn't hesitate to give himself to both of them, his dead best friend's son and the poor child's stricken mother. He stayed for as long as she needed, building his strength daily. He didn't ask where she lived, where she borrowed the rings, what she would do once he left as they planned.

A shard of wood, as long as a workman's pencil and many times as sharp, was now lodged so deep in his breast he was told it may never work free. It had pierced the tissue of his right lung deeply enough to win him an honourable discharge, a thick scarring, a lifetime of pain on exertion. A 'Blighty One' Bert would have called it, bad enough to get him sent back home.

He gave Mathilde two month's wages, his chocolate ration and another photograph of Bert. When she asked for one of himself, he realised he had none to give. Instead, he pulled the regimental badge from his jacket and gave her that. Outside the registry he peered into the pram, pretended to shake the baby's tiny, curled fingers and asked her, embarrassed, not to try to contact him before he sent a sign, if indeed she ever did want to contact him. He took her mother's address and said he would send what he could.

Strong women. 1993. Emily's story

There are so many lives in Jim's tin of memories and keepsakes. People I will never know. A row of women in fox stoles and summer dresses stare out, unsmiling as they wait for the photographer to finish. Several men pose with waistcoats and pipes. A group of young men, all with the bottoms of their trousers rolled, laugh directly at the camera. People sit in sagging deckchairs in front of bandstands, line up along the railings of a sea wall, stand in front of garden gates. I imagine the bloodlines, examining the shape of a nose or the ghost of mischief in a smile. There are limitless possibilities in these stories.

There are four news clippings about the Ministry of Information. Two photographs of someone who could be Jim with an older man, both wearing long coats and trilby hats standing in front of a tall white building that I think I recognise. They're standing half in front of the sign but it looks as though it includes the word Ministry. Perhaps he worked there? It's a start in my search for clues.

Nan, perhaps in her late teens, has been photographed sitting on a bench in what looks like the garden of Jim's house. She appears happy. What changed that? When did they lose each other? I felt so close to Nan when I was small, now I feel I never knew her at all. I used to be eager for our stays with her in Norfolk, all long flat beaches and wide skies. With Carrie there it was the best time of my life. Even after Carrie it was easier to breathe there, away from Mum and Dad's constant work. Nan always had time to play, and she always seemed to know how we felt without having to ask.

Before Nan got ill, the three of us spent the whole summer

once, playing in the stubbled fields around the cottage, baking in the kitchen when it rained. I remember her teaching us to make paper strings of ballet dancers, joined at the arms and the edges of their tutus. We spent all day competing over who could get the most in a line, covering the floor in little nicks of paper like snowfall. She glared at us when we fought or sulked, telling us we should be thankful for the sisters we had. It was the only time we ever used to see her cross. 'It's *family*,' she insisted, setting her face in that way that meant she was not to be argued with, whatever Anna may have done. If she set such store by family, why did we never know her own father? So many questions I have no-one to answer.

'Are you eating toast?'

'Granola.'

'Of course.' The word annoys me. I want to talk about Nan's cottage, our summers, feel the cosy pull of the past. Were we happy then? I want to huddle together and work out what other family we might have, speculate about our great-grandfather.

'You called at breakfast time, what am I supposed to do, starve?'

'Eat something English, have some self-respect.'

'English is pretty much the only food you can't get here, and with good reason.'

'You know you miss bacon butties.'

'Ohmigod I do! Remember when Dad used to do those Saturday specials? Before piano lessons?'

'He knew how much we hated those lessons!' We both laugh. Neither of us has any music in us. Those lessons were for Mum. Another thing I couldn't give her. Does she think I wasted the chances I was given? She's never said.

'He used to wipe the buttered bread over the pan, so it soaked up the bacon grease. That's worth a visit in itself.'

I pause for a moment, savouring the image. When did I last eat?

'Mum said you might be going to Spain for Christmas.' It would be good to see her. All these photos and memories and phone calls are making me realise that family can slip through your fingers before you realise they're gone. I wonder if we might be better friends.

'Did she? I'm not sure when we talked about that. You know I almost forgot they were there. When I think about them it's always at home, real home.'

'Yeah, I know.' I almost tell her that I'm at the house now, but I don't want the inevitable questions about why I keep staying here. I catch sight of my smudged panda eyes in the hallway mirror. Looks like I cried in my sleep. I bet Anna looks good even at this hour, all perfect nails and glossy hair. One-handed, I pull my hair back into a ponytail and grimace. Mum's pale grey eyes, good skin even in adolescence. When I was younger it was enough. Now I look tired. I drop the ponytail.

'How's Jim?'

I wasn't expecting that, but I'm pleased she's asked, showing she's thought about me. No doubt she thinks if she was here she'd have sorted it all out by now. She might be right.

'No change. I haven't been able to find out much about his life yet but I've met a few people who might.' It's a lie. What I mean is Daniel and I know he can't really help. Something stops me from mentioning him to Anna.

'Any other relatives pouring out of our closets? Should I be worried?'

'No. Let me know what you think about Christmas, it might be fun.'

'Sure, I'll call you soon.'

It's only after I replace the receiver that I remember what it was I wanted to say to her but, as I go to retrieve it, it rings again.

'Ian. It's early.'

'It's not early at all.' He sounds cross.

'It is for Saturday. Are we supposed to be somewhere?'

'Apparently *you're* supposed to be here. You have a house guest.'

Who would show up unannounced? Another relative? The hospital wouldn't have the address of the flat. Daniel? Did I tell him? I can't remember but I don't think I would have.

'Who?'

'One of your hippies.'

Vanessa, it must be.

'Is it Vanessa? She did say she was coming, but she didn't say when.'

'No. I expect she didn't. What would you like me to do with her? Other than give her a shove in the direction of the shower. She smells like she's been sleeping in a hedge.'

I've only ever seen her author photograph, but I'm guessing she's in her late thirties, with wide henna-coloured dreads that Ian will dislike.

'I need to get dressed. I'll meet you in Kensington, it's about half-way. Give me an hour and I'll see you in that funny coffee shop, I can't remember what it's called. The one that looks like a log cabin on the outside.'

Ian hangs up. There's not much point in talking to him when he's in this sort of mood. I hope he's not being rude to

Vanessa. Sighing, I brush my hair out, smooth on some tinted moisturiser. I still don't have many clothes here and I don't want to look too smart. Jeans annoy Ian but he'll have to lump it today. To go with them I choose a loose-fitting blazer and floppy silk t-shirt, some heeled boots. I've seen Cindy Crawford dressed the same and if I don't look in the mirror I can imagine I've pulled off the look.

When I arrive, they're both standing outside the café, Vanessa with her hands in the pockets of her dungarees and Ian, some distance away, talking into a payphone. He's frowning as he speaks, showing the hard line between his brows.

'He's leaving you another message,' whispers Vanessa. I go to shake her hand and she pulls me into a hug. It feels surprisingly good, and I hold it for longer than I should. Either he's made her shower or he was making that up earlier. She smells of soap and tea roses. It's a sharp reminder of Carrie, the days we'd spend adding rose petals to water in an old garden tin, making 'perfume'. The scent was amazing, briefly, before the petals softened and turned to a brown mush.

We both smile brightly as Ian stomps over and the three of us walk in. Vanessa is spectacularly underdressed for the weather.

'You didn't mention you were coming, I might have been a bit more organised,' I say.

'No, God, this is nice and I hate ceremony.' We smile at the anthropologists' joke. 'It was a pretty spur of the moment thing. Mum's not well and she's not young so I thought I'd better visit and I wanted to see Harrison while he's tiny. I'm glad I did, he's amazing. I want to be the best auntie in the world for him.'

'Are you staying with your sister?' I navigate my way to the table with a tray of mochas and pastries.

'She's brilliant with him. I was there last night but their flat's kind of small and filled up with baby.'

Ian makes a show of stirring his drink until Vanessa looks away, then he gestures furiously at me behind her back. He won't want her at the flat.

'Come and stay with me, I'm at Mum and Dad's place at the moment so there's loads of room.'

Vanessa looks nervously between me and Ian as though expecting something more to this story and I take a deep breath and begin. She seems genuinely intrigued by the tin of memories and I feel myself getting excited to show someone who's interested. When she excuses herself to visit the bathroom, Ian leans over.

'Why the hell does she have to stay with you?'

'Because I didn't think you'd really want her staying at the flat.'

'I can give her a list of hotels. I could get her a good rate through the firm.'

'Why should she stay in a hotel?'

'Why shouldn't she?'

'Because we've got four spare rooms between us at the moment. She doesn't earn a lot from her royalties.'

Ian rolls his eyes. 'All that nonsense about elders and comas.'

'It's nice to talk to someone who's interested.'

'I'll leave you to it then.'

I should stop him but I'm too tired for peace-making, I just want to talk to someone.

'Don't forget we've got lunch at my parents' tomorrow,' he says without turning, leaving without saying goodbye before

Vanessa returns. I'm embarrassed but if she's noticed tension she doesn't say.

We walk, from the Serpentine to the Tate, in search of art for Vanessa, who doesn't know London well and is hungry for culture. In the evening, too tired to cook, we eat takeaway curry. Sharp spices and warm conversation permeate the house. Lying back on the sofa, red wine in hand, hearing stories, I'm content. Vanessa's talking about her tribe, the Edaben. She looks relaxed, good in the weird, weathered way that British people do when they've lived in the sun for a long time.

'I think living with the Edaben is doing you good. I like the chapters you've sent so far.'

'I've got more for you here too.' She holds up her tattered holdall.

'Impressive. Amazing not to have to chase for every word. If this is as good as what you've sent already, I'm pretty sure we can get some genuine interest in it.'

'I've only been out there for a few years but already I'm beginning to see more sense in the way they live than anything here. Even the stuff that seems odd at first is perfectly rational.'

Well my life certainly isn't rational. Maybe I should just go and write an ethnography of my own. 'What was the stuff you wrote about vengeance in your letter?'

'Vani, their oldest member, offered himself as a vengeance kill to another hill tribe.'

'Is that common? I thought it was a peaceful area?'

'No-one seemed surprised. He struck a deal for two months of life, so I guess it'll happen a few weeks after I get back. He gets treated like some kind of deity for that whole time and he seems to be happy with it. He hasn't been well for a long time, so secretly I think it's like a kind of voluntary euthanasia, although his family won't talk.'

'That's incredible. Are you able to witness? Is that how it works?'

'Not sure. I would have thought so, there's no point in exchanges like that unless they're highly ritualised or where would it all end? I'll try to get some images for the book.'

I can't think of any other ethnographies that show or detail case studies of vengeance offerings and I say so, becoming more excited by the prospect of this book, perhaps even a chance to have something on the bestseller list. It's better not to mention that. Despite the engaging way Vanessa writes, she doesn't like the idea of popularising her work. If it's something that will make people think then I'm all for it.

'Have you sorted out all your technical issues?' I pour two more glasses of wine and stretch out my legs. I feel comfortable and safe. 'I thought you needed to buy more equipment. Let me know if you want an advance on the book or anything, it's got quite a bit of support so far.'

'Thanks, it's minor stuff really. Most of the problem was the satellite signal. It's been flaky over the rainy season, storms in the mountains, they affect the signal and the atmospheric pressure. Gave me headaches and made the lowlanders seriously jittery. They've been having a lot more of these storms this year for some reason.'

Vanessa takes a sip and leans back. She's wearing Mum's pink velour dressing gown over her clothes as she's feeling the cold. She is entirely unself-conscious.

'The elders are blaming my boxes for the storms or they were for a bit, the sat and recorders and stuff, God knows what they think I've got in them.'

'Is that going to stop you getting photos?'

'I don't think so. They love the cameras, they never get tired of watching themselves on the replays and they insist the whole village comes to watch after I've filmed an interview. They dress up for it too. Mybwen—she's like the grandmother of everyone—spent hours putting on her ceremonial bangles and having her face painted in tiny dots that made looping spirals across her cheeks and forehead. I'd interviewed two of the men before she was ready.'

'Glamorous grannie!' I smile at the image.

'The older you are the more paint you get to wear, the more extravagant your jewellery. Interesting to people who think youth is the only beauty and spend fortunes trying to halt the spread of wrinkles. I did try once to talk about it over there, but I gave up pretty quickly. They'd never get their heads around it. They think we're all mad anyway.' She pulls a photograph from her holdall and hands it to me.

'She's gorgeous,' I say honestly. 'And we *are* all mad.'

'She's unbelievably strong and resourceful… she reminds me a little of you,' Vanessa replies.

Later, after we've gone through Jim's tin and talked about my phantom bloodlines, I push Vanessa off to bed. I pick up the evening's rubble, tidy away the plates and glasses and think about this person that she seems to think I am. I must come across to my authors far better than I do to myself. Carrie was the strong one. She chose our games, our clothes, the girls we would allow to sit near us in school. Without her I am still lost. How could I be like her? Like the woman in the photograph? Strong and resourceful; I hug the warmth of the words to myself, wanting to believe they're true.

A confidence. 1918. Jim's story

'You should have let me write to him.' Ma stroked Pearl's hair, trying to try to calm her down, but she paced between the two rooms on the ground floor like a caged animal.

Jim watched her, full of concern. No-one knew how the fire had started but it was clear she'd had to choose which child to save. Frank Harris told him that when he'd rushed round from next door with his wife and daughter, all carrying buckets of water, they found her rocking back and forth, still clutching Ruby's body, though her arms were burned raw and stuck fast to the blanket, while Alfie still slept peacefully, safe in the drawer she'd grabbed and carried him out in. Since Jim had been home she seemed to have got worse rather than better, though Charlie would be here soon. Charlie would get through to her.

'You can't put something like that in a letter!' Aunt Violet settled into the kitchen chair with the best view of the lane and ignored her sister's vicious glare. 'It's better this way, he'll understand, love, that it wasn't *really* your fault. What time are we expecting him then?'

'Depends on the trains.' Ma took a long, deliberate look at the clock on the mantel. 'Won't Billy be wanting you back?'

'He'll be sitting in the garden on a nice day like this. Why don't we all go outside? We could welcome Charlie together.'

'That might be too much for him, Vi, it's his first leave in two years and who knows what a time he's had out there?'

Whatever he'd been through he'd be looking forward to seeing his daughter. Her face might have been the only thing keeping him going. Jim could hardly bear to think about what this would do to Charlie. Jim couldn't even say her name without a visceral pain twisting his gut, he heard her voice everywhere and Ma must feel the same; Aunt Violet wasn't helping anyone.

'He'll be pleased to see us all. I'm looking forward to seeing him anyway. I wonder if he's got a beard? They do, you know, in the navy.'

Ma shook her head and turned back to the stove, banging the door a little too hard. Aunt Violet would never take a hint, Ma should just tell her to go. Jim shifted himself up slowly to set the kettle again, not really knowing what else to do. As he rose, a stab of pain in his chest buckled his knees and made him cling to the tabletop, gasping shallow breaths until it passed. It didn't happen so often now, perhaps it was settling as they said. When he'd first got back, he could hardly walk ten paces without falling.

Pearl turned tight circles in the hallway, wringing the ends of her dressings between her fingers. On her forearms and hands, the skin was almost healed. Jim had heard Aunt Violet asking what she was doing with a lamp lit in the middle of the night, sparking gossip, suggesting that perhaps she'd turned to drink in Charlie's absence. 'You wouldn't be the first one, dear, you might as well tell your family.' She wouldn't be the first one to be scared of the dark either, would she? There were plenty of women who left the lamps all night. Maybe it was Ruby, she used to wake in the night, maybe she knocked the lamp, no, stop thinking about it, it did no good. He closed his eyes and saw her skipping down the garden to the chickens, then lying limp across Pearl's lap, her nightdress charred. It felt like the end of everything good.

'Oh, look! I think he's coming! Jim, sort that kettle out!' Aunt Violet called. 'Pearl! Annie! He's here.' Jim gave Pearl a smile of encouragement. She was so thin, she was barely eating. He looked around for Alfie so that Charlie could meet him first, before he knew anything was wrong, it was important for him to bond with the boy before he associated him with anything from that terrible night. But Violet had already seized him and was carrying him out the other door, singing happily at the prospect of some drama, promising him a trip to the chickens. Jim opened his mouth to protest but perhaps it was for the best to have his aunt occupied.

Jim felt a quick excitement run through him at the sight of his brother, safe and well, returned to them against the odds and looking so different in his uniform. He seemed older, broader across the shoulders, holding himself with a bearing of stoic pride. He resembled Pa. Standing back from the window he watched Ma pushing Pearl along the garden path to meet him then return to her spot by the door, bowing her head slightly as if pleading with some unforeseen power.

Charlie dropped his bag, held out his arms. For a brief moment the reunion seemed happy but, as Pearl shuffled forward, the smile on Charlie's face died out. The two stood facing each other. Jim strained to hear the conversation then he watched in horror as Charlie grabbed his kitbag and turned back along the path without seeing his son, without a second glance at his brother's face by the window or his sobbing wife on the ground.

'It wasn't the easiest thing to do but Florence said she thought it would suit me and we both agreed it might be what I needed to perk me up a bit, after the way things have been.' Lilly paused briefly, as if to gauge Jim's reaction, but he let her carry on. 'I asked her to do it last Saturday, just like that! I did feel sick when I saw the scissors. She said I was ever so brave in the end, once I'd stopped crying. It feels funny not to have to brush it a hundred times every night or curl it all up into loops. I think I must have a lot more time now. I can see why so many women are doing it. Have you noticed many?'

Jim looked up, unsure whether it was a genuine question or a way of testing him. Sometimes she tried to catch him out and it made him nervous. Sometimes he drifted off mid-conversation and couldn't remember what she was talking about. Since he'd returned, she seemed more often cross than not and he was never sure why. He found it hard to focus. Even Ma said he lived in a dream world but she said it softly, passing her hand over his head to marvel at his thick-ridged scar.

When he looked at Lilly's new bob it was hard for him to respond. It was just hair, but shorter. What was all the fuss about? The style wasn't particularly attractive on any woman, but it didn't look awful on Lilly. With her neat face and slim figure she could pull off new fashions as well as anyone.

'None of my hats suits me now, I'm going to have to save for some new ones, can't go wearing anything old fashioned with this. If you *were* thinking of a present for my birthday it would be *nice* if it was a new hat.' Lilly examined his face, checking he was listening. 'One of the ones that pull right down over your ears, they're ever so smart. Lizzie Jones was wearing one to church the other day but then she was wearing trousers as well and I'm definitely not that brave. You should have seen the look she got from Reverend Hubert! I'm not even sure that trousers suit women. And she's so tall anyway! I mean I like having short hair, but I don't want to look like a man.'

Jim nodded and shifted his weight onto his other elbow; it was hard to lay on his right side. He felt the splinter, hard and ungiving. What was the date of Lilly's birthday? He must have known once. There was a birthday tea he remembered vaguely, four different types of cake and two of Lilly's friends giggling at him over their tea-cups. It was a lifetime ago.

'No,' he agreed, 'You wouldn't want to be like a man.'

'I said *look* like a man! I wouldn't mind *being* a man. Seems to me that you lot have it easy, being taken care of all your lives.' Lilly tossed her head and carefully tucked the ends of her bob around her ears so that it made a neat curve when she took it out again, the tip brushing the collar of her dress.

'Is that so?' said Jim.

'Yes. I had to help out on the farm again this week, though I absolutely refuse to do the harvest again. I worked at least five hours every day without a break and when I got home I had to get Father's tea because Mother's poorly again. They wouldn't expect my brothers to do that. Stanley's only sitting in school all day, you'd think he might be able to help.'

'What's wrong with her?' He was fond of Lilly's mother. She was quiet and she went out of her way to feed him well whenever he visited, always using the front room and the best china in a way that embarrassed him, though he knew it was kindly meant.

'More headaches. They're bad this time too, she sees things that aren't there. Doctor Farrell says it's migraines and there's nothing for it but total quiet and a dark room. She seems to spend longer in bed every time.'

'Send her my best. I hope she's better soon.' He meant it.

'You could do worse than come to visit. Dad was saying yesterday that they've only seen you once since you got back.'

Jim thought about the stone cottage beside the cowsheds with its leaded windows and tiny rooms full of heavy dark furniture, and he knew he couldn't be there with Lilly. It was hard enough out here in all this space. She made him feel he couldn't breathe.

'If she's ill maybe I should wait.'

'He thinks it's odd that you haven't been over.' She narrowed her eyes, 'I might have to agree with him. You haven't gone off me, have you?' She affected a laugh and Jim knew she was fishing, that it was more likely her own thoughts than her father's, who never said more than two words together. Lilly didn't take after him. Always on at Jim to talk to her about the war, as if he could. Always digging, as though he had something to hide.

Jim shook his head. He couldn't offer reassurance. He stared out over the edge of the dune where they sheltered from the wind, eyes tracing the wavy lines of seaweed along the bare sand, the neat parallel tideline of pebbles. Every day the sea washed the stones to the same place, beyond the deep line of sand that never fully dried before the tide returned. The scene was comforting, unchanged. But he would never be the same again. He could have been gone twenty years, not two.

Home was his beach now, not Ma's cramped cottage. Pearl and Alfie occupied his old room and half of Ma's too, because babies seemed to need so many things, and Pearl refused to throw anything of Ruby's away, partly because she was still grieving and partly because she secretly harboured the hope that when the war was finished Charlie would come home for good and they could have another girl together. Pain stood like walls between all of them and there was nothing anyone could say.

'Penny for them,' said Lilly, laying her cool hand lightly on his forearm. His skin raised little goosebumps, surprised by the sudden touch. 'Your thoughts! Maybe sixpence actually they look interesting.'

Jim stared back out over the sea. 'I'm thinking that you can actually see the air. It isn't clear at all. It's sort of greeny grey. It is here anyway. They say that you can see the air in the northern countries, Iceland I suppose, and Norway, and it can be full of coloured lights.' He was stopped by a violent memory of green and yellow flashes lighting the sky.

'You really do come out with some strange comments sometimes, James. You might at least *pretend* you were thinking about me. You've been back for a while now and practically everyone we know is getting married, no-one waits long anymore. War does funny things to people.'

Funny things. What was he supposed to tell her? That he caught dysentery because he stood waist-deep in trenches filled with bloated bodies. Should he describe the stench of unattended wounds? Tell her that all uniforms looked the same on corpses? Jim stared at Lilly with such intensity that she stopped talking and began to pull at the tough strands of seagrass that grew through the dunes. Others might be happy to tell their families what they wanted to hear. Maybe for some it helped to block it out, or pretend it happened to someone else. He couldn't talk about anything without telling the whole story and what then? Would it have been better for everyone if he'd followed Pa?

Jim never felt like this with Grace, never ran out of things to say. He'd broken the news to her here, on this same stretch of beach. Her grief for Bert was terrifying and he wished he could grieve for Ruby in the same violent way instead of tiptoeing around Pearl and Ma. Grace fought it with her fists, her wild, undressed hair flying out in the wind. It whipped around her face in great snakes, making her look like an angry goddess while he held her, ignoring the pain in his side. Somehow he'd managed to calm her and get her home, late and tearstained. He'd visited since, more than once. Maybe there was a chance for him. Maybe happiness wasn't always for other people. Except there was Lilly. And her constant hints at marriage.

It was sheer frustration that made him do it. Why else would he tell his secret to the one person in the world he knew he couldn't trust with it? It was the only thing he could think of that might make it easier to free himself from her. So he confided, told her he was technically a father, then made her promise never to tell, never to shame Bert's family or blight his memory. Even as he spoke he knew it hadn't worked. If only he could take it back. Lilly listened, her face impassive. She selected three long strands of seagrass, concentrating on weaving them into a tight plait. What had he done? Brought them closer together with secrets? She was spoiled, used to life's small luxuries; there was still time to convince her she'd be better off with someone else. Little enough room in Ma's cottage now and where else could they live? Not at the dairy. His wounds made him useless with animals and his work was now with the feed crops, the lowest farmhand status. He thought of the thin cows that saved him during those first months in France. Lilly finished plaiting the length of seagrass and twisted it into a circle, fitted it onto the ring finger of her left hand and then splayed her fingers, turning them in the light.

Dead living. 1993. Emily's story

Vanessa has gone to complete her final research with the Edaben, promising to stay in London longer next time and it's comforting to think she'll be back soon to deliver her final chapters. I enjoyed getting to know her better. Her positive spin on life is infectious and she believes that finding Jim will be life-changing. 'These things always happen for a reason. Maybe he was sent to heal you or to help you find peace?' It made sense when she said it, but I know what Ian would say.

Before she left, Vanessa gave me a reference and I take it to the British Library, my favourite place for research with its blue leather seats and green lamps full of history. Cloakrooms check my bag and I carry my pass to order up the book, *Shamanism and Second Sight in the Plains Ntoyi* by Dr Ralph Sanderson, an author I would like to poach from Bloomsbury and who still writes at least a book a year though I suspect he'd be too old to travel much these days.

When the recommended text arrives, I can see it's been well used. Must have been on a few essential reading lists; its blue cloth cover has been carefully mended and its spine is curled with yellowing tape. I scan the index and begin with Chapter Two:

Most of the Ntoyi live in hilly areas; they are fiercely tribal and fight over scarce resources. But there are some who have established themselves on the plains, built shelters, developed sophisticated agricultural techniques and begun to specialise in their daily labours. Ntoyi plains elders are sought-after as shamans amongst other clans. Women mostly depend on basket making, though a considerable number have developed a good living from their reputation for second sight and wander from village to village as fortune tellers. Their status as seers and shamans has been heightened in recent years by their possession of a man said to embody the spirit of 'dead living'. As a young man of 15, just initiated into the warrior hunter clan, he went into the forest and didn't return. He was found asleep a week later, under a banyan tree, four of its wide leaves spread across his torso. He proved impossible to wake. The search party brought him back to the meeting house, strung from poles like a kill, and laid him on a date palm mat where he lives to this day. The elders argued for many weeks over whether he was untouchable, consumed by the pollution of death, but eventually they agreed that, because he was still breathing, that could not be the case. He receives small offerings daily, as well as liquid food in a reed pipe tube which the women take turns in administering. In this way the Ntoyi have kept their Dead Living for many years and believe he has rewarded them by bringing peace and prosperity to their settlement.

Poor boy. Extraordinary to think he could be kept like that outside of modern medicine. Dead living. Is that how I should see Jim? How long can Jim really last, even with life support? Will he bring peace and prosperity? No other sections on the young warrior offer explanation and I close the book, push back my seat. Dead living. It's the same phrase Vanessa used to describe the Edaben view of Western life. 'They think we're asleep, unconnected to the world we live in.' Are they right? We've changed our environment so far beyond its nature that most of us could never live so closely to it again. Or to each other. Her villagers live in long huts in huge family groups. They would never lose an elder because they couldn't shut each other out if they wanted to. We're the opposite, pushed apart and disconnected, no time to sit together and unable to talk about the things that matter.

Perhaps it's unfair to assume all families are the same, but it seems ours stopped living when we lost Carrie. Dead living—the phrase could be meant for me. It's what Carrie is too; she has never really gone away.

I could scan the indexes for more text. It's what Shona would do. She's always on the lookout for more books to add to her series, which is why her list is so successful. In our monthly projection meetings she puts the rest of us to shame with her innovative ideas. That's business though. Anthropology's a little different, more niche, but no less important; my list has so much relevance to the way we live now and with books like Vanessa's I could really start to make some big sales. A vague outline for a book on coma, myth and magic starts to form and then fades. It's a silly idea, of no interest to anyone but me. I should pack up and head to The Bloomsbury. All these thoughts have brought on a melancholy mood and it might be nice to have a glass of something before I meet Ian for lunch.

At the returns desk I hand back the book, shake my head as the clerk asks to check my notes. There's nothing to see, I haven't written a word, and he gives me a suspicious look. I pick up my bag and coat from the lockers and step out into the gardens at the front of the building, past the security guards in their broad-ribbed jumpers and belt chains. After the warmth of the library the chill air feels uncomfortable and I stop to pull my scarf from my pocket and wrap it around my neck.

'Emily.' I startle, almost bumping into Daniel, and the surprise makes me cry out.

'I didn't know you'd be here.' What a stupid thing to say.

'Any news?' he asks, leaning closer.

'One of my authors, she gave me a reference to follow but

it didn't give me much to go on. She's writing about another tribe now. She gets very immersed with the people she lives with.' He looks confused, maybe we didn't talk about my job but I thought we did.

'Any news on Jim?'

He must think I'm mad, rambling like that. Of course he was talking about Jim. I'm about to apologise when I remember the state of Jim's house. How could they have left him living like that, not called anyone to help?

'He's… his eyes opened.' I try a frosty tone.

'That's great!'

'Doesn't mean much according to the doctors.' I tell him what Dr Iqbal said, everything I can remember, and he listens carefully, nodding occasionally as though he understands. He seems concerned and I don't want to stay cross with him, but I have to say something. 'I went to his house.'

'It's the big one with the checked path isn't it?'

I nod. 'It was horrible inside. Covered in dust and mould, can't have been cleaned for years. I don't know how he could have lived like that.'

His face falls. 'I'm sorry to hear that. Mum used to offer to help him, quite often I think. But like I said he was private, a bit defensive. He never wanted anyone there.'

'All the food in his kitchen was out of date.'

'He had his meals delivered. Once a day anyway. They used to come every afternoon but he'd never let them inside, he used to make them leave it on the doorstep.'

'You didn't say before. So he was looked after by social services?'

'I don't know, might have been a private thing. I only know that because I called Mum at her hotel, to tell her. She blames me for his accident.' He looks worried.

'She shouldn't,' I say gently. I'm going to be late for Ian, but I'm touched at his concern. I wish we could talk for longer. 'I'm going to be late.' I say lamely.

'Don't let me keep you. Here,' he fishes in his pocket for a pen and scribbles some details onto a clean folded tissue. 'If you find out anything else let me know. I'd like to see him pull through.' He shakes his head. 'The brain choose to shut down. You wouldn't think it, would you?'

By the time I reach the pub I'm kicking myself for not asking more questions. Daniel knew Jim, he knew where he walked, where he shopped. There are things I could ask now, things that no-one else could answer, like when his wife passed, which newsagents he used; things that could lead to information. I finger the tissue in my pocket. It would be a shame not to contact him again.

'You OK?' Ian's lips and teeth are stained purplish red. He raises a wine glass and I order him another, myself a gin and tonic. I hope it's his first. It's only one-thirty and I'd like us to do something later. I enjoyed the galleries with Vanessa and it's a long time since Ian and I have played at being tourists in our hometown. We used to like the walk along the South Bank, seeing old films at the BFI and finding book bargains on the outdoor stalls. It would be fun to do that.

'Nice morning?' I've already decided not to tell him about Daniel, or the dead living, if he asks how I've been.

'Gym, picked up some cheese from the deli on the way back. Finished my list.' He points to the folder on the table. 'Did you finish yours?'

I don't know who he thinks I should be adding. All my friends are his, or partners of his friends.

'Vanessa, if she's back. I think she'd come back.' A friend

who'd travel all that way to see you get married—that would be something. She didn't seem to like Ian much but they weren't together for long and she didn't see him in his best light.

'Really? You better give her an advance so she can get something decent to wear.'

'She's interesting.'

'She can be interesting in nice clothes.'

'Shona.'

'Have I met her?'

'From work. She's the only one you have met. Short dark hair, I can't remember her partner's name, David?'

'Good friends then.'

'We don't talk about boring stuff like boyfriends. That's it, except family. I think Anna might come back, I haven't checked the date with her though.'

'Will she bring anyone?'

'Probably. Can't give you a name though, she won't have met him yet. There's a new one every few months.'

'Very New York.'

The waitress brings across two plates and I'm about to wave her away when he thanks her and sets them in front of us. I'm irritated that he ordered for me but pleased with the macaroni cheese. It looks good, bubbling in a copper skillet with a fresh salad and warm bread on the side.

'How did you know I'd want this?'

'You always order that when it's on the menu.'

'I might have fancied a change.'

'You wouldn't. It's freezing out there. You'd always go for this.'

'How predictable.' I try to shake the feeling of annoyance.

It's good food and I should be happy that he knows me so well.

Another couple asks to share our table in the crush of the pub, pulling off thick coats and scarves, draping their bags across the chairs. We shuffle across and eat in silence. They're oblivious to the room around them, talking loudly about the book they're both reading and laughing in a way that grates when you're not joining in. I try to read the cover upside down, *Trainspotting*, doesn't look much to laugh about.

When Ian goes up to the bar for the third time I can see he won't want to do much else this afternoon. His friend Paul is there with another two I don't recognise and soon they're all deep in conversation. Would he mind if I went to see Jim later? Maybe I could go back to the house, I might feel brave enough to look at some of the upstairs rooms. I'll give him fifteen minutes to remember I'm here and then I'll go and tell him that's what I'm doing.

I pick up the newspaper he's left on the table. Graham Taylor has resigned as England Manager, more photographs of Princess Di with her personal trainer. The pages seem back to front, celebrities in the main features and the real news buried inside. Conflict in Bosnia has turned to war. Two thin columns detail horrors traded between countries that didn't have names a few years ago. Such rage and violence after the revolutionary spring. Ethnic cleansing, systematic rape, thin soldiers with schoolboy faces wielding huge automatic weapons. Cruelty beyond comprehension. Is all war the same? I know the soldiers in the Great War refused to talk of it, that it changed them. What happened to Jim? What might happen to Daniel? British troops are massing in the Baltic regions, unsure where allegiance should lie. Will Daniel be joining them? If he's to go it seems important that I should see him first.

I'm not entirely sure what I'm doing back at Jim's house. Searching for clues? There must be some of Jim's friends and family left. I could look for details, lists of people to inform, names to bring to the hospital but I don't know where to start. I wish I'd asked Daniel to come with me. In the pub I wrote his number in my book, threw away the flimsy tissue in case it got damaged and I lost the chance. I tried to call him once I got here but he didn't pick up and I didn't want to leave a message.

Imagining how beautiful the house was once I wander through the rooms. Traces of grandeur shine through—elegant windows, high cornices and sweeping stairs. Almost every item of furniture is mahogany or deep red lacquer. Despite the damp and decay, the rich colours are unfaded, protected by heavy drapes. Windows are muffled; in the upstairs bedrooms, thin sun-bleached strips of blackout fabric still cling to the frames. I'm surprised at the amount of clothes in the wardrobes. Jim must own a dozen suits in tweed and worsted. Some are pristine, some are heavily darned; his generation never got rid of clothes, just mended and kept them for second or third best. There are women's clothes too: his wife's belongings? Some of them are beautiful. The rails are full of raw silks and pure wool and I trail my fingers across the hangers, watching them spring back. The clothes seem to have escaped the pernicious mould that creeps across the house. There's a lovely three-quarter length astrakhan jacket, soft black curls lined with pale blue silk and cut with deep pockets. A coat to hug yourself into on cold days. I want to try it for size but something stops me; I shouldn't really be rummaging through these things, I'm more likely to find what I'm looking for downstairs.

Four stiff chairs confront each other across the gloom of the parlour. Low tables are strewn with scraps of lace-edged cloth and the grey wallpaper has a delicate pattern of green bamboo. This room seems particularly formal. Thick cobwebs stretch over the threshold as though no-one has crossed it for years. Maybe something happened in here. The thought makes me shiver.

There must be an address book somewhere. Mum always kept hers in the dresser, by the boxed-up formal tableware that was only used at Christmas. Bureau drawers slide open easily, releasing a churchy mothball smell. None of them holds much, aside from tablecloths and placemats, but the last one is locked and there's no sign of a key. When I fetch a knife from the kitchen and gently ease the blade along, trying to catch the lock from inside, I'm surprised at my own stealth. It only takes a couple of tries. When the drawer springs open there's nothing but a stack of old pamphlets, brown at the edges. Public information booklets from the Ministry of Information.

Did Jim write these? Why else would he keep them? From the cuttings and photos in the tin I'd already assumed he worked for the Ministry but I'd forgotten they produced such things. They remind me of the mint copies of the books from my list, lining my office walls, untouched. Someone has certainly gone to some trouble to keep them pristine, there are leaves of tissue paper between them and they are laid out in numbered order. Not a single issue appears to be missing. Why would these harmless pamphlets be hidden away in a locked drawer? I take them out carefully, *Dispatch on the Far East*, *Report on the People of India*, *How to Keep Well in*

Wartime, Make Do and Mend. I sort them into piles by subject; advice books, war effort, ethnography. Vanessa will be interested in some of these, social documents that chart an era with more insight than historical texts. They probably belong in a museum.

Fading light makes the thin typeface harder to read. It's growing dark outside and I have no idea what these shadows would do to my nerves at night. I can't stay but I don't want to go either, to be alone at my parents' empty house or face an evening with Ian's wedding spreadsheet. Gathering up the documents I wedge them awkwardly into my shoulder bag then lock up and leave.

Before I know what I'm doing I'm ringing the doorbell of Daniel's mum's flat, hoping Daniel is still here. He seems neither surprised nor delighted to see me, but he asks me inside. I'm not sure what I was expecting. Indicating a sofa in the sitting room, he gazes sheepishly at the clutter. His mum is either very tolerant or still away.

I refuse a beer and he makes hot chocolate without comment. He tells me his mum's on holiday with a friend, I remember him saying he called her at her hotel, and he's taking some leave from his barracks so he can spend some time with his daughter. Her name is Evie. Her mother is with someone else. Neither of them liked the family life of barrack towns because he was always away and they were left to deal with everything else. We question each other, openly curious, and the conversation seems easy. There's no point in small talk because the way we met defies social convention and in my world of limited friends that makes us close, but I can't assume anything in case he takes it the wrong way. I may not have understood at all.

'I can't stop hoping that he might wake up and be OK.

That he'll tell me about what happened to the rest of our family.' I thought maybe Jim would fill the emptiness I feel. I don't share that part.

'When my father died I was furious I no longer had the chance to ask him questions.' Daniel's face is serious, thoughtful, his grey eyes darkened. 'He wasn't around much, not at all really, when we were growing up. When we were teenagers he wanted to make amends but we wouldn't let him. We'd seen what he'd done to Mum, running out on us and everything. But the point was we never heard his story. I didn't exactly grieve when he died. But it did hit me, the realisation that I'd never know him. I still often wonder what I've missed.'

I'm so pleased I was brave enough to come. There was something about Daniel's manner that first time, something humble and honest, that made me think he'd understand how Jim makes me feel. Right now I need someone that understands.

'Do you have any siblings you could talk to about him? My sister Anna always seems to know more about people, she's older than me, so…' I trail off, unsure of what I mean to say. The cocoa is good, made with real chocolate and swirled with cream. Not the way men usually make it.

'My sister, Ellen, passed away a couple of years ago, two years and three months in fact. Breast cancer.' He looks visibly shaken. If you really love someone, two years is as raw as two weeks.

'I'm sorry.'

'I don't know why everyone apologises, like they're somehow responsible for death.'

'Just us. Other cultures are far better at articulating the pain of grief.'

'I think I prefer 'sorry' to wailing.'

Perhaps he's served in a Middle Eastern country? I open my mouth to mention the funerary customs that mark a year's end to mourning, the haunting that follows if they're not carried out properly. But I think better of it.

Our gaze locks for a moment, then he stands up quickly, offering more cocoa. I accept and he takes my cup, goes out to the kitchen while I glance at an odd collection of toys I assume belong to his daughter. She stares down from the photographs on the wall, a pretty child with a wide smile and big eyes. Feeling guilty I check for photos of family groups, looking for the child's mother. There are none. It doesn't matter to me. As he brings back the cups I ask if he would come to see Jim with me and he nods, looking directly at me in a way that draws me in and makes me braver. His eyes are the colour of the English Channel.

A letter from the King. 1919. Jim's story

'Maybe she *is* cursed, maybe they were right after all!' Aunt Violet raised her eyebrows pointedly at Ma and pulled a face that Jim thought made her look like a turn from the music hall with those thin painted brows and disapproving pout. How could she talk about Pearl like that after everything they'd suffered?

'Who's they?' Ma looked furious too.

'The whole village! Wouldn't surprise me if it went further either, she's always been what you'd call 'well known'.'

'What do you mean by that?'

'Don't pretend innocence with me, Annie Rose, you said it yourself: no good could ever come of beauty like that.'

Ma's nostrils flared but she had said it. Jim remembered clearly the first time Charlie walked Pearl proudly up to the cottage to meet them, a bunch of spring flowers in his hand and a soppy smile on his face. Like everyone else they'd been stunned by the girl's uncommon good looks.

'Why else would all this have happened to her? Do you think it's right that she was half seas over that night? Never did shake off those London ways.'

'Hold your tongue, Violet Chase! I have never seen her take a drop in my life. I hope you put them right.'

'Don't blame me, I'm just telling you what they're saying!' Aunt Violet shifted on the hard-seated chair and set her cup back onto the table, helping herself to another scone. 'These are lovely, I don't know how you manage what with all these extra mouths to feed.'

'You know I like having them. Alfie, come and have some tea before your great aunt eats it all.' Alfie trundled obediently into the room with his truck full of wooden bricks and beamed at them.

'Good boy. Are your hands clean?' Ma lifted him on a chair so he could reach over the high stone sink, drying his hands carefully on a tea towel before settling him at the table.

'Goodness me, doesn't he look like his father?' Aunt Violet's hands flew up as though she'd been struck.

Jim nodded. The little boy looked so much like Charlie, and Pa, that sometimes it seemed ghosts moved between them. Pearl must struggle with that too, especially now the war was over and Charlie hadn't sent a word.

'Father,' said Alfie, testing the word and spraying a fine shower of crumbs on to the floor.

'Does he know? About Charlie I mean?' asked Jim.

They stared at the child with his greenish eyes and floppy hair that always seemed to need cutting.

'He's got a point,' said Aunt Violet. 'A boy does need his father after all.'

'Who knows what will happen?' said Ma brightly, eyeing Jim. 'It's early days yet.'

Why the warning look? Ma needn't worry. He wouldn't tell Aunt Violet that Charlie had promised never to set foot under this roof while his wife and child were there. He'd even left his faded photograph of Ruby, now safely stowed in the tin under Jim's bed. As if Jim didn't already see her face every night before sleep, every morning when he woke.

'Finished,' said Alfie, rubbing his mouth with the back of his hand. 'Alfie get down?'

Filled with a sudden rush of love, Jim seized and hugged him until he wriggled free and ran, giggling, into the garden. Aunt Violet waited before continuing her interrogation.

'It's common knowledge that she's been seeing a lot of Mr

Hardacre. I'm only asking because I'm concerned.' She held her hands up in mock surrender but they couldn't dispute the number of times the man came to the cottage, bringing little gifts, extra food, things for Alfie. It broke Jim's heart to think about it but he understood. What did people expect Pearl to do? Was she supposed to just give up on life? Grief was one thing, not living your own life was quite another.

'He's been good to us,' said Jim, not wanting any more of that talk here, where Charlie still watched them all from photographs.

'He's well connected. Nice to have some help with feeding the family, especially until they sort out your pension.'

'He's just being a friend. Things will work themselves out. Charlie needs some time to get used to it, that's all.' Ma didn't sound convinced.

'Do you really think Charlie might come home? After all this?' Aunt Violet's eyes were bright and searching as she leaned forward in her seat, mouth gaping. Crumbs spattered her blouse.

Ma busied herself with the bunch of sweet peas she'd picked that morning, cutting the stems and breathing in their heady scent before arranging them in a blue-striped custard jug. Carefully she set the jug in the middle of the table and glanced at the clock. 'Been nice to see you, Vi, but I need to get on with Jim's tea now and Alfie needs to come in and rest.'

'Good job I'm not too far away.' Aunt Violet pulled on her cardigan and eased her swollen feet back into their shoes. 'You'll be lonely when she goes and takes Alfie with her. Jim won't be here long once he pops the question to Lilly. Unless he already has?'

God, she was prying, always poking her nose into everyone's business.

'No, he hasn't but I'm sure you'll be the first to know if it happens. We'll see you soon. Goodbye.' Ma held the door open and watched Aunt Violet waddle through, stopping to give Alfie a mint from her handbag. She waited a few moments before calling Alfie indoors, her smile fading into an anxious frown.

'She's not such a bad thing, Jim, I know she needs to watch her tongue but she's right. You probably won't be here long.'

'I'm not getting married, Ma, if that's what you mean.'

'I'm not going to tell you what to do. I'm here if you ever decide you want to talk about anything.'

If only he could. She worried so much about them all and still he couldn't tell her; he didn't know where to start. Was he turning into Pa? It terrified him that their world was shrinking, they were fast becoming the only ones left. If they ever spoke about it they might drive each other away too.

Touching the skin gently, with the tips of her fingers, Grace traced a circle around the bruise of Jim's eye, deep purple in the centre, spreading yellow where it reached his cheek.

'Is it sore?' she asked.

Jim shook his head, tried a lopsided grin. The swelling made it hard to see properly.

'Have you put anything on it? I think steak is supposed to bring out the bruising.'

'Imagine Ma letting me use good meat for that. Anyway I think it's doing quite nicely, I'm not sure I want it enhanced. She put a cold compress on it. And the ice she found in the watering can this morning.'

'There was ice on the inside of my window this morning, I could have saved it for you.' Grace smiled. 'Looks like it's going to be cold for a bit longer. The seals are still here.' She pointed over the end of the next breakwater to where the wide expanse of beach was so covered in slick dark bodies that it was hard to see sand. A cream-grey baby seal heaved to the shoreline and tried to launch itself into the foam to be dashed back against the breakwater. Its mother bobbed anxiously nearby.

'Was your ma there? When he did it?' Grace touched his eye gently again.

'She was.' It was odd that Ma hadn't seemed surprised. When he broke up with Lilly he wasn't expecting a visit from her father. Red-faced and furious, Sam Bramwell had refused Ma's invitation to come inside, instead demanding that she send Jim out to him, which she did, in her usual calm and polite way, turning back into the house to give them some privacy. She must have heard the double smack of his fists, one at the edge of the jaw and another square in the eye, but she didn't come running out. Good thing too. Embarrassing to see her war hero son slumped against the wall, watching the enormous dairyman striding away along the lane. Even without the element of surprise he probably wouldn't have fought back. He had too much respect for the family, that and Bramwell's considerable bulk.

'What did she say?'

He watched the baby seal batter itself against the breakwater a second time, determined to push through the danger to reach what it knew instinctively was safety. Such a small creature, such fight. If it survived it would end up as huge as the great bull he'd seen dead and beached. Better to go fighting.

'She said it was a shame how you still couldn't get iodine, that some things were taking too long after the end of the war to settle down,' Jim laughed. It was typical of Ma. Always practical in the face of drama. 'And then she told me I probably deserved it.'

'Did you?'

He shrugged. He'd been spending an awful lot of time with Grace even before he found the courage to tell Lilly he could never marry her while his heart was elsewhere. Surprising how badly she took it. She never showed signs of truly caring before. Even Ma had said it was all for the best in the long run.

Undaunted by the power of the waves, the seal launched itself out to sea for a third and fourth time before catching the current right and being washed towards its waiting mother. Grace clapped her hands, delighted, swirling around to face him with a glimpse of her old self. She hadn't been happy like this in a while. Maybe she would be able to imagine a life without Bert after all. It gave him hope. If he couldn't have her, after everything, then he could never bring himself to marry anyone else. United in loss and grief, it seemed they hardly need speak to understand each other. As the months passed they'd spent more time together, forgetting the excuses that Grace was 'missing Bert' that Jim was 'struggling to settle'. They met and walked and sometimes talked. She never asked him about the trenches or what happened to him, didn't question his bravery or imagine him having adventures. Though he would have answered her, he was grateful not to have to.

Once, only once, she asked what happened to Bert. On the day Bert's mother got her dead man's penny and a letter, confirming the body wasn't found, signed by the King, Grace had looked Jim right in the eye and demanded to know. After the tunnel, the flashes and the sandbags, the missing men and the tears, she had simply nodded her head and sat beside him, breathing out until all the air disappeared, taking with it her anger. She never asked again. But when she was quiet, or thinking, her face took on a hard look that wasn't there before. Jim would go to great lengths to avoid anything that upset her.

'I suppose I did deserve it,' he said eventually. 'I'm not sure I deserved to lose the job though. He went straight from ours to Kearsey's apparently, said he told him I wasn't to be trusted anymore. The message from Kearsey himself was that I shouldn't bother showing up on Monday.'

'You can talk to Kearsey though. You've been with him a long time now.' Grace looked at him in concern. 'I hope it's not because of us.'

'What do you mean because of us?'

'Spending time together.'

Jim caught his breath, knowing there wasn't a way back, that there may not even be a way forward. '*Are* we together?'

'Yes,' she said. 'I think we are. I want you to be happy, Jim. Are you still afraid?'

Jim leant over to kiss her with his swollen mouth, feeling suddenly old. All he'd been afraid of was that this would never happen. Now that it had the fear was worse.

Dear Annie,

Thank you for your letter and for the photographs. Jim does look smart in his uniform.

I talked to Samuel about him and we'd be delighted to have him stay with us in London, I'm surprised a fine young man like him, and a war hero too, can't get work near you, it's a shame, you'd think the farms would be desperate for help. Samuel has found him a job working with him at the Ministry of Information so they can travel to work together. We will be happy to provide full board for 10 shillings a week, so he'll be able to send a little back to you.

We're looking forward to having some company, the house is always so quiet. It's hard for Samuel and me without Jack, I can still hardly believe he won't be coming home and sometimes I set a place at the table for him, like I always did. I know it was God's will that he was our only blessing but it seems so hard now that he's been taken.

We must come to see you as soon as we can, we could do with some fresh air, especially Samuel. He's been working so hard lately, still it keeps his mind off things. I have a lot less to do these days of course. Do send us your news. If you let us know which train to expect him on, we'll meet Jim at Liverpool Street.

Your loving sister,
Hilda

'I haven't seen them since I was little.' Jim turned the letter over in his hand. It was written in a delicate looping script on thick, cream writing paper, slightly scented with lavender. He raised his eyebrows as he held it up. 'Are they rich?'

'I think Samuel has done alright for himself.' Ma chose her words carefully. 'He's quite high up in the Ministry. I know they've got a nice house, a proper London house. Me and your father went to see them a few times before you were born and when you were smaller. I never liked London much, can't see why Hilda does, it's not surprising she wants some fresh air.'

'What are they like?'

'Hilda's a good woman, Jim, she'll look after you. She's a good cook too.'

Ma lifted the lid of the tattered cardboard hatbox she'd asked him to reach down from the top of her wardrobe. It was covered in balls of dust and she wiped it with the corner of her apron before placing it next to the box on the table. From the pile of photographs inside she selected a handful, passing them to him one at a time.

'There's your Aunt Hilda, with Samuel, in front of their house. It must have at least four bedrooms. She always wanted a big family. She loved children.'

Jim remembered Aunt Hilda as quiet and kind, the aunt who gave him apples and patted the top of his head. Nothing like Aunt Violet with her smothery hugs.

'This one's the two of them with little Jack,' said Ma. 'I think he would have been about four when this was taken.'

'How old was he when…?'

'He was born the year before you so he must only have been twenty or twenty-one. Terrible. Look, here he is.'

Jim took the photograph and found himself staring into the serious-looking face of a boy about fourteen, dressed in an odd suit with contrast piping around the collars and cuffs, a shirt with rounded collars and a bow tie. He held a small pile of books under his left arm.

The clothes were ridiculous. 'Why's he look like that?'

'He went to a posh school. They could afford it, only having one. Hilda never did find out why, never had any *trouble* if you know what I mean, they just weren't blessed with any more.'

'I'm glad you never dressed me up like that!' Jim thought of the village school he attended until the age of twelve. Would he be expected to be like the boy in the picture? He didn't want to go to London and live with strangers but there was no work for him here now. Lilly's father had seen to that and the general animosity towards Pearl hadn't helped. But London? How would he manage there? Would Grace wait for him? He wasn't sure what the Ministry of Information was. Aunt Hilda hadn't said what the work was in the letter, just a job. Perhaps he could do better than the farm after all.

He imagined walking along the Strand in a suit and a bowler hat like the men in the news reels.

'Hilda doted on that boy. I remember the letter she wrote when he joined up, she was so pleased he went straight to Captain, because of his schooling. He was a nice lad, quiet, loved his books.'

'What do you think I should do?' Jim couldn't listen to her talking about Jack anymore. Did they think he was going to wear a dead man's suit? Wasn't he already doing that? Surely once was enough for anyone. And what if Mathilde tried to contact him? Or his 'son'? Ma would never understand. She'd open his post too, he could imagine that, she still thought he was a child. Would she tell Grace? Hard to picture Grace's reaction, they usually avoided talk of Bert altogether.

'It's an opportunity, Jim. Your Uncle Samuel is well connected and it's good of him to have got you a job. I don't know what you think there is for you here.' Ma spread her arms, gesturing helplessly around the crowded cottage; Jim followed with his eyes. A pile of laundry sat on the table, steaming sheets dried by the fire, Alfie's toys were strewn across the floor and boots cluttered the hallway. Silently they agreed there was nothing else to be done.

Jim spent two days putting his small affairs in order, tidying his things, writing letters—to his old employers, Charlie, the war office. He opened a bank account and bought a train ticket, both for the first time. He wrote to the virtual strangers that were his aunt and uncle and wondered if they'd all get on, if his presence would be a comfort to them or a sharp daily reminder of Jack's absence. Ma cleaned his good shirts and nightclothes and packed them neatly into a cardboard case with a faint mildew smell. Only when he

119

really believed he was going did he cycle round to Grace's house and tell her what he planned.

Jim had imagined a dozen ways for her to take the news. In front of the dim bathroom mirror he'd practised words and phrases he'd thought would help. He didn't need to say any of them. Grace, quiet, raised her calm grey eyes and said it would be for the best, that they wouldn't get much peace around here the way things were.

Jim hoped she knew how much he didn't want to go. His heart was pounding in rushes that filled his ears and he felt dizzy standing on the low wooden porch at the front of her parents' house. There were a million things he wanted to say but he knew they'd turned down the wireless as soon as they'd heard the knock at the door and made no pretence of turning it back up again. No doubt they'd be delighted. They'd probably tell her to prepare for the worst, find someone from their tennis club to take her out.

'What do you think? We can marry when I'm settled and it all seems such a good chance, a good start for us.'

'It's a long way. But it's better than having you at war.' Grace held his arm, tied her scarf to his wrist. 'And when the time comes won't it be wonderful to leave these flat fields behind? We'll be glamorous, Jim, living in the capital.'

Jim's future felt clear, settled. It was only after he'd left that he realised she hadn't asked how long he'd be gone.

History lesson. 1993. Emily's story

Nurse Evans raises an eyebrow as we walk in together and I make a weak joke to cover my embarrassment, 'No flowers this time.'

'I can't be getting complacent, can I? You timed it right, they've just finished changing the sheets. I'll get a second chair.'

Daniel holds up a hand. 'I'll get it. Would you like tea? I'm going to get some.' He looks at me. 'You have a few moments first.'

Thoughtfulness shouldn't be so overwhelming. 'Milk, no sugar,' I smile. I may not need the sweet tea but the sympathy can stay.

Jim's eyes are closed again. Is that a good sign? Movement, at least, and I find it easier to be here with them closed. It's less disconcerting than seeing him staring into nothing. Dried tear tracks show where his eyes have watered. His skin is less pale.

Daniel brings tea, placing it carefully on the wheeled bed trolley, then fetches another huge chair that scrapes and scuffs the floor with a painful noise.

He winces. 'Sorry.' Was it unkind of me to ask him to come? He seemed willing to help and he clearly knows it's for me and not Jim. Two giant chairs don't really fit in a room this size and we are forced to sit wedged together. The intimacy is broken by the sound of Nurse Evans talking softly on the phone and I clear my throat.

'I've brought some photographs. From the house. In case he wakes. I read somewhere that it's less upsetting if there are people you recognise when you wake. He wouldn't know me and he doesn't know you all that well so...' Would he remember Daniel as the driver? Can you see through a windscreen as you hit it? The driver of Carrie's bus was a middle-aged woman, probably a mother herself. I don't remember what she looked like, but I remember the sound of her screaming. I pull out an envelope of photographs that I found in the tin, picking out the largest and clearest. There's one of Jim with someone I assume to be his wife, another of a young pretty girl that I'm sure must be Nan, and one of Jim in uniform standing next to another lad that looks similar enough to possibly be a brother.

'Good idea.' Daniel props them on the cabinet under the window so they're at Jim's head height. 'Better to look at these than a blank wall. If he's frightened when he wakes up it'll only take him longer to get better.'

'You think he'll get better?' It's so good to hear someone else say it.

'I don't know. He's old. But he's a proud man, that I know, and he's a soldier.' He points to the photograph. 'He'll be made of tough stuff.'

'They didn't have a choice then. They were all soldiers.'

'Look at his face in that photograph, he's proud to be wearing his uniform. Probably taken when he joined up. I don't think you can fake that.'

What about you, does the uniform make you proud? It would be different I suppose. Soldiers look so casual now in comparison to the stiff khaki drill. I try to imagine Ian in a camo suit and big boots like the photos in the news and find that I can't. You can't tell much from Jim's uniform except that it looks new. Was he just a private? I had wondered whether he was something more glamorous, a reason for all the secrecy.

'There was a point when, silly really I know, but I did start to think, after you said he was moving quickly, that he might have been being chased or something. That he might have been a spy.' Immediately I wish I hadn't said it, but Daniel stops for a moment and gives me the benefit of his quiet, considered response.

'I wouldn't think so. Who would want to hurt someone like him? Even if he was a spy or something, it's all too long ago for anyone to care. I can see why you'd come up with explanations though. What's the alternative? That you'll never know anything about his life or death. That would be unbearably sad.'

I could weep with the relief of his understanding. 'Have you seen active service?' I ask, in a quieter voice.

'Of course. Back out in a fortnight.'

Is he going to Bosnia? Am I allowed to ask? I barely know where it is. Two weeks doesn't seem long. I can feel my cheeks redden and I pick up the photograph of Jim in uniform.

'Everyone in this country's so nostalgic about the world wars. It must have been awful really, living through that.'

Daniel looks at me as though I've disappointed him in some way. 'People have an odd idea about war,' he says slowly. 'I think when a whole country knows that there's a war on, then it makes people calmer, they get less involved in creating their own small dramas. When everyone has the big stuff to worry about, then the little dramas get put aside.'

'Those wars are the only time this country's ever been affected, first-hand anyway. These days it all happens in places people only read about.'

His smile is thin-lipped, precarious; I hold my breath. Have I overstepped a line? Where did he serve? Northern Ireland probably, which makes me feel stupid for saying conflict's always far away. The Falklands? He'd have been young but maybe. Although that was a far-off war people did care about, weirdly, because it was a matter of national pride. Is Bosnia worse? It sounds it. More civilians, more women and children in the crossfire.

'If you want to know about Jim you should go to the National Archives at Kew, near the gardens. They'll have lists you can check, especially if he worked for the Ministry. They were good jobs. He's likely to have come home with some sort of honours if he worked there.'

It's a long way, too far to go now but I feel I must seize the opportunity. If he's going in two weeks there may not be another chance to spend the day with Daniel.

'What time does it close?'

Daniel laughs. 'You'll need an appointment. And plenty of time. I remember going with Mum to look up my grandad's records for a school project. It wasn't anywhere near as exciting as she promised.'

'Isn't there anywhere else?'

'The Imperial, maybe? They have all the personal stories and diaries, mostly from the second war I think, but we could look. The diaries are more interesting anyway and they're bound to have information on the Ministry.'

It turns out you need an appointment for the Imperial War Museum too, along with more personal details than I know. The artefacts are still being catalogued, says the imperious curator, but he hands me a number, says to call when I've found out more and the library will run his name through the system, see what they have. He doesn't sound hopeful.

I'm disappointed and close to tears as we sit in a cafe on the Lambeth Road, with oversized cups of watery cappuccino and buttered teacakes. Concrete streaks of sugar scar the plastic table. I pick up a battered *Time Out* that someone has left on a chair and flick to the listings, hoping to find another museum that will keep Daniel with me. There's nothing he wants from me and yet he's choosing to help; I don't want today to slip between my fingers so easily. It feels important to know that we can be friends.

'There must be somewhere else,' he frowns, trying to read the pages upside down.

I turn over the concert listings, Simply Red, All Saints, a Living Dream weekender. What music does he like? We skipped the small talk. I know that, like me, he feels abandoned by the loss of his sister and yet I don't know what gig he would enjoy.

'I'm not sure I've ever heard of anywhere else. The Imperial is massive, I remember going there with school. We all thought it was the most deathly boring trip at the time.' I was made to hold hands with Emma Pheelan the whole day, because she was a liability for the teachers and they knew I wouldn't give them any grief about it. I was a biddable child. I did what adults told me to do, not because I wanted to please them, but because, after Carrie, I didn't care anymore what I did. Part of me is still the same, pushed along by events as though life doesn't need me involved. I try to ignore a sudden mental image of Ian's wedding spreadsheet.

'Children never think history's going to affect them. You don't think about anything properly until you've had a good dose of all the emotions, do you?'

He looks up and gives me a smile that's infectious. A young waitress with long legs and a lank ponytail is throwing him sideways looks. I sit back and try not to stare at him. Two other couples sit at nearby tables, one silent, staring absently at the brown wall before them, and the other huddled together in conversation so urgently whispered it must be illicit.

'I don't really know what I'm expecting,' I'm nervous in case this turns out to be fruitless and he sees it as a waste of time, 'but It would be nice to find some sort of clue to the person he was and the things he did.'

We sit in slightly awkward silence for a while until he says triumphantly, 'What about the Cabinet War Rooms? I remember them opening, all that Churchill renaissance. Must be ten years ago now.'

'Never heard of them.' I peer across at the guide, moving close enough to brush his coffee cup with my sleeve, catching it slightly, causing him to reach out and steady my arm with his hand before I quickly draw it away. I think we both know this place won't do anything to help me find Jim. 'But they're not too far, we could walk over Lambeth Bridge and across to the park, it's a nice enough day for it.'

'Yes,' he says, 'it is.' The waitress with the ponytail watches us gather our coats and leave. I feel Daniel's touch on my skin like a fingerprint gently moulded in clay.

The walk took longer than planned. I hadn't seen St James Park since I was small; Daniel had never been. We took a lengthy detour to circle the lake, carried giant ice creams to a partly collapsed bench and made up stories about the little fairytale house on the island. In between fits of laughter, I told him about the infamous murderous pelican, crouching in its rockery nest, waiting to eat the exotic ducks. He told me that squirrels can see behind them, and that they're mostly trying to fool other squirrels when you see them making a fuss over burying nuts. We spent so long in the park that

Daniel had to leave before the museum. Now I'm trying not to read into that, wondering what it was he rushed off to do. See Evie, perhaps. And her mother.

The War Rooms give a vague impression of austerity and mystery, like Jim's house. A converted basement, no safer than the average London building and not bombproof at all. The brick walls have been painted in cream and green, like a stage set. As a place where wars could be designed and won, it's almost laughable.

This famous bunker was just as open to attack as the surrounding walls, another smoked mirror in the game of chance and determination that wins wars. I try to imagine Jim here. Would he have taken his chances in the blackout rather than bunk down here with the rats and worse? Perhaps he chose to watch the raids. I know he worked for the Ministry but I have no idea what that might have entailed. He could have caught a bus directly here each day, probably the same one I'll catch tonight. Was he one of the PM's detectives? A despatch rider? A secretary? Did he hide from the fighting as a civil servant or orchestrate the action on one of these pin-studded maps? I want someone to tell me who the real man was, the reason he ended up alone, so I can protect myself from all those years of dead living.

Inside the underground rooms everything is neat and sparse, like Jim's house. Every surface is hard, the beds are scarcely more than boards on legs, little different to the table or the unpadded chairs. Unthinkable furniture. We're all too soft now for this kind of a war. Most of us wouldn't even survive the hardships of civilian wartime life that affected Britain. Was that what Daniel meant earlier? War that doesn't affect us doesn't matter.

The map room holds a web of pinned string that binds the

globe in an energetic march of miniature flags. Unceasing activity. It's how I always imagined wars to be designed and won, how central intelligence always looks in films. Is it the same now? I try to imagine Daniel behind this desk, barking orders into this mouthpiece.

For once the gift shop isn't a mandatory part of the exit but a detour through the small café with its attendants in period costume and I squeeze through the crush of tables to the stands of books and publications. Two of the texts are the same as the ones in Jim's drawer, reprinted with retro-kitsch covers and matching posters and I buy them both, intending to compare their contents with the materials I have.

'Do you have any more of these texts for sale?' I ask.

The woman at the counter is friendly and eager to help, though she looks a little out of place with her curled horns of braided hair and silver piercings. Her eyebrows are beautifully painted in 1940s arcs.

'There's a whole archive. Most of it's on our micro-fiche index, you can look at it here or in the British Library.' She glances at the oversized clock on the wall opposite. 'You'll probably have to come back though, we're closing in about half an hour.'

I thank her and stow away my purchases, take a contact card of opening times. Why would these texts be locked away in Jim's drawer as though they're top secret? What did they mean to him?

'I don't really want to read them, I have copies, I wanted to know why they were written.'

'The Ministry of Information had an official stance on everything. It was actually set up in 1918, replacing the propaganda work at Wellington House, but it only came into its own after the second war broke out. The government was worried that morale would be low, so they set it up to be a controlled source of propaganda.'

'And lifestyle advice?'

'Even that was propaganda. Spoon-feeding. They probably had teams of people working on them all.'

'You know a lot about it?'

She laughs. 'This is what a history degree does for you: a brainful of interesting knowledge and a fine career in a gift shop. What's your research about?'

'I wouldn't call it research.' What would I call it? I just want to know more about Jim. These texts were important to him. Did he write them? Did they get him through the war? 'I found a whole bunch of them, they belonged to a relative of mine and I think he might have had something to do with them.'

'Can't you ask her, or him?'

I shake my head, should I tell her? I know what Ian would say, 'Doesn't do any good moping around, Em, you need to get on with things.'

'OK, I get it. If you hang around for ten minutes you can buy me a pint and I'll tell you everything I know about the Ministry.'

Unfamiliar clothes. 1920. Jim's story

Jim's aunt and uncle were decent, quiet people. They left him alone and that suited him as he grew used to his new life. Working indoors drained his energy in a way that farm work never had; his eyes burned from the strip lights and his shoulders ached from sitting. At least he wasn't running errands and messages anymore. His injuries had earned the respect of poor-sighted and asthmatic civil servants who'd stayed for the duration. They were also the reason he'd been given The List—sole charge of compiling a definitive record of deaths in service from the Great War, a role that came with its own tiny office, complete with leather chair and neat filing trays.

Each entry had two paragraphs, into which he was supposed to detail the facts and figures of a soldier's life: regiment, corps, battalion, place of birth, service number. Though he tried hard to make them unique, it was difficult in restricted space and with the requisite details. Each entry included key life dates—born, enlisted, died—plus a line or two on the theatre of war. Officers were set aside for the list he'd work on next. Sometimes it seemed that he'd spend his entire life detailing deaths.

When the rains came it was bliss to be in his warm room, with tea and biscuits at precise two-and-a-half-hour intervals, free of the chafing wet fields. Sunny days were different; he gazed through the glass, trying to remember the smell of fresh-cut hay, the sound of crows following the plough. He should write to Ma for some pictures. The little office could do with brightening up. He hadn't asked about its previous occupant; some men's misfortunes created opportunities for others.

Jim felt uncomfortable in his unfamiliar clothes, an old jacket and shirt of Uncle Samuel's and a new pair of trousers. They were fitted with six pleats on each side at the waist and tapered to a neat turn up at the bottom, which sat snugly on the new leather brogues that he cleaned every evening. His hat and overcoat were brushed daily too, to raise the nap and keep them 'good'. He'd never had so many responsibilities. Independence unfurled in the spring of his step as he walked to the bus stop, in the deferential nods as the tea ladies pushed their trolleys through, and in the political conversation he began sharing with Uncle Samuel. At first, he'd craved the coastline then Aunt Hilda reminded him that the sea was cruel, that it had ruined her family when it took her brother. 'It's only the air I miss,' she said, 'there's no fresh air here.' Still, she'd moved a seascape painting into his room—a Turner print—and he'd thanked her, admiring the fine detail on the lines of foam that burst up above the harbour wall. Sometimes he sat up in bed and stared at the picture, imagining the sea spray wild in his face. He missed home, and Ma too, but it was good for him to be finding his feet—hadn't she said that herself? It didn't do to think too much of it. Before long, it seemed that whenever he visited Norfolk things there were strange and awkward and not the other way around. He saw Grace only once every two months, when she took tea with them in the kitchen before Ma pushed them gently outside to walk together.

Hilda cooked a roast every Sunday and, after church, Jim and Samuel put on their hats and walked down to the Black Lion. Jim insisted on peeling the potatoes first, growing embarrassed at the way his aunt filled with tears, as she did over all small acts of kindness. He was glad, though, after helping her, to be escaping the muffled still of the house, with its heavy velvet drapes secured in thick corded tassels. Aunt Hilda considered net curtains to be common, something slovenly people hid their dirty rooms behind, and none of the ground floor windows was covered during the day. It was odd to see nothing but other houses as he sat at the table facing onto the street.

They walked briskly, stopping briefly to empty a bag of stale crumbs into the water for the geese that circled the footbridge, and reached the pub in under twenty minutes, settling onto high stools in their usual place by the beam. Jim was pleased to buy the drinks and sipped his first with pleasure, feeling like a grown man as he raised his glass and surveyed the busy room.

'Your good health,' he said.

'Likewise,' replied his uncle, carefully dabbing at the beer foam on his moustache with a spotless handkerchief. He was a tidy man, not tall or handsome, but neat in appearance and sparing with words, possessed of a quiet dignity that served him well on the battlefields and earned him the respect of his colleagues when he returned to work. Jim was grateful for the way he was. He hadn't needed to help a nephew he barely knew.

'Weather held out then.'

'Yes.' Jim nodded and set his glass down gently on the towel that spread over his end of the bar. 'I expect the rain will hold off until tomorrow.'

'How's the work doing this week?'

'Steady progress. I worry it'll never be finished. Every day there're more names and files and especially more unknowns or missings. I don't know what we'll do with those. It's going to cost an awful lot of money to print once it's finished. There's a lot of discussion about the right cut-off date. It would be terrible if people were missed off.'

'Or if they were missings that came home, or showed up dead... might cause some upsets.'

'Can that happen?'

'Suppose so. Can't go on forever though, old boy. Have to draw the line somewhere. Been almost two years now since the whole damn shooting match finished. I'd say another twelve months should be enough.'

'If I can write it a bit more quickly! At the moment it will be more like two years unless I get some help.'

'It's a fine job you're doing, not the sort of thing too many people should be involved in. I did plenty of similar things when I joined the Ministry too, not as important as this, of course, but it's better for accuracy if you do most of it yourself.'

Jim nodded. He'd been given an office so he could set up his own system of filing and retrieval that would make omissions or repeats impossible. With his lack of experience, he'd done a good job of creating a unique system that most of his colleagues would find impossible to unravel.

'Let's keep it to ourselves though.' Samuel gave a sad smile.

'If you think it's for the best.' Jim was doubtful. He understood why discussing his job might make his aunt upset but he'd been so excited about the new office he'd blurted it out and, when they'd agreed not to disclose any details about what he was doing, she'd decided he must be engaged in top secret activities, unravelling the lessons of the war and planning for future conflict. Since no-one contradicted her, the silence turned to untruth. It was like Ma always said, 'Once they take hold, lies, like ivy, tend to grow where they're not wanted.' Now the rest of the family believed it too, although he planned to tell Grace the truth as soon as they were married.

'I do. I don't want her to ask to see it.' Samuel took a packet of Capstans from his top pocket and offered them across, forgetting, like everyone, that Jim didn't smoke. He lit his cigarette and inhaled deeply, holding his silver lighter up for another customer who'd wandered over to ask for a spare.

'Hilda's stronger since you've been with us, Jim, I'm grateful for that, but she still can't talk about the damn war and it's not our place to make her, whatever people say. It's not always good to get things off your chest. She had a terrible war and that's that. People ought to leave her alone.'

Was that for the best? Ma wouldn't say so. Hilda seemed to spend most of her time indoors and was nervous if they ever had visitors. He'd tried to explain it to Ma, but their worlds were so different it was hard to find the words.

They sipped their drinks in silence while Jim, facing over the long curve of the bar, surveyed the room. Tall sash windows were lowered at the top, bright trailing blooms of hanging baskets showing through the gaps. He ordered another with a little nod of his head and the barman nodded back, taking his time with the pumps, giving the brass a polish with the end of his white cloth before wandering over to their end of the bar and setting down the new glasses. Samuel picked his up without bringing it to his lips and sat contemplating it for a moment, tilting the glass as though weighing it in his hand.

'After Jack ... after she got the telegram, she used to sit for hours on one of the dining room chairs, looking at that painting. We never liked it before, always said it didn't look much like him, we had it up in the study for years. But she brought it down then, without asking, had Roberts hang it in the middle of the room.'

Samuel paused and Jim cleared his throat. Was he expected to say something? He didn't like it either. The oil-painting showed his cousin at five years old, wearing a serious expression and clutching a wooden boat, painted in red and green with tall white sails and a trailing string. The same boat stood on the windowsill of the room Jim slept in, along with dozens more treasures from Jack's life.

'She's different since you've been with us, though. Changed, in a good way. Not as active as before Jack, she doesn't see too many friends, but sort of... distracted from grieving all the time. She's always in the kitchen now.'

'I'm not complaining about that,' said Jim. 'Aunt Hilda's an excellent cook.' It hadn't taken him long, in the end, to succumb to the fuss she made over food. The extravagance of several courses at each meal and the sheer number of dishes to clean. Aunt Hilda continually experimented with new recipes, and she would never use leftovers or put the same meal on the table two days running. 'Waste not, want not,' she said as she wrapped it in paper for the gardener or Mrs Roberts, who came to clean in the mornings. But it *was* wasteful. Was she trying to fill her days? It was hard to ask Ma without seeming disloyal.

'I don't know where all this is going to end.' Samuel patted his waist. 'She thought it should have been me. Has she told you that yet? I hadn't been back two months and she came out with it, like that, said it should have been me.' He shook his head and Jim leaned in to protest.

'She wouldn't have meant...'

Samuel held up his hand to stop him. 'I understand, Jim. I

do. I know she's heartbroken. But it's hard to forget when someone says something like that.'

After the party. 1993. Emily's story

It's still raining after three heavy, wet days. Huge raindrops roll down the wooden shutters of the villa and I watch them through the window, wondering why rain in Europe is always more beautiful than at home. I made the mistake of mentioning this at yesterday's dinner and received a lecture on atmospheric refraction. My parents' new friend, Bob, is an expert on most things.

Anna didn't make Christmas in the end but, to assuage her own absent guilt, she managed to convince me it was a good idea to travel to Valencia to have the conversations I wanted face-to-face. Ian refused to come, partly because he works for a firm that fails to see the benefit in taking holidays and partly to make the point that it's his parents' turn. They'll be holding a stiff series of drinks parties that I'm not sorry to miss and their idea of festivities is awkward. There's always charades and they open presents at suppertime when the day seems finished.

I brought Jim's tin with me, and its contents are spread all over the kitchen table because I came to find answers. I wanted Dad to tell me who they all are but he recognises no-one except Nan, can't remember relatives ever visiting them. How can people split apart and never find each other again? Alice, the friendly goth from the gift shop, was incredibly knowledgeable about the Ministry and its publications; she even promised to help me find out more and I'll take her up on it because I liked her a lot. But she can't help with these questions and, apparently, neither can my own family.

I've brought photographs of Jim's house, too. If he ever wakes up he can't go back to living there as it is. The place seems full of sadness and I want to peel away its layers until it's a home again. Perhaps I'm naïve about what that would take but at least I'm prepared to try. Dad, who gets alarmed by the threat of any kind of home improvement because that means change, is unconvinced by my attempts to borrow money from him for fixing it up.

'It would be an investment, wouldn't it? If you're the only living relative, then you'll probably inherit the place anyway.' I dip a hard, sweet pastry stick into my coffee and sneak a hopeful glance at Mum who has strong opinions on the security of property. She looks shocked. Both sit holding photographs as though they can't quite believe what they're seeing.

'What do you think?' I try a light-hearted tone.

'It's a mess, Emily.'

'Not really. I think with a bit of modernising...'

'It would cost more than the property is worth!'

'Not in that part of town, and anyway we could do lots of it ourselves.'

'No,' says Mum firmly, 'your father's not well, he can't be worried with all these things.'

I look from one to the other of them. There didn't seem much wrong with Dad when he was laying into the beer last night. I should fix up the house myself, prove I can be practical. It would be the right thing to do. Then I could be there to look after Jim when he gets out.

'I'm not asking you to do the work, just lend me some money for a few improvements. It would be really helping him. We could put in some rails and I could be there when he comes round.' I'd have a huge amount of cleaning to do first but I really want to do that, I want to make it a home for Jim again.

'You don't know the first thing about looking after anyone, Emily.'

'Thanks. I think even I might manage to find some nursing skills if I really tried.'

'You know what I mean. It's not going to be just a question of cooking and cleaning for him. If he ever comes out of the coma, don't look at me like that, *if* he ever comes round, he's not going to be back to normal. Whatever normal might have been for him. He'll probably need someone helping him with the toilet, washing him. You're not up to all that.'

Four days with Mum has left me feeling ten years old again. I want to argue but I know it'll come across as sulky and childish. Can I see myself looking after Jim like that? When I think about him getting out of hospital he's unharmed, chatty, pleased to get to know me. We have long heart- to-hearts in his newly renovated house and I cook him dinner.

'The hospital will want social services involved.' Mum speaks as though this is scandalous, like having the police round.

'There's no harm in making it a bit easier for him to manage. We can't let him go back there the way it is and he's family, Dad's grandad. Don't you want to get to know him?' I pick up the tin, start to replace its contents. 'I want to know about all this.' I wave a photo of strangers who are probably relatives. 'I want to know everything.'

'When I was growing up I didn't think about it,' Dad says. 'We didn't have any family around us. I never thought anything of it at the time, and there were plenty of families in Winterton who'd lost everyone in the wars, but as you get older you do wonder.'

'I remember staying at Nan's. I loved it.'

'So did your sister,' Mum adds.

Is she talking about Anna or Carrie? I don't remember Anna loving the beach, she used to complain about the sand, how it got into everything. She spent most of her time looking for stones with holes in, to thread on a shoelace. Witches' stones, Nan called them, she said they should be thrown back into the sea in case they brought bad luck. 'It was so different, to us. I remember watching the seals on the beach. Must have been hard to leave all that air for the city.'

'Not really. It was exciting, full of people like me who'd left to find work and forget their troubles and what-have-you. People who couldn't stand the peace and quiet anymore.'

What must he have been like then? A young man on the verge of adventure. About the age of Jim when he went to fight. Did he ever think he'd end up in an open-plan villa full of cane furniture, in a motley ex-pat community? Aside from know-it-all Bob there's Deirdre, his wife. Alan and Brenda seem well meaning enough when they actually sit and talk but their perpetual enthusiasm for any and every activity is beginning to grate. There's Celia, who lost her husband to lung cancer a few years ago and never quite got over it. Besides them there are three or four couples who seem good for my parents in a bombastic, drinks party way. Perhaps Dad has finally found family of sorts. In the last few days they've barely been out of one another's houses. Life seems to be one long round of brunches and bowling, tennis and lunchtime cocktails. It's a social life I never thought they'd have. All the long minutes of each day need to be filled in retirement.

Mum picks up the tin and gingerly places it back inside its carrier bag. She beckons me through to the kitchen and asks me not to upset Dad with all my questions. 'I wouldn't go digging around too much in the past,' she says. 'You're not always going to like what you uncover. What's done is done, isn't it?'

How are they not interested in their own pasts? It's not digging around because the past won't stay where it's left, it follows you until it wears you out.

'Are your parents quite well, Emily?' Ian's mother inclines her head as she speaks, as though she's eager for answers, but her eyes dart around the room, making sure everyone is exactly where she wants them, neatly positioned on the cream leather sofas and chairs. There are several smart older couples, women in dresses, men in jackets and ties, all looking odd in stockinged feet that won't mark the thick cream carpets. Small tables have been brought out from storage, each balancing china bowls of cashews and sour-cream flavoured crisps.

'I'm never too sure. Mum's always hinting at some medical problem with Dad, and I know he takes pills for his blood pressure and angina but he seems OK to me. He brushed it aside when I tried to ask him about it. They were both in the party mood really.' I can see by her look of distaste that I've made the mistake of thinking she wanted an answer other than 'fine', and a move on to other topics.

'Do send them our regards. We all need looking after a little more each year.' Her face rearranges itself and she turns to smile brightly at Sarah, smoothing down her green silk dress as she stands. 'Elegant' Mum calls her, impressed and perhaps slightly envious. It looks exhausting to me. I've never seen her dressed in anything other than beautiful, tasteful clothes, perfectly groomed. She has her hair styled and nails manicured weekly. Will Ian expect the same relentless routine of maintenance for me? I try to picture us together in a house like this, his parents' age, parents ourselves. It's not an image that comes easily.

I found a kind of peace with Mum and Dad, did some thinking on the plane home. For a long time I thought Carrie's death had closed them off, but they both lived in small family units all their life; Dad with just Nan in their little cottage and Mum with her parents dying so young and the rift that somehow put between her and Aunt Samantha. Whatever the damage was, it was done before Carrie was even born. Losing people is a gradual thing. It makes sense to me now, their stiffness, the way the house felt too quiet. Mum's constant cleaning and surrounding herself with soft furnishings. They've done nothing wrong.

'Did you manage to settle Sheldon?' Ian's mother asks and Sarah smiles brightly back.

'After a fashion,' she replies, practiced at the art of small talk.

Her eyes are dark-ringed beneath concealer. Sheldon is a colicky baby, unlikely to settle well. Getting him down now will no doubt mean he's up in a few hours and Sarah will be walking him round the house, trying not to disturb anyone else's sleep. It would make more sense to let her bring him down now, to cheer up the party and pass him round to everyone, tire him out for bed. But that's not how Ian's parents are.

'It's tough the first few months.' I put a friendly hand on her arm.

'It's really not.' She pulls it away. 'It's much easier than everyone imagines.'

'Good girl,' Ian's mother pats her thigh. 'Emily will find out for herself soon enough. Though goodness knows I'm not at all ready to be a grandmother so perhaps you could leave it ten years or so, dear.'

'You'll never *look* like a grandmother,' says Sarah.

Why can't I think to say things like that? Ian's mother laughs, pleased, catching Ian's attention. He wanders over to our corner, bringing a plate of vol-au-vents filled with prawns in a violent pink sauce.

'I suppose you're talking about me.'

'Goodness no, you'd never be so amusing,' I say, hoping it strikes the right tone. Ian gives me a puzzled look, Sarah and his mother exchange glances and then select their vol-au-vents. I give a high false laugh. 'We're talking about your mother being a glamorous grannie.'

'Is there something you should be telling me?' Ian asks.

'No!' My reply's too forceful. 'Nothing like that, just... a silly comment.' I take one of the prawn puffs in a conciliatory gesture, struggling to eat the chewy pastry without upending its horrible innards onto my skirt.

Sarah joins Andy and Ian's father while his mother reaches over to smooth Ian's collar.

'First things first,' she says. 'There's a wedding to plan. I've booked you an appointment at Morley House the day after tomorrow.' She takes a napkin printed with holly leaves and dabs at the sauce on my thigh. 'Don't eat that, dear, if you don't like it.'

Ian is enthusiastic about Morley House, a large country estate turned luxury hotel about a mile from his parents' house, where the children of most of their friends have been married. It's expected. Ian thinks it's suitable. Ian's parents consider it to be reasonably priced, have offered to cover most of the expenses and have actually allowed us to visit without them. We stand in the lobby, and I feel the weight of heavy tapestries and whispered secrets. The room is autumn coloured.

A heavily made-up woman talks to Ian while leafing through some pieces of paper on a clipboard. There is some confusion over timings.

'Why don't we have a coffee and wait?' I suggest. 'There's nothing else going on today.'

'Because Mother booked an appointment,' he replies, his shoulders stiffening.

I hold my tongue. He's already irritated, and I don't want us to view this place barely speaking to each other. The woman is still looking through papers. Perhaps there's a double booking? But there isn't a likely looking couple hovering nearby. Two well groomed, older women with hard faces are talking at each other intently, leaning forward in vast leather chairs. Gathered around the small table behind them three men with good haircuts are discussing golf vocally. The hotel has a course with undulating greens that stretch around the building.

'I do apologise, sir.' She speaks in exact, clipped tones, but the traces of an accent remain and I wonder how she came to end up in this genteel palace of gloom. A large blue badge over her left breast reads *Sonja, Duty Desk Manager*.

'It's quite alright, Sonja,' I say. 'These things happen.'

'I don't see why this is so difficult,' Ian snaps. 'All we want is to look at the ballroom.'

Sonja's face is impassive. Poor woman is probably used to rude people; it's the kind of place that attracts them.

'Where's your manager? Perhaps you could tell him that I'd like a word?' Ian asks.

'I'll get her.' She doesn't correct him. She turns towards the front desk, picks up a telephone and begins to speak, still watching us.

'If she doesn't hurry up, we'll be late for Mother's lunch.'

'We've got ages and I'm not that fussed about this place. It's got actual stags heads on the walls. I don't like the way they watch you.'

'It's called the Huntsman's Room, Emily, what are they supposed to have on the walls?'

'I thought we'd agreed it would be simple.'

'It will be. It just gets awkward once you start leaving people out. We've been to so many in the last few years, we can't not invite them back.'

I don't want our life together to start off in a room full of strangers, but, despite his mood, I put my arms around him because I know why he wants this. A grand gesture, the idea of company and parties, of belonging to close-knit groups that stay together. His own family is small, no siblings and parents with snobbish ideas that mean everyone falls into the mutually exclusive categories of 'too common' or 'too grand for us'. Ian, too, can be judgmental. We don't often meet new people ourselves.

Sonja is coming back with another woman, younger and taller with a straight-backed walk and turned-in toes. She's also heavily made-up but it suits her better. Her voice is a high, nasal singsong.

'How can I help you today, Mr Mason?'

'I assume that's already been explained to you, since you've been talking to your colleague for ten minutes.' If she's taken aback, she doesn't show it. Sonja lurks behind her, watching the floor.

'Sonja has indicated that there has, unfortunately, been a little mix up with the date. But if you're OK to do the tour now I can take you round myself?'

'Emily, do we have time now?' His mouth is twitching slightly, his irritation deflated by the hug. I shrug, acquiescent, and we follow the manager through a series of three reception rooms, each larger than the last, ending in the enormous ballroom where, she assures us, the most prestigious parties are held. With a wink she tells us she couldn't possibly reveal names but we'd definitely recognise them. We end our tour back in the lobby, where she hands us a shiny brochure with her business card before disappearing.

'What do you think?'

'It's not really my cup of tea.' I'd prefer something a bit less pretentious. You knew that though. I leaf through the brochure. 'There aren't even any prices in here.'

'She said they'd have to quote for us, there are too many variables, weren't you listening?'

'I thought there'd be some indication.'

'I liked the ballroom, I could see that with round tables, and there's a good space for dancing at the end, if we have those folding doors pulled back.' Ian hands me his folder and I juggle it with the brochure. 'I'm going to ask them to do the quote now.'

'I thought we were going to be late?'

'It shouldn't take long. And we can show Mother then.'

The Manageress is all smiles as she settles us into huge wingback seats in the bay window, fussing with papers, ordering complimentary drinks. The chairs remind me of hospitals, of Jim and Daniel too. Silently I finish the grainy coffee and stare out at the grounds. I find the sculpted landscaping as oppressive as the decor inside. There's a small folly to the right of the lawns, twisted with ropy vines and half hidden by the sweeping curtain of a willow like the one I used to hide inside at home.

I can clearly hear Ian's mother's voice as he talks to the manageress, his fear that our wedding might not pass muster. It's hard to blame him for wanting all this. His parents are serious in a way that, despite their tragedies, my own are not. Ian's mother and father care what others think of them, social occasions must always be carried out 'properly'. If we could talk about why he needs this crowd to belong, he might change his mind or I might feel better disposed towards the plan. It is, after all, just a party. But he would be hurt, in his silently furious way. He'd feel compelled to offer some judgement on my own family; things I don't want to hear. Better to leave things unsaid.

A second-hand ring. 1922. Jim's story

'It was a grand do, Annie.' Aunt Violet leaned back into the chair with her feet stretched out on a stool, a fresh cup of tea balanced carefully on her bosom. 'I'm fit to drop now. Have to get Billy to fetch me home.'

'Some hope,' laughed Jim, jerking his head out to the front bar where his uncle lay slumped and snoring over a table, his fist curled firmly around a beer glass. Ma, laden with used plates and cups, tugged Grace's arm and they both joined the laughter, leaning against each other as they tried not to drop anything. It was good to see them together like that. Ma deserved to enjoy herself after all the baking, sewing the bunting, arranging the flowers. Jim would have been happy to go back to the cottage after the ceremony. 'No,' Ma had insisted, 'if they're going to talk let's give them something to talk about.' She'd persuaded George Evans to let them use The Jolly Sailor for nothing. It was no longer busy, even on Fridays. Not enough young men with wage packets in their pockets. 'Might as well open the doors to something happy,' she said, and he'd agreed.

'You mind that dress, Grace, you don't want to get any stains on our mother's wedding gown. Lovely material that. Be good to keep it nice for Eleanor, when she's ready of course. Family heirloom.' Aunt Violet put her teacup down with a clatter. 'Like the rings,' she muttered.

'I'm so glad it's being used, too,' said Ma, walking through to collect more plates. She threw a sharp look at her sister. 'It's important to keep things in the family.'

'We were all wondering when it was going to be used, Jim. Have to work fast now to start that family, eh?'

'That's enough, Auntie Vi,' he said. It would take more than his aunt's loose talk to upset him today. He took the plates his bride was carrying and set them down on the table, taking her hands in his and holding them high. 'Let's see how different you look, Mrs Avery.' Grace smiled and bowed her head, as though she was admiring the ring. He hoped she wasn't disappointed. Grandma's thick gold band was heavy and Victorian, the dark border around the matching garnet ring was another lover's threaded locks of hair. Women could be superstitious about these things. If she'd set her heart on something else it was certainly too late to ask.

Hard to believe they were married. Grace was beautiful in the dress he'd asked Ma to alter, using the spare material to make a small gathered veil. 'Blushers' they were called, apparently, though Grace's cheeks were pale as milk all day. Maybe she'd expected more. A girl like that, she could have had her pick. Before the war she did, didn't she? And now she made do, like everyone else. Her shoes were the only new thing she wore, pale kid leather with a bar across and heels that made her almost the same height as him. She'd been so excited when they'd bought them, justifying the expense by saying she'd get lots of wear out of them when they moved to London, as though they'd be out every night with a busy social life. Would that end up disappointing her too?

Neither of them had wanted him to wear Pa's good suit; it was one of the first things they'd agreed. 'Disrespectful,' said Aunt Vi, 'with all your father's medals too.' But Ma said it was up to them and she meant it. The church was already full of ghosts.

'It was a wonderful day.' Grace smiled at Ma. 'We're so grateful for everything you've done.'

'I'd do more if I could,' she replied.

Grace's own parents, who made no secret of the fact they considered Jim beneath their daughter, had barely stayed for half an hour after the ceremony. Samuel had to leave Hilda at home, 'Unwell,' he said in a way that made Ma sad. He made the journey from London alone to see his nephew wed. He'd helped for a while but didn't like to leave her alone for long and he'd already walked to the station to catch the last connection to Norwich. Jim wanted to hug him when he left, but settled for a hearty handshake with a slap on the back in return. He was still trying to forget that Charlie hadn't shown up. Perhaps the letter never reached him. Perhaps he didn't want to see Pearl and little Alfie because it hurt too much to see Ruby in them. It didn't feel like that anymore to Jim, though; Alfie ought to be the only thing Charlie cared about.

'The spread was lovely, Ma, you were right to do it like that.'

'I know you wanted a sit-down thing, Jim, but no-one's like that round here.'

Jim pictured the villagers, the farmhands and fishermen who'd danced with a beer in one hand and a pie in the other. It was strange after living with Aunt Hilda to see how carefully Ma separated out the good food to be saved and re-used, wrapping it carefully in bowls and cloths, stacking the packages on the barrel trolley they were borrowing to wheel it home.

'What are you to do with all that?' he asked. 'Give it to the poor?'

'We *are* the poor, my boy,' said Aunt Violet and Ma laughed.

'She's right, we are, we'll use it all up, you'll see. I'm surprised there's such a lot left to be honest. I made too much I suppose.'

'You always do go overboard, Annie. I'll have some of that cake if it's going?'

'Sorry, Vi, we're taking that back,' said Ma firmly. 'Jim will want some to share with his new friends at work. Here.' She threw her a cloth. 'You've taken the weight off long enough, go and help Pearl out the back or we'll never get home.'

Violet heaved herself up with a sigh and an envious glance at her still snoring husband. When she'd disappeared out of earshot, Ma reached deep into the pocket of her handbag and drew out a small package, handing it quickly to Jim.

'What is it?' He turned it over in his hand. A fat envelope. He opened one side gently and a little gasp of shock escaped as he realised it was stuffed with ten-shilling notes. 'I can't take this, Ma! Where on earth did you get it? There must be hundreds of pounds here.'

'It's yours and I won't hear another word about it. I didn't need the money you sent home so I put it aside for you until you needed it, for a day like today. I did spend some on the food, but the rest is yours and Grace's, you'll need it too once you have a family of your own.'

Jim stared at the money. It didn't feel right. For a moment none of it felt right. Would this all work out? They'd only stay here for one night, the two of them in his own small bed, Ma next door. They couldn't manage like that for long. But what would Grace do in London? Had he been honest enough about his life, his prospects? He tried to imagine her with Aunt Hilda in those rooms filled with Jack. What would they find to talk about when they were together all the time?

On the way back to the cottage they stopped on the beach, Jim feeling shy, wanting Ma to go to bed first so that things weren't awkward. Above their heads the entire night sky spread out like a glittering web and they climbed onto an upturned boat, laying back to watch it. Jim could pick out one or two constellations, the ones Bert used to call the plough and the giant, the great bear. He listed their names, Grace smiled to remember and, just for a moment, he felt the intoxication of their beginning, before the thought of Bert and Mathilde dragged him back to the earth.

'It's a beautiful sky,' said Grace.

Jim felt the weight of it pressed down upon his shoulders. Back in the London smog Grace might find, like him, that she struggled to be without the vast coastal sky.

'I miss the sight of stars,' he said. 'You can't see them at all in town. On nights like this here it seems all you have to do is reach out and touch one.'

They leaned as far back as they could across the wooden hull and lay there with their heads touching. Jim thought of the flat, windswept strands. How could he be nervous of the future? He was already terrified of the past, worrying constantly that Grace would find him unexciting and begin to compare him to Bert. What would happen if Mathilde or her son tried to find him? He hadn't even been able to tell Ma, he could never explain it to Grace now.

More than three years of Jim's life was lost to The List. When it was finished and printed by the Ministry without a single mention of his name, it seemed somehow pointless to enlighten everyone about his work. The publication itself hit eighty volumes, their largest ever. It was much acclaimed and admired by reviewers, earning a parliamentary mention and several paragraphs in *The Telegraph*. Initial copies were bound in leather with soft vellum pages, but so many libraries requested their own versions that eventually they were reissued in a cheaper format.

Lack of public acknowledgement was a relief; he wasn't forced to tell his family what he really did for a living. Jim liked that they never asked questions. He didn't want to upset them by telling them anything about his work. He'd planned to bring Grace to his office, tell her everything, draw her into his life there. After a while, it seemed easier not to. Whenever Aunt Hilda mentioned his top-secret role Grace looked at him with respect and he liked that. Uncle Samuel never spoke much at home so Jim's secret was secure. That was that. His cosy office was a haven where he could pore over the relative mundanity of his tasks without having to worry someone would put a value on them. There was great potential in anonymous work.

With the war over and The List finished, the Ministry itself had little useful work to do; core staff were co-opted into other departments. Jim found himself engaged with a series that focused on countries of the Empire. The publications were, he supposed, intended to reinforce the sound national belief that, despite the continuing post-war austerities, Britain was still the best place in the world to live. After a while the descriptions of daily living all merged into one. The images, mostly grainy photographs of chiefs and their multiple wives, were a constant source of amazement. Who could imagine ever meeting anyone like that? Or seeing the places they lived? Mud houses with palm-fringed roofs and the thin bark canoes that might tip a man overboard on a whim or a light breeze. Spare images decorated the pinboard wall above his desk, making strange, compelling worlds. Impossible to imagine a climate so warm that leaves and beads were the only necessary clothing. Some of the photographs were indecent, embarrassing. He took those ones to the central office and swapped them for small bars of chocolate, wrapped in brown paper that carried the Ministry's official stamp. These he took home to Grace and Aunt Hilda. Secretly he would love to travel to such places, but it was hard to talk about that with Grace. She'd already moved for him and she must be thinking of children.

It was effortless to keep secrets in the huge, dark house. Day in and day out, as they lived side by side, each with their own deep wounds and the deeper fear of re-opening them, Jim and his family learned only to talk of small incidents, cementing a tacit understanding that feelings and dreams would not be discussed.

History. 1994. Emily's story

Daniel has gone. He came to see Jim without me, left a note with Nurse Evans that she hands me when I visit. Perhaps the last time was too intense. I can't blame him, Jim's not his family after all, but I had thought he cared enough to visit with me again or to call; he has the details. The note is written on thin pink paper with a border of painted fairies, probably Evie's. The fairies remind me of Nan, and Carrie. He doesn't write much except that he's off on active duty, can't say where, likely to be several months. The newsagents on the corner of Barrett Street is where Jim bought his paper, he wants to point this out as it isn't the nearest, he forgot to mention it before. He hopes Jim is fine. He hopes I find what I'm looking for.

I fold the letter back into the small pink envelope and put it inside my jacket pocket, ignoring the fact that Nurse Evans is peering in. She knows more about me than almost anyone else, a realisation that I find depressing.

'How's he doing?'

She pulls a face. 'His eyes are moving a lot. Best not to read anything into that though.'

Jim appears to have shifted position, although that's probably some of the orderlies changing him again. His arms are over the bedclothes, showing huge dark bruises round the ports on his hands. Fluid in, fluid out. His breathing seems calmer through the narrower tube. Dreams flutter beneath his eyelids; a whole life being revisited in his thoughts.

'We need you to talk to your family, Emily. Your dad in particular. There will come a point when we can't keep him like this.' She holds up a hand, showing me it's not her choice.

'Not yet. But we need you all to talk to each other so you're ready to have that conversation. When it comes.'

I nod. I don't want to know when that will be. Neither do I want to discuss it with Dad. I'm more interested in talking to him about Jim's future; or discovering his past. I don't want to discuss deciding he's not coming back. We don't know him, so we can't presume to know what strength he might have to pull through. We don't even know what he looked like. These photographs around the room may not all be of him; from childhood to old age we're so many different people, everything changes us, even if we don't recognise it. Nan always used to say she felt the same at eighteen as she did at sixty, though she hinted she was wilder in her youth and when we walked on the cliffs she would wince at the pain in her knees. Is Jim the same? Daniel says he walks to the shops, that he manages, but his house tells a different story. His life seems to have slipped away long before he ended up here and, unless he wakes up, I will never know why. It feels as though it could easily be my story. Nan and Carrie are gone, Anna and my parents are halfway across the world, and the rest of my life feels like it's happening to someone else.

Nurse Evans finishes taking Jim's observations, straightens his covers, pushes one of the photographs closer to the edge of the locker, by his bed. Then she gives me a tired smile and leaves, pushing the door slightly to behind her.

I can't sit round waiting for Dad to make decisions. If Jim is going to pull through, and he has to, then he could wake at any time. I should go to his house later, clean the kitchen, buy some sensible store cupboard items to get ready for his return. There are a few things I could do to make it nicer. Even so, it's not a comfortable house and I worry about him being there. I think about what Mum said at Christmas, that

I couldn't look after him. But could I? I've never had to. I've no idea what it would entail, or what it would cost. No doubt he would need some professional help too. Briefly I imagine myself moving in with him and then remember the wedding.

Mum and Dad have refused to spend money on any real improvements to the house and I won't argue, they seemed quite annoyed by it all. Yesterday they called to ask me to help put their own house on the market and I'm not surprised by the news that they won't be coming back. They're clearly happy in Valencia. It means I'll have to stop using it as a second home, but staying there isn't good for me anyway. It makes me feel as lonely as it always did. Perhaps they were running from their thoughts too, but they never spoke of Carrie, never even mentioned her name, and they wouldn't at Christmas either. Did something similar happen with Nan and Jim? Did Dad have a brother? Mum says I'm attention seeking. 'You have such an overactive imagination, Emily. Why don't you just focus on your wedding?'

On the way back from the hospital, I walk to the shop on Barrett Street, a small corner terrace with garish signs covering the windows, trays of okra and yam at the front. Above the door is a hand-painted *Evening Standard* masthead, a brick with '1926' carved into its side. Maybe Jim walked all the way to this shop because it's always been here. My parents got their paper delivered.

A small bell rings above my head as I push the door and a pretty woman in a headscarf looks up from arranging magazines to smile at me. She's wearing an orange shalwar kameez top over wide jeans and making it look stylish.

'Hi.' She straightens up and walks to the other side of the counter, ready for business.

'Hi.' I go to the fridge, take out a can of drink I don't want and set it on the countertop, examine the rows of sweets below. Daniel's letter bulges from my bag. Thinking about it makes me feel awkward.

'I've come from the hospital,' I say, and a look of concern crosses her face. 'Nothing worrying,' I add quickly, 'I have a relative there, he got knocked down by his house, nearby.'

'We don't have a car.' Her voice is firm; she doesn't want trouble. Perhaps I shouldn't have come. This is hard and I don't really know what I think she can help with.

'Jim Avery. He's my great-grandfather. I didn't know him very well and I just wondered if you might be able to tell me anything about him. He got his paper from here.'

'*The Times*,' she says. 'Every day but not weekends. We wondered why we hadn't seen him for a while. Is he OK?'

'I'm not sure. He's still unconscious.'

'I'm very sorry to hear that.'

I give her a thin-lipped smile, waiting.

'He's seems like a very nice gentleman. He doesn't really talk to us though, just 'Good morning' or 'Nice day' or not even that. He is quiet.'

I nod, fumble for my purse, I'm wasting my time here.

'Have you come far? To see him?'

She can't imagine it, a family living broken just a few miles apart.

'Kind of,' I say, suddenly emotional. 'Quite far. And thanks.'

Alice has spent the best part of an hour enthusiastically encouraging me to undertake some sort of genealogy. We're in her favourite vegetarian café, a lot safer for me than trying to match her for drinks in the pub. Apparently she can let me borrow the PC at the war rooms, which she thinks has the same software package her mum used to do their own family tree.

'Mind you, it did take over her life,' she says, taking a sip of green tea. 'She was doing it all the time, used to drive us crazy.'

'I guess it's hard to understand when you're small.'

'It's not funny when you're teenagers either! We had a weird family crest with three bees on it. Everyone used to laugh about it, we got called all sorts.'

'I never had a nickname at school. I wanted one though. I think it means you belong, everyone knowing you by a certain name, and where it came from.' Anna's nickname was Rory and she never would tell me where it came from. Dad said it was all the shouting but she only did that at home so it must have been something else. I should ask her, she might tell me now, but it won't be so important to know.

'Yeah, right. Unless it's Sting.' Her expression is pure disgust. I'm laughing too much to hold my cup of tea properly.

'Did you find out much about your family?'

'Not that much. I mean it showed up a few interesting characters, someone who got transported to Tasmania and a man who choked to death on a bread crust. We've got a former mayor of Lambeth too. But that's not why. People do it because they want to be connected to their families, because they want to find out *who* they were, what they were like, whether they were like them. We just want to feel part of something like it's all meaningful.' She shrugs and tails off.

I think she's trying to reassure me that this is all normal. She certainly doesn't seem surprised that my family can't help with any information. It would be good to think that we're not the only ones in the world to have found an elderly relative living around the corner as though he's nothing to do with us. It breaks my heart to think we could have made each other happier.

'Do you think skeletons lurk in every family?' I blurt out.

'I wouldn't know,' she says, 'that being in the nature of secrets.' She gives me one of her full-beam smiles. She's really far too cheerful to be a goth. 'Why don't you try some local societies or war groups or something, a history group? Bound to be some. Look on a neighbourhood noticeboard, or try the local paper.'

There are four local history groups in my postcode alone. I circle the nearest, fold over *The Evening Standard* and hold it out to Shona, who's making me tea.

'What's that for?' She's made a point of choosing the *carpe diem* mug for herself, explaining that it's because she scored a record five approvals to progress with book ideas in today's meeting. She waves the mug in my face.

'Well done. We'll get you a big trophy to drink out of next time,' I smile. She deserves the recognition, no one works harder than Shona. 'It's a local history group. I want to go and find out about research, about what my great grandfather did in the war.'

'Why do you need that? Can't you just ask someone in the family?'

I still haven't told her the full story. 'They're a bit vague. My nan was the kind of person who liked to clear things out and throw them away. We don't have a lot to go on.'

'What is it you want to know about him?' She pulls up a stool and starts to leaf through the classifieds.

'What he did in the war, his career. I've found some

photos but I want to be able to talk to him about things he'd know.'

'He's still out cold then? Poor thing. It's supposed to help if you talk to people while they're unconscious, isn't it? Like they can hear it on a different level or something.' She pauses a moment, twists one of her giant earrings. They look like liquorice allsorts. 'Those groups are a bit weird, aren't they? I imagine them full of retired colonels.'

'Why don't we find out?' I'm feeling brave. 'Come to this one with me?'

'You have to be kidding. That is not my idea of a fun Tuesday evening! Tell you what, I'll come if you come to the Hampstead Ponds with me.'

'Let me think about that for a moment… Er no! It'll be absolutely freezing! Try me in July.'

St Margaret's Community Centre is almost as old as the church itself; a lovely early Victorian hall built from soft red brick. I walk through a doorway ridged in decreasing arches and dotted with carved brick flowers. In the room behind the lobby, untidy with piles of local flyers and parish magazines, are two trestle tables laid out with green-glazed cups and saucers and plates of custard creams. A short woman with a stern grey cap of hair beckons me into the next room.

'Chairs at the back,' she barks in a stage whisper.

I shuffle towards one, avoiding the gaze of the handful of people who've turned to watch me come in. I try to sit gently on the plastic seat but it creaks slightly on its tubular legs and I stare straight ahead as though it wasn't me, surreptitiously placing my bag on the floor and hoping Alice won't be too late. I couldn't wait outside any longer.

An overhead projector shows grainy images and I squint

to see. It looks as though they're discussing the odd stone and wood structure on Broad Street, which I'd always thought was an ancient well of some sort, but apparently is a public torture device last used as recently as 1850. Alice slides in with a cheerful wave around the room. The slides run on for about another twenty minutes and then the speaker, a bearded, middle-aged man in a velvet blazer, opens the floor to questions.

'What's the meaning of three?' asks Alice. She's the youngest here by miles.

'Interesting question, thank you, a new member too, I think? Welcome. A question that's puzzled us. Three, of course, is a known magic number in pagan rites, and early Christian belief. But that doesn't really explain its use here. A closer examination of the structures themselves show that this one on the left is built in a slightly different way. So that when all pulleys are being leveraged at the same time, by the weight of the bodies on the plinths, one of the structures is not working in the same way, it's not giving the same pull on the skin.'

'Why?' Alice has a spiked bag on her lap that looks as though it's made from medieval armour.

'To allow redemption. We must bear in mind that despite the persecution of anyone likely to be slightly different, or sharp tongued, or inconvenient to someone in power as all these so-called witches no doubt were, the people who put them in these contraptions were extremely God-fearing folk. More than anything they feared His wrath, in case they had it wrong. So they put in a get out clause, a means for God, Him- or Her-self, to choose the one who might get off unhurt.'

'But didn't they see that as a sign that the victims really

were witches? Like the ducking stools... and then do it anyway?' This time it's an elderly lady with close-cropped white hair, a long grey velvet scarf wrapped elegantly around her throat. Her eyes are piercing, intelligent; probably she would have been accused of witchcraft in the dim and superstitious past.

He thinks for a moment, actually stroking his beard, a fact I store up for Shona. 'Interestingly, not in this instance. We must bear in mind that ducking stools were for less sophisticated societies than this. Even in 1850 we would have been close to the centre of London.'

'Proximity to London town not being a terribly clear-cut sign of sophistication, in Victorian times or otherwise,' mutters the elderly lady.

Alice grins at her. I sense some kindred spirits. The speaker wraps up questions and invites us outside to talk further. Armed with cups of milky tea we introduce ourselves to the possible witch-lady, who seems delighted at the prospect of other females in the group. I'd imagined such local history gatherings to consist predominantly of women.

She rolls her eyes. 'There are so many divorced men and *metal detectorists*, I'm afraid. You'll need a strong constitution.' Her name, she says, is Florence, and 'definitely not, on any account, Flo.'

'We're not really joining, Emily just wants some help,' Alice explains and Florence leans in to listen. For fifteen minutes we're absorbed and it's wonderful to talk about Jim with people who don't know me well enough to judge or make unspoken assumptions about my sister's ghost or my state of mind.

'That is fascinating,' Florence speaks carefully. 'What have you got to go on?'

'Not much. His address, his age, no other family details, but I think I know where he worked and from some of the letters and things I found in an old tin, I'm pretty sure I know which battalion he was in. It sounds like he got sent back injured from the war, there's a letter from a hospital and...'

'But that's a lot to be going on. You need to start with dates,' says Florence, 'all of them. Get the tin and put every letter and news clipping out in order, write the dates and the names and the places and any other bits of detail you can get from those things and then you'll know where to go from what year. You shouldn't have to look too hard to find what you need.'

Keepsakes. 1923. Jim's story

'What's the matter?' Jim sat up in bed and tried to keep the irritation out of his voice. 'You've been tossing and turning all night!'

'I'm not tossing and turning, I can barely move.' Grace struggled to sit up and Jim placed a pillow behind her back, to support the growing weight of her stomach.

'Is it painful?'

'Not when I'm lying down, but it's kicking a lot. I had a long walk today, blowing the cobwebs after all that rain. It was probably asleep all day. Now it's wide awake. Got strong little arms and legs. Think it must be a boy.'

'I don't mind what it is.' Jim yawned. He'd be fit for nothing in the morning. 'As long as it's healthy.'

'Nothing wrong with this one,' grumbled Grace. 'Going to be a prize fighter I should think.'

'Should you be walking that far? What does Doctor Elliot say? I know Aunt Hilda thinks you should be resting more, she said so yesterday, while you were helping Mrs Roberts.'

'She has a few too many opinions if you ask me. Anyway, I was mostly trying to play with Jane, or Primrose or whatever you call her.'

Mrs Roberts came to clean three times a week though the house barely needed it, always accompanied by her daughter, Jane, a small and wide-eyed child who clutched a pale brown knitted dog by its neck and looked half terrified of everything, including Grace. She adored Jim from the first time she saw him, though, when he sat on his heels and told her that her name wasn't pretty enough for her, renaming her Primrose-Jane and finding her a toffee in his pocket. After that she would always look for him, making him little things from card and paper, handing them over shyly and then running back to her mother's skirts. He used to bend down to talk to her as she hid behind the furniture and when he stood up there would always be a toffee or a coin on the floor and he would pick it up and exclaim loudly that someone had dropped it, making her smile and play along. Sometimes he would pretend to pull a coin from her ear, the way he'd seen Charlie do with Ruby.

'I think you've gone soft since you've been in London, I'd be walking everywhere at home. I'm just so uncomfortable! This bed is nowhere near big enough for us.' Grace struck the side of the bedframe as though she meant it harm.

Jim knew what was coming. She wasn't wrong either. They shouldn't really be living in Jack's old room. Aunt Hilda had replaced the single bedstead with a mid-sized metal frame, borrowed from a widowed friend. But the mattress was thin, worn and lumpy, taking vicious digs at their ribs in the night, and her fussy satin coverlets slipped off continually, leaving feet and elbows frozen.

'If we had our own place it would be different, Jim. We could have our own things.'

What could he say? It was true. Grace would never spread her wings until she had her own house. It was all she really wanted: their own place. She had these silly ideas about inviting people to tea, feeling she couldn't do that here. As if that was why they were finding it hard to make friends of their own. Aunt Hilda had been good to him, she'd hate it if they left, and he wasn't ready to rush into anything. He'd been raised on a tighter household budget than Grace and was terrified at the idea of having debt of any kind.

'That's what we're saving for, it costs an awful lot of money to set up house, Grace. We're comfortable here. They've been good to us and they've said we can stay as long as we like. I don't think they want us to go. Might as well wait until we've enough money to do it right and get all the furniture and things we'll need. I thought we'd agreed?'

Grace sighed and nodded, shifting her awkward bulk against the pillow. 'I just feel like… a stranger. All the things in the bathroom and the kitchen and everywhere, we use them but they're not ours. I'm not allowed to cook or clean. What's the point of a housewife without a house?'

'Aunt says you should be resting. You haven't got long, you shouldn't strain yourself.'

'I'm not likely to. All I do all day is read.'

Grace pulled at the pillows, her jaw set, hard. Jim didn't like seeing her that way. But it was easy for him. Off to work all week. What must it be like alone in the house from morning to evening with Aunt Hilda and her grief? Not even allowed to help Mrs Roberts or play with strange little Primrose-Jane who spent all day crouching down beside her mother when she looked old enough to be in school.

Without family, for all its faults, there was no closeness, no constant, no one who owed you the time. Maybe he was wrong to have brought her here. Back home there was always someone popping in, always neighbours and family, or both, and Grace had several younger sisters. If you no longer lived in the thick of family, if no-one shared your life, then only the mundane was left; a polite chat, a note on the weather, a comment on one's garden, 'Good morning, Mr Avery, lovely day,' before a hasty walk back down the street.

'Are you unhappy?' He stroked her hair in a way that he hoped was comforting. Ruby had liked her hair stroked. A sudden image of the little girl sprang into his mind. What would it be like to walk along holding the hand of his own daughter? Or maybe a boy, someone to kick a football in the park, teach to ride a bike, to sail boats. A sudden image of Bert and Mathilde walking past the boating lake stopped his thoughts. Those children he'd helped with their sticks and boats would be grown now, so would Bert's son. Would he ever try to get in touch?

'I'm just tired of waiting. Tired of being on my own all day.'

'Everything will change when the baby comes. You won't have time to be bored.'

'I'm not sure they even want the baby here. I feel like I'm upsetting her even more. I'm taking up more than my share of their house and the bigger I get the more she ignores me.'

'It's not long now,' he said, though he wasn't altogether sure. 'Things will be different then. You know how hard I'm working to save. And they *are* good to us, they don't ask much for bed and board.'

'I know that, the last thing I want is you spending even more hours at work, we don't see you much as it is.'

Why did she always say that? They were together every evening. They didn't talk a lot because it was hard when everything you said was overheard. Besides, after everything they'd been through, there were things they no longer needed to say. Surely those things were just understood.

'You think he's a boy?' He rubbed the swell of her belly through her cotton nightgown, smoothing it where the thin cloth was caught and twisted into folds.

'Everyone says if you carry high it's a boy. I think that's why my back aches so much, it makes me sort of lean backwards.'

'Have you thought about a name? A boy would be easier

than a girl. I can't quite decide between James, after Father of course, and Samuel, I think he'd be delighted, he's been so pleased about the baby and then there's Charlie, God knows if we could get Charlie excited about the baby it might mean... what is it?'

Grace had batted his hand away roughly and turned away from him, struggling to free her caught nightdress. 'There's my father, too. And we lost my brother. We've all been through a war, Jim.'

He was silent for a few moments before saying, 'But your father's name is Albert... is that... would that be right? To call him Albert?'

She looked away, towards the clock sitting on top of her book on the nightstand. 'It's not even midnight,' she said, 'and I'm starving. This one thinks it's breakfast time already.'

'Do you want me to get you something?'

She nodded and sat back heavily on the pillows. Jim pulled on his slippers and belted the cord of his dressing gown before opening the bedroom door with one hand at the back, pressing on the hinge to stop it creaking loudly in case it woke Aunt Hilda. She was a light sleeper and had possibly already been woken by their conversation; if she had, he also knew that she would never bring it up. She reminded him of Ma like that, knowing everything and keeping it to herself.

He knew the stairs well enough now to change the side of the tread he put his weight on, which ones creaked and which were silent. Gripping the bannister with his left hand he steadied himself with his right on the thick flocked wallpaper. Albert. Why that name? She'd never seemed close to her father. Maybe she really did want to build bridges. No point in discussing it further when her mind was so set, but he didn't like it. Every time he looked at his son he'd remember his friend, the reason he was able to marry and have a family in the first place. He couldn't say that to her either, though, could he? She'd tell him not to be silly, that it was the past and it belonged there. But it wouldn't stay there, and he was acutely aware of how different his life would be if Bert had survived.

Deep in thought he wandered into the kitchen and lit a candle, walked over to the pantry and fetched the remains of a pork pie. He brought it back to set on the table while he looked for a plate and a knife. Aunt Hilda was sitting there in silence in her nightclothes, the side of her face lit up by the shards of moon that spiked the room, and Jim started in such shock that he dropped the knife to the floor where it rang out against the small red tiles.

'I'm sorry, I didn't expect… Grace is hungry. Do you mind?'

'It's quite alright, dear, I often sit here in the night. Samuel doesn't seem to have much trouble sleeping. I suppose he has more to occupy him, but I can't sleep well anymore.'

'Isn't there anything Doctor Elliott can give you?'

Aunt Hilda shook her head. 'I just have to get up and walk around, don't worry about me, take Grace her pie.'

'She's certainly hungry!' said Jim. 'We'll need to start paying you more for our board.'

'Those last few weeks are always the worst.' Aunt Hilda looked wistful. 'They say the baby puts on a pound a week at the end. You can believe it too. With Jack I…' She tailed off and pursed her lips, as though she didn't trust herself to speak.

Jim put a slice of pie onto the plate with a chunk of bread and two tomatoes from the bowl on the table. He was about to walk away when Aunt Hilda took hold of his sleeve.

'I miss him so much, Jim. Everyone said it would get easier but it gets worse. Sometimes I sit here and it feels like the whole world rushes round me while I cling to the edge of the table and breathe slowly, trying to imagine him coming through that door with the coal. And when he does, when I can picture him, I know it's going to be alright.' She raised her head and looked at him. 'What am I going to do, Jim, when I can't see him anymore?'

Jim covered her hand in his. How much energy did the country have left for this? It was all very well writing booklets about how people lived halfway across the world. Someone needed to tell the people here how to live or where would they all end up if it happened again.

London was always going to change him. Ma must have known that, despite her pushing him to go and better himself. She'd as much as said so on the day he left. But each time he came back, on his increasingly infrequent weekend visits, it felt like *she* was the one who'd changed. Was she less interested in him? All she ever talked about was village life, gossip about people he no longer knew or cared for. It irritated him in a way he couldn't hide. She never asked him anything about his life or his work and it infuriated him to think she didn't care. Now she was gone it struck him that maybe she just didn't have the questions to ask.

Not once had she visited Aunt Hilda's, always making some excuse until she really became too ill to travel. The stomach pains that had plagued her for years finally stole her appetite completely, taking her strength and her fight. But in those years, without him and Charlie, without Pearl and Alfie too once they'd moved to Yorkshire with Mr Hardacre, her frame of reference had shrunk to a few fields, a handful of conversations a week. How could she have known what to ask? She couldn't imagine what he did all day. Jim covered his face with his hands and clung to himself, wracked with guilty sobs.

It felt wrong to be here without her, an uninvited guest in the cottage where he was born. An interloper, trespassing. He perched awkwardly on the worn coverlet, pushing his feet into the floor as it tried to slip him off, pressing down hard to relieve the dull ache in his instep from his new leather shoes. Ma would never have trusted the wearer of such shoes he thought sadly, too pointed and expensive looking. 'People in shiny shoes bring bad news.' He heard her voice and he stared at his reflection in their liquid surface. She was gone. Everything around him was a poignant reminder of her wise words and the gulf that had grown between them.

Below him, in the kitchen, a dozen or so people were still saying their goodbyes, reminiscing, becoming maudlin as afternoon drew further into evening. He could hear the low rumble of voices, broken by chinking sounds as glasses were refuelled and plates stacked. They were probably speculating about the obvious absence of Charlie, the fact that Jim was there without Grace, and 'wasn't it all such a shame?' Aunt Violet would still be holding court in the biggest chair, attempting to keep the little gathering going for as long as possible, although most of Ma's real friends had left after an hour or so. Aunt Violet was in charge now, she'd said as much this afternoon, reminding him pointedly that he'd abandoned his home, that he 'was a Londoner now.' She'd gone straight to the landlord to request the tenancy for her eldest daughter, Eleanor, who had recently married and outgrown her room at home. 'Nice to keep it in the family,' she'd said. 'And it's much less trouble for you if the furniture and things stay where they are instead of you having to get rid of them.'

He was never coming back here, naturally. There was the Ministry for one thing and, even if it wasn't for his injuries, he was too soft to farm the land for a living again, still too faint-hearted to fish the sea. He was sure Grace wouldn't hear of it either, though they'd never discussed it. He no longer felt the pull of the brutal coastline and there was a tacit understanding that they were better off now. After Lilly there were people who didn't approve of him and, besides, there was little work to be found. He had hoped that Charlie might want the house, that at least he would come back for the funeral, but no-one had managed to find him. It was as though he'd sunk without trace. Jim had no idea if he'd stayed with the navy, as he'd planned, or rejoined civilian life when the war ended. At some point he must have returned, because there was no mention of him missing or killed in The List, the final count. In their different ways they had both lost the chance to return home.

Eleanor had sweetly told him he could be there whenever he liked and he had thanked her and pressed her cold hand though he knew this would be the last time he'd ever set foot in the village. There was nothing here for him now. Ma would have been pleased that, with her sons gone, it should be her favourite niece who took the cottage. Maybe she and her husband could fill the place with children, chase away some of its sorrows. He hoped they'd be happy.

On the way back from the church he had stood aside to let Violet lead the party in and stopped for a moment to look at the cottage, trying to commit it to memory so he wouldn't forget. From there he could see the ridges of flint, shiny chipped surfaces that never needed cleaning and glinted silver or deepest black in the tiniest thread of sun. There were only three windows on this side, disproportionately small and so darkly leaded they looked like watchful insect eyes. His old home stared defiantly from this angle, circled by shrieking gulls.

There wasn't much of value in the cottage and Grace wouldn't thank him for taking back anything old or worn. He took the baking things though, the green enamel pie dish and the rolling pin made of thick glass with bubbles inside. Ruby had never tired of turning it over to see them. Her little hands seemed to hover over it and it made him smile to think of his own child using it to roll biscuits. Jim felt like a thief as he placed it carefully in his knapsack in the washroom, hefting the bag to check its weight, the kitchen things clanking against the gold-plate clock and Pa's watch.

Pearl had asked for the brass door knocker, shaped like a curled fish with a fine detail of scales and fins and always polished until it gleamed. Perhaps it reminded her of Charlie as well as Ma and the cottage, he didn't ask. Jim had quietly found the box of Pa's tools, scraping the thick layer of polish carefully from the screws before using a chisel to lever off the brass plate from the groove where its weight had sunk it into the wooden door. It was good of her to come all this way for the funeral; a good idea for her and Alfie to sit in the front pew with him and Aunt Violet while Mr Hardacre sat at the back to deflect any malicious sniping. Alfie had fidgeted his way through the whole service and it struck Jim with a pang of sadness that the boy, who moved far away as a tiny child, probably couldn't remember them at all. He'd seemed to remember the house though, walking through the little rooms with a wistful look on his face, stopping to stroke a fabric draught excluder in the elongated shape of a dog. 'You can keep it,' said Jim, 'if you like,' and he'd picked it up straight away, hugging its stiff body to his chest and giving Jim a familiar flash of his little sideways smile.

Strange how it affected everyone in the same way, young and old. Inanimate objects become personal after a death, perfectly ordinary bits and pieces alive with the spirit of their deceased owners. It was hardest to bear in Ma's bedroom. Perhaps because these things had been kept in the privacy of Ma's own space. On the dresser, clustered on a lace-edged linen square, sat a silver-backed brush and mirror, little coloured-glass lidded pots, a bulbous bud vase with a painting of irises. It was deeply feminine, indicating a girlishness he'd never seen her display. Nothing here to associate with his hardworking mother in her serviceable clothes, her pinned back hair, hands red and chapped from the soil or the laundry. Even the yellow satin coverlet and the wallpaper, with its deep brown-yellow pattern of tea roses, seemed frivolous. It was spotted with damp here and there, curling away from the wall where it reached the ceiling. He opened the closet door, wondering if Pearl would know what to do with the clothes, and then slammed it shut in shock when he realised it was completely empty. Violet, it must be. Probably thought she was helping as it was unlikely any of Ma's clothes would fit her.

Jim breathed in deeply and checked the clock. He should stop all this playing for time and find what he'd come looking for; it was getting late and though he had to stay and organise things tonight he didn't want to miss the first train tomorrow and have to leave Grace for another day. She'd looked so ill when he left, he'd never noticed before how weak she was. Carrying their child had made her ill from the start, too fragile to help with the preparations, too nauseous to talk much. Lately she always referred to the baby as 'Bertie'. It made him nervous and uncomfortable, but how could he tell her? She was easily angered at most things these days and Jim was too cautious to say how little he liked the name, fearful of unpredictable reactions. Sometimes they tried to guess which of them it would take after, if it would be clever, funny, loving. 'Your looks and my extraordinary brains would be best,' Jim laughed, 'and of course my overwhelming modesty, what more could we ask?' Secretly he hoped for a girl.

Eventually he found the hatbox on top of the wardrobe, where it had been pushed too far back to be visible. With the lid slightly lifted he could see it was still full of Ma's documents and photographs, the pictures and ribbons of her life. The last time he'd seen it was when she showed him the photographs of his aunt and uncle. Carefully he carried it down to the kitchen, where he fastened the lid with a length of string then stowed it into his bag before slipping into the parlour to rejoin the others.

'There you are! We were going to start a search!' Violet had clearly been free with the sherry he'd ordered. Only Pearl and Mr Hardacre were without glasses in their hands, she on the stool next to Violet's chair and he standing by the mantelpiece in conversation with John Barley, the organist, who'd carried a torch for Annie most of his life and was so overcome at the service that it was hard to tell what hymn he was actually playing.

'Don't tease him, Vi, he's got a lot of goodbyes to say here... haven't you, Jim?' Pearl threw a warning look. 'Would you like some tea? I've just made it fresh, seems that not too many of us are drinking it though.'

He nodded and crouched down beside her, trying not to stare at the thick, wavy ridges of skin on her hands and wrists as she reached over to pour the tea.

'How is Grace?'

'Doesn't seem to suit her much I'm afraid, she's tired all the time. Keeping her chin up, of course, but I think she'll be glad to have it in a crib.'

'She must be getting pretty big now?'

'Mmm,' he mumbled. Why did everyone say that? She wasn't really. She seemed to have stopped getting bigger a while ago. Was that something else he should be worrying about?

'Can't be long now; you must be excited. I know it doesn't feel like it, but it will help when the baby comes, it will make everything less sad. Babies are the most wonderful time wasters.'

'I know, Ma used to say that too, she loved children so much.' Jim looked around the room, wondering how he could clear it without seeming rude. 'You can stay here tonight if you need to.'

Pearl shook her head. 'That's kind but Arthur's arranged for us to stay with his cousin in Horsey, it's not far. We can help you to sort things out if you like?'

'No, you've done enough, thank you, and you've come such a long way.'

Pearl shrugged. 'She was my ma too. The only good one I ever had.'

'I know. If you wanted to take anything else, something a bit more personal, there are lots of things in her room, perhaps you'd look before you leave? I've got no use for them and I'm sure she'd rather you had them.' Pearl pursed her lips and nodded as though she was fighting tears. It felt cruel to do this to her, but he wasn't sure he'd get another chance and it was the right thing to do. 'I had hoped that Charlie would... but he didn't and I don't know how to get in touch with him now; he's completely disappeared, like a ghost, I'm sorry.' Pearl was really crying now. He should make this quick before Violet stuck her nose in. 'I've got Pa's watch, should have been Charlie's but there we are. I just thought that if you wanted it, if he wanted it, it should go to Alfie really, because he would have had it.'

Jim took Pearl's hands and turned them over, shocked by the hardness of her scars against his skin; he placed the gold watch in her upturned palms and then gently closed her fingers over it, putting his own finger to his lips and gesturing over to where Aunt Violet sat with her head turned in conversation. He rose and stood behind Pearl with his hand across her shoulders in awkward comfort. It was no use now telling her what else he'd found, the little box with Ruby's things folded neatly inside, stored under the bed. Perhaps he could give the box to Mr Hardacre before they left, ask him to find the right time to talk about it, as if such a time could ever exist.

'Aaah, she's all overcome. It was a lovely service, wasn't it?' said Violet, eyes watery with alcohol. 'Won't be long before it's me, you know, I can't get about anything like I used to with these ankles.' She held them up awkwardly to demonstrate, falling back in the chair with a puff of excitement. 'No, it'll be me next and I ask God to make it quick so I'm not a burden to the family. The wonder is that Annie should ever go first, she was a fit woman.'

No, she wasn't. She was strong though; I only hope I've inherited half of what she had. But Jim said nothing and nothing was expected.

'It was a lovely service,' agreed the neighbour she'd been talking to, who pointedly glanced over at the reverend before adding, 'because she wasn't really what you'd call a *religious* woman, your mother, was she?'

'She used to thank God for her bed every night,' Jim said with a small smile, deflecting the blow.

'Don't we all, boy!' called the organist.

'I asked her once, when I was about ten, what she thought God was,' he said quietly, 'and she laughed and said straightaway: 'A woman, I can't see a man making all this in six days, can you?" It had made perfect sense to him then, that God should be a mother's unconditional love, maybe with the face of the painting in the church. Now he wasn't sure what he thought.

There was a burst of laughter from the half dozen or so people round him and he waited patiently for it to die down, unsure how much more was expected of him. It was becoming exhausting to perform. Most of his day had been spent on show, trying to remember warm, funny stories to tell this gathered crowd, to make them feel better about their loss when his own was taking all the warmth from his bones. He had wept with them and held them and shook their hands, he'd made them laugh and now, at the end of such a long day, he wished he'd not been forced to come alone.

'And what do *you* think, James… is God a woman?' The voice pounced as he was trying to escape to the kitchen and he stiffened before turning: only Lilly called him that. He'd expected her at the church and was pleased that her newly widowed father had come too, pleased they were respecting Ma. After all it was years ago, that nonsense, and Lilly was apparently engaged now, to a man who'd invented a milking contraption that he made for local farmers. Why would she come back to the house though? Why would she still be here?

He spread out his hands like a white flag. 'It wasn't my

intention to start a debate.'

'I'm sorry for your loss, James,' she said primly, standing before him, poised and fashionable in her black gabardine coat, a dark red hat pulled down over her head. She clutched a strange flat bag like a shield and he nodded warily, not knowing what to say.

'I was surprised that you didn't feel able to come and tell me yourself, I had to find out through Violet's grapevine.' A sudden gasp of shock and indignation indicated eavesdroppers on their stilted conversation. 'It was a petty thing to leave us out and my own mother still almost warm in her grave.'

'I didn't inform many people directly, but there was a notice. You came to the service and that's the thing, isn't it?' He didn't add that she hadn't informed him about her own mother because he wouldn't have been welcome there and they both knew it.

'I hear that Grace is blooming. Or have I heard wrongly?'

Suddenly swamped and overwhelmed, Jim cursed his wife's weakness. He shouldn't even be here without her, yet here he was, unprepared and alone. He nodded.

'Still, it's not like it's the first time for you. I'm sure Grace takes comfort in that. You have told her? I wonder if he'll ever come looking for you? You really should be prepared.' Lilly's smile widened, triumphant. Jim swayed on his feet. Muttering behind him told him everyone had heard. What would be worse? To turn and correct the story, bring out all those ghosts, or ignore it and pretend it had never been mentioned?

'We should be leaving, Jim, will you come and say goodbye to Little Alfie?'

He looked at Pearl gratefully.

'Can I have a forwarding address? There's some paper in the kitchen, a notebook, I'd, we'd... like to keep in touch if that's...'

'Of course, and send your news, too, won't you? Send me news when the little one arrives, it'll be so nice for Alfie to have a cousin.'

'Yes,' he agreed, 'It will.' Although with Grace the way she seemed to be, it would fall to him to try to hold things up. Without Ma to bind everyone together his family might already be lost.

The brotherless. 1994. Emily's story

Every time I chop red onions I think about Aunt Sam. I remember her telling me once that, because their skins are papery and thick at the same time, the only true way to skin them is to cut off the whole outer layer and throw it away. Any small pieces left on by mistake can ruin your meal. She whispered, in the kitchen of her mansion house flat, because miserable Uncle Bill would have dismissed it as another example of her wastefulness.

It's the first time in ages I've cooked for Ian, a tray of Mediterranean vegetables that I plan to roast with olive oil and a sprig of the rosemary that grows in such abundance in Mum's old garden. The witches' plant. Aunt Sam said it only grew in the gardens of strong women and I wonder which of us attracted it there, Anna probably. I feel a sudden urge to have her here sorting everything out. I used to find her bossy; now I think she would just rather act than 'sit around moping'. If I could, I'd explain that I understand, but there's no more reason for her to listen to me now than there was then. She was always confident, able to separate all the loss from herself; she still laughed and played and joined in, still made and dropped friends as easily as washing her hands. 'Hide of a rhino,' Dad always said. Carrie's absence defined my adolescence and it was easier to be alone than explain all that to anyone I wanted to befriend. I should have spent more time with Anna, she must have missed Carrie too. On the surface she seemed so together but she was just doing what she had to do. Same with Mum and Dad. Everyone clinging on, keeping it together because what was the alternative?

I slice the aubergines the way Aunt Sam showed me, thin

enough to cook evenly and not so thick they'll soak all the oil away from the other vegetables. I take my time to make them all the same size, enjoying the feeling of domesticity in simple tasks. The flat's atmosphere isn't entirely relaxing, there's a tension between us, and I know I'm stretching out the preparation of the food. I don't know what we'll do after eating, we can't seem to talk without disagreeing. Tonight I don't have the energy to argue so I'll find a film in the TV guide, say I've wanted to watch it for ages.

Aunt Sam and Mum fell out over her choice of husband a long time before she left London and moved to Cornwall. They were never particularly close and so we didn't see her much after that. She came back when Nan was in hospital, different somehow, changed. I remember thinking how thin she'd become. But then, as so often happens at emotional times, the sisters fell out over something small enough for Mum to have forgotten, or so she says. I was never told exactly what was said but suddenly we never saw Aunt Sam again and now apparently the only bond we have is a tip on cutting onions. Every onion peeling reminds me how unbearably sad and ridiculous families can be, with our skins that are papery and thick at the same time.

'It wasn't all that useful but the people were lovely,' I tell Anna. I've forgiven her for Christmas because she's remembered to call and she's even asked about the searches on Jim. 'And it's made me notice things round here a lot more. Like the statue of George and the Dragon by the park, did you know that was there?'

'Of course! Don't you remember how we used to fight about who got to sit on the dragon's tail first? We used to race each other all the way there. I always beat you.'

How does she remember this stuff? Our childhood is as clear as day to her. I remember little except Carrie. When I looked at that statue the other day I could have sworn it was for the first time.

'I thought I might go to another meeting. I could ask them about the statue.'

'Ask them about that tower, at the top of Henry Street, the one everyone used to say had someone locked inside.'

That I do remember; I also remember the nightmares it gave me, waking in sharp cold sweats with the image of some poor child behind those high stone walls. I tried to imagine her with long blonde hair, but it didn't work; the girl's face was always Carrie's.

'Maybe I will.'

'You'd probably find it easier over here; I've yet to meet anyone who's not obsessed with their family tree, they seem desperate for some history, hang on…' She breaks off for a moment and I can hear a muffled noise followed by a short laugh. 'Sorry, that was Jacob, he's refuting my allegations. It's true actually, he does refuse to think about the past, that's one of the things I like about him.'

'Is that because it's painful?' I have no idea why I say that but it seems to amuse Anna enormously.

'Not all New York Jews are Woody Allen, Em.' She raises her voice, leaning away from the receiver. 'Emily wants to know if your past is painful, Jacob?' The line goes quiet for such a long time that I wonder whether she's disappeared but she adds, 'No, he says the present is painful, his family is a living museum with a daily audio tour. He says we should be grateful ours isn't.'

She's in a good mood, her guard down; I take a deep breath.

'Sometimes you have to ask those questions anyway, Anna. Tell me what happened to Mum and Aunt Sam.'

Nurse Evans is waiting for me when I arrive and I can't work out if she's nervous or excited. She makes a show of asking me to sit in one of the chairs by the nurses' station and I wish I'd asked Alice to come today but eagerness kills friendships.

'What is it?' My stomach clenches into a ball. Tell me the worst if you have to but get it over with.

'He's conscious, Emily.'

My eyes, prepped for tears, open wide in disbelief. I jump up to see but she puts out a hand to stop me.

'He's regained consciousness, he can focus and he's sitting up, but he hasn't spoken and he seems dazed. Don't expect too much.' She's serious, calm. She reaches for a clipboard on the desk and turns it to show me his observational chart. The ticks and figures are code, I haven't learned much in the last few weeks. 'He's stable, doesn't seem distressed. Eyes reacting, pulse normal.'

'Can I see him?' I want to see his face without the tube.

'You can go to the doorway. See how he responds and take it from there. I'll be with you in case we have to react quickly.'

I rise, slowly, and walk to his room. The lights are off and the gloom is lifted only by a small lamp clipped to the top of the washstand. Nurse Evans says harsh strip lighting might hurt his eyes. I stand in the doorway and watch for a while. After such a long sleep he looks exhausted, propped on fat pillows, staring straight ahead. Something about him reminds me of Dad. If Dad could see him like this, wouldn't he want to come home? Jim's fingers twitch across the blanket with a life of their own. He looks completely different without the heavy breathing mask to obscure his face and I stare at his features for a long time, trying to remember the others in the tin of photographs. He has a long straight nose and high cheekbones, like Dad's, like mine. I see the sensitive length of his fingers, the determined set of his jaw and the weary droop of his eyes. I try to invent a personality for him from these shreds and patches.

Behind me Nurse Evans clears her throat and I walk into his room, moving softly, take the chair by the wall and place my bag on the floor. Jim doesn't turn his head; his forearms begin to twitch like his fingers. How does a body wake when it's slept so long? How many days, weeks, will it take before we know if he'll get back to normal? I don't know what his normal is so how can I ever be sure if he gets back to it?

'Hello, Jim,' I say softly, leaning forward. 'How are you?'

There's no response except the twitching of his arms. I try a few more times, repeat his name, then stop, feeling foolish. I walk in front of the bed, to see if motion will attract his gaze, but nothing stirs and I return to my seat, to watch him.

'It's going to take time.' Nurse Evans has brought me tea in one of the thin plastic cups from the vending machine. It burns my fingers and, in trying to put it down on the tray table, I manage to tip it over, spilling hot liquid onto my tights and shoes, making me cry out. Nurse Evans grabs the jug of water and throws the whole thing over my legs. We're still mopping it up when Jim turns his head to look at us. His eyes are bright beneath heavy lids that seem to want to close.

'Look at us, making a circus in your room.' Nurse Evans' ward voice is back, bright and forceful, in charge of everyone. 'Sorry about that. You've had enough fuss lately, haven't you? All this business with your accident and now we can't even let you have a bit of peace and quiet.' She nods at me. 'You alright? Look, Emily's here to see you, Jim. She's been coming nearly every day.'

As if he understands her words Jim looks from Nurse Evans to me. Why did she say that? Now he'll be expecting someone he recognises.

'It's good to see you.' I give him a big smile. He bursts into tears.

It's hard to concentrate knowing Jim is awake. Shona is out of the office and there's no-one else I can tell but all I can think about is ways to get his mind working again—more photographs? Things from the house? I still haven't tracked down anyone he might know. It's possible he would recognise Daniel, or his mum, though I don't know how or where to write to him and the idea of contacting her makes me tired. I don't how much he's already explained. When I left Queen Mary's I tried to call him but I wasn't expecting him to be there and the answer phone was full, I couldn't have left a message if I'd wanted to.

There's a pile of post on my desk; author royalties, a few magazines and a badly written submission for a book about the Korean comfort women in the Second World War. Interesting idea, would be easy enough to sell. Absolutely not the right author though, if the letter and synopsis are anything to go by. Vanessa has sent another section of her book and attached a pretty detailed outline of the rest. I skim through it quickly, imagining her life in Peru.

There's a geography to ageing. Where food, water and shelter are easy to come by, there's time for the distractions of youth. The Edaben are cultivators but the climate is harsh here, the soil tough. Often they say the land is 'angry', and in angry years it takes the whole village to feed each other, everyone must help. To age without family would be incredibly hard. You have to be part of a group to survive. They have a saying that can be translated as 'bare is the back of the brotherless', which means many misdemeanours and faults are tolerated as families must stay together to survive. It is possible to move off and live with strangers, but to the Edaben such actions are not entirely to be trusted. People who live for themselves are treated with a good deal of suspicion, as though they live alone or apart because they are difficult people, hard to live with.

She has clearly absorbed our conversation about Jim and I like the exploration of the geography of ageing. It's controversial enough to attract the attention of the more literary broadsheets and I think the Board will approve. Timely, considering I have a meeting with our fiercest publisher in twenty minutes and if Meredith Winter asks for progress you'd better be able to show it. I make a mental note to thank Vanessa and read through the rest.

For elders, to be lonely is not an option, they're never left alone and this often annoys them. Ramal, in particular, would like to sleep all day but no-one lets him because he's the best at making weapons—that's kept him alert and vibrant well into old age, and prevented the slide of the mind that the developed world considers natural. No-one is alone here. The Ano, who live across the river at the foot of the Tembe hills, have a shaman figure who lives apart from the group in a cave that he's painted inside and filled with skins. But that is his choice and helps to create his aura, it's not obligatory for his rituals, and he's not seen as polluted. Everyone else stays in the group, with their children, their siblings, there are always people around and there is always noise, always something going on even if it's just helping with food preparation.

There are two good chapters here as well as the outline and I copy them in triplicate for the meeting, stapling them all together separately. We don't usually discuss such small books in detail and Vanessa's won't be on a major list or part of an ongoing series but I have a feeling I can it sell it as a featured title, one that will get extra PR help on publication and a showcase author interview in our newsletter, or even *The Bookseller*. If Vanessa keeps up this work rate she should be home soon. I make a note to write to her about Jim. I'll tell her about the history group too, she'd find that funny, would probably want to come along. Alice is keen to go back; she's taken a liking to Florence and wants me to show her the tin. But I can't contemplate running around with his things, talking about him. I'm hoping he'll be able to speak to me when I visit tomorrow. Jim's awake now, and he's real.

An uninvited guest. 1924. Jim's story

Notice of Death
Requiescat in pace et in amore
Albert Charles Avery, passed away peacefully
with his mother, Grace, and father James
(Jim) at his side, on June 30. He was born
at 9.41 a.m. and passed straight into the
arms of Jesus. The family wish for no other
mourners at the funeral, to be held on
Saturday, but flowers may be sent via Williams
& Son funeral directors of Barnes.

At first people were kind to them, in ways that surprised Jim. Loss was so common that generally it wasn't mentioned. You were supposed to ignore it until it was bearable, because it was the only way to survive. Speechmakers may still be congratulating the country on the pulling together that won the greatest of all wars, but the shells and guns had pushed ordinary people further apart. Grief was hard to share. There was nothing to be said. Broad shoulders and stiff upper lips were worn by men and women alike and it became hard to form meaningful friendships because nothing of any consequence was ever discussed.

So when neighbours broke their hard won reserve to be kind, the attention caught him off guard. Jim wished they wouldn't ask Grace so many questions, they made her cry. Everyone reliably informed him that it was good for her to do so. 'She must let it all out,' they said, as though her tears would finish but she never seemed to get any better or cry any less. Visiting armies, in twos and threes for courage, brought endless cake, which Aunt Hilda left in tins for other visitors, gave to Mrs Roberts or simply threw to the pigeons by the fountain at the end of the road, until even their interest waned.

Over time the armies grew smaller, retreated, their forays becoming less frequent, their questions less concerned. It was really time for Grace to 'snap out of things', they agreed. 'It might be best if she moved on and got out of herself a bit more.' As if he could do something about it. Grace stubbornly refused to even try to get over her beautiful stillborn child. Eventually the flow of visitors trickled to a halt. 'There's nothing to be done for her,' they said, it was too sad to be there when she couldn't talk about anything else and, besides, the year was moving on and there were things to organise. 'Why don't you try for another one? Wouldn't that help?' they asked and they looked at her as though death was catching and the strength of her grief might cause their own bright-eyed children to be snatched away from them.

Samuel, with his rational mind and practical manners, refused to believe that the loss of a baby could equate to the loss of his son, a grown man with a personality, someone who'd lived with him for years. Jim should make his wife 'just get on with it', something Jim felt hopelessly ill equipped to do. Samuel began to take walks in the evenings; Jim suspected he was unwilling to sit with her tears. Aunt Hilda touched Grace knowingly on the shoulder every time they passed in the silent corridors of the house. She added Albert's birth announcement to the growing shrine on her mantelpiece and each time Jim looked at it he pictured the tiny fingers curled into fists, puffed eyes tight shut in a wizened face.

The baby was supposed to save them, all of them, and without it they had nothing to say to each other. What they'd waited so long to welcome became a space in their lives that grew bigger each week. London's thin grey air was the colour of unhappiness, seeping into Jim's skin and taking the breath from his damaged lungs. All the things unspoken hung between them for a while and then faded. In that silence his wife slipped away.

It became easier to spend longer hours at work. At the Ministry no one dreamed of mentioning home-life. No questions were asked. The work itself was interesting and important. Jim began to be prized as a conscientious compiler of texts and pamphlets and he relished the chance to set about them with his lists and pens, bringing order to chaos and simplicity to the most unreadable of manuscripts. Departments started to ask for him by name and he brought home his finished products with increasing regularity, always smoothing them neatly before locking them away in the bureau drawer. He was developing an idea for a series giving lifestyle advice that could change the role of the Ministry, making public health more about prevention. 'People are leading their lives wrongly,' he said, and Uncle Samuel agreed that there was a weakness creeping into everyday life, people complaining about their lot. 'It's got to change; if the rumours are right, there might be another war on the way.'

Jim was just the man to write the lifestyle series. All he needed was the opportunity. If he could make it work then maybe he'd reach Grace, find some control over the rest of his life. Was that too much to ask? If he set the nation back on its feet, then he could find his family and put it all right again.

There was just one thing left to fix. While Grace had been labouring upstairs, cotton rags clenched between her teeth, a man had come to the house and pulled on the bell-rope as though it was on fire. Mrs Roberts and Primrose-Jane had come to find Jim pacing the drawing room, fervently wishing for a girl. 'It's bad luck to have guests at such a time,' insisted

Mrs Roberts, but Jim refused to have him sent away. Whether the visitor had really brought death no-one would ever know. But it did seem more than coincidence that Bert first reappeared on the day Jim's son wasn't born.

'It's really you then,' Jim felt dread and happiness. Bert was alive at least; it was a miracle after so long.

'Could say the same about you. You've scrubbed up alright.' Bert took the collar of Jim's jacket between his thumb and forefinger and stroked the cloth in an exaggerated gesture of admiration. 'Can't see you surviving on the old injuries pension.'

'Uncle Samuel helped me to find work, when I first came here.'

'I heard that Kearsey gave you the push.'

Even now, he had the ability to make Jim feel somehow less of a person. 'It's all a long time ago. Can't say I miss the farm though. It's nice being indoors.' Jim tried hard to keep his tone bright. The room was horrible. How could Bert be living here? No wonder he was aggressive and resentful.

'I heard you came off worst to Lilly's old man as well.' Bert flashed a sly smile. 'Where you working?'

'At the MOI, with my uncle. Desk job.'

'Don't suppose there'd be anything there for me? I'm sick to death of people telling me I can't work with this.' Bert held up his left arm and Jim looked closer at what he'd first seen on the unhappy day of Bert's reappearance. The sleeve of his jacket was pinned across itself and held together over his wrist at the bottom, to cover the gap where his hand should have been. 'Just ask anyway. I think perhaps you might do that for me.'

'I saw it was like that, the day you came. I'm sorry I never thought to ask. It was such a time for us.'

'How are mother and baby doing? Scene of domestic bliss no doubt?' Bert's voice was bitter, cold, and Jim felt himself stiffen. He looked down at the dirty linoleum. Where were the words to answer?

Bert stared hard at him and began to pat his right pocket in search of a cigarette. 'I'm sorry... I did wonder. Never saw a baby carriage come out of the house.' He pulled out a crumpled pack with his right hand, flicked the silver paper to one side and pulled a cigarette out with his teeth. 'What happened?'

'He was stillborn. Grace is OK but she's not strong, her mind is... it's unsettled her a lot. I haven't told her yet. About you, I mean. I wanted to wait until she was better.' Or at least until she stopped getting worse. What if she'd known Bert was spying on them? 'Why were you watching us?'

'You did promise to get in touch. I got fed up waiting. I came lots of times. Could never quite find the courage to ring again. I never saw anyone come and go.' Bert threw the pack onto the table and lit the cigarette that dangled from his mouth. Sour smoke filled the room.

'I leave the house early.'

'And get back late, I suppose?' Jim nodded. 'What does Grace do with herself all day?'

Did Bert's voice catch on the name? He could just be imagining things. Jim shrugged.

'She keeps herself busy, like any woman.'

'She's not any woman though,' Bert muttered softly. 'You know I *would* like to visit you, I remember your Aunt Hilda too. It looks like a fine house.'

The bedsit was uncomfortably close, almost filled by the single bedstead and another small camp bed pushed in beside it. Bert was perched on the end of it as they talked, Jim leaning up against the small gas stove in the kitchen area next to the scullery sink. A faint smell of gas and boiled vegetables lingered. Jim felt the rift between them growing. Without his aunt and uncle he would be living in a place like this too, perhaps without work, certainly without Grace, and all the biggest questions were still unasked. He should never have come. Should never have stopped listening to Ma's voice. She would have told him to stay away.

'Is this John's place?' He remembered Bert's cousin, a good lad, fine fast bowler. 'Is he well?'

'He planes furniture all day. Factory. Still it's a job and it's nothing I could do now. He's good to put up with me.'

The landlord had painted the splintered walls in a serviceable greyish green that could have been war surplus. Along with the camp bed and thin green curtains it made the flat look like a makeshift barracks. Even the bedding was a pair of rough, grey, military blankets. What horror did Bert dream there? He should offer some sheets, Hilda would have plenty to spare. Jim was hopelessly out of his depth, still grieving for his child, his absent wife. There was nowhere his eyes could rest without widening in further shock. What could such poverty do to someone? No wonder Bert seemed to be cracking under the strain.

'I know what you're thinking, and you can save your pity, I don't need a scrap of it.' Bert finished his cigarette and reached over to stub the end into the open mouth of a whale-shaped brass ashtray, the only decorative object in the room. 'But, since we're both sick of looking at these miserable walls, maybe we should step out for a pint?' He rose and picked up his hat from the kitchen shelf, his bearing still tall and straight, his movement quick. Any other injuries must be reasonably minor. The thought afforded Jim some relief.

He followed Bert out onto the dark communal landing, watched as he carefully pushed the key inside the letterbox on its long string, ready for John coming home after his factory shift. There was a lot you could learn to do with one hand. At the bottom of the steep flight of stairs, as they emerged into lamplight, Jim brushed from his fingers the flakes of paint left by the handrail. He was ashamed to realise he considered the neighbourhood to be rough-looking, too embarrassed to ask if they were heading for a local. They walked in silence for a while along the backstreets, passing the blocks and the bedsits, the backyards with their lines of grey washing and debris. Gradually the buildings became smarter, turned into houses, then bigger houses and garden squares, and they came to the door of The Apprentice. Both tall, they ducked slightly under the lintel, knocking against each other on the uneven step without smiling. Inside they waited for their drinks in silence; Bert made a big show of paying for them and Jim tried not to make a show about having to carry them both to the furthest table from the bar where they sat side by side with their backs to the wall, instinctively unwilling to be overheard.

'I don't know where to begin,' said Jim eventually.

'Let's just carry on with the small things then, like everyone else. Let's talk about the weather, shall we? Or the price of bread?'

The snarling spite in Bert's voice was frightening.

'It's like sitting with a ghost. It took us forever to get used to you being gone.'

'And now I'm back. Like a bad penny.'

'You know that's not what I mean.'

'I kept thinking you'd come home, back to Winterton, I

kept thinking that if I stayed long enough you'd eventually come, to see everyone.'

'To see who? I haven't been back since Ma died,' Jim protested.

'My ma said you'd gone up in the world and left everyone behind. Looks like she was right. She told me about everything, about Lilly and Charlie and poor little Ruby, about you and Grace and your ma too. We all liked Annie. I'm sorry for that. I don't know why she always thought I caused trouble.' Bert smiled and for a moment his old self shone like a needle of sunlight through a storm cloud then, just as quickly, vanished. 'I couldn't stay at home. There's nothing I can do on the cars and bikes now, not with this. And what work is there at home? Isn't that why you're here yourself?'

Why was he here? If it wasn't for Grace he could have stayed. He'd probably be running the dairy now, would have been a real father.

'When John came up here he asked if I wanted to come and there wasn't a reason to say no. I tried not to contact you both but it was hard knowing you were so close.'

Did he mean it? Or was it just Grace Bert wanted to see?

'How long have you been back?' Jim asked.

'A few years in rehab, place in Scotland where they fixed my arm properly and had me helping men to make bloody baskets. Tried a place in London with a fellow I met there but he'd no reason to put up with me. Home for a bit. Not much point in keeping count of years. Nothing changes. No-one wants to employ an old soldier with a disability. I'm finished. I'm not 30 yet and I'm finished.'

'But you get the pension? They do that for you?'

'Single man allowance. Enough to live on if you get your bed and board from family. Doesn't increase if I marry now so, even if a woman would look at me twice, we'd have no chance at living.'

'The next company said no-one got out alive.' Jim had put every one of their names in The List.

Bert shook his head slowly from side to side, wetting his lips with his tongue as though trying to coax the story from his throat.

'Got captured by Fritz. I'd been in town all day with The General, on business. I missed the order but when I drove her back I could see it wasn't pretty, I stopped a way back and tried to take cover but everywhere was holes already. I took a shell square on the arm as I tried to leave. Serves me right for trying to run. You might as well say it, I know you're thinking it.'

After all that heartache, he wasn't even in the tunnel. What kind of business he'd been on was anyone's guess. Better not to know.

'Bit of butchery in the prison hospital and there you have it. Seems they weren't too keen to let me go.' There was no trace of his smile left now. 'They made us clear the rubble, all the bombed-out buildings, we cleared it by hand. Load after load after load. But the worst thing was always wondering what was happening. We knew not to trust what they said but still, not to know, and then to realise when they come to let you out that the war had been over for months. That was the worst part.'

'The others were almost all lost that day,' said Jim gently, trying to bring him back. 'Everyone except me and Nissington. We're lucky to be...'

'If only I'd been with them.'

'Come on, old man, that's not right, you mustn't talk like that. You've got your whole life ahead of you.'

'And what a life. What have I got left? I'm finished, I'd be better off dead.' Bert stared into the dregs at the bottom of his glass as though he could read the future. 'I'd always thought me and Grace would be together. It's hard, really hard, to think of her with someone else. And you, well, it's funny really, all that time the thought of her kept me going out there.'

'You hid that pretty well.' Jim spoke sharply, unable to hide the rising irritation he felt at Bert, for disappearing, for returning, for changing into this bitter, self-pitying man. For letting him down.

'No-one's a saint, Jim, not even you.'

'What do you mean by that?'

'We've all got our secrets.' Bert was smiling again now, a broad grin that pushed the sides of his trim moustache but seemed unable to reach his eyes. 'I know what you did. Lilly was quite happy to tell me, though she says it's a secret. You like your secrets, don't you? You always did.' He took his time to remove a cigarette from his case with one hand, place it between his full lips and light it, drawing the smoke in deep with his eyes half closed as though it might be the only pleasure he had left.

Jim sat motionless. He could almost see the look on Lilly's face. Why had he been so foolish?

'I only did it for you, Bert.' And to assuage his own survivor's guilt. What would Grace say? She was so fragile, so weak. 'Grace doesn't need to know. She's been through a lot.'

'I just want to see her again, Jim. I want us all to be friends.' Bert set his jaw. 'You can't stop me.'

Jim balled his hands into fists under the table and held them there, as though the temptation to leap over the table and strangle this ghost with his threats and his hard luck was almost too great to bear.

'I don't think that's a good idea, old boy, she's still weak after all and it's better that we wait until she's stronger. It might be too much of a shock.'

'I can't believe you didn't tell her I came.'

Bert's face was incredulous, as though he was the only news there was. He could sit there like that, in his rage and his self-pity, and he hadn't asked a thing about the others, how they'd gone, how he survived. 'God's gift', that was how Ma used to describe him and she was right.

'I will, when the time is right for her. You wouldn't want her to see how you're fixed. Better for everyone if we wait.' Jim thought of Lilly with her savage threats, of Mathilde's tears. He thought of Grace on the beach with her wild hair flying around her face. He tried to remember the last time she left the house.

Rites of passage. 1994. Emily's story

'Have you managed to speak with your dad yet?' Nurse Evans stops me as I walk along the corridor. Jim is still awake, propped on cushions and staring at the photograph of a young girl that he's holding out in front of him. I think it's Nan. I hope it's bringing back memories so I don't disturb him today, leave him with his thoughts.

'A few times,' I reply. Nothing practical though, which is what she means.

'What does he think?'

'He's not very well at the moment.' I fall back on Mum's excuse. 'I think he'll probably just agree to whatever I think.'

'Not going to come and see him then?'

'He's not well,' I repeat. How long will Jim stay on this ward now he's awake? Does his confusion still count as serious? I haven't seen Dr Iqbal to ask. 'Is Jim going to be moved?'

'Not yet. He's been out for a while and he'll need all the usual tests. He seemed quite agitated in the night. I wasn't here but I've seen the obs.'

I nod, relieved. 'It might worry him even more if he's moved.'

Nurse Evans folds her arms across her chest. 'He can't stay there forever. He's going to have to be moved sooner or later. And when he is he'll have to be assessed.'

'Assessed?'

'By social services.'

Mum was right. I suppose her own parents might have needed the same but I barely remember them. They lived up north and we didn't visit often. They died within a couple of weeks of each other, when I was a teenager.

'And the outreach team. We don't know what injuries he's going to carry, if he needs physio, if he's going to need help walking.' She looks at me, choosing her words carefully. 'He's probably not going to manage on his own.'

From the side-room Jim starts to talk to himself in a low, hoarse voice.

I hold my breath and push through the crowd at the bar to reach the table where Ian is sitting with Andy, Doug and Becky. He looks drawn and even thinner, his jacket seems to hang off his shoulders. I feel a stab of affection at the sight of him. I'm slightly late. I stayed with Nurse Evans, listening to see if we could pick out something from Jim's words, but it was impossible to make sense of any of it. A normal reaction, she assured me, to the process of coming back to life. Upsetting all the same.

They're already picking antipasti from a wooden board as I join them at the table. Nothing's really edible here but MidHouse is Ian's favourite, a club for people who pretend not to like private clubs. Everything is subtle and muted from the hard, grey velvet benches to the conversation.

'Where's Sarah?' I ask.

'Babysitter bailed, little man's obviously getting a rep already,' says Doug, draping his arm around Becky's shoulders. She's under-dressed for the weather in a wispy silk kimono top that shows off her delicate arms and wrists, her hair a perfect halo of curls. Sometimes their smugness irritates me but they can be good company, animated and funny, especially when talking about work; Becky's a nutritionist and Doug's a lawyer who made partner last year. He's been Ian's friend since secondary school days. He has confidence and privilege, a manner that belies anything other than getting his own way, and he takes up as much space as possible, sitting with his legs far apart and his arms flung around the chair of whoever sits next to him. They're friends, I remind myself, Ian's friends anyway, and I shouldn't feel intimidated.

'That's not funny.' Becky pokes Doug in the ribs. 'It must be awful to be so tied, to have something relying on you for everything. We should go and see her, Em.'

'What about Sammy and Vodka? Don't they rely on you?' Doug and Becky have two white Samoyeds. Cruel to keep them in our climate, their thick coats are bred for below zero temperatures and they are misery itself in the summer heat, open mouthed and panting.

'That's different, Em, dogs aren't like babies.'

'Aren't all pets just surrogate babies?'

Becky looks slightly confused and Doug roars with laughter.

'You want to be careful there, Ian, mate, sounds like the old clock is ticking.'

'We haven't seen *you* for ages either.' Becky leans in and puts her hand on my knee.

'I'm fine, thanks, busy. Been spending a lot of time in the hospital, I've got an elderly relative there.'

'Ian didn't say.' She looks at him meaningfully and he rolls his eyes.

Why does Jim make him so uncomfortable? Perhaps he fears old age. I know his own grandmother unsettles him because I met her, only once, at my insistence, when we first started dating and I was desperate to feel closer to him, hoping his family were all wonderful in a cosy TV drama sort of way. Something to feel part of. We went to her nursing home, an expensive place in Oxford not unlike the hotel he favours for our wedding. She was so tiny, the size of a child, wrapped in a huge brown cardigan and a stained skirt. She was smiling, listening to music in a room full of old people listening to music, not many of them smiling. Perhaps, I thought then, losing memory is a good thing; she seemed happy.

Ian wouldn't sit down while we were there. He paced between the garden and the coffee machine while she told me about the man in the next chair who could change the channels on the TV with his eyes. She asked if I liked dancing, if I was her mother, if I knew the sun wouldn't rise on Thursday. Then she fixed her eye on me and asked me if I really loved the man I'd brought with me. On the way home Ian apologised. He said he wasn't the best visitor for her and hated that she had no idea who he was but any stranger could make her smile. He feared it was hereditary, that every time his mother forgot an appointment he could see it was only a matter of time.

'He's not really family. You've never spoken to him and he's out cold.'

'What's going on? Some kind of mystery?' Doug wears a look of intense amusement and I don't feel like talking about it in front of him.

'No mystery. Just a relative that's back in our lives, that we want to help to get better. He was in an accident and that's how they contacted us.' And he is awake now, I add silently.

'I hope he gets better soon,' says Becky.

'I reckon he's some old chancer looking for a new family,' says Ian and Doug roars with laughter again.

Becky looks nervously between us all, searching for a way to calm things down. 'Ian was telling us about Morley House earlier,' she says.

'Yeah, that was awful.'

Becky frowns. 'Oh. But I thought… Ian, didn't you say that was the one you were going for?'

'It's the only one big enough to hold everyone and they'll be able to accommodate with bedrooms,' says Ian.

'Round of golf should sort out the head next day,' adds Doug.

'We haven't decided though,' I say, hoping he hasn't already booked.

After dinner we all walk back across the park and, although I would really like to be alone now, our flat is too close by for me to go all the way back to my parents' house without causing tension. I undress and change into pyjamas with the bathroom door locked. When I venture outside Ian is sitting on the bed, still fully clothed.

'Sorry about Doug.'

'It's fine,' I say, though Ian was worse. 'I'm used to him.'

'It wasn't fair. I know this whole thing with Jim means a lot to you.'

I shrug, I don't think I've heard Ian say his name before. He sounds insincere.

'I'll come with you next time. Maybe he'll wake soon.'

'Maybe.'

I can't face telling him about Jim's garbled words, the idea of social services and how we might have to care for him. I get straight into bed and lie still, feigning sleep, every muscle stretched taut with the effort of not moving. I think about the faces in the tin, their loves and children and dreams, and wish fervently that I'd lived among them, a tangible branch of that family tree. Here, lying still as a corpse beside my fiancé, I am alone.

When I first met Ian, I was impressed by his easy charm; 'bowled over' Mum would have said; she didn't though because she was impressed by him too, his expensive suits and manicured nails, the obvious smell of success. She was delighted to think I could attract a man like that and it was fun at first. We'd go on long, freezing boat trips down the Thames to Richmond, visit the Tower, climb up to the Whispering Gallery in St Paul's. Breathing slowly through my mouth, I wonder whether Jim was happy, whether he ever boated down the Thames or danced in the moonlight at the top of the tallest building in the City. I wonder if he ever lay in bed at night, trapped in the headlights of a blank white future, fearful of change but even more scared to stay the same.

Sheldon's eyes are rolling back under the thin amphibian skin of his eyelids, veined in blue, lifting every now and then to show their whites. He's gripping the fingers of my left hand with his, periodically arching his back and then settling down with a roll of his shoulders. As he sleeps, every muscle in his tiny body moves constantly, flashes of emotion rage across the plump skin of his face, turning from fear to outstretched smiles in an instant and I watch it all, fascinated. A quick look at my watch tells me I've been doing this for almost an hour and I look up in guilty realisation that I've been ignoring Sarah all that time, only to find her smiling across at me holding her son.

'Time wasters, aren't they?' I say, embarrassed at what must seem like broodiness on my part. 'All the way over here I was thinking I won't go gooey over the baby, I'll make a fuss of Sarah, she's the one who's starved of attention, and look at me!'

'Babies just do that to people.'

'He is particularly cute though.'

'All babies are cute, it's just that until your family or your friends have them you don't really have much to do with them. Then all of a sudden you're holding them all the time.'

I rock him gently, wondering if I should put him down. Mum used to say it was bad for babies to be allowed to sleep on people, that it made them fretful in their cots, but I'm enjoying the cuddle. I had no idea babies could make you feel calm, I thought they only brought stress and mayhem. There are cups and plates on the floor, piles of washing in various stages all over the dining table and small oval-shaped pads scattered on the sofa. Dozens of colourful, crinkly, noisy things, shaped like animals and crazy insects are mixed up with cloth books and roll mats and other signs of the fun they seem to be having together. Sarah follows my line of sight.

'Sorry,' she says half-heartedly, 'I did mean to get around to tidying up today but there's always so much to do. It feels like a major achievement if I get him to sleep long enough in the afternoon to cook something for dinner. But then there's always something I need for the recipe and it's a mission to dress him and get him in his buggy ready to get to the corner shop. By the time I've got all his clothes on he needs changing again.'

Despite the moans she seems happy, different to before. Perhaps children put everything into perspective, whether they fill your world with this new, all-encompassing kind of love or tear you apart like Ian claims. Perhaps it's both. Perhaps the way you navigate it is the key to staying together.

'And there's the amount of work they create. I have never done so much housework in my life. Seriously, Em, I feel like a drudge, I spend half my life hanging miniscule socks on radiators and sterilising things and feeling horribly guilty if I don't iron all the creases out of everything he wears.'

I feel suddenly guilty myself. All I've done is sit here and cuddle the baby.

'Let me help,' I say. 'Here you take him, he probably shouldn't get too used to going to sleep like this, it's only going to make trouble for you in the end. I can tidy round in here, let me know what would be the most help.'

Sheldon is starting to wake and fuss and I realise my back is aching from the odd way I've been holding him. Sarah takes him from me, a muslin square ready on her shoulder.

'He's quite a weight after a while.'

I stretch my left arm as though I've been there for days.

'Are you guys still free on the 19th? It's going to be a proper christening now, at St Margaret's, it seems like the right thing to do. We've been to a couple of naming ceremonies and they're a bit weird.'

Tucked in between the lists of funerals and marriage announcements there are three christening notices in Jim's tin. One of them is pinned to an order of service with a small blue ribbon, faded at the tips, and I try to remember the name of the child.

'It's the right thing to do. Our rites of passage. That's all life becomes in the end. We just muddle through them as best we can.' It's a moment before I realise I actually said this out loud and before I can explain Sarah is asking me if I'm OK. She settles Sheldon in his basket again and looks up at me with concern.

'I'm fine. Honestly, it's this business with Jim making me think about things a bit too much.'

She starts to ask me about it when a loud rapping at the door wakes Sheldon with a start, causing him to cry. Sarah wearily picks him up again and answers the door to Andy wearing a large grin and looking unsteady on his feet.

'Greetings earth people!' He lurches forward to plant a big wet kiss on Sarah's face. She looks unimpressed.

'How long have you been drinking? You smell like a pub.'

'That's a nice welcome for your favourite husband. Ian stopped by after work and we just, I don't know, what time is it? It's not late, is it? Little man still up?'

'He was asleep until you woke him.'

Andy flops down on the sofa next to me and I move up to make room for him. He holds his beer slightly better than Ian but he's breathing with some difficulty. There are red marks like wheals on his cheek and his eyes are watery. My evening is over.

Talk of escape. 1930. Jim's story

Weeks of relentless rain carried the murk of winter through to spring and early summer, dampening the air and smearing the windows with tear tracks. Grey light lingered from morning until night, leaving the house in a fug of dusk. Grace, stricken with grief, wore the weather like a cloak as she wandered between rooms, unable to focus on the small domestic tasks she was permitted to undertake. She wanted to scrub the floors, she told Jim, to pound the washing and bang the dust from the rugs but he gently ushered her to the drawing room and told her to rest, frightened by her anger.

Mrs Roberts brought her a letter, holding it out with her usual mixture of deference and disdain. Peeping through her legs was Primrose-Jane in an oversized pinafore, a tiny feather duster in her hand. It was the first letter addressed only to Grace since they were married but she didn't mention it and Jim didn't ask. He was pleased when she started to take shopping trips. It didn't matter that she often returned without bags, exhausted, and took herself straight off to bed. It was natural that she should feel like fresh air, despite the weather. No-one could expect her to stay indoors forever. He bought her a coat, a beautiful soft curled astrakhan jacket with a sky-blue lining, so she wouldn't catch chills.

Throughout the long grey summer, the rain kept pouring, covering windows with a layer of droplets that distorted the view and clouded Jim's thinking. He told himself that he would sort things out when the rain stopped, but where could he start? Grace barely talked to him. She drifted in and out like a ghost. When he got home from work she looked far-away, and Aunt Hilda shook her head, pushed them through to supper where Grace picked at the food on her plate and looked at the window while Jim lied about his work. She became careless, untidy, leaving beds unmade and cushions unplumped. When Jim found her astrakhan coat in a crumpled heap at the foot of their bed he was not surprised. He picked it up and draped it on a padded hanger, noticed something heavy in the right pocket as he went to hang it in the closet. A china pillbox, painted with red and peach roses, edged in gilt to match the clasp. He'd thought Dr Elliot had stopped giving her pills, concerned they made her worse. But it was empty of pills, held only a thin piece of paper torn from a letter, the address of Bert's bedsit. He opened it out very flat, smoothing it down against the coat, and then very carefully folded and replaced it because he did not know what else to do.

Had she kept the letter? Was she so determined to see Bert that she would sit in his dirty bed-sit? How could Jim ask her? Secrets and resentments burned until there was barely anything to say. When the rains finally stopped he walked back to Bert's flat. There was no-one to answer the door, no key on a string, no sign at the window. A red-faced man leaned from the downstairs window. 'You can rent the bloody room for three shillings a week or bugger off with that infernal banging.' Jim shook his head, breathing hard, and walked back through the front garden with its jumble of junk. Sitting on the low brick wall, he watched the weak sun dry the last of the glittering drops from the pavement. Bert had disappeared again but things could never be the way they were.

Maybe Grace would be better off back home, by the coast, in the sea air. The sharpness of the wind might pull her mind back to earth. Though she seemed healthy carrying this child she wasn't sleeping properly and in her dreams she talked of escape. Often she talked of the sea. Water called Jim too, drawing him to the park's oval lake, the fountain in the nearby garden square with its rim full of impotent pennies.

Most nights he lay awake with the feeling that a heavy weight was crushing his chest, anxious that they knew nothing about each other, fearing that even the baby might not bring them together again. For a long time, his nightmare was that Bert would try to come to the house but now that he knew Bert could never contact them again, well, that was no less of a secret to carry and he still worried that Grace might find out, even though he'd hidden the tragic newspaper article in the drawer with his own writings. Easier not to talk about it. Guilt for Bert would fill his words, muddle his thinking. Grace would blame him too, he knew that, and it would make him feel worse. Better for her to think that Bert had simply moved away. She didn't need to know what he'd done. She was better off thinking he didn't want to see her. The details of the coroners' report were at once too much and too little detail. Poor John was the one to find him, in his own room, overcome by the gas that poured from the stove. After everything John had already faced, little wonder he'd given up the flat. But what of the real detail? What did Bert feel in his desperate pride—relief as he slumped? If Jim thought of it too much he might wish for the same.

When Grace grew too big to walk far she sat by the pond below the rockery in the garden's cool shade; shuffling slowly through the sun room and across the lawn, hands clasped across the smooth hill of her belly. Jim sometimes lay next to her, on his back on the moss-filled grass, listening to the rush and trickle of the tiny waterfall. In Aunt Hilda's sheltered

212

garden, flanked on all sides by tall houses, he could look directly at the sky without the light hurting his eyes. He would lay still in the bright afternoon, watching the clouds scud across and disappear behind brick walls, wondering where they started and where they would finish their journey. Just tiny droplets holding on to each other in the rush of a chance wind.

Dearest Cousin

I do hope that this letter finds you and Grace well and safe. We thought you would like to see this picture of our new arrivals. Twins! Who would have guessed? Not another pair in the family according to Mother, so we feel that we are especially blessed. They're dear little things and they know each other already, they even cry when they're separated and sleep with their arms linked together. I expect I must have carried them like that.

Harry and William are not much interested in babies now, they're too busy playing at soldiers out in the fields all day. They're growing up fast and both starting to look like their father. I can hardly keep up with the food and clothes they need. The money you send does certainly come in useful and we are so grateful to you for everything.

They've had a new roof put on the cottage and finally the leak above your old room has gone, it drove us mad in the rains. They've painted the door too and it's looking smart. You must come and see us when Grace is feeling well and strong again.

Please do pass on our best wishes to Aunt Hilda and Uncle Samuel. Mother says she would dearly like to visit them but for her legs, she does seem to suffer so in this weather and doesn't get much further than the church most weeks. She seems lost without Father and spends a lot of time here with us. She says it makes her feel closer to Annie and I know we all still miss her very much, as, of course, must you.

Please keep in touch with your news and let us know when the baby arrives, you will love being a parent, Jim, it is the greatest happiness of all.

Much love

Your cousin Eleanor

The young girl from the post room had thrown the letter onto his desk and turned to rush off without even so much as a 'good morning'. He should say something, but what? Was he even supposed to get personal mail at work? He'd asked Eleanor to use the office address, worried in case the postmark upset Grace, but he'd never checked if that was allowed. Did he have to anymore? Sometimes the weight of his new-found prestige sat uneasily on his shoulders. Now the post girl, with her defiant eyebrows and scarlet lips, stood rudely in his doorway, chatting with Peggy who started her rounds on this level. While he read his cousin's letter he was treated to a muffled stream of gossip about the rest of the building.

These were desperate times for such big employers he thought vaguely, they had to take whoever they could get. He'd often heard Aunt Hilda discuss this with her neighbours, berating the loss of a decent serving class and the impossibility of staff in these straitened times. He'd seen Grace roll her eyes at them too, seen her take on the gardening herself dressed in one of his old work shirts, sleeves pushed up. At least she wasn't afraid of a little hard work, despite the life that was swelling inside her.

'Honestly, she does go on so, Mr Avery, I'm sorry, she's just a young thing, no harm done.' Peggy stuck a testing little finger into the cup surreptitiously. 'Your tea's quite cold! I'll make you another.' She fussed over the urn on the trolley that she'd parked outside in the corridor, polishing its tarnished surface with a limp cloth while she waited for the heavy tea to drip from the tap. Placing the fresh cup onto the old saucer with a clatter, she added a welsh cake on a small, green plate. Jim saw Ruby pushing currants into biscuit dough and a wave of nausea came over him. He wouldn't eat it. He'd have to smuggle it out so he didn't offend her.

'Bad news, was it, Mr Avery?' Peggy asked amiably, setting cup and plate on the side desk next to his main work area. She tried to move a large stack of his precious papers to make room and he rescued them carefully, straightening their pages and placing the manuscripts on the wooden cabinet shelves along the wall. The shelves were colour coded for his latest advisory pamphlets. They always gave him a stab of pride lined up together in their graded jackets. It was good to see them out in the open instead of hidden away in the drawers at his house, unseen by anyone, unpraised. His current project was another great list, this one a record of all the vessels lost at sea in the Great War, an overview of the navy's role, a constant reminder of Charlie. It was important not to lose hope. A separate file of information sat next to the folders of The List, a chance to maybe track him down. It slowed his progress and kept him in the office, catching up time at the end of the day, because he knew his lists were awaited, were perhaps the most important things being written.

Promotion had been offered, on several different occasions, across the desk from the formidable, titled heads of the Ministry. They shook his hand and congratulated his sense of industry, the hours he put in to make sure he hit his deadlines; they offered him a better job, a bigger office. But they didn't smile at him or use his first name and he knew that wherever he was put he would always be the hired help, a private in their Officers' mess. So he thanked them but he'd rather stay where he was. Besides, he liked his office with its pale green walls, its wide, leather-topped proofing desks and banks of shelves and titles. Most of all he liked the work, the neatness of collating and the satisfaction of completing a definitive repository of information and fact in a world where little else seemed certain.

'Not at all, Peggy, thank you. A letter from my cousin in Norfolk, actually.'

'That's where I went on my honeymoon! Wells-next-to-Sea, I think it was, took ever so long to get there on the train.' She fiddled with the cups and saucers on the trolley, stacking them in noisy piles. Jim's fingers itched for his list. 'Why do they call it that then, I wonder? Isn't it all next to the sea there? Is that where you're from then? You always did have a funny accent.'

'I think there are other smaller places called by the same name. Us East Anglians seem easily confused.' He smiled in a way that he hoped wasn't too encouraging. Peggy was nice enough, but she could stand there all day and he must get on.

'It was nice, cold I remember, windy, mind you it was a long time ago now. We had crab, never had it before, didn't suit my husband, God rest his soul.'

'It's an acquired taste,' agreed Jim, taking a sip of his tea before that one, too, turned lukewarm.

'Got lots of family there, have you, Mr Avery? I expect that's making you home sick.'

Jim was about to nod when he realised that, no, he didn't anymore. His parents, Charlie, Pearl, his poor niece and little nephew, all gone and how powerless he'd been to prevent that. If it wasn't for Eleanor he'd have no contact at all, no ties, no news of his relations. It made his head swim for a moment and he set his tea down, rattling the cup against the saucer, thrusting the photograph of his cousin's newest arrivals into Peggy's hand to divert her attention.

'Little darlings! Twins are they? Boys or girls?'

'Both, Annie and Freddie, that makes four children for Eleanor now, she sounds happy, comes from quite a big family herself.'

'How many?'

He shrugged, surprised he didn't know and hazarded a guess at nine, wondered briefly where the rest of Violet's brood were now. Her two eldest were lost in the last war of course, poor bastards, but the others he couldn't place at all. He made a mental note to ask Eleanor when next he wrote.

'My mother was the youngest of 14! Imagine that in a little two up two down. Goodness knows how they managed. Mind you, she said some of them were married and off before she was even born.'

He remembered the last cup of tea he'd had with Ma, in the kitchen at the cottage, when he'd told her about his fear of fatherhood. 'We're all already born with responsibility,' she'd said, 'there's nothing there to fight or fear.'

'And when will your happy day be, Mr Avery?'

'Sorry?' He'd almost forgotten Peggy was standing there.

'Your wife, Mr Avery, she's also expecting, I believe?'

'Oh! Yes, of course. Not for a few weeks, I think.'

'Could be any day then, couldn't it? Don't expect it to be convenient, they have a habit of surprising you. Make the most of now because you'll have no peace at all when it comes along; it'll turn you all upside down.'

That sounded good. They could do with some shaking up in that dreary house, a bit of fresh life. He would like to have invited Eleanor and her family to stay, but he knew it would never work; they were too different, too poor. She would make her excuses; it's too far, too expensive, too dangerous; we'll wait until the babies are older or there's a bit of spare money. And even when those things happened, they still wouldn't come.

'Do you want another one now, before I go?' Peggy looked at him for a few moments. 'You should go and see that family of yours. A bit of sea air might do you some good.'

Another tin. 1994. Emily's story

When I arrive at my parents' to let in the estate agent she's already waiting in her car, thirty minutes early. I'd have preferred to go in and check around first but she gets out as soon as I open the gate, rushing forward with one hand outstretched and the other clutching a briefcase. American soft rock hair and white stilettos. Her jacket is heavily padded at the shoulders, her handshake damp and limp. 'Donna,' she tells me, and we step over the pile of post on the front mat. One envelope is hand-written, standing out from the junk mail and bills, and I scoop it up. The postmark is foreign, blurred, the paper as light as air. It's not Anna's writing so it can only be from Daniel.

'Take as long as you like to look around,' I say, wanting to read his words. But Donna has questions before she can measure up, some of which I'm unable to answer. Do we have any covenants? Outstanding mortgages? Debts on the address?

'It does help to have sofas and beds in the photographs. Is it all being listed in the price or will they want any of this furniture?'

'Probably not.' None of it's expensive, nothing older than their marriage except the sewing table that came from Nan's house and I'll take that. It won't look right in the flat though, our things are too modern.

We walk through the rooms and Donna gets me to hold the end of her measuring tape, speaking the metres into a small recorder, presumably to be typed up back at the office. She adds other things to the dictaphone too. 'Lounge, large, double aspect. Wide picture rails and skirting.' This is going to take hours. The letter is burning through my pocket.

'Second bedroom. Good size. Fitted carpet. Fitted cupboards along left hand wall, wood, white painted.' Donna opens and closes each of the doors, stepping slightly back as though she expects something to jump out. There are posters stuck to the insides of the doors, Anna's favourites; Depeche Mode and Duran Duran. They're all shirtless; Mum must have made her put them there instead of on the walls like the rest of her posters. I pick up a postcard of The Thompson Twins that's lying on the cupboard floor and the carpet sags, gives way beneath my hand. A false floor.

Wishing Donna wasn't watching so intently, I push my hand under the square of carpet and peel it back. Underneath is a lid-less cardboard shoebox filled with postcards, sketches and photographs. I draw it out carefully and a photo flutters to the ground. Anna, me and Carrie, arms around each other, mugging for the camera, sitting together on the sea wall in front of Nan's cottage, looking as though we hadn't a care in the world. The box is full of photographs and we are no older in any of them. A snapshot of our childhood. Did she hide these for my sake? To spare Mum and Dad? We'd have been better off keeping them together. After all these years I don't know where we'd start now. If it wasn't for Donna I'd probably push them back again but I turn and say, 'My sister's. I'll put them in the packing crate.' There's an old camera there too, one I remember Nan using. I carry it all back down to the lounge, where Donna sits to finish her notes.

'Would you like to list it straight away?' She pushes back her glasses and looks at me expectantly. She's used to getting things done.

'Won't it take a while to sort out?'

'Couple of weeks to get the details written up. But we can

add it to our list inside, so if we get any callers looking for something similar we can bring them round. Once the owners have signed and faxed the agreement back.'

That might buy me some time to think. Mum always panics with legal forms, it'll make her double check everything.

'How long does it usually take to sell a house?' If I can't stay here, I'll have to find somewhere else. I can't think at the flat and I don't even want to admit what that means. I just want to get Jim right without worrying about myself and what I might need.

Donna shakes her impressive mane and hands me a few listings of houses a bit like ours. 'This one took three weeks. We sold this one before the photo even went up in the window. Popular road this, popular with families. The houses are well built, solid, good size bedrooms.'

It wasn't popular with families when we lived here. I remember most of our neighbours being ancient. They've probably all passed on now, the houses full of new folk with children and cars. I won't have long to keep this house from joining them and, when it does, I'll have less of an excuse to be hanging around. Unless Jim picks up. Unless this letter is friendly. I tell Donna I have an appointment and nudge her gently through the front door, still talking, promising, telling me to call Mum and Dad for a fax number she can get the details sent through.

The letter is airmail, the kind of blue paper that folds in on itself and seals. It's hard to open without tearing. There isn't much text, just a few paragraphs, no terms of endearment.

Dear Emily,

I hope you don't mind me writing, it's easier than trying to call. Most of the time it's pretty busy here and there's no time on your own. I can't say where we are but you can probably guess. I can't say much about plans either, and I don't know when I'll be back. So you can see it's much better to get news from home! Write and tell me how things are going.

I've been thinking about Jim. I hope he's better now and that you're getting to know him. If that's the case you can probably ignore this, but I know you wanted to find out more about him and I remembered that I met him, waiting in the doctor's surgery, with someone—Lilly? Rose? She had the name of a flower. She was much younger, maybe young enough to be his daughter. Sorry, that probably doesn't help much. But I was thinking so I thought you should know.

When I get back I'll get in touch and we can visit together if you like. If you did want to write to me, this is the address.

All the best,

Daniel

I read it through four times and his voice is the words in my head. Is this all he's allowed to say or all he wants to say? I'm confused. He's clearly doing a lot of thinking, but is it about me or Jim? He's remembered someone Jim was with once. But he can't remember her name. What sort of spurious reason is that to write? Now I'm going to be driven half mad with a fact I wouldn't know where to begin checking out. Even if I went to the doctors, they wouldn't be able to tell me anything about any of their patients. Would they? He has written, though, to me. He's been thinking, just as I have been thinking. And when he gets back, we will meet.

Water cascades over my head, waking my senses. I am

conscious of limbs, muscles, skin. My body is awake for what feels like the first time in weeks. It's good to be swimming outside, on a crisp winter morning, steam rising up from the water like mist on a lake. I had no idea this place was here, an outdoor pool in Covent Garden. A strange oasis flanked on all sides by offices, apartments and shop fronts. Water as warm and bubbling as a Jacuzzi. Though the pool is busy it's not crowded because these are serious swimmers. They plough down the lanes in neat furrows, never touching. Pushing through the water I feel strong, alive. Shona was right, this is a brilliant way to start the day.

One arm holding the deep end wall, treading water, I watch for a while. Shona looks sleek and feline in a black one-piece and cap, her goggles streamlined and watertight, wrapping the sides of her eyes. She's a serious swimmer, a Hampstead Lady. Every day she visits one of her favourite outdoor swimming spots, one of them is in the Serpentine. I think I'll pass on that. This is good though, I could make it a habit. Anna would be impressed to know I'd been exercising before work. 'Growing up', she'd say then try to set me times to beat. I haven't told her I found her box of photographs yet; I don't know how to start that conversation and it's possible she's forgotten it was there. In some ways I hope she has, it would mean she's moved on. But I do need to let her know I understand.

'You giving up?' Shona suddenly appears and showers me with spray. 'How many lengths have you done?'

'I have no idea. Don't tell me you count?'

She holds up her wrist, showing an expensive-looking black rubber watch. 'Race timer. Looks around 50. You can't be far behind.'

I rub at the goggle marks on my forehead. 'In that case I've definitely had enough. I haven't been swimming since I was about ten.'

Shona stretches out luxuriously, pushing her legs straight against the side of the pool, back muscles taut. 'This place always makes me feel like I'm on holiday. You get sun beds around the side in better weather, even in the early sessions people lay there sipping cool drinks.'

'More coffee weather today! I could do with one actually but I'm scared to get out of this warm water and face the cold air.'

'I'll grab your towel.' Shona pushes herself up on the pool edge and out of the water in one deft movement. There are no steps or hand-rails. When she gets back, wrapped up and holding out my towel, I'm still struggling to drag my legs over the side.

'You'll get used to that,' she laughs. 'Bit more swimming will improve your upper body strength too.'

'You might convince me once or twice a week. Here though, not one of your ratty river holes. They must be freezing at the moment.'

'More refreshing.'

'This'll do for me. Thanks. I enjoyed it. If you don't mind me tagging along I think it'll do me some good.' I feel suddenly emotional at the thought of doing anything regularly, with a friend, someone who has actually chosen my company. The kind of thing that makes you realise you can look forward with pleasure. A lump appears in the back of my throat and I jerk my bag out of our shared locker too quickly, causing its contents to fall out on the wet, grubby floor.

I dump the bag on a bench and start scrabbling for things; purse, hairbrush, travel card. Shona, helping, picks up some papers, the airmail letter among them. I hope it's not soaked.

'You don't talk about him much.'

My neck flushes with heat before I realise she has picked up a photograph of Ian that was in the side of my purse. It was taken a few years ago, after the snow, when we'd been sledging on binbags in Battersea Park, laughing at the wildness of wet jeans and gloves. A good day. He's wearing an orange beanie and an orange and navy striped scarf and, although he's not smiling, you can tell it was a good day. His face is warm.

'You want to hear all the domestic details?'

She gives me an odd look. 'I'm not prying. Just haven't heard his name come up much, that's all. Everything OK?'

'You'll be getting your invite soon, don't worry.' I give a forced laugh. 'We're quite laid back about the plans.'

'He doesn't strike me as the laid-back type.'

'That's not such a bad thing given I'm the other one helping.'

'You're incredibly organised. I would love my desk to look like yours.'

Not everything in life fits a project plan. I wish it did. I take the photo and put it back in the purse, pile my clothes on the bench.

'We should get going. Did I tell you I had some new chapters from Vanessa? The publicity team loved them, so you won't be the favouritefor much longer.'

Water has soaked through the thin paper and blurred the writing into fuzzy blue lines. There's no chance now to read and re-read meaning into the words. Thankfully the return address has survived; I pull it away and hide it in a side pocket.

'You came back.' Jim's voice is hoarse from the breathing tube but much clearer than I expected. The last time I visited he'd stopped mumbling and was back to staring mutely into space. To hear normal speech come from his mouth is almost miraculous, and he seems to know who I am. He knows I was here before. This time he is looking straight at me, intent and serious.

'Of course I came back. I had to see how you were.' I sit down on the chair by the bed as quietly as I can, not wanting to break the spell.

'I'd given up.' His pale eyes search my face intently.

'I've been coming to see you every day,' I reply.

'You haven't changed a bit.'

He thinks I'm someone else. Nurse Evans, sitting outside, has repeated that I shouldn't expect too much, and I'm worried if I correct him he'll get upset. Is it better to carry on? Does he think I'm his wife? I don't look anything like the photograph I thought was of her, on the top of the washstand. Someone else from his past?

'How are you feeling?' I stall.

'Head hurts. Throat hurts. Everything aches. They said I'd been asleep for a while. Doesn't feel like it.'

'Do you need anything?'

'Not now, Molly, not now you're back.'

He thinks I'm Nan. What age was she when they lost touch? Dad says he never met him at all, so she must have been young. I know she had Dad when she was really young. Is that what drove them apart? He's reaching out his arms now and I stand up, move to the bed. I take his hands and he holds them with surprising strength. There are tears welling in his eyes, and mine, though I have no right to be crying with him. I'm only misleading him.

'I never stopped loving you, Molly, whatever you thought, when they sent you away.'

'I know that,' I say instinctively and he sobs.

'Your mother wasn't well.'

'What was wrong with her?'

'She wasn't well. Her mind…' He carries on gripping my hands, shaking his head. 'She had a hard war, Molly. She couldn't come to terms with it all.'

'What happened?' I ask gently and he looks up at me for a while.

'It's done,' he shakes his head. 'All done.'

'Is Mother…?'

'She wasn't strong, Molly. She couldn't take what happened with you and that terrible man.'

What man? Was it her that sent Nan away? 'Tell me.' I need him to keep talking. I don't want to break this spell but I have to find out what I can.

'It was Harrington-Green, his family. They made her do it, she said. But she didn't want to know you either. She felt it was her fault, her fault for everything else. She could hardly bear to look at you, even when you were a baby.'

All the things Nan hinted at before, that Dad was born out of wedlock, not wanted by his father, were they true? It must have been so hard for her on her own. It must have been so hard for Jim not to help her. But if I push him for answers he'll know I'm not Nan then the likelihood is that I find out even less. I sit quietly for a moment, still holding his hands, waiting for the past to catch up with us.

'She always said you'd be a monster.' Jim is calmer now, he's loosened his grip. Why would she think Nan was going to be a monster? 'She never told me why but I knew as soon as I looked at you. You were Bert's child. Beautiful like him. And

227

she said he was a curse but I knew you weren't. You were always beautiful and perfect. I loved her and you, Molly. I loved you with all my heart. I loved Bert too, we all did.'

The room tilts suddenly and I am so overcome with the need to cry out that I bite down hard on my lip, drawing blood. Jim is not Nan's father, not Dad's grandfather at all. No bloodlines connect us. All the heartache, all the hunting for meaning in his house, going through his things. I lean hard into the chair, afraid that I will faint. Where does this leave me? All the soul searching and anguish. Nan wasn't even his daughter but the product of a difficult affair. Even now I haven't found family and I have no idea what this all means. Ian was right, Jim is nothing to do with me. And yet we are connected. Jim is still holding my hands tightly, as though he never wants to let go and I'm pulled by the force of his emotions. He's not Nan's father but he loved her as though he was. He loved her fiercely and she was taken from him. What have I found? It only makes sense here, sitting by this bed and listening to Jim's heartbreak. Only Jim can tell his story. He can only tell it to me if I'm Molly. And it will have to stay in this room.

'You were a perfect baby, a perfect child. So patient with your mother. She wasn't well, Molly, you can't blame her.'

'I don't.'

He smiles, leans back on the enormous pillows. 'She's proud of you, I know it really. And I'm proud of you.'

'Why?'

'You're such a strong girl. You're going to make a name for yourself. No-one takes photographs like you, I don't know where you get it from. Such a headstrong girl. That's how I knew you'd be alright. It would have finished your mother off if you'd stayed.'

Nan loved her cameras. I don't remember ever seeing really old photos of hers though. I make a mental note to ask Dad next time we speak.

'Thank you for the photos of your boy. Where is he?' Jim looks around on the floor as though expecting to see a child playing there. He's been speaking so lucidly I've forgotten how confused he really is. To him it's fifty years ago and Dad should be rolling a wooden car along the tiled floor. Would Dad have been different if he'd had a father, a grandfather? What I know now is so unbearably sad. How can this be our history?

'He's at home. He's fine.'

'He looks like both of you. I hope he takes after you more.'

'I think he must do.'

Jim gives a deep sigh and presses his head back into the pillow, his eyes drooping closed. Nurse Evans appears and I wonder how long she's been listening, whether she will tell me off for my deception.

'He needs rest now. That was a tiring visit.' She pats Jim's hand on the way to check his observations. 'I'm sending your visitor home, Jim, she can come back tomorrow.'

'Tomorrow,' he repeats in a sleepy voice.

As I gather my things and turn to leave he calls, 'They should use your photos, the Ministry. Yours was the real war. I'll tell them to make the book, Molly.'

Moonlight. 1931. Jim's story

Jim shifted uncomfortably against the hard-stuffed sofa in the lounge, suddenly aware that he'd been sitting in the same position, with his arm crooked and his neck bent to the right, for several hours. Everyone had told him that babies were timewasters, but he still found it incredible how long you could actually spend staring at them, even while they slept. Especially while they slept.

He scooped her weight in the soft blanket and leaned over to set her down in the crib beside him, keeping her close to the heat of his body and holding her still long after he laid her onto the covers, back aching, breathing shallow. Everyone said she was probably hungry, that it would be easier after she was weaned and went to bed with her stomach feeling fuller. But it didn't seem to help with Molly and anyway she fussed over the little spoons of rice and rusks so much that Jim worried whether any nutrients got through at all. They must do, though, because she was certainly growing. His arms and shoulders were sore with the effort of carrying her from the moment he came home from work until she slept. Maybe if Grace had been able to feed her as nature intended, she might be a calmer baby. Was it too much for her having a baby at her age? He hardly dared to mention it, but Hilda had said so often. 'You shouldn't have waited so long, not for the first one.' Was that why Grace struggled to feed her, grew so tired and turned to sleeping all day? Should they have thought about such things? Pointless to dwell on what couldn't be changed.

Molly was a nervous baby, needing constant warmth as reassurance against abandonment. Settling her every night was a drawn-out performance. It was necessary for Jim to hold her tightly and then somehow ease her into the crib that had been saved for Jack's children and which moved around the house, to keep her always close to other people. The slightest sudden movement could wake her and the whole performance would start again. Jim eased his left arm out from under the weight of his child and pushed down his shoulder blades to relieve the tightness across the top of his back, leaving his hand across the span of her chest for reassurance. She looked so peaceful with her head thrown back and her mouth stretched into a lazy smile.

Slowly he took his hand away, stroking across the downy hair on top of her head, but immediately Molly's eyes popped open and she began to wail as though she had been struck, crying in intense crescendo, while Jim crouched by the crib with his head in his hands. Was it even possible to feel more weary? Battlefields were good preparation for babies. The sleep-deprived patience with which he'd dug tunnels had served him well, giving him the strength to clean and fill bottles and hold them to her again and again before she finally decided to drink them. He tried to lift her before she woke the rest of the house.

'You should be in bed, Jim, it's gone midnight and you've got work in the morning.' Aunt Hilda stood in the doorway in her wrap and gown, her hair covered and the low light from her candle casting stern shadows across her face. 'You've been down here for hours.'

'I'm sorry Molly woke you, she's fussy tonight, doesn't want to be put down, I've only just settled her.' Were they outstaying their welcome? His aunt always insisted they needed the company. The thought of having to look after Grace and Molly alone was too much to bear.

'Don't worry about me, dear, you know I'm always awake

anyway. But it isn't right you living like this. You barely touched your dinner; you must be exhausted.'

'I'm alright, she'll go down in a moment. She was sick earlier so she might be hungry. I'll go and fetch another bottle.' Really he should ask for help but he never felt comfortable handing Molly to Aunt Hilda because she held her with stiff, awkward arms which the child disliked and which made her fussing worse. He turned to walk towards the kitchen, Molly now contentedly snuggled against his chest.

'And where is Grace?' she asked.

Jim knew she knew the answer. 'She's tired, Aunt Hilda, I've left her sleeping tonight. She said she had another of her headaches today. Did you see her at all?'

'I did not. And neither did Molly. Poor little thing. She spent most of the day in her carriage with Mrs Roberts and Primrose-Jane. Grace should be up and about by now, it's not natural Jim, Molly's over ten months old. She needs her mother.'

'I know. But she seems so weak, I don't know how many hours a day she sleeps. I think I'll get Dr Elliott to look in tomorrow.' Worried as he was about Grace, Aunt Hilda's questions always had an accusatory edge that made him defensive. There was little point in another visit from the doctor but what else was he supposed to do? Some weeks she would flatly refuse to get up, talk to him or look at Molly; she would lie on her side in the bed they shared and stare at the plain blue wall ahead. When she lay there like that it was impossible to rouse her or penetrate her thoughts.

'He's already seen her several times. There's nothing wrong with her, Jim, she needs to stop wallowing in it and spend more time out in the fresh air.'

'She does try, Aunt. She doesn't like not being able to take care of Molly.' Perhaps it was the flicker of the candle shadows, but Aunt Hilda appeared to toss her head. Grace *did* love their daughter, however her behaviour might look. Sometimes she would go for days without letting anyone else near her and he would find them curled up together smiling into each other's faces, or sitting together in a lukewarm bath marvelling at the trickle of water between their fingers and he would have to scoop them out and dry them, fearful of what might happen. He didn't know exactly what was wrong with Grace but her sickness was real. She didn't choose the way she was.

'Perhaps it would be easier if we were in a house of our own?' he started, softly cautious. 'You've both been kind but it's not easy now that we're three. And we'd hate you to feel put upon.' He held his breath, waiting for her usual protestations. A house for their family of three was what Grace wanted and they could afford it now too. But who would take care of Molly when he was at work if Grace was having one of her weeks? At least here there were people to rely on. Primrose-Jane adored Molly and was always glad of an excuse to drop her duster and mind the baby. 'We don't want to be a burden, Aunt Hilda.'

The old woman's sharp snort almost snuffed out the candle. 'Don't be ridiculous, I couldn't possibly let you manage on your own. Besides, we'd be lost without you, rattling around this place on our own.' She gestured helplessly. 'You're all we've got.'

'If you're sure? It would help so much if we knew we could stay until Grace is better.' Molly was sleeping again now, her cheek creased and her round nose pressed up against his shirt. Jim sat down hard on the sofa; he was weary enough to sleep here for one more night but he didn't want Aunt Hilda to know that.

'It isn't kind, Jim, whatever you think. You're running yourself into the ground but the longer you let her do this the less likely it is that she'll get better.'

'Maybe you could talk to her?' Jim looked up, hopeful.

'I'm afraid she doesn't listen to me or Samuel. Doesn't she have friends you could invite over, that you could talk to? She used to go out quite a bit, before the baby came.'

Jim thought for a few moments but not a single name came to mind. He had no idea who she knew. The address in the pillbox popped into his head and he pushed it away.

'Of course,' he tried to keep his voice bright. 'Of course. Good idea. I'll get onto that tomorrow.'

'Let me take Molly so you can get some sleep. I'll settle her down, don't worry.' Hilda held out her arms as if to take the baby. Jim shook his head and held her tighter.

'It's fine, go to bed. I'm happy here for a while but I'll get her in the crib soon.'

Jim sat, smiling, until she'd taken the candle and disappeared into the gloom of the corridor then he snuffed out the lamps awkwardly with one hand. When the house was silent he swung his legs up onto the sofa, supporting Molly's weight with his palms in case she stirred, and eased his back into the unforgiving pad of the seat with a sigh of relief. It was easy here, with Molly like this, close and warm. In the quiet house he listened to the small indignant huffs of her breath. It would be different when she grew, when the questions came, but for now there was nowhere in this muffled house he felt safer.

The weight of knowing. 1994. Emily's story

For a few days the knowing burns holes through my life. Avoiding the office, I walk through the parks, past Daniel's mum's flat, spend hours sorting papers and packing boxes at my parents' house. I visit Jim, armed with clever questions, but he is silent again; his eyes are dull and his hands lie still on the stiff blanket. Nurse Evans tells me he was agitated after my last visit, sleeping in ten-minute bursts before jumping up as though something terrible had happened. Then he fell quiet and he hasn't spoken since. 'I can wait,' I tell her, 'I waited long enough to meet him.' She gives me a sad look.

I feel have to speak to Dad; how can I keep Jim's secrets to myself? But how on earth would I start? 'You were born out of wedlock so Nan's parents kicked her out, oh and by the way, you know I thought I'd found your grandfather? It turns out he's not Nan's real father anyway.' Dad's old-fashioned and he'll hate it all. Is it better to wait and find evidence or to keep it to myself? Should I run it past Anna first? And if I do, will it bring us closer together or push us apart in our disagreement over how to deal with it?

I try to practice the conversation in my head as I wait for them to answer. They always take an age to pick up, whatever time of day I call, but mid-evening guarantees they'll have already had a couple of drinks; I'm hoping that might make it easier for us to talk.

'Yes?'

It's Mum, now I have to find an excuse to talk to Dad, which won't be easy. He's not a big phone talker.

'Hi, Mum.'

'Emily? It's late, is everything alright?'

'It's not that late, I wanted to catch you in, I know what your social life is like.'

She laughs. 'We had dinner with Bob, you remember? He does cheer us up. We've been back a while though. We had a call from the estate agents yesterday, what's the lady's name?'

'Donna?'

'That's it. She seems nice. She said they'd had a couple look round who really liked it. I got Dad to fax her the forms back.'

'You need to tell me what you want done with the rest of the stuff. You're not going to want it all in Spain, you won't have room.'

'We'll think about that when the time comes.' Classic Mum, not committing.

'Dad there?'

'I think he's gone to sleep, hang on I'll call him.' She calls for him without moving away from the phone, louder each time. 'What d'you want him for?'

'I went to see Jim again.'

There's a long pause before she answers. 'Don't go dragging that up with him again Emily, you know he's not been well. He doesn't want to be bothered with you asking him for money.'

'I wasn't going to… it doesn't matter. I'll speak to him another day.' It's not the right time, and what good would it really do for him to hear the truth?

'He talked about Nan. I think he thought I was her, he kept calling me Molly.' Since I can't talk to Dad I call Anna, telling myself it's to see if she knows anything about Nan's photos. In reality I think I'm hoping that if I share Jim's story it will bring the two of us closer. We should have been like that as

236

children instead of always playing our parents against each other or vying for their affection.

'Makes sense I guess, if he hadn't seen her in years. You do look a bit like her.'

'He was pretty confused about that. But he spoke clearly enough. He was pleased to see me.' Can I trust her with his words? It seems too hard on the phone, all these miles apart. It might be better to wait until she visits.

'He talked about Nan's photos of the end of the war. I don't remember ever seeing something like that, do you?'

'Vaguely. I remember Mum and Dad going through a few boxes of black and white photos when they brought all the things back from her cottage.'

'I don't.'

'You were probably with Mrs Matthews.'

Being made to sit on her cream sofa eating fig rolls off a saucer, terrified to spill crumbs.

'And you were going through Nan's things?'

'Not really. I remember making a lot of cups of tea. Put me off for life.'

'I don't suppose you'd know where they put them? I've been through most of the rooms now. The estate agent thinks it will sell pretty quickly.' I tell her about Donna, which she loves. She's less keen to hear about the empty rooms. I almost mention her own box, but something stops me. Like Dad's story it's too intimate for telephone wires.

'Nan's stuff is probably in the loft. I don't recall seeing it since it I was at school. There *were* some strange photos though, now I think of it, rows of soldiers and dole queues and things. I wanted to use them for a project, when I was at uni. The boxes were in the lounge then.'

'That can't have been long after she died.' I'd just started sixth form with the dread that every new phase in my life would bring the death of someone I loved. 'What was the project?'

'Can't remember. I know Mum wouldn't let me use them anyway, said they were weird, that I wouldn't want people to think my nan had taken them. You know what Mum can be like. She never wanted us to draw attention to ourselves.'

Alice is all agog. I haven't really betrayed my family secrets because I haven't told her everything. I wouldn't. It would feel like a betrayal to Nan if I shared secrets she didn't even know herself. I couldn't resist finding out who she fell for though. Anyway, I need some facts if I'm going to explain it all to Anna, or even Dad, one day.

'Harrington, I think the name was,' I say, hopeful. I wouldn't have known where to start without Alice, didn't even know libraries kept local records. 'No Harrington-Green.'

'If he was as bad as Jim said then he'll be in the newspapers, surely.' Alice rifles through the library's microfiche with an expert's eye. 'What sort of year do you think we're looking at?'

'After the war? When Dad was born, 1947.'

'Let's start two or three years before that and work our way through. If we don't find anything we may have to look further.' Alice frowns at the screen. 'Two local newspapers, plus *The Standard* and then maybe the nationals. Text was small then, not many photographs. We'll have to blow these up.'

Alice has uncurled her horns of hair. Now it hangs in two high bunches woven through with blue and purple wool and tied with streamers of black lace. Her skin is looking pink and fresh without its customary white foundation, but her lipstick and nails are black. She's attracting sideways looks from the woman behind the desk and the others in the library: a young mum with a buggy, her toddler happily chewing the cover of hardback book as she flicks through the shelf of videos; two old men reading newspapers at the next table, one nodding off in front of his broadsheet, the other intently scanning the racing pages. Perhaps Jim came too, for company or warmth.

I haven't been in this place for years. We used to come after school on Thursdays, to kill time waiting for Anna to finish judo. Carrie liked the green armchair. It was big enough for both of us but I wasn't often allowed in with her. She liked to curl sideways on it, reading through her favourite Asterix or Tintin stories. Books that I can't bear to look at now.

'There are way too many articles here, we're going to have to take a year each. Have you used these things much before?'

'The ones in the British Library, copied ethnographies and things though, not newspapers.'

'Same principle.' She shows me how to find the year, month, week, and then enlarge the text so each article is readable. 'Shall we go through these years and then get a coffee?'

Trawling through the pages begins to hurt my eyes after a while. The curled fonts and letterpress print require squinted attention, even under the glare of strip-lights. What if I'm missing something? Headlines don't lend much clue as to whether his name will be in the story, it could be anything at all. If I find out Dad's father was some axe murderer or something then I'll have to keep it to myself, but I'm sure it won't turn out that way. Nan was the type who always saw through people.

In the small back page columns another name catches my eye. Albert Baxter. Bert—the one Jim said everyone loved? Wasn't this article in Jim's tin? There was a headline too, in fact I'm sure it was this one.

OPEN VERDICT RETURNED

MYSTERY OF MAN'S DEATH NOT SOLVED

FOUND LYING IN A GAS FILLED ROOM. The mystery of the death of a man, who was discovered by the police lying in a huddled attitude in a gas-filled room after they had broken their way into his home in West London was left unsolved at the inquest, which was held by the East Surrey Coroner at Mortlake yesterday afternoon. The inquest was on Albert Francis Baxter, a disabled veteran of the Royal Norfolk Regiment, age 31, currently residing at Number 4 Victoria Mansions. Mary Victoria Baxter, 26, of Winterton, Norfolk, gave evidence of identification, saying her brother lived with their cousin John Rowley, who had been visiting relatives. Aside from his disability, a missing left hand sustained in service, he was a healthy man and in good spirits.

FORCED WAY IN
Police Constable Barton said that at 9.30 p.m. on the 18th August, in consequence of information received by Mr Rowley who had been unable to gain admittance to the flat, he went with him to the address. Being unable to gain admission he broke a pane of glass in the door and made his

way to the first floor where he noticed a strong smell of gas. He discovered that the oven of a gas cooker was full on and the door of the oven wide open. He immediately turned off the gas and opened the windows. The windows were not sealed in any way.

PC Barton said then he saw the deceased, who was lying in a huddled position between the sink and a dresser, with his head turned to the left. He had apparently been vomiting in the sink and appeared to have collapsed. There was no sign of life in the body. After calling a doctor he searched the rooms, but found no letters or communications left by the deceased. PC Barton said a frying pan was on the top of the stove, with a small piece of bacon in it and none of the rings on the top of the stove were turned on.

The Coroner concluded that there was no clear evidence to suggest that this poor man intended to commit suicide and returned a verdict in accordance with the medical evidence—that death was due to asphyxia from coal-gas poisoning.

The Coroner extended his sympathy with the relatives.

I don't know how to get this without Alice seeing so I take out my notebook and copy out the main details. Albert, was this the Bert that Jim was talking about? Is he Nan's dad? Why would he kill himself? Jim said they all loved each other. But did Bert love Jim's wife more? Could that drive her slowly mad with grief? These days they would split, live together, follow their hearts. But someone will always be the one to suffer. Poor Jim. He seems to have carried everyone. And none of them was happy. Is it better to stay together because it's expected or to hurt one person's feelings to save a family?

Lost in thought I almost jump out of my skin when Alice tugs at my arm. I flick my screen away from Bert's story and move over to hers.

'What do you think? Harrington-Green, look, he's a politician. Must be him.' Alice enlarges the photograph to reveal a dark-eyed man with a mop of dark hair and a sharp three piece-suit. Despite the grainy image I can tell he is beautiful. His smile looks dangerous. He holds his cigarette like a magician's wand.

'At first I found this one.' Alice pulls up another photograph of an older man with a wide paunch. 'Same name, also an MP, but it's his father. I think from the year, and their ages, it must be the son.'

The woman behind the counter tuts to herself, making the loose skin under her neck wobble. I try to whisper more softly. 'I guess so. Maybe it was bad because it was the father? I feel so awful that he told me all this. He wanted to tell Nan. He must have wanted to tell her for so long.'

Alice sighs. 'It doesn't matter, does it, if he thinks you're her? You've absolved him, Emily, it's what he'd want before...'

A lump rises in my throat. I know what she was about to say before she stopped herself. 'Are there any more stories?'

Alice flicks through a few more editions of *The Standard* and then stops at a front page. 'New Era Politicians—he's the one on the left, look.'

She zooms in on the picture and there's Nan's name in the credits—Margaret Avery. No wonder Jim was proud. No wonder he was devastated. Nan must have met this guy on the shoot. We trawl through the articles on him, there are dozens. By all accounts he was a charmer but an unscrupulous man. Perhaps, after all, Dad's life was better off without him in it.

My eyes are strained from the flicker of the screen. I'm keener than ever to find Nan's photos so we walk straight to my parents' house. It's only a few streets away. We pick up sandwiches at the shop on the corner and devour them as though we haven't eaten in weeks. Alice walks quickly. She's wearing striped purple and black tights with huge black platform boots that I rather admire. They look comfortingly fierce and I briefly wonder whether I count as too old to wear them. I know without asking that she would say 'no'. I make her take them off to climb the ladder to the loft and she laughs at my fussing, though she'd never fit them in between the rungs.

The loft is full of boxes and it takes a while to find Nan's photographs. They're stuffed into a wooden stool with a hinged lid, padded and covered in a tapestry cloth and edged in deep pink tasselled silk. It's probably protected them. Some of the papers in here are damp and spotted with age but the photos are clean. They still smell of the chemicals she would have used to process them.

All of the photographs are stunning, some are heart-wrenching. Alice is silent as she looks at one after the other, holding up one of three soldiers sitting in the street, two slumped against each other, one passing a cigarette to the lips of the man on the end who's arm stump ends in a pinned jacket. I show her my favourite, three small boys dancing around a soldier on crutches. He's trying to join in their game of football, gamely waving one crutch in the air, a huge smile on his face. His right foot is missing. He looks barely older than the children playing.

The photographs are clear and simple. Their message is plain. They speak of ordinary people trying to make sense of the way war has changed their lives. The violence that shows in the bodies of these broken boys and men, and the silence in which the civilians go about their everyday business when they should be screaming in pain. They are terrible and wonderful and they make me love Nan even more. I would push ahead with publishing them even if I thought it would be hard, but it won't. If my publishers can't do it there must be dozens who would.

'They're probably hand printed on glass plates.' Alice runs a hand along the edge of a print. 'I don't think you'd get this kind of clarity without. It would have been quite a painstaking and old-fashioned way to do it, even then. Worth it though. They're amazing. What a brilliant family history, I wish I had someone like that in my family.'

Momentarily I'm shocked to hear her say it. As I've got to know Alice over the last few weeks I've been jealous of her own huge clan, the five younger siblings and bohemian parents. Her stories are crazy. They're as close-knit as you could want a family to be and she is envious of *this*? Maybe this is it, our family. There is something to be celebrated after all.

Under the box of Nan's pics I find our old copy of *Pookie*, a beautifully illustrated book about a winged rabbit. Instantly I think of Anna. Delicately painted in a lovely 1930s style, the rabbit has red shorts, long ears and silvery fairy wings. We used to trace these pictures to make our own books, so that the rabbit could have new adventures that were happier than the ones in the book, where he always seemed to be getting captured by wizards. I put the book aside carefully. I will post it to Anna. The winged rabbit will mean more to her than any of my heart-pourings.

Inheritance. 1939. Jim's story

A new photograph of Hilda and Samuel was placed in the dining room, centred over the mantelpiece in a fine, gilded frame that had cost Jim half a week's wages. It was worth it. They were dressed for Uncle Samuel's department's New Year dinner dance, in timeless black tie that sharpened the image and made him look commanding and imperious in a way he never quite managed when he was alive. Aunt Hilda was elegant in her black dress and pearls, a small bag in one gloved hand and the other resting on his shoulder. Both of them were smiling for the camera, so Jim guessed it must have been taken before Jack went, some time before he came to London himself. He liked it and he knew his aunt would approve of the choice.

A second, more recent, photograph was added to his tin. Slightly overexposed and faded where the frame had held it, the image bled into the background in pale grey and white, but it captured his aunt and uncle in a pleasing, familiar way. The two serious people standing by the tea rose in the front garden were the people he'd lived with. He placed it carefully into an envelope along with the deeds to the house and a picture of Jack in full uniform, and tried to ignore the rising feeling of dread that he'd taken what shouldn't be his.

No-one was more shocked than Jim to find that he had inherited the house; what would happen when Samuel passed away had never even crossed his mind. Between his job at the Ministry, raising Molly and attempting to bring Grace back to life he hadn't had much time to look around him, hadn't realised how ill his aunt had become. Brave Aunt Hilda, suffering in silence. She'd been let down by everything.

Deep down she'd always believed that a little more money, a few more nice things, could solve all the problems of the world. All the things she collected, all her genteel manners, hadn't afforded her any protection at all. Uncle Samuel had faded away without her. Less than two weeks after the funeral he had followed her and Primrose-Jane had been the one to find him, sitting stiff and lifeless in the parlour, wearing a slightly bemused expression, as though he didn't want to trouble anyone.

At least they'd known Molly for five years. They were good years too. As she grew, Hilda seemed to take to her more, spending time with her out in the garden or making wardrobes for the paper cut-out dolls that Molly loved. They'd been happy in those years. He was glad they were spared the angst of another conflict.

War broke out barely a week after Samuel was laid to rest, while Jim and Grace were still reeling from the overwhelming shock of home ownership and financial stability. This time there was no waiting, no gentle easing in from a state of peacefulness to the constant roar of war. Within minutes of the announcement everything changed; warnings were issued, instructions given, food rationed and men seized. Jim's injuries were mostly hidden, and those who didn't know him well had little respect for the fact that he wasn't rushing to the front to volunteer. There were plenty of men older than him who'd already gone.

Jim felt no guilt himself. He was needed at the Ministry because British citizens relied upon his information sheets and advisory leaflets. The war would never be won without them. He kept panic from the streets and food in the pantries. He protected children, urging the public to make hasty arrangements to send their little ones to safe rural places.

That was something he couldn't apply to himself. Life without Molly was unthinkable. She'd grown into the hole between him and Grace and given meaning to his days; without her he was terrified of what they would become. So he convinced himself it was a decision he didn't yet need to make. Depending how long the fighting went on this time, well, he'd see how they managed. There was always Eleanor if needs be. 'It'll all be over soon,' everyone chanted, but no-one believed it this time because war was no longer something that happened far away; it came to the doorstep.

'I don't think I want to do it now.' Molly spoke in a small voice, eyes staring down at her own feet in their new red leather shoes.

'Go on,' encouraged Jim. 'There's only going to be one first time isn't there? After that we'll be switching them on and off all the time.'

'What if it makes fire and we all have to run outside?'

'School has lights, doesn't it?'

She nodded, still looking down, shuffling slightly from one foot to the other to admire the sides and backs of the shoes as well as the buckles on the front.

'Has that ever happened at school?'

She shook her head from side to side. Her hair slides were decorated with enamel daisies. His beautiful child. He should never have fussed her so much, Aunt Hilda had been right, the poor child was scared of her own shadow. 'It's perfectly safe, Molly. You said you wanted to be the first one to turn them on.'

'For goodness sake, Jim, she doesn't want to do it, leave her alone and try it out yourself.' Grace had been the one who wanted to wire the house for electricity, wearing him down until he'd agreed to dip into their savings. She'd never liked the gloom and dark of the house but Jim was reluctant to change the style of his uncle and aunt. Whenever Grace removed ornaments and knickknacks, stowing them away in one of the spare upstairs bedrooms, he always noticed, often replacing them out of respect for their benefactors, as though their spirits watched in stern reprove from beyond the grave. She'd won the electric argument by cruel means in the end, asking what he thought would happen if Molly knocked over one of their many lamps. Jim thought of Pearl's scars and Ruby's smile and he booked the workmen the following day.

'She'll regret it if she doesn't turn them on herself.' Why was Grace so harsh? It hadn't helped the poor girl that her mother was so absent half the time, unable to find pleasure in caring for her. She never knew which mother she would find.

'Come on, Molly, we can't waste time. We need to know if they work before the men leave.' Grace walked briskly over to the window and pointedly raised the heavy net curtain to check the van was still parked outside.

'They haven't been paid yet, so I expect they're still there.' Jim smiled hopefully at Molly, who looked from her mother to her father and sighed.

Grabbing hold of Jim's hand, she led him over to her mother at the window and clasped her hand in the other. In a ragged line of three she dragged them back to the black, square switch and raised their hands to turn it on together. Eyes closed tight shut, they pressed it down, fearful of some vengeful explosion. But when they opened them again the room was calm, bathed in a yellowy light that illuminated even the darkest of corners.

Dearest Eleanor,

Thank you for your letter and please do thank Sofia for her note, she sounds so grown up and we barely recognised the pictures of the boys. You must be proud of William, he looks smart in his uniform and we're wishing him a safe and speedy return home. It's hard to believe how fast the years have passed, the last time we saw him he was only three and of course we have never met the others, nor you with our Molly. She is growing rapidly but still a good girl, enjoying school and making us proud. When I look at how the years have passed it's so hard to believe. I don't like to write this but we were so sorry to hear about Harry. I dare say you are better off without him but I know it can't be easy for you so we wanted to send extra this month and, if you are willing, to pay the rent until you get yourself on your feet. We have been more than fortunate with our circumstances in London and it is certainly what our mothers would have wished. There, that is settled.

When this blasted war is over we will definitely come for a visit. Molly has never even seen the sea, if you can believe that! She is a real town girl. She was pleased to receive the postcards for her scrapbook, thank you.

With much love,
Your cousin, Jim

It was the least that they could do. After all, hadn't he and Grace been handed everything on a plate? He was the only one in the family who had a right to be happy at all. His good fortune embarrassed him, carried the guilt that, despite everything, it couldn't make his little family happy. A good wage and a big house didn't stop him lying awake at night, wondering where he'd failed.

Eleanor's last letter had broken the pact implicit in their formal correspondence that just because they were the only family still in contact did not mean they should burden each other with letters full of their troubles. They knew little of each other's lives. News that Harry had left her for the newly widowed landlady of The Jolly Sailor had not been much of a surprise. Harry had always made him feel nervous, concerned for Eleanor. A huge man, with a low, fierce brow and a reputation for fighting, he was initially given the benefit of the general assumption that he was ready to settle down. Jim had always found his company uncomfortable.

Harry was one of the reasons they hadn't rushed to visit before. Then one thing happened after another—a baby, a bad week at work, the first day of school—and, before you knew it, fifteen years had passed. Just like that. Eleanor would probably move on after this. Fifteen years he'd been thinking of the cottage, the sea. Now he'd probably never see either of them again.

Someone was standing in the kitchen when Jim returned from work and it took him a few moments to realise it was Primrose-Jane. She wore a new dress with a long tight skirt and a low-cut neck, high heels she could hardly walk in. Her face was plastered in make-up and a clematis flower was tucked behind her left ear. Perhaps she was auditioning for a theatre group? He smiled at her.

'What's all this in aid of?'

She threw her arms around Jim's neck and put a finger on his lips. 'Would you like to kiss me?' she asked, her eyes pleading.

For a moment he was frozen. The feel of soft skin on his own flesh was something he'd almost forgotten and he breathed the scent of gardenia from her neck. A speck of mascara had fallen onto her cheek and he was transfixed by its shape. Did Grace ever wear mascara? He remembered seeing Lilly spit into a cake of it, whirling it round with a little

251

brush to make it soft enough to apply. It had made him feel queasy. What was Primrose-Jane thinking? All that make-up only made her look more of a child. He removed her arms gently, shaking his head.

'Where's Grace? And Molly?'

'Upstairs,' she said, a sulky look coming over her face. 'Molly went straight to her after school. She's been in bed all day again.'

Poor Grace must be having another one of her turns. He should go to her, find out what Molly was having to see this time. He took off his jacket, hanging it on the chair, and turned to go up.

'She doesn't deserve you. You're too good for her,' blurted out Primrose-Jane, before she pushed past him and ran out of the house, banging the front door behind her. The clematis flower fell to the floor and he picked it up, stroked the stripy middle of its petals. He understood. She'd been shown so little kindness in her life. What experience of men did she have? Her three brothers had raced to war to escape their father's fists, and she'd no one else to guide her now. It was down to him to help her or she'd end up in trouble.

He went up to see Grace, and found Molly playing a game of jacks quietly on the floor of their bedroom while her mother stared at the wall, eyes glazed, wearing a thick dressing gown over a silk dress.

'Mummy's tired,' said Molly, holding out the jack. Jim took it, held her hand and squeezed it.

'Yes,' he said, 'she is. How was school today?'

'Walter Bridges says we have to move away and leave our parents. Is that true?'

'It's not true. We'll be perfectly safe together here.' Molly nodded and pushed him to throw. 'Only two Daddy! I got six. Look.'

What would they do without Molly? He couldn't bear it if she went to the countryside. She was scared of her own shadow too and that was Grace's fault, she never tried to hide a thing from her. How could Molly go to a farm? She lived worlds away from his life in Norfolk and she'd never even seen a cow, she'd be worse than the men of his battalion in France. It was better this way. He'd ask Primrose-Jane to keep an eye on her too, that would give her something to focus on. It was hard on them all trying to live without family.

'Shall we leave Mummy for a while? We could look through the tin?'

Molly nodded eagerly, scooping up the jacks and packing them into their drawstring bag. She patted her mother's hand but Grace did not stir and Jim pulled the door to behind them as they left the room. The tin would help to calm them both today. Molly could happily spend hours going through the photographs, talking quietly to all the people she was related to but had never met. Once she had told him she imagined they lived a long way away, in towers or prisons, and asked if they were safe. 'People didn't used to smile in photographs,' he had told her, 'it didn't mean they were unhappy.' Now, as they spread out the contents of the tin across the kitchen table, he wondered whether any of them was happy at all. Were they? Was happiness a thing that ran away as soon as you began to question it? Better not to ask.

'Nana.' Molly held out a photograph of Ma, standing by the chicken coop, and Jim nodded. He couldn't remember now who had taken it, Pearl perhaps, she liked photographs and often asked to borrow a camera from Lilly's father, the only person in the village, except Kearsey, who owned one.

'Where are the chickens? Are they in heaven too?'

'Chickens don't go to heaven. Animals don't have souls.'

'They do. Dogs have souls. You can see them in their eyes.'
Jim smiled. 'Well, maybe dogs.'

'Can we have chickens? Mummy likes eggs, she'd like to get the eggs in the morning with me.'

Would she? It was hard to guess what Grace would like. Molly seemed to have more faith in her than anyone and she'd seen less of the woman she used to be. 'We don't have enough space for chickens. Your Aunt Eleanor has them though.' He held up a photograph of Vi with four of her children, Eleanor standing at the front looking solemn with a doll clutched across her chest.

'She's just a little girl.'

'Not now, this was taken a long time ago. Eleanor is grown now, she lives in the house your Nana used to have, where I grew up.'

'I want to see it.'

'One day, Molly, one day. Shall we look at some more pictures? Look, here's Mummy and Daddy at the Yarmouth dance. We used to cycle all the way there. No buses like you have here.'

'I like buses, when can we go on a bus again?' Molly was busily pulling out the photographs and putting them out in some sort of order, people she liked the look of. She was fascinated by the styles of dress, the way the photographs changed over time, some so pale you could hardly see the faces and more recent ones in stark black and white so the shape of a hat or a facial expression was clear.

'Who's this with Mummy?' Lost in thought Jim hadn't noticed Molly digging to the bottom of the tin. She held out a photograph of Bert, his arm draped around Grace's shoulder, smiling into the camera looking handsome and carefree.

'That's your Uncle Bert.' He swallowed hard. There was never going to be a right time to tell her the truth.

'Primrose-Jane,' Jim called softly as he walked to where she fussed with the washing line, carefully hanging the pleated silks that Grace dressed up in to stay in her room alone. In place of the garishly glamorous dress, today Primrose-Jane wore an old striped shirt with men's trousers that drowned her shape, her hair covered by a length of cotton tied into a knot on her forehead. In her face he could see the plain child who marvelled at his coin tricks, the child he'd renamed Primrose, because Jane was not a beautiful name.

'Primrose-Jane,' he tried again and was rewarded with a glance. 'I'm sorry.' He held her gaze as he spoke, still walking towards her, as though she might dash away at any moment. 'Please, can we start again? I don't want you to run away from me.' He had to tell her that he understood. It would be good for Molly to have her around.

'I think it's probably best that I go.'

'Heaven forbid you should leave! You are family to us. We won't talk of it. Soon you'll find a nice boy who isn't the age of your father.' Though she tried to hide it, Jim couldn't help but notice the visible flinch caused by the word. God only knew what she was suffering at home, without a man left in their row of cottages capable, or willing, to stand up to her father. Night tears were clearly visible in the rabbit-pink of her eyes.

'Why don't you move in with us? It's not as though we don't have the space and Molly and I would like it very much.'

'And Mrs Avery?'

'Yes, of course, Mrs Avery too.' They both knew this was a lie. In fact, he was already dreading telling Grace. He smiled and put his hands on her shoulders as though comforting a child, not moving even when the gathering skies finally broke in a burst of torrential rain.

Primrose-Jane said nothing. She bit her lip and stared back at the line of newly heavy sheets and clothes, watching their fabric darken and drip like clouds.

It was poor Primrose-Jane who gave him the idea in the first place; her and the others like her who'd been left alone by war, widows and orphans. It wasn't enough that their sons had been taken and wasted, now everyone was fighting as the battlefields were drawn across towns and cities, bringing bombs like the one that killed Primrose-Jane's mother as she crouched in her local church's makeshift shelter. How long could they last? How long could these people be expected to last in the face of this? If they gave in, was the war to be lost at home?

A nation without family to cheer them on, without sons and daughters to live for and parents to tell them how to live. They needed looking after more than ever. It was the Ministry's duty; if Jim couldn't be their cannon fodder this time he could do better. He took two months to write a guide to life that might keep them all fighting until the war was won. A guide that showed them how to get the most from what plain food was available, how to care for colds, why they shouldn't drink too much. He added sections on how to keep up spirits and maintain a happy family life. Silently he allowed himself to admit that most of it was forged from an altogether contrary experience. As a parting note he added more advice on how to keep a healthy sex life, within marriage, how not to get carried away with the 'end of the world' mentality that made people all around him act, like poor Primrose-Jane, with such reckless abandonment.

He had already experienced the warm glow of pride from seeing someone reading one of his books, *Make Do and Mend*, the book which had been featured in almost every available women's magazine. But this was more important. Jim felt he had a vested interest in ensuring that every man and woman in the country read it and that, if they followed its heartfelt advice, this war would be won. At home, at least. Bound in serviceable green and printed with a cheerful motif, three pristine copies of *How to Keep Well in Wartime* arrived at his desk that afternoon, as requested. He wrote inside the cover of one and handed it straight back to the post girl before she left, telling her to treat it as a handbook for life. Another was placed in the clear glass box above his desk which housed his latest works. And the final copy was put carefully inside his briefcase, wrapped in a brown paper bag, ready to be locked away in his bureau drawer at home.

Arrangements. 1994. Emily's story

Even in death the body is strong. I have to ask Nurse Evans
for help closing Jim's eyes as they stubbornly refuse to shut for
me. Although she's busy, she stays to remove the cannula on
his left hand; she does it gently, holding the skin to brace it as
the metal draws out, even though she knows he can't feel it.
Briefly she touches me on the arm and tells me to take a few
moments. She pulls the door behind her and I think she
understands that I'm grieving as much for the life I didn't
know as the one I did.

Through the door crack I see a waiting cleaning trolley. I
don't have long; they'll need this room for other patients,
people with a chance of life, but I have no idea what I should
be doing. I know the death rituals of every culture but my
own. Roma would tip the reflective water from its jug; Ibo
would take on his name. If I were Yanomamo I would drink
his bones in soup to make him part of me. But I'm none of
these things.

Death is too hard to bear alone, too raw to discuss with
someone who doesn't share your sadness. I don't want to call
my parents and I don't want to make the arrangements on my
own. Daniel is the only one who might understand. And he
isn't here. I wrote to him when Jim woke, though I couldn't
put much of what he said on paper. I will write to Daniel to
let him know Jim has gone, invite him to the funeral. Nurse
Evans tells me it can take weeks to organise at this time of
year because the cold is hard for older people. She also said
there would need to be an inquest, because of the way he
died. They'll need to establish that his death wasn't Daniel's
fault, something else I don't want to put in a letter, unless it

would bring him home quicker.

'We are so sorry for your loss.' Dr Iqbal has slipped into the room. He perches delicately on the end of the bed, at a respectful distance. Any questions I wanted him to answer seem irrelevant now.

'Was there any reason why he… why now?'

Dr Iqbal removes his glasses and pushes them to the top of his thinning head, rubbing his eyes with both hands.

'It is simply as I explained to you before, there were lasting effects from his injuries. His brain tissue was considerably swelled, we are not sure what might have caused this to happen, possibly the damage to his spine due to the build-up of blood from the internal injury and contusion.'

He pauses for a moment, as if thinking of something, or someone, else. Would this be like Carrie? If she survived that crash? Just a shred of life.

'When we grow older the body does not always behave as it should. Such prolonged unconsciousness, we have no way of knowing what effect that would have on a person. It is kinder to him this way.'

I've been doing some research on prolonged unconsciousness myself, reading medical terms that laymen are not supposed to see. I ask if he thinks Jim was lucid when he was hit, whether he could have been drunk.

'Absolutely not.' He's categorical in his response. 'We run blood analysis on all accident victims as a matter of course, it is a legal requirement; if there was anything unnatural in his system we would have found it.' He looks down at Jim's notes, frowning. 'But there were no traces of any medications at all in him, which is unusual because he had been prescribed several.'

I take a deep breath. 'How was he supposed to remember

to take them? If he had dementia or memory loss or whatever? Didn't anyone check? What about social services?'

'There is no need for social services if a patient can take care of himself.'

'But you said he was known to the hospital.'

'Yes, he had been admitted before, for a fall. We are not completely barbaric, we do follow up these things. And if he can get to the surgery for his appointments and take away his medication, what would they be needed for?'

'He couldn't take care of himself.'

'But we had no reason to believe that. With all due respect, Miss Green, your family was not close, it is difficult for you to understand these things now. I know you are upset. But I do hope you realise that it's kinder this way?' Dr Iqbal looks me squarely in the eye. 'It is highly surprising to us that he did not die straight away.'

I look away. At least I had some time with Jim and, though it would probably seem stupid to anyone else, this brief time with him has changed me in ways I don't yet understand.

Vanessa arrived in Manchester yesterday, to visit her own mother in hospital, and she's flown straight down to stay with me tonight. I'm grateful for the gesture; she'll be leaving early in the morning, but, for tonight, it's good to have company. There isn't really much to do. I don't feel like going to his house yet and his body won't be moved until the hospital has run tests and established the exact cause, 'polished the paperwork', as Dr Iqbal said. I've called Dad, let him know, been angry and then sad at his lack of his response. If he's hiding a reaction then he's doing a good job of it.

Neither of us feels much like eating; I think Vanessa, worried about her own mother, is almost as melancholy as me. She looks drawn, older. There are deep white grooves in the crow's feet around her eyes, stark against the tan of her skin. Her face lights up when I ask about her book and we talk for a while about how much she'll miss her adoptive family in Peru. They've extracted from her a promise that she will visit every five years. 'They threatened to curse me if I don't, so you'd better make it a bestseller or I'll never afford the airfares.'

'We can manage that. I'm thinking about a book of my own actually.' I pull across the first of Nan's boxes and watch Vanessa's face as she pulls out the reportage photographs. Like Alice, she is delighted with them, passing them to me as she goes. A suited man in a bowler hat picks his feet carefully through rubble at Queen's Park Road; children in gas masks bend down to play marbles on a chalked pavement grid; a woman scrubs the step of the last house left standing in a row of terraces. I wonder where the street is, whether the house stands flanked by prefabs or if they knocked them all down.

'I'm not sure where to start with putting them all together, whether to write anything to go with them. There's so much I still don't know.'

'I love these. I don't think it matters if they're not explained. They speak for themselves. You could do a biog of your nan as a foreword and then maybe get an expert to do a piece on the importance of this kind of reportage? Talk to some of the museums, or universities, there's bound to be a professor of it. There's an expert for everything these days.' She gives me a suddenly serious look. 'It might help with things, doing something to celebrate your family. Sad to be thinking about funeral arrangements when you should be planning a wedding.'

'I'm not sure where to start with either.'

'Can't help with the wedding, but funerals here are generally quite straightforward, aren't they? I remember sitting in the Co-op with Mum and we sort of picked things from lists all in one meeting. Mind you, my dad had been pretty clear about what he wanted, he had a lot of time to think about it while he was ill.'

Poor Vanessa, her dad must have been young. And now her mum's ill too. Families change constantly, the people we lean on disappear. 'That's it, though, how am I supposed to choose for Jim? I've no idea what he'd like.' All the things I wanted to do for him, to save him, to bring him back to our family and now the only thing left is to give him a good send off and I'm not even sure I can manage that. 'What should I do?'

'I've only ever been to three funerals, apart from Dad's, which was so awful and sad. Aunt Joan's was fairly traditional apart from the fact that she only wanted Cher songs throughout…'

'I don't think he'd like that.'

'Who would? And the other two were while I was with the Edaben and they were different occasions because one was for an elder and the other for a young man who caught a fever. His was sombre because his life was cut so short, the other was more of a celebration of a long life.'

They didn't let Anna and I go to Carrie's funeral. I remember her holding me back from the window as I howled and raged, doubled in agony and grief, the horror on the face of Mrs Matthews and her cleaning fluid smell. I remember Nan's, the snow on the earth as they lowered her down, the cold that shook our bones.

'I like the idea of celebrating life, but it's hard to do when you don't know someone.' Vanessa knows that he's not blood, and she doesn't think it matters. 'Why would you care?' she said. 'You should care who he loved, and it sounds as though he loved your nan.' She's right, too, it's how I feel. I want to make this ceremony right for him for so many reasons. We can never make amends but we can lay things to rest, and that's what I'm trying to do.

'I don't think the vicar would approve of the Edaben burial customs anyway. Mourning dress for the family is to go completely naked except for the ancestor necklaces—they're like long strings of beads, each of which represents a dead ancestor, shell for women and wood for men. They're painted in different colours to signify things like how long they lived or how many children they had, whether they had a dog or liked fishing. In this way they remember them all. They go naked to show their grief, apart from the beads that the head of the family wears.'

'I don't fancy that. Bit nippy at this time of year.'

'They do hill burial as well.'

'Because the land's too rocky to dig?'

'Sort of. If you can dig a hole in it it's better used for crops not bodies. They just peg out the corpse and let the air dry it or let scavengers take it.'

'Seems brutal.'

'They have a ceremony, with music and dancing. And the family takes a soup made of dried leaves and herbs, which they say stops the pain of grief but which I suspect is hallucinogenic. I haven't tried it though.' She pulls a face. 'It smells horrific.'

'Maybe you should get me the recipe. Might help get me through. It's so weird feeling like this.'

'Just remember that the death of someone as old as he was is a reason for celebration, not sadness, OK? And you tell that man of yours to look after you. Times like these are meant for people to pull together.'

Because I have no real alternative, I ask Ian to help me with the arrangements. I've leaned on Alice too much already. Vanessa is back in Manchester with her mum, who's poorly, and I'm trying hard not to miss her. When I dropped her at the airport she told me I should make the most of this experience, that it's a healing time for the family; but Anna hasn't returned my calls and Mum says Dad won't be well enough to travel for the funeral. I suspect they've convinced themselves it's too much effort. I have no intention of trying to persuade any of them to come home.

Before we sat down with the brochures, Ian came with me to the laying-out room, to watch me while I said goodbye, when, for once, I wanted to be alone. Half-screened by the heavy velvet drape at the head of the temporary casket, the Assistant Funeral Director lurked too. What I'd really like is someone to take an interest in the things I'm choosing—the casket with its dozens of different silks and handles, the flowers, the transport. These catalogues are endless. What's appropriate for any of this? What's tasteful enough for a man of his age? Why do we assume all elderly people have conservative tastes? For all I know Jim would want heart-shaped bouquets and a Harley Davidson hearse. Ian is non-committal and approves every choice with a standard 'fine' that makes me want to throw things.

'Vanessa says we should be celebrating his achievements.' How can we do that? I suspect he wrote those pamphlets, I know he fought in the war and he definitely carried enough peoples' grief through life. I've tried to write it all out but I need help.

'She'd probably want you to get him a tie-dyed shroud.'

'Vanessa isn't a hippy,' I reply.

He raises an eyebrow, puts the catalogue back on the marble table. 'Who's paying for all this anyway?'

I'm irritated at how handsome he looks today. He has kept his hair slightly longer and his work stress seems to have subsided, his skin is glowing, he looks younger. He is clearly not losing much sleep. 'Me. Who else is there?'

'Have you got some secret savings pot set aside for accidental relatives?'

I glare at him. How can he make this about money? He earns way more than me and it wouldn't hurt him to offer to help.

'No.' I don't trust myself to say more.

'We're supposed to be saving for the wedding. You haven't given me your totals yet and I need to get back to Morley House soon. Can you actually afford to do any of this?'

If he mentions his bloody spreadsheet I may scream. 'What would you like me to do? Peg him out for the eagles like one of Vanessa's tribesmen? He has to have a funeral.'

'What about your folks? Aren't they doing anything about this?'

'Nobody else seems to care that much. He needs to be sent off properly.'

'I suppose your precious roaming tribal societies all love their elderly?'

'Actually that isn't true at all,' I speak quietly. 'Reverence for the wisdom of elders is something for settled cultures, tribal societies are usually warring or migrant cultures, they don't have much use for people who can't fight or travel.'

'Really?' Ian picks up his pager, checking for calls.

'Really. Most nomadic tribes don't mourn the deaths of

elders, only people who die in their prime, who leave holes in the community.'

'Sensible,' he mutters, still fiddling with his pager though I can see there are no messages.

In a moment of total, decisive clarity I know that we can't get married. I think he knows it too. The only thing left is when to tell him.

A careful lens. 1947. Jim's story

'That one.' Molly pointed to the silver scarf pin in the middle of the display. Shaped like a dragonfly, it had delicate filigree wings over a heavy body.

'Excellent taste,' said the shop assistant as she carefully removed it from its velvet cushion and began to wrap it in tissue paper. 'Is it a gift?'

'For my mother,' Molly smiled. She clutched her first week's wages in a small brown envelope. She pulled it open to remove a ten-shilling note and it caught Jim's breath to see her so grown up. It didn't seem long since he was desperate to pull away from Ma and now he was on the cusp of losing his own child, proud of the way she'd turned out and terrified for her independence. Children never understood these things until it was too late.

'It reminds me of the dragonflies in the garden pond.' She looked at Jim and he felt his heart melt.

'It's lovely, Molly. But you don't have to spend all your money on Mother.'

'I want to. I want her to be happy for me.'

'Of course she's happy for you.'

Molly said nothing. She took the pin in its box, tied with silky brown ribbon, and placed it carefully in her satchel with her camera and lenses before they left the shop. Outside she took Jim's arm and leaned against him lightly as they walked home.

'I hope she likes it.' Molly seemed nervous and Jim prayed that Grace was in a good mood when they returned. She hadn't spoken to him when he left for work this morning but that was nothing unusual. Perhaps she'd be better now. Molly could sometimes get through to her, but she was hard on the girl too. She didn't approve of her choice to work as a photographer, despite the fact that she was staff on a prestigious women's magazine. Jim felt he could burst with pride. To think that his daughter was doing something like that, so clever. Whoever would have thought taking photographs could be a job? She'd loved photographs, always poring over the tin. He'd bought a Brownie camera for her sixteenth birthday and she'd brought him the advertisement for the job, shyly, wanting his approval. He'd gone with her to the interview and collected her every day on her first week.

Grace was in the garden when they reached home, sitting upright on one of the heavy metal chairs by the pond. Jim squeezed Molly's arm as she pulled away to run down with her gift and then followed her slowly. The pin was pretty and he knew Grace liked nice things. She wanted nicer things than she had. It wasn't something Jim thought of much, he was practical, like Ma, and didn't like to waste money, perhaps he should think of it more often. She might be happier if he did.

'What's this in aid of?' asked Grace, opening the box. The brooch threw a dagger of reflected light from the pond's surface.

'My first wages,' said Molly proudly, looking from her mother to Jim. 'I wanted to surprise you.'

'You've already surprised me,' said Grace, putting the pin back inside its box and closing the lid firmly. 'Taking a job like that. It's common. And you should never have encouraged her, Jim. It'll be your fault if she turns out wrong.'

Was it so wrong to try to give his daughter choices? Surely it was better for her to rely on herself than have to find a husband before she was ready. And she loved her photographs so much. If only Grace could see that.

Molly wiped the large lens carefully. First with cloth soaked in an anti-fogging chemical that helped to clarify the image then, with a soft, thick piece of material, rubbing the glass until it was completely dry. The chemical solution, a sharp, noxious fume, was originally developed for the windscreens of fighter pilots. Jim thought it must make life inside those suffocating cockpits even worse for the poor men flying them, though he knew that she'd still have given anything to be there with them, that she wanted to know what it was like or at least to reproduce the experience in such a way that everyone viewing her photographs would understand.

War records, 'all those lists and numbers and arrows', she'd made it plain she considered those a waste of time. 'Photographic records, Dad, that's what we need, everything captured in black and white.' He'd seen some of her pictures of shattered soldiers, airmen and marines snapped alone or in pairs, with facial expressions that would tell the story of the war from the point of view of this cast of thousands, not through sterile numbers and lists. He'd tried to get her work with the Ministry, though it wasn't their idea of things and no-one took her seriously; a woman, a girl, what would she know? But, when she wasn't working at the magazine, she recorded the aftermath of wartime all the same. She took her camera and followed women standing in food queues, counting their coupons and staring into shop windows that were artfully dressed to hide the lack of goods. She shot children playing in the street, being soldiers with sticks for guns, or clambering over the wrecks of bombed-out buildings, looking for souvenirs, raising their prizes high above their heads as they looted. And she took dozens of

269

pictures of soldiers, broken and limping or slumped on the kerb, filling time by joining in the games of marbles that carried on regardless around their feet.

No-one would publish the photographs, none of the newspapers she petitioned and certainly not the respectable monthly magazine that employed her. Jim had helped her turn one of the spare bedrooms into a darkroom and spent hours there with her sometimes, breathing in the scent of silver bath and dilute acid, and listening to her talk openly about her work in a way that he envied.

In the soft red glow he watched her painstakingly tweezering sheets of paper through the trays of solutions and holding them up close to her face to examine.

'Anything happen today?' He turned over a lens in his hand.

'You know that book Esther gave me? The one I asked you if you knew who wrote it?' He nodded, *Make Do and Mend*, published by the Ministry and written by himself, was full of clever household tips on how to make things go further. In this confidential atmosphere it was as much as he could do not to confess everything. 'I said we should do a column, like the book but with lots of photographs and the news editor agreed. We're going to call it *Re-use*.'

'Great. What are these for?'

'Don't get fingerprints on that, Dad!' She took it back and gently polished it before stowing it inside its case. 'It's a fisheye lens. They invented these as a way to photograph clouds, they're brilliant for other stuff too, they make everything look sort of... melancholy.'

'Did you use it on these?' He reached out to pick up a print of what looked like a group of men, but she moved it quickly to a shelf.

'That one needs to dry, Dad, it's for work.'

'Doesn't look like one of your usual ones?' Her job was to take pictures of the casseroles and thickly iced cakes that they described in their recipe pages. In the six months since she'd started, she had only photographed food, clothes, beautiful baby competitions and several different craft projects, all in the stages of being made so that the publication's readers would be able to recreate them easily at home.

'No. I did some food shots today, though the Food Editor got pretty annoyed with me. I kept getting bits on my lenses, it took forever.'

'Is that why you were late?' He'd been worried. Grace, who rarely ate with them now, was oblivious, resting in her room as usual, but Jim had paced the front room for almost an hour. When he heard her key in the lock he'd been about to put on his coat and walk up to look for her, though he feigned nonchalance now. In recent weeks she'd been coming home later, kept behind to finish something at work. If anything happened to her he would never forgive himself for persuading her to apply for the job at the magazine and telling her she should be able to live independently from a husband, if that is what she wished. He couldn't bear the idea of her in an unhappy marriage.

'No. I was hoping to make this a surprise when it was printed but you're all questions today! Look at this.'

Jim peered at the sticky paper photographs of twelve young-looking men, mostly dressed in sombre, black, tail-coated suits and dress shirts. In some of the prints they were staged in formal groups and in some they gathered round trays of tea and scones, wielding floral cups and laughing wildly as though they were attending a high-profile funeral party and behaving rather badly at it.

'What's going on? One of these young men looks quite familiar.'

'They should all do, that's half the Front Bench according to the Editor. They were interviewing them today, a group thing about the newest politicians. 'You can't imagine what a privilege it is to have them all in here together, Margaret."

They didn't look like privileged guests to Jim, they looked like a band of pompous boys. Young, able-bodied men hiding in offices and drinks parties and getting up to God only knew what else. 'I thought I recognised them, you never said you were doing this today.'

'I didn't know. Both the men were out on other jobs, some demonstration in Trafalgar Square, and they couldn't hang around so they asked me.' She beamed with pride, with a new-found sense of confidence. She was slipping away from him even as he watched. He cleared his throat.

'Congratulations. Bit different from cakes, isn't it?'

She laughed, taking back the prints and passing over some more for inspection. The sound of her laugh was so much like Grace's used to be, a laugh he hadn't heard for years. He bent his head low over the pictures to steady himself. They were close up images of the same men—the round-faced one with the little black-rimmed glasses, one with a fine aquiline nose. She always took the same shot several times because a slight turn of the head, a chance raised eyebrow, or a curve of the mouth could alter the composition and make you consider the sitter in a different way entirely. The last image showed one of the young politicians leaning back with his arms folded to give the impression that his eminence at such an age was the most natural thing in the world. Perhaps for him it was. He was painfully beautiful, with a cold expression and a finely chiselled bone structure that gave him the look of a movie-star.

'Who's this one?' he asked.

'Rupert Evelyn Harrington-Green,' she answered, a name that was somehow as difficult to forget as it was to remember. Her voice was reverential, as though this arrogant boy was the only person in the world who mattered.

'It's nice to see you again, Rupert.' Grace held out a plate of buttered teacakes. Jim had warned her not to serve the tea herself; she'd replied tartly that Primrose-Jane could not be trusted around such a man in the slightest. A man who could take your breath away.

'Likewise, I'm sure, Mrs Avery, thank you.' He selected a teacake and sat back in Jim's wing-backed chair, completely at ease with the greatness of himself in this sheltered world. 'You're looking charming today. I do believe you've been walking in the sunshine, I can see you've caught some colour.'

'Oh, fancy you noticing!' Grace patted her hair and Jim felt a spike of irritation that she'd bothered to dress nicely for this, never for him, then immediately felt guilty. He should be pleased that she felt better, though he'd pay for it tomorrow when the effort took its toll and she stayed in bed. 'I've been doing some gardening, trying to brighten the place up. We haven't had a gardener for years, you know; we must all make sacrifices, mustn't we?'

'Indeed,' he answered gravely, smoothing the embroidered white linen cloths that covered the arms of the chair before balancing his plate on one. 'And how are things at the Ministry, Mr Avery?'

'Quite well, thank you, Rupert, we are busy of course, and under staffed, what with some of our best men away, but we all do what we must.'

'Important work you do there, Mr Avery, even us Government chaps are kept in the dark about some of it.'

'Indeed.' Was he fishing for information? Jim wasn't sure how long the two of them could string out their small talk.

'Are you managing to maintain morale?' asked Rupert.

'Sorry?' Jim had heard him perfectly well and was trying to buy himself some time. Perhaps Rupert suspected after all. The first time he visited the house he'd appeared to be impressed with Grace's overwrought description of her husband's job. Perhaps, despite the deferential hinting, he'd done some research of his own. Perhaps the game was up, the bureau drawer open.

'Your staff, Mr Avery, I believe your wife mentioned that you had quite a big department... it isn't easy in this day and age. Trying to keep them happy, getting them to leave their sorrows at home.'

'Quite.'

'I expect you've a lot of women there now too.' He laughed jovially at this suggestion.

'The women in my department are not a concern,' replied Jim, feeling the need to deflect some attention from himself. Molly's young man unsettled him, he couldn't imagine what his parents might be like. 'And how is the excitement of the Front Bench?'

He listened to Rupert talk for a long time about his career, his hopes and ambitions. Was it all for their benefit, to impress them for Molly's sake? Or was his career more important to him than marriage or Molly at all? He left Jim confused, feeling somehow slighted. He over-compensated with a deference that Rupert barely noticed and took as his due.

'Father thinks the new bill will be passed without much trouble.' He smiled triumphantly.

Jim wasn't sure what response was expected. He'd been paying more attention to the way his daughter watched this man, dreaming with her eyes open. She watched the curve and curl of his lips as he spoke, the slight protrusion of his canine teeth that made them visible before the others, giving him a dangerous animal look that instantly disappeared when he showed the rest of his straight, white teeth and smiled. She watched the wave of his hair and the grey strands that grew uniformly on each temple and served only to highlight the luxuriant black gloss of the rest. There was something about it that scared Jim. Molly looked as though she had lost all reason, and absolutely didn't care.

'He was Secretary of State for a while,' she added quickly, as though sensing Rupert's good mood may be about to disappear. 'And he is still active even though he's not Cabinet anymore, so he *does* know what he's talking about.'

'I'm quite sure that he does, Molly.'

'You know we would be honoured to meet your parents,' said Grace suddenly. 'We could invite them for tea... or dinner, or... well perhaps you could ask them when they might be free?'

'Yes, of course,' Rupert answered carelessly, 'I'm sure they'd be delighted. He *is* rather a busy chap though, so I wouldn't get up your hopes that it would be this side of Christmas.' He smiled to deflect the slight. 'I really must be going, thank you again for your kindness, Mr and Mrs Avery, perhaps I could trouble you for the use of your telephone before I leave? I'm due at the House later and I need to make a call to Mother first.'

An embarrassed hush fell upon the room as he retrieved

his cigarette case and gloves from the table and brushed down his jacket.

'Surely you're not expected to work on Saturdays, Rupert?' Jim eventually broke the silence.

'There are no weekends in Government, Mr Avery, I am expected to work whenever work needs to be done. No need to trouble yourself if your maid has left, Molly can show me where it is.'

'We don't have a telephone here,' said Jim, ashamed, not for himself but for Grace, who cared deeply about the form of such things. He hoped Rupert never did invite his parents here because he doubted that Grace would ever recover.

'We are getting one,' said Grace. 'It would make it so much easier to stay in touch with everyone.' Jim nodded amiably though he had no idea who could possibly want to call them or what anyone would want to say on a line that was overheard.

Tributes. 1994. Emily's story

At the suggestion of the Assistant Funeral Director, I place a notice in all three of our free local newspapers as well as *The Times*, because Mrs Khan said that was Jim's paper of choice. My head is full of Ian and the conversation we must have, so it takes a long time to decide what to write. I'd like to add my name and details, ask other relatives to come forward but it's impossible to do in a way that doesn't sound creepy or mysterious and, as Alice pointed out, I don't want to deal with 'inheritance-fakers and hearse-chasers'. In the end I leave the information to the bare minimum, taking his full name and age courtesy of the hospital records.

MR JAMES ARTHUR AVERY (JIM), AGED 96

Passed away on February 16th after nine weeks in Queen Mary's Hospital, near to his residence in Hall Road. Family would like to thank the hospital staff for their care. Funeral will be held at St Mary's Chapel, Church Road Crematorium, SW13 9HL, on Friday 23rd at 2.30pm. All who knew him welcome.

It reads a little oddly sandwiched in between so many heartfelt goodbyes and tributes but I can't add anything about the accident as I don't want Daniel to feel bad and I do want to thank the hospital, as much for their care of me as Jim. I consider a charity collection instead of flowers, but a hearse without beautiful bouquets is unbearably sad and I'd like to see some colour in the crematorium. I'd like to see it filled with flowers. The most I can hope is that a few people will attend.

On some Indonesian islands, if a person dies at an inauspicious time, or if the village doesn't have the money or ability to give them the send-off they want, they can wait years to rest properly. Bodies are buried simply first and then exhumed for the celebration later, as if to wake them up for their own party. A bit like a memorial. Perhaps after a while, if I can find out more about Jim or if lots of people come forward, I could arrange a memorial service of his life.

I try to keep the surprise out of my voice, in case it offends her. Like all big personalities Anna is easily slighted. I'm touched that she's called to hope the day goes well; it feels comforting to talk to her.

'I wanted to say thanks for sorting it all out on your own. I've been so distracted... I realise it must have been a weird time for you.'

'Thanks, I appreciate that.' What's she been distracted with? Work? Jacob?

'I'm sorry I couldn't get back. I did think about it. I talked to Mum as well. I was a bit surprised at them. Did she tell you why they aren't coming for the funeral?' Anna's voice is low and hoarse, as though she's pretending not to whisper.

'She said Dad's hernia was playing up.'

'Right. I guess he's worried about the flight then. God, they seem so old. They're getting worse.'

'Did Mum tell you they're out permanently now?'

'She said you were sorting selling the house for them. Rather you than me. They're going to want every single last corn-on-the-cob holder shipped over there.'

I laugh and remind her about Donna with the mane and

padded shoulders. 'I'm too scared not to obey the hair. She's already found a couple of interested buyers. One's put in an offer but she only talks to Mum and Dad about that. I was hoping Dad would call today, I'll ask him.' In some ways I'm glad he hasn't called. I don't want to hear any pretence that he cares. The last conversation was a painful reminder of the distance between us all.

'I wouldn't hold your breath, he probably hasn't even thought about it.'

There's resentment in her voice; it's never far off when she talks about them. They didn't go to either of our graduations because the train was too expensive and Dad got too tired driving. Or see her off at the airport when she moved to the States, in case Mum got too upset.

'They don't like their routines shaken,' she adds. I feel a stab of fondness for her.

'They're way worse since Dad retired. I was hoping being over there might change them but…'

Anna snorts loudly and I hear someone, Jacob? stirring from the sudden noise, Anna's whispered encouragements for him to go back to bed and then a slight buzz on the line as she wanders to another room with the phone.

'It's early for you, I can hear you've got someone.'

'Just Jacob, don't worry about him. He's terrible in the mornings but it's time we were getting ready for work anyway.'

'Name crops up quite a lot these days?' Anna could do with a steady influence, someone calmer. If this call's anything to go by, he's having a positive effect already.

'He's turning into a bit of a permanent fixture… is that bad?'

'Not as long as he's gorgeous and solvent.'

'He doesn't do badly.'

I like the way she talks about him, she sounds comfortable, happy, as if being with him has made her that way. It's infectious and I wish again that she was nearer so I could meet this man. He has brought back much of what I like about Anna and I don't think she's even noticed the changes.

'And Jacob's making you happy?'

'I don't think anyone should really be the cause of someone else's happiness, Em, that's ducking out of taking any responsibility for yourself, it's not a good idea.'

'I didn't mean it like that.'

'I think if you're with the right person,' she says carefully, 'that person will make you feel so at home in your own skin that everything else in your world naturally falls into place.'

'Like a halo effect?'

'Yeah, I guess... now who sounds like a Yank? You're OK, you and Ian?'

I can't tell Anna over the phone, I can't tell anyone until I've told Ian and I'm not ready to do that yet. When will I be ready? 'We're fine, he's not been the most supportive over this but basically it's OK. I'm not sure whether we mightn't need some time apart.' We've been together for years. Sometimes it feels as though my whole adult life depends on us together and the idea of changing it all is exhausting. I can't think about moving my things, changing my address, losing most of the people I hang out with, whether they're my friends or not. I can't think about any of that until after the funeral.

'That doesn't sound basically OK.'

'It's fine. Thanks for calling, Anna, it means a lot.'

The celebrant is professional, warm in his condolences and tactile in contact. His presence fills the small, modern room as we wait for the proceedings to commence, he calm and me peering anxiously through the door in the hope there'll be some mourners to dignify the occasion. He seemed surprised when I asked to come in and sit down, though he knows there'd be no point me standing outside to welcome anyone in. It was hard enough travelling in the hearse alone, hard to understand who, or what, the tears were for. The end of something. Ian didn't think I should go with Jim and he stubbornly refused to travel with me. I was glad of the peace. In such oppressive confinement I may not have been able to hide my heart and the back of a hearse is not the right setting for such a conversation. I want to tell him properly. I owe him that, at least.

Celebrant—the word implies that ceremonies should be, as Vanessa says, a celebration of life. He clearly expected more to work with. When I met with him to discuss the music and his words I sensed a note of accusation in the questions over the kind of man Jim was, his life, the whereabouts of the rest of his relations. I suppose my lack of knowledge must have made it difficult for him to write his piece. As he walked me to the front row he suggested I wait around afterwards so he could introduce me to the organist, who's in his eighties, and seems to know everyone. 'If you have the time to do that, of course,' he added, in a tone that made me sad. Is family breakdown so unusual? A small incident or perceived slight, a lack of motivation for long motorway journeys or fewer phone calls and suddenly years have gone by and you don't even know where these people live anymore.

Ian arrives, together with Sarah and Andy, and they sit on either side of me in the narrow pew, penning me in. Ian drapes his arm across the top of my shoulders, a gesture that might once have been reassuring. Now the weight of his arm makes me silently scream. I feel pinned down and I wriggle in my seat, fighting the urge to escape. He doesn't ask me how I am. I don't ask him either. I can feel him and Sarah exchanging meaningful glances above my head and I wonder how long I really have until I break my news. I don't want him to guess, to start a confrontation. I want a meaningful exchange and a proper end to this part of my life. All of them have eschewed respectful black for navy, Ian's a thick chalk pinstripe and Sarah's a naval blazer with more gold buttons than it can possibly need. I want to scan the church behind me to see who's here, but the heaviness of Ian's arm is stopping me from craning my neck so I sit silently, head bowed.

Rich light streams from the single stained-glass window, a setting sun, and it tints my hands red. I dressed carefully, grimly, this morning. A new black suit with a fitted skirt and a neat, short jacket covered at the neckline with a grey and black scarf. Feeling need of confidence, I've forced my feet into towering heels that I'll probably regret when we're standing outside.

Wavering organ chords fade and stop. As the celebrant shuffles his papers, clears his throat, Ian drops his arm to his lap. I take the chance to turn and survey the rows of seats. It's not as empty as I'd feared. A good handful of elderly people, about seven or eight, who I assume are Jim's friends but may well turn out to be my relatives—or non-relatives—too. Mr Khan from Jim's newsagents is here with his beautiful wife; and I am touched to see that Nurse Evans has arrived, a black cardigan pulled over her uniform. In the row behind them is an odd-looking man in his late forties, unsuitably dressed in a camouflage jacket and dark blue jeans. He's looking straight ahead, avoiding eye contact, and clutching a worn, white carrier bag; it looks as though he may be here to keep warm.

Finally, I spot Daniel too, several rows back, in a black jacket and tie, and my heart leaps in my chest as if to prove to my denial that I've missed him. I'd hardly dared to hope he would come, even as I wrote the letter. He can't have come back just for this. A lucky coincidence, perhaps. Either way I'm more pleased to see him than I could ever have imagined. My emotions are running dangerously high. How will I introduce him to Ian? To Sarah and Andy? He's smoothing the fabric of his jacket self-consciously; I guess he's borrowed a suit that doesn't quite fit. I imagine him struggling to pull the tailored trousers up over his muscular thighs. He has joined Nurse Evans and I'm pleased to see that she presses his hand. He is not to blame.

Alice arrives, in her usual black, with tight, neat horns of hair and smart pointed boots. Huge silver rings run up each ear and across both hands. She wears barely any make-up but for bright red lips and exaggerated black brows. I have never seen her look more beautiful. To her left is Florence from the local history group, an unlikely but game companion, looking wonderfully poised in a sleek black velvet opera coat, her grey hair fixed with a diamante slide. They are deep in a conversation that I wish I could hear.

Shona sits at the back with a man I assume is David, a good foot and a half taller than her. They lean against each other as though no-one else is here. Just before the service starts, Vanessa comes flying in and takes a seat at the back, by the table of leaflets from various charities offering help with bereavement. She beams round at the congregation as if she's looking for people she knows. I'm hugely touched, especially given what's happening with her own family, that she's travelled all this way to give me support. They all have. I suddenly realise that these splendid, wonderful women are all here for me. They're my friends. Not Ian's, not Ian's friends' wives, but *my* friends. They've seen something in *me* that they like; so much so that they are here when I need them the absolute most. And Daniel is here too. No doubt for his own reasons, but he is here. Today could not go better.

When the last hymn is sung we take a few moments to remember Jim. No-one except me is crying, but I'm glad to see a respectful display of flowers on the casket; some beautiful arrangements and one so ostentatious that it must be from Becky and Doug. There's another, smaller wreath that uses exactly the same flowers as mine, pure white chrysanthemums laced with iris and delphinium, the flowers in the photograph I took to Jim in hospital. The same flowers that grow in Jim's garden.

The casket pulls back, the funerary curtains close in jerky stages. It's an awkward moment, accompanied by more wavering organ music, but it's better than watching him lowered to earth. Burning and ashes seem kinder on the spirit, better than eternal darkness underground. Plenty believe bodies are harmful to the earth and, in many societies, the empty shells of the dead are left outside the village to be devoured by predators, to fulfil the circle of life.

As we file outside Vanessa catches my eye, gives a sympathetic smile. What rituals is she imagining? She says hello to Ian and he returns a curt nod, moving away to stand by the far wall of the remembrance garden with Andy. I see him take out his pager to check his importance and I wonder if he even had it switched off in the service, or if it was luck that kept it silent. I don't know how much longer I can keep up this pretence that we're a couple. I don't have the energy for him now. 'You've done enough,' I say to Sarah. 'There's no need to stay now. Tell Ian I'll call him later.' She gives me a look of concern but I push her gently towards them, relieved as Ian waves agreement and begins to walk away.

Not knowing who was coming I haven't organised a wake, just tea and cake in the wooden hut by the gardens and the guests, apparently familiar with the protocol, amble back towards it. There are neighbours and friends, perhaps relations, that I ought to thank for coming. Several of the elderly people bend stiffly to take my arm and pat it, knowing what will help, not asking me to talk. I feel a tap on my shoulder, turn and face Daniel who hands me a small bunch of white chrysanthemum laced with iris and delphinium. I breath in their heady scent, before placing it gently on a table. Alice and Florence left already, promising to call me tomorrow, but I see Shona and Vanessa and all I really want is to introduce them to Daniel. If I was unsure before, this fact tells me everything I need to know about my feelings for him.

Standing with him is an elderly lady.

'This is Mrs Delaney, my mum's neighbour,' he says and I'm grateful for his introduction.

'I'm sorry for your loss, dear.' Mrs Delaney walks with difficulty, her eyes milky, knuckles swelled as she grips the canes she holds in both hands. 'Jim was a decent man.'

'Thank you'. The weight of aching bends her almost double, yet she is smartly dressed in a draped black suit with matching purple leather boots and gloves. 'Your gloves are lovely.'

'Doesn't take old people long to scratch around and find something to wear for a funeral.' I'm not entirely sure how to take this and, as she smiles, I run her face through the images from the tin, trying to find something familiar about her. She is so old that I can't imagine she would remember anything; when she speaks the inside of her mouth looks shockingly red against the pallor of her skin.

Daniel tells me that she's lived next to his mum since she moved in. Mrs Delaney adds that she's lived in the same house for almost sixty years, that her husband, 'God Rest His Soul', used to take the same bus as Jim to work every morning. I'd been hoping she'd tell me more and I try not to look disappointed as Daniel asks her if she'd like a lift home.

'No, dear.' She indicated a young man with lank hair scraped back into a ponytail. 'my grandson, Neil, brought me, he's a good boy.' Neil raises a hand and shuffles awkwardly as she drops her voice to a stage whisper. 'Wish he'd cut his hair though.'

As Mrs Delaney leaves, Vanessa walks over and smothers me in a hug that makes me tearful all over again. I feel my cheeks burn as I introduce her to Daniel but she's too good to comment. I have noticed though, the pride in my voice as I point to him, his obvious kindly gentleness and the way he seems to know how to handle this whole afternoon, perhaps he's been to too many of these already. There is nothing I want more than to get to know him better. Whether he has room in his life for me is uncertain. I'll have to wait and see.

We speak to various residents and shopkeepers of Hall Road and nearby and, as we're all about to say goodbye to one another, a slightly younger woman walks up to us and introduces herself as Mrs Oxley. 'But call me Primrose-Jane... Are you relations? Sorry to be nosey only it's unusual to see young people at funerals unless they're relations, and I wasn't aware he was in contact with any.' Is Primrose-Jane a relation? She doesn't look anything like the family I know. She's shortish, almost as wide as she is tall in places, dressed in black trousers and coat and covered in an enormous black wool wrap.

'It's alright.' Daniel instinctively knows to take the lead today and I am grateful, emotionally exhausted. 'My mum lives nearby, I know you by sight, but this is Emily, she's related to Jim.' I nod and smile awkwardly, wondering where to start, knowing it won't be with the truth. I'm not related to him at all, not by blood or life, and I haven't even had a chance to tell Daniel that.

'I didn't know about him,' I say, as though I'm being accused of some kind of neglect, 'I didn't know until the accident.'

'I always did wonder where his family was. I knew him a long time, all my life, dear. He was a good man, he didn't have it easy.'

'I would love to hear about him, anything about who he was, the kind of person he was, if he was happy, did he have a good life?' I trail off lamely because she has turned her head to look over the gate, a distant look in her eyes.

'Sometimes people aren't completely happy, whether because of things that happen to them or whether that's just their way, I don't know, but he's at peace now, isn't he? Filthy weather to stand here chatting. Such a sad day. Why don't you come and see me sometime, when you feel like it? I can tell you whatever you want to know about him then.' Primrose-Jane hands me a piece of folded paper with an address neatly written with a real ink pen in a leaning, shaky hand and I realise she must have prepared it to bring. Such age must bring weary familiarity with funeral obligations. As we watch her leave, Daniel slips a hand into mine, squeezes hard.

'I didn't know you were coming, I had hoped.'

'I'm glad I could be here. Mum's over there, I'll introduce

you in a moment.' He indicates a young-looking woman with his colour hair, deep in conversation with Mrs Khan, then he smiles down at me, and I am lost. I know I must join Ian and the others; I have to bring myself to deal with things that will pull my life into pieces for a while and the weight of those actions is heavy on my heart. If I could, I would stay here forever.

'Have you… where have you been?' That came out wrong, I wanted to know how he'd been feeling. I don't need the details yet.

He shakes his head. He's had a haircut, the dirty blond fringe replaced with a neater style.

'How are you feeling?' he asks and I burst into tears at the idea that someone would care. Poor Daniel. I haven't even spoken to Ian yet and here I am throwing myself before him. His life is complex enough. It's not even as if I know for sure what I think. Since Jim brought his ghosts, I am crying out for a sensitive broad shoulder. Daniel may just be in the right place at the right time. All I know is my whole life I've been quiet and I am tired of it all.

Making do. 1947. Jim's story

Even holding the diary felt like a betrayal. Jim stroked its pale blue leather cover. It looked as innocent and beautiful as Molly herself, reminded Jim of her birthday when he'd handed it over wrapped in tissue and told her she must learn to write as well as take pictures, so she could be a true record keeper. As always, she'd laughed at his seriousness, but she'd started using it all the same, had written in it most days ever since, forever leaving it around the house safe in the understanding that it was hers alone and no-one would touch it. He had never intended to read it, but he had to know what was going on.

Yesterday he had watched her as she sat before the mirror on the dresser in her mother's bedroom, staring hard at her reflection in the three panels as she practiced with creams and colours. All the while she looked slightly surprised, as though she'd been expecting a different reflection, measuring her looks against some unknown prize. To ward off any potential vanities, there had never been a mirror of any kind in Molly's own bedroom and she usually made do with the one in the bathroom, which had an antique silver backing that was worn out from years of dampness and made skin look grey and ghostly, eyes dark and hollowed. Yesterday was the first time he had ever known his daughter to be concerned over what her true image might look like; she had always preferred to capture the essence of others in her photographs.

A mirror image is only true while the watcher is still there, he thought; once a person leaves a mirror they might imagine themselves to be anything they wished. Perhaps that was what she'd always done, but the truth was incredibly important to him now, to know if she'd really fallen for Rupert's practiced charm. He began to turn over the diary's neatly written pages, ignoring the sickening feeling that rose from his stomach.

17th March: R told me I was beautiful today. Me! I've been looking in the glass for hours like some enchanted princess, trying to work out what is special enough about me to have attracted someone like him. I have no idea if he means it or even if it's true, but perhaps in a small way I am. Even thinking of him now, the warmth of his skin when we kiss, is enough to make me blush, he makes me feel weightless, and I do not care what our future might be, so long as he is there. He has a fierce ambition. Sometimes it frightens me. Today, as he walked me home, he told me a strange story, about one of his colleagues, a man he's known since school and is supposed to like and yet a man he seems to have ruinously betrayed, to further his career. Then he stopped by the lime tree at the end of the road, held me so gently as we said goodbye that his cruel streak vanished as quickly as it appeared. The sun made shadows of his eyelashes on his cheek and he looked so beautiful. Surely a man like that, a man whose eyelashes make such perfect shadows across the angle of his cheeks, could never really be cruel.

With some effort Jim closed the diary and placed it, precisely, on the corner of the table where it had been left. He was right to be worried that she might leave them soon, perhaps in some way she already had. What would be left of him without her? The drained hull of his body might simply slide to the floor and disappear.

There are almost endless possibilities to be considered once you start looking at old clothes with the idea of remodelling them. Panels inserted into blouses and dresses that are too tight or too short can bring years more wear when material is scarce; ties and scarves can be joined to make tops or tunics. Blending two garments together can sometimes make an entirely new person.

Almost two years after war there was no indication that rationing might end. Jim told himself that the girl was only keen to have the latest fashions, though he knew she was letting out her clothes at the waist and chest. *Make Do and Mend* had become Molly's bible. With the advice from its pages, she became adept in the arts of sewing and camouflage and was rarely to be seen at home without a pile of unpicked material and slashed stitches, silent Primrose-Jane sat helping by her side.

Jim's old shirts became roomy shirt-waisters, the button-through coat dresses she wore for work looked somehow smarter and more stylish with the bands of contrasting fabric run through them. Covering up was easy thanks to the pink-bound book. It was easy, too, for Jim to keep his suspicions to himself. If Grace observed a change in her daughter's shape or style on her rare forays downstairs, then it barely registered with her, preoccupied as she was with the past.

The band show on the radio had finished and the airwave silence before the medical hour made the whole house seem expectant. Jim felt alone in his house full of women. He felt awkward listening to this broadcast in the same room and he offered them both tea, walked through to the kitchen to set the kettle on the hob. The advice they needed from the Radio Doctor was hardly likely to be discussed on air; if he didn't do something soon, he might not save her at all. He peeked through the crack in the door, watching them together. Aunt Hilda's ancient treadle machine was sitting in its painted wooden case on the windowsill and Molly climbed slowly up to it, reaching at an angle to lift it back down to the table.

Primrose-Jane immediately sprung up from the chair and reached the machine before her. 'That's heavy, let me do that for you.'

So she knew too. She must do. Sharp smells of lavender and beeswax caught at the back of Jim's throat and he stood by the door while the girl fussed over the machine, making sure it was in the right place, making Molly comfortable. Jim felt nauseous, hardly daring to breathe in case he gave himself away.

'I won't say nothing you know,' said Primrose-Jane.

His daughter stared straight ahead, lips pursed. 'Anything. I won't say anything.'

Primrose-Jane nodded. 'Yes, ma'am,' she said.

Why did Molly feel the need to put her in her place? All the girl wanted was to offer support. Molly could have a good friend in that young woman. Why couldn't she see that? Why couldn't he find the words to tell them both that he loved them? His house seemed destined for nothing but secrets and sorrows. Grace spent so much time upstairs she didn't even know that Primrose-Jane was living in one of the family's spare rooms and now here he was hiding in the kitchen because he wasn't brave enough to talk to his own daughter about something they all pretended wasn't happening. He made his mind up to fix it, and he knew how.

'It isn't your fault,' said Primrose-Jane quietly. 'It isn't nothing to be ashamed of.'

'Anything.' Molly's reply was instant. 'It isn't *anything* to be ashamed of.' She picked up her cloud of sheeting from the floor, gathering it round her like a billowing cloak of invisibility.

Even the entrance seemed deliberately designed to be intimidating. Twelve stone steps reared up from the pavement in a steep row, plump with history, their bowed middles worn down with the weight of distinguished guests. Jim climbed them slowly, breathing heavier with the effort, then pulled hard, twice, on the brass chain to the right of the door that would announce his presence deep within the house. Perhaps the sound would cause a stir, it didn't seem like the kind of house that received visitors unannounced. But he hadn't called ahead, partly because he did not want his conversation overheard at work and partly because he knew the Harrington-Greens would politely claim to be otherwise engaged.

It was time to set things right, and it was down to him, because it was his fault. He'd encouraged her love of photographs by sharing with her the faces in his tin and talking to her about the lives it held inside. Molly had spent hours looking through them as a child. He blamed himself. If they hadn't spent so much time with the tin; if he hadn't pushed her into that job…

Looking down to pavement level from here made him feel slightly giddy. He'd never seen Rupert's parents, other than the images of his father that appeared in *The Times*, but he imagined them now, leaving their house at this level every day, pausing on this step to survey the rest of the world, so far beneath them. Below the glossy black railings he could see three levels of building, a cellar, basement and ground floor, and, if he took a step back and craned his neck slightly, he could see that above were a further four stories plus the pointed attic gables where the housemaids were banished after their day's work. The house was almost as wide as it was tall, with two grand sets of bow-fronted windows thrusting out from each side of the black front door. A house that could swallow you up.

Jim shuffled awkwardly on the step, looking down at the cobbled side passage, the mews that held a row of cars. A stately picture of wealth so incongruous in this decade of austerity that it reminded Jim of one of Molly's photographs, the one of the rag and bone cart, the children dressed in hand-me-downs and borrowed boots and the grand house seen through the curve of their skinny limbs. Lost in the image, he didn't notice the well-oiled door swing open until the parlour-maid actually spoke.

'May I help you?' A tall spectre in a neat black dress and white apron asked. Her starched face gave Jim a sweeping glance of appraisal, eyes lingering on the hand he clasped across his chest.

'I'm here to see Mr Rupert Harrington-Green,' he answered; staff here were clearly employed to keep undesirables out and the poor woman was only doing her job.

'He's not at home, sir, would you like to leave a card?'

'Oh, perhaps I have the time wrong, he did say today before dinner. Now what time would he usually dine?'

'He generally dines at his club, sir.' The maid was still holding the door, standing with one leg slightly buttressed against it as though this interloper might decide to barge in at any moment and she wished to be ready.

'But he's due back to dress first, perhaps? May I wait?' Jim was insistent. The maid's eyes narrowed to the width of a grass-snake's.

'Who is it, Amelia? Stop time-wasting out there, we have guests this evening!' A woman's voice called down the hall in the booming tone of someone who believes that everything they have to say is of the utmost interest to the rest of the world.

'Someone to see Master Rupert, ma'am,' the maid replied without moving from the door or removing her gaze from Jim.

'Well, send them in!' The ma'am of the house sounded exasperated. 'Roo won't be long.'

'It's a man, ma'am.' She stepped back reluctantly to let Jim through the door and did not offer to take his hat or coat, but indicated that he should follow her through to the sitting room at the back of the building, where the grand house's lady was currently engaged in re-checking a huge list of arrangements for the evening's meal. She whirled around and began to offer an apology for the slight disarray in which he found them. If the sight of Jim standing behind Amelia in his work suit and heavy overcoat surprised her she gave no sign of it and showed him to a large floral chair.

'And to whom do we have the pleasure of speaking?' She extended a gracious hand that she withdrew as soon as Jim's fingers had brushed her own. She wore a burgundy velvet day robe that skimmed the floor in a little pool of material at the back and was cut higher at the front to reveal a pair of shapely legs in jewelled Moroccan slippers. Her features echoed Rupert's, the aquiline nose and sculpted cheekbones, though they were set off by her arched brows and rouged cheeks, by the velvet turban that swathed her hair. Jim had never seen anyone pull off such a complicated, theatrical look so effortlessly; it must be exhausting to dress like that all the time.

'James Avery, Jim, my daughter, Margaret, is a friend of Rupert's, perhaps he has mentioned her?' Jim's legs were aching from the walk. He badly wanted a glass of water. Why had he been stupid enough to come? He felt as though he was drowning.

'No, I don't believe he has. Do tell me how they met.' Mrs Harrington-Green leaned in with an expression of amusement.

'She's a photographer. He came to her magazine and she photographed him with some other members of Parliament.'

'I see. How modern of her. And she has sent you perhaps to request a picture of him at home for her readers? She couldn't come herself?'

Before Jim could explain further Mrs Harrington-Green had swept across the room to the doorway and was calling Amelia back to fetch them some iced tea.

Attempting to affect a manner of ease in his surroundings, Jim leaned back in his chair. There were no signs of austerity here; freshly cut flowers and bowls of fruit adorned the scattered tables and two roaring fires flanked the room, despite the warmth of the day. Clearly they still ran a large staff; the house bristled with the restless atmosphere of a building crammed with unseen servants, listening and watching with sharp ears and bright eyes.

The sitting room was stiff with furniture and littered with photographs in heavy silver frames, all of which, on closer inspection, and despite his certain knowledge of at least four siblings, revealed themselves to be images of Rupert. Evidently he was the favourite, unless there were several other sitting rooms dedicated to other children in the family. Any such thing seemed possible here.

'So...' Mrs Harrington-Green perched on the arm of a chair, as though she was far too busy to sit, and lit an American cigarette, which she placed in an ornate silver holder before offering the case to Jim, who shook his head quickly. 'Rupert should be here in about twenty minutes. I hope it's not too uncomfortable for you? Splendid. I would usually leave him to tell his good news himself but we are all so pleased there isn't much else talked about here and anyway I assume that's why you're here?' She blew out a long spiral of smoke and watched its satisfying curl up towards the ceiling. 'It's all terribly exciting, he's one of the youngest ever members of the Cabinet. Daddy's awfully jealous of course, the old fool, and furious that we're making such a fuss with this dinner, but, as I told him, we have to announce the engagement sooner or later.'

'Sorry,' said Jim, 'I'm not sure I understand.'

'Of course, he's been engaged to Rosie, sorry, Lady Stoneleigh, for ever but finally the time has arrived when we can announce it to the papers. Perhaps your daughter should photograph them together? It might make for a nicer story.'

A great wave of nausea rose in Jim's stomach with the realisation that his very worst fears were true. There was no hope for Molly, and all he had done by coming here was make his family look even more foolish. Rupert was never going to marry her, whatever the poor girl thought. His beautiful, wonderful daughter. The child he'd raised as his own. What was to be done? Grace would never get over a scandal like this. He had to find a way to make this work, for Molly.

'My dear, are you quite well? I'll go and chivvy along Amelia with that iced tea, she's terribly slow I'm afraid, been here for ever, of course, and thinks she's family.'

Rupert's mother hurried off to find her truculent maid and Jim took the opportunity to see himself out, taking care not to cause any upset with the heavy door and holding tightly to the rail of the steps along the way.

A pill box. 1994. Emily's story

'Glad it's all over?' Ian removes his jacket and tie and stretches back against the soft leather Midhurst sofa, pushing his arms behind his head. He gives me an appraising look. 'You seem better anyway. Maybe we can start to move on now.'

I had hoped that they would all go home after the funeral so that I could speak with Ian quietly, sensibly, in our flat on our own. But they decided it would be good for me to have a drink and insisted I meet them here. I'm shaking with the effort of showing it's all OK and pretending that whole last bit with Daniel didn't happen. But it did. And now, despite all the years with Ian, I am itching to take back my life.

I'm leaving you: the words flash neon across my brain, blocking normal conversation.

'He doesn't mean anything by it,' Sarah soothes, passing me a glass of wine that I stand on the table.

A huge convex wall mirror runs around our table, so we can see ourselves a hundred different ways. Our waiter wears red braces, a dusting of glitter across his cheek. He fusses with the drinks and I brush him away, impatient.

'Can't I pay you a compliment?' Ian smiles. 'We've all been worried about you.'

'But you look great today,' says Sarah brightly. 'You just need your hair done and you'll be perfect!'

'What's wrong with my hair?' I know very well what she means, that I've skipped the highlighting. I never did have the time to waste while someone painted individual strands of my hair with a tiny brush and now it all seems so utterly unimportant. They won't be coming back. My hair is longer, too, and I like the defiance of its swish when I turn my head.

'Maybe a bit of colour. Anyway, the funeral went off well,

didn't it? Who were all those people you were talking to, you've been living some sort of double life!' Now he notices.

'The nurse was Debra Evans, Jim's nurse, she's been amazingly supportive, I can't believe she came, it was really kind.' It strikes me that she may have been professionally concerned about me. Perhaps I could do something for the unit to show my appreciation. 'Mrs Delaney, a neighbour of Jim, she had a stick with a white band... my friend Alice was there too and you saw Vanessa and Shona. And I met a friend of Jim's called Primrose-Jane.'

'Who were the young guys? The one in the suit and the sort of tramp?' Ian appears unconcerned that I introduced him to no-one, there's an arrogance there, a certainty about his place in my life that will make things hard for me. I don't even want to speak his name in case I give myself away. I think about the broadness of Daniel's back, the white chrysanthemums and irises. I think of the sea in the colour of his eyes.

Dropping my gaze into my wine glass, I shrug. 'I'm not sure. Funerals are public events. There are plenty of people with nothing better to do who show up to strangers' funerals.' Not exactly a lie. But there may come a time when this finds me out and already I feel guilty for that.

'Rather them than me, weirdos. Still it keeps them off the number 18 bus.' Ian launches into a story about his route to work and I sit back, trying to find the words I need. The mirrors along the walls reflect different versions of myself, some of which I like better than others.

Ashes to ashes. From the Book of Prayer, the celebrant said, not the Bible as everyone assumes. Being in hospital with Jim has both given me time to think and brought a sharp reminder of the need to live a fulfilled life. How long before I return to dust? I am almost breathless with the need to get this done, to rush back to Daniel and find out if there is a chance we can begin, however slowly.

'When do you want to get all your stuff? I can borrow Andy's van so you can get it all at once, make it easier for you, you must have tons there now.'

Ian is looking at me, my mind is blank. 'What stuff?'

'*Your* stuff, silly. Clothes, shoes. You don't need to stay near the hospital anymore, you can leave your mum's place.'

'Where is Andy?' I ask Sarah.

'Oh God, I said I'd call him when we got here. He went back to the office. Hang on.'

I wait until she's standing on the far side of the bar, trying to persuade the barman to lend her the telephone, before leaning in. Being unkind to Ian won't make me happy but being true to myself, ultimately, will.

'I'm not sure I'm going to be coming back to the flat.'

'You won't need anything today, we can help you over the weekend.' Ian's arm is unsteady as he pours another glass and I realise I've picked the wrong moment but it's too late now. I can't stop.

'I'm not sure I'm coming back at all. Ian, we need to talk. All this time I've had to think has made me realise things about myself, things I wasn't sure of before. But I don't want to get married, I know that.'

His eyes widen momentarily, then he smiles, pats my shoulder. 'You're upset from today. Seems to have messed with your head a bit, all this nonsense. It'll blow over.'

Blow over. He sounds like his mother. People getting upset over silly things, they shouldn't talk about them, it's better not to dwell. If I stayed with him I'd be living half a life.

He is never going to feel anything deeply, he's never been allowed.

'It's not nonsense, Ian, it's the way I feel about my whole family and you can't even pretend to care. Today of all days. I don't want to get married to you. I want things to change and I'm not coming back to the flat.'

Ian's face drops and then picks up brightly as Sarah walks back over to us. How easily he acts.

'Sorry but I'm going to have to take Emily home,' he says, full of mock concern. 'She's a bit upset.'

Shona sits on the grass, arms wrapped around her. I know she feels cold too but she won't admit it. She was right though, a swim in freezing water does feel as though it has done me some good. My body tingles, dry and comfortable now and my mind feels clear.

'I'll get you in the river next, you'll see, it gets addictive.' She pours coffee from a wide red thermos, hands me a plastic cup. I shake my head, laughing.

'No way. This is absolutely cold enough for me.' The Serpentine Lido opened this week and is almost empty aside from a few hardy wild swimmers. Part of the condition of staying at Shona's is to join her on adventurous swims. She's been kind, handing over her spare room for as long as I need, giving me space without questions. I've begun to open up to her, slowly, and it feels better than I'd thought possible to share all the things I've pushed away. Natural. This is what friendship means.

'I can't remember seeing that tracksuit before, looks good.'

'It's new, they called it 'lounge wear' in Selfridges. Yoga style I think, maybe I should take that up too. It's comfy anyway.' I've been buying quite a lot of new clothes, returning to things I preferred before Ian's creeping disapproval changed my style. I like more casual outfits, jeans with nice shirts and trainers. He liked me to wear dresses and heels, the clothes, I realise now, his mother would like. When I returned to the flat, to remove my belongings, he made sure he was out. He left an inventoried list on the kitchen table, marked in different colours to show what he felt it appropriate for me to take and I was grateful, because the sight of it sealed my decision and made it easier for me to go. In the end I took very little. Everything seemed to belong to a different life, a different person.

'What are you up to for the rest of the day?' Shona screws the lid back onto the thermos, puts the plastic cups on top and checks the seals, holding the flask upside down and watching for drips.

'I need to pick up a couple of things from the library but I thought I might walk there, it's quite nice from here, do you fancy coming?'

'I'm meeting David at the Royal Academy, he wants to see the Hockney before it finishes. Come with us if you like?'

She's being kind. I need to give her some space or the fondness we have will spoil.

'I need to go to Mum and Dad's actually. They've got a buyer and there's loads to sort out. I'll probably stay there tonight, too, give me a chance to start early tomorrow.'

'If you're sure? Bit depressing being there on your own.'

'Needs to be done though. Won't be long until it's sold, then I can make some decisions about what I'm doing. Can't stay under your feet forever.'

'I like having you, Em. You know I do.'

I know, and it feels good. 'Go on. Enjoy your culture and I'll see you later tomorrow afternoon. How about a roast in the Albert? David too if he's around. Say 'hi' for me.'

We stand up and she gives me a quick hug before she leaves. They're a good couple, easy in each other's company and fond of the same things. They're always off to museums and galleries at the weekend and watching them I realise how important it is to have common interests. Ian never shared my excitement in a finished book or a walk through some damp woods, any more than he understood my need for Jim, and all the time I told myself it didn't matter I was wrong.

Now that their house is under offer, I don't have much time to sort out Mum and Dad's things. In a panic I've turned every kitchen cupboard out onto the floor when I hear the neat double chime of their doorbell. I curse the timing, assuming it's the buyer again. They've been back several times already, always unannounced, to measure for curtains and check the carpets and generally act like it's already theirs. This time I'm determined not to let them in and I march towards the door in my yellow rubber gloves wearing such a fierce expression that Vanessa giggles when I yank it open.

'That's a good look. I never knew you were so domesticated.'

I give her a hug and half drag her in over the threshold, apologising for the mess as she picks her way through the rubble of the hallway.

'They're really doing it then? Good for them. Big thing at their age.'

'S'ppose it is.' I'll go and see them soon, when the house is finished. Maybe I could ask Vanessa to come with me, she's probably missing warm weather. 'Cup of tea?'

It's good to see her and even better to be able to talk without hiding anything. Now everything's out in the open, I feel the rest of my life has been restored, as though it's been on hold for a while. I wonder if that's what it was like for Jim, all the silence and lies, the strain that might make a brain simply wish to shut down.

Vanessa has found the astrakhan coat that I couldn't bear to get rid of and she's trying it on, twirling round and hugging it to herself.

'Gorgeous, isn't it? I've been clearing out the cupboards at Jim's house, sorting out things to take to the charity shop. Thought I might keep that one.'

'You must, it's lovely, looks hardly worn too.'

'Come over to the house and have a look in the wardrobes if you like, I don't need to get rid of everything and there's some beautiful vintage stuff, more your sort of thing than mine mostly.'

'I'd love to!' She twirls again and then squeaks excitedly as she pulls out something from the right-hand pocket of the coat. It's a pill box in with a rose design on the lid, like all the things in the bedrooms at Jim's house, small and fussy.

'Open it,' I say but she passes it over to me reverentially. The lid is stiff but when I eventually prise it up I realise it was wedged by the folded piece of paper inside. There's an address written on it, but I suppose I'll never know the significance of that. I turn to the tin, thinking I might match the words with something in there and Vanessa picks up some of the contents with a wistful look.

'Amazing you have this. I was thinking about it, when I was going through some of the piles of paper at Mum's house.'

'Is she...'

'She won't get better. She knows she won't go home again. I'm trying to face the inevitable. After Dad, she never cleared anything, not a thing. Our grandparents' and parents' homes, they're full of all this aren't they? It struck me, looking at your tin, that everything meaningful is stored out of the way now, on hard drives and discs that will probably never be viewed or downloaded. Never left for future generations to look through and wonder.'

She's right. I am grateful for the chance to see the faces of my history and I have something to try to piece together. If my own family has shrunk to the point of extinction at least I can feel the weight of my history behind me. But I'm no longer looking for answers there.

Still life. 1973-4. Jim's story

A white shard of moonlight pushed its way through the kitchen window and fell across the table, illuminating everything on its surface and throwing the rest of the room into sharp relief. The dish of apples was lit like a still life before another cloud blocked the light, leaving Jim in darkness. It must be almost dawn. Most nights ended sitting on a kitchen chair, in the early hours when his thoughts ran free. Ma and Aunt Hilda were often to be found like this. Was that all life really gave you in the end? Just the fears that keep you up in the middle of the night? He was supposed to retire, to finish at the Ministry for ever. What good would it do him to stop work? What might things be like when he was continuously home? He'd been due to retire two years before and had simply not acknowledged the fact, making his journey and taking his seat in the same calm way, every day, waiting to be found out. He had practised his response; if they ever told him he'd outstayed his time he would stand down gracefully, feigning ignorance over the procedure and pretend he found it all as deeply amusing as everyone else.

The prospect of endless silent hours stretching across the house filled him with dread. Impossible to imagine a routine without leaving and returning at the same time every day. If only Molly had come to him first he could have made it right. It was so hard to get that thought out of his head, even after all these years. How differently everything could have happened. Why were none of them ever as close as he wanted? He'd spent longer and longer at his desk, throwing himself into work, and it wasn't even ambition, because what had he achieved? Everyone in the country knew his words, but not his name, and besides, when he saw how she'd managed her disguised thanks to *Make Do and Mend*, where was the pride in that?

Molly had gone to her mother, despite the way Grace was. Their childhood bond cut through Grace's illness and drew Molly to her room in supplication, to ask forgiveness. It still pained him to think how roughly she must have refused. Given every opportunity to right the wrongs of the past Grace had simply turned away. When he'd returned from work, late as usual, his daughter was already gone, her little case lay abandoned in the hallway and he had cried when he picked it up, so light it felt empty.

He had pleaded with Grace, begged her to let them take the baby and bring it up as theirs, but she wouldn't even speak of it. If she knew where Molly was, she refused to tell him. They should do as Rupert asked, she insisted. After all, he was a prominent man and she entirely agreed that the shame to be brought on all of them was too much to bear. If Molly had really done as they'd planned she'd be thousands of miles away, alone and maybe frightened so far from home. But, even if he had known, or knew now, where to find his daughter, there was no arguing with Grace as she was, confused, weak and fragile in mind as well as body. Before Molly's departure even the slightest upset had sent Grace to bed for days on end; now she rarely came downstairs at all.

Primrose-Jane, too, had offered to bring up the baby as hers, a typically selfless gesture. Grace had told him that while he stood there with Molly's abandoned case clutched in his hands, sneering that the girl was no better than she should be and 'would likely end up that way herself if she wasn't careful'. Little did Grace know that Primrose-Jane almost had, but for his intervention. If only he could have helped Molly like that.

Grace told Jim that she knew about the secret room in the attic and had asked the girl to leave, made a point of saying she had to ask twice. It was clear she saw the poor thing as a threat. If she'd had any choice, he knew, Grace would have dismissed her altogether but she could hardly go and find another to help with the housework. So Primrose-Jane still came, but only twice a week and all Jim could do was provide her with good references and contrive to give her as much extra pay as he could.

Another strobe of moonlight fell across Jim's thin cotton pyjamas, still neatly pressed, uncreased by sleep. The clouds were fast moving tonight, blown over the sky with a tailwind that must have come straight from the sea. He saw himself walking with Grace on their beach, heads bowed together, laughing as the wind whipped their hair and stole their words. He saw the three of them switching on the first light together, laughing and clutching each other. Molly wouldn't be gone forever; she would find them, come back, when she was ready. He had to keep hoping.

On the dark wooden stand in the hallway stood the little suitcase, in case she ever returned. Grace removed it every now and then, leaving it out by the bins for collection. But he always found and replaced it. Eventually he won, and there it stayed, like an accusation, freshly wounding every time he entered and left the house.

Jim was starting to panic when they found her. After she sent Molly away, the depression that Grace battled most of her adult life had finally won. In the years that followed, Jim had watched the energy ebb from her bones until she spent her days sitting hunched under a thick, checked blanket in the high-backed chair by the dining room window. On bad days he would find her, surprisingly supple, curled into a tight ball on top of her bedcovers staring, unblinking at the papered wall.

Grace so rarely left the house that he hadn't thought to look for her in the garden until he saw a flash of colour through the French doors. He'd expected to find a cat, one of the dozens that criss-crossed these backyards, each convincing themselves that they encircled their own territory and ignoring the others until forced to fight. London cats, with all the rage and hunger of the farm who seemed to favour the wilderness of their overgrown garden. Slowly Jim picked his way along the path, feeling for the flat stepping-stones underneath and wishing someone was with him. Primrose-Jane had her own family to consider and she disliked bringing her son too often, partly because she resented the fact that her own childhood was wasted here and partly because Grace seemed to frighten him so much. They really should get someone in to do the garden, but taming the shrubs had always been Grace's job and there was still the hope that plants might bring her back to them again. Besides, a gardener would be a wasted expense, they never sat outside and he didn't want strangers here, the inconvenience of trusting people he didn't know.

The flash of colour was Grace. He exhaled deeply. She was sitting on the damp grass in a thin cotton dress, without shoes, her stockinged feet smudged wet with earth. How had she managed to struggle down there? One arm was wrapped around her knees to hold her upright, in the other she held an object, turning it over and over between her fingers. Jim crouched down beside her, balancing on a large flat stone at the rockery's base, and saw that it was an oversized camera lens, its rounded glass cased in ridged black plastic. Gently he took the lens from Grace, who began to rock slightly forwards and back, hugging her knees, still staring straight ahead as though Jim might conveniently disappear if she did not see him directly.

The lens was one he remembered Molly describing as a fish eye, with a tumescent glass bulb curved inside the case. A lens designed to distort and deform the images it made, invented to capture clouds. Molly's room, just as she had left it, was full of such things but Grace must have been in there to find it. She shivered. She was poorly dressed, had obviously struggled with the buttons and ties, but she'd managed to put on a pretty scarf and fix it with a silver pin in the shape of a dragonfly. The sight of it stabbed Jim with memories as he put his own cardigan gently around Grace's gaunt shoulders.

'You should be more careful, it's chilly today and this grass is damp. Perhaps we should go in now?' Jim looked at his watch with a slow deliberate movement, as though coaxing a child's attention. 'How long have you been out here? You're cold, we should go in and have some tea. There's Madeira cake, your favourite.' He'd given up taking her lunch, she never touched it, but she usually stirred herself for afternoon tea, could sometimes become quite talkative at this time of the day.

'I'm quite alright, thank you, I can manage quite well.' Grace still stared straight ahead. 'I felt as though something was going to happen, can you feel that?'

'A storm on the way perhaps,' answered Jim, though he knew this was not what she meant.

'All day I had the feeling that something was about to happen. I wanted to be out here to… *feel* life.'

'Would you like me to help you up? You must be stiff. I

don't know how long you've been there. I'm afraid Dr Forrester will think badly of me for letting you.' Jim tried to affect the business-like tone he used to chivvy Grace in one of her slumps, in the weeks when she washed her hands until the skin bled or pulled out great fistfuls of her translucent hair and bunched them up on her lap.

Grace turned her head slowly and contemplated Jim with a gimlet stare that blackened her eyes.

'It's my fault,' she said. 'All of it. It's my fault she's not here.'

'You mustn't blame yourself. Rupert is the one who should bear that.'

'I didn't love the people I should have loved, don't you see? If you don't love the people you have a duty to love everyone suffers. We both know that's the truth.'

'Love isn't a duty,' Jim said softly. 'We can't help who we love.'

'We can. We can put others' needs before our own and not make bargains and promises we can't keep. We can stop trying to rearrange the world until it's too late to go back.'

Jim pressed his lips together and exhaled sharply; it was by far the longest speech Grace had made in years and he was shocked by its confessional nature. 'Maybe,' he said cautiously, 'but love isn't a duty.'

'It's my fault they're not here.'

Jim moved to her side, breathing the thick, fresh smell of earth and crushed grass as Grace shifted slightly to let him sit down. They sat side by side in the damp. Jim stared at the tendrils of clematis as it curled through the undergrowth, marvelling at the contrast of the slim green shoots that burst from the gnarled dead wood of the stem. There was a sad sort of beauty in their climb, the insistence of fresh life that it must grow at any cost. We all survive, he thought, Molly will too, and maybe she'll be happier elsewhere.

Everything changed again on the day he returned from his retirement party. Finally found out, he succumbed to the inevitable, three years after his time and with a grudging acceptance. He left the party early, disliking the kind of conversation people made when they stood around with sherry in their hands in the middle of the day. He wasn't good at accepting presents and good wishes. The gold watch for long service reminded him of Pa's, the one he'd given Pearl for Alfie, and made him melancholy at a time when people wanted him to smile.

Jim opened the front door, batting away the strands of wisteria in irritation. He passed the lonely suitcase in the hallway, with its gathered shroud of dust, and hid his retirement gift, a full bound set of his publications for the Ministry, inside the bureau. He heard the scream from the garden just as he closed the drawer and stood bewildered as though a particularly confusing dream was unfolding.

Primrose-Jane ran into the house, one hand above her heart and the other over her mouth. She looked old, he thought, surprised, because in his mind she was always a girl. Motherhood had not been kind, her body was heavily padded under the housecoat, her legs and ankles thick in their carpet slippers.

'Jim! We need an ambulance. Grace has fallen by the pond.' She grabbed for the telephone and pushed him out of the way, towards the garden.

It felt as though something had slowed time, his ears rushed with blood and he struggled to move towards the door, not wanting to face what was out there. He didn't want to look. Grace was lying on her side, a deep cut on her forehead that stained the paving stones red. The sleeve of her dress was torn and her left arm covered in scratches. She hadn't put out her arms to stop herself. It looked as though she had simply toppled sideways from the chair. He knelt down beside her. She was breathing, but her eyes were empty.

'Don't move her, Jim!' called Primrose-Jane. 'They said don't move her. In case we make it worse, in case anything is broken.' She produced a cushion from one of the kitchen chairs and very gently eased it under Grace's head. 'That's all we can do to make her more comfortable. They won't be long.' She squeezed his arm and they waited.

All the way to Queen Mary's he tried to make pacts with God. Let her live and I'll make things right. Let her live and we'll finally talk, we'll sort out everything. We can find Molly, bring her back, bring our grandchild home. We can invite Eleanor to visit, find Alfie and send him presents. We can fill the house with family. Just let her live and I'll change everything.

Thirty minutes later a tall man in blue scrubs was breaking his heart. A stroke they said, a massive haemorrhage to the left side of her brain that rendered her speechless and took away the last of her soul. 'It's unusual,' the doctor said, 'for such a frail woman to survive such a thing. You're lucky to still have her.'

Looking forward. 1994. Emily's story

Primrose-Jane seems genuinely pleased to see me again. Initially I consider it a vote of confidence that she allows me to make the tea, but when I emerge, carrying the cups and a packet of biscuits that I bought on the way, she's leaning back in her armchair with closed eyes and furrowed brow, as though she's in pain, and I realise she didn't have the energy to do it herself. I set the tray down carefully on the sideboard, so as not to disturb her, but she eases forward at the sound and thanks me, settles herself for a talk.

'Are you OK? Can I get you anything else?'

'No, dear, it's alright. I've got some new pills from the doctor and he says they'll take a while to work. I don't know that they're not making it worse. Mustn't grumble, plenty of people worse off.'

'Was Jim?'

'Not in his physical health, dear, no, he was fit as a soldier. Apart from his war wound, of course.'

'Oh, I didn't know. What happened?'

'Splinter of wood, right in his chest. From the first war, shell in the trenches. Stopped him going back, which he always felt guilty about. He used to joke that it made him hard-hearted. Couldn't have been further from the truth.'

A shard of wood. It's how losing Carrie left me, hardened in a way that made me weaker.

'I'd rather have my mind though. Least I know what's wrong with me,' says Primrose-Jane, looking sad. 'Poor thing, he was so lonely, even when Grace was still here. She never liked visitors of any kind.'

'They said at the hospital it was likely he had dementia.'

'When you get to my age you won't like that word either.'

'I didn't mean...'

'Not your fault. Just an excuse to write us all off. If you want my opinion, I don't think anyone's strong enough to fend off the troubles he had. Sooner or later if you live with your troubles, they're going to get to you.'

'Was he depressed?'

'Always got to be a label. He was a troubled soul, I know that.' Primrose-Jane holds the back of her hand to her forehead and presses it against her hairline, as though she's weary of thinking about it. 'I don't really know what depressed means, another reason to fill us all with pills. S'what they did to my poor Robert. Spent years on antidepressants or sleeping pills or whatever. It's to make people fit a diagnosis. To excuse odd behaviour. That was more like Grace.'

Again, I sense her bristling at the mention of Jim's wife and I wonder whether Primrose-Jane and he were lovers. Would she have given him a happier life? She looks so tired; I should leave her in peace.

'But you and your son, Robert, you were kind to Jim. I'm sure that kept him going.'

Primrose-Jane shakes her head. 'Not really. Robert said it was like he didn't want to remember things properly, like he was blocking it out. He used to get confused and think Robert was all sorts of people from his past. First he thought he was Alfie, his little nephew... did I tell you about his brother Charlie? He never saw him after the first war. There was something there too, but I don't know exactly what happened. Alfie had a big sister who died, and the family never really recovered. He was navy, Charlie, like their dad.'

'Did he die in the war?' There's a photograph of someone

in naval uniform in the tin, only one, a young man with a serious face which must be Charlie. There are several photographs of an older man wearing trawler's dungarees.

'His dad did. They don't know about his brother.'

'That's sad, not to know.' It must have eaten him up, not knowing what happened to him. Imagine if Carrie had just disappeared. I would have spent my whole life trying to find her. In many ways I have, something I've realised far too late.

'Then he thought Robert was someone who'd come from France. Because he did a good thing for his friend, Bert, who died in the trenches. Bert fathered a child in France and Jim gave his own name to the baby, after Bert died. He hid that from everyone for a long time, especially Grace. For some reason he was terrified she would find out about it. I wouldn't have minded, if it'd been me, I would've understood him, been proud of him even, but not Grace. She wasn't like that.'

Another dig at Jim's wife. Perhaps she deserved it, but Grace wasn't immune to all the tragedies of their lives either. Primrose-Jane was certainly fonder of Jim than might be expected from someone who cleaned his house. Could it be the same Bert from the news clipping? He didn't die in the trenches and Jim knew that, so maybe he wasn't as honest with Primrose-Jane as she thinks.

'He always thought that child would contact him, and it never did, and I think in a way he was sad about that. Then he kept insisting that Robert was Molly's baby but, well, we didn't know what happened to her. He always thought she'd gone to Australia, that's what Grace told him, but she certainly lied about other things so maybe that too.'

'What things?'

'She hid that book of photographs from him for a start. I found it under her bed and when he saw it, it was too much for him. I only found it a few days before his accident. Lovely album it was, Molly had obviously kept up her photography. Full of pictures of her little boy, your dad, right from when he was tiny.'

So it was Dad in the album. I listen as Primrose-Jane explains how she found it hidden away among Grace's things long after she died. The note with it was from Nan, written when Dad turned eighteen, the age Nan was when she was sent away. Nan must have agonised over it, did she want Jim to find her? Did she leave a forwarding address? What sort of missed chances and regrets live all through our lives?

'That must be the one I found, in the house. It was under the kitchen table, like it had been dropped.' It should have been a time of revelation and forgiveness, but they never had the chance. Poor Nan. It makes me even more determined to publish her photographs and use them for good, to draw our family together in the way that she wanted.

'He took it hard. Cruel thing to do to him, Grace keeping it from him like that. To think she'd tried to contact him and he never knew. That night... who knows what he was thinking?' Primrose-Jane heaves herself up from the chair and walks to the sideboard, takes a stack of magazines from the drawer and passes them to me. 'He was so proud of her. Her photographs. She worked on these, they were her photos of the cakes and food. We used to work on the recipes in the kitchen sometimes. She changed though, when she met *him*.'

The magazines are pale and faded, their covers rough to the touch. Stylised images of perfect housewives in curled hair and pearls are drawn around the photographs. Nothing in their pages feels real.

'What's going to happen to it? The house?' Primrose-Jane sits back down, breathing heavily, and contemplates me through mystic-thick spectacles.

'I don't know. Depends on Dad and what he wants to do. I'd like to take it on but it's up to him, really.' I explain what's happening with Spain, their move and she nods though I can tell she's not really listening. Her heart's with Jim, and the house she grew up in.

'Going to need a lot of work that house, a lot of work. Been too much for me for a long time, but like I said, he wouldn't have anyone else in. Be good to see it looking nice again.'

'Can't promise anything, but I'd like you to come and see it,' I say and I mean it too, I like Primrose-Jane. She smiles a little wistfully as though she doesn't quite believe she'll make it to next week. Tears prick my eyes again and she stares at me intently.

'It's not your fault. It's easy to end up alone. We're everywhere. Old people, in our flats and houses and chairs, sitting on our own.' Her voice becomes softer. 'You'll see. When you get old. All the things that fade away and leave you. Your house changes, neighbours move. Friends, first they stop wanting to go out or do anything different and then one by one they begin to disappear and you find that you can't make new ones because where on earth do you start?'

'I don't know,' I say, because the way she has described it Jim's life sounds just like mine was until recently: dead living.

'You mustn't be sad for him, dear. I meant it when I said he's probably happy now.' She speaks slowly and deliberately, as though she needs me to fully comprehend. 'When you stop interacting with the rest of the world, that's the end of life, not when you stop breathing.'

'But when sad things happen to people… sometimes it's easy to hide, isn't it?'

'We're all fallible dear, it's what makes us human. But so does the way we try to make up for our accidents and mistakes, the way we live, the choices we make. The end is when you stop all that and for some people it comes a long time before they die. When they stop doing new things, looking always back instead of forward.'

She's right, and I need to stop all these tears, whether they're for myself or for Jim. I may not know where my journey ends but I know where it starts, and it's not in the past.

A Life in pictures. 1993. Jim's story

Living with a silent, unmoving Grace was worse than living alone. Jim felt suffocated by the need to tiptoe around in quiet. By the time Grace slipped and faded away completely, ten years after her stroke, he was already old. There seemed little point in talking with no-one to listen. He felt his mind sliding faster without anyone reminding him not to eat straight from a tin with an unwashed fork, or rinse the tin to drink from as though living on a battlefield. A slow and subtle shifting of perspective. Primrose-Jane was the only person who ever came inside the house and he never ate in front of her. She didn't clean much, her knees were worse than his, and most visits they just sat in the kitchen, for company. Without Primrose-Jane he might forget how to speak completely. No-one else was close enough to notice any different. In the silent brooding years, Jim slowly separated from the world.

Jim's waist disappeared and his shoulders grew round, his eyes hollowed. Winter brought stiff swelling to his knuckles, making feats of endurance from everyday tasks—lacing shoes, fastening buttons. His body seemed to fold in on itself; every time he went to the bathroom, he struggled to re-buckle his belt. Easier to stay in bed longer, to wear pyjamas under his suit.

Before Grace died, he used to push her chair to the lake in the park, flushed with the effort of moving its creaking wheels. He refused any help. He was happy to do it, he told the doctor, he would care for her properly. Sitting by the water, watching the waterfowl's petty squabbles, he would look around, amazed to have lived so long with a chest full of wood. He wondered if exertion would dislodge it, but by the time his visits to the doctor were regular, he'd forgotten the question.

After Grace, there seemed little point to the park, or the lake, and his walks became shorter and less frequent. Soon he only walked to the corner shop. There were fewer faces he recognised each year. From the dining room window the seasons changed and blurred together in a restless march of weeks that seemed at odds with the painful length of one evening. Was he really hanging onto his mind? It was hard to focus on reading or keep his fingers painfully bent to write.

In the overgrown garden Jim watched the copper gold frogs, remembered Molly catching them to examine in her jam jars. He watched the paper wasp queens work themselves almost to death, chewing and building their fortresses, weaving back and forth patiently to finish the fragile dome that would keep them in solitary comfort. He left their nests in peace. Jim was tired of his body's relentless need to function. He could feel his mind closing down, rejecting new information and selecting the memories he viewed over again, enlarging and distorting them like Molly's lens that captured clouds.

When Primrose-Jane found the photograph album hidden among Grace's things, at first he'd been confused. A young man's entire life in pictures, and such familiar features. He thought it must be Alfie, the first name his memories provided, and he was pleased that Pearl had not forgotten, pleased to think she had looked for him and found him. Until Primrose-Jane pointed out that Alfie would be grown by now, an old man. Whoever he was, thought Jim, he was family and Primrose-Jane had no right to be here, when he wanted to remember things she couldn't understand. He sent her away then, to give him space to think, but the boy rose from the book like a spirit and it was hard to place him. It was hard to work out what he wanted.

His name was Henry the spirit-boy said, or maybe Henri. A French name. The boy grew angry that he'd been left and so Jim told him he could stay. He was welcome. But the boy turned away in silence. Could it be his own grandson, come to look for him from Australia, from right across the world? Where was Molly? She hadn't survived her broken heart and it was his fault, for not standing up to Grace. Jim sat at the kitchen table, upright on the ladder-back chair, like his aunt in her grief before him, watching as the boy left like so many others had before. If Jim went now, chased after the boy he could find Molly. He didn't stop to think or put on clothes or let his mind be changed. This time he wouldn't be stopped.

Living. 1994. Emily's story

An important aspect of the veneration of the dead among this group is the appeasement of ancestors via ritual chanting and offerings of food and small valuable items. Ancestor worship is built into the fabric of daily life and rules are followed strictly as neglect of duties can quickly summon the anger and menace of ancestral spirits. Among families the deeds and personalities of their forebears are told and retold continually so that their names and faces, their stories, will not be forgotten.

Vanessa Barton,
Religion and Ritual in the Edaben of the Lowlands

It's time for me to accept that Carrie's gone, time to open up to others, because I don't want my life to be like Jim's, just existing with a truth I never mention. Daniel may or may not be the person to push me from the place I'm hiding, and if I'm honest I have no idea how this relationship will work out, but I have to try. We can't choose who we love, or what we receive in return, but we can choose to live rather than exist. I know that I've begun to make the right decisions, looking forward with an open mind instead of worrying about what might catch up with me.

This time, when I walk up the path, I test which tiles have uneven wobbles and make a note in the green-covered notebook where I plan to store all of my lists. If I'm going to restore this house, like I promised, everything must be right, from the plans to the painting. Though I wasn't looking too closely before, I've convinced myself that minimal serious building work will be required and I'm hoping today's checks will prove me right, partly because my budget is so restricted and partly because I can't outstay my welcome at Shona's. She's been kind but I need a home. It's one thing to stay here while I fix it up and make it pretty, quite another to camp out in a building site.

Daniel offered to come again today but he's already helped enough with the searches for paperwork, dealing with the legal stuff that I dislike and which he handles confidently, like everything else. He has phoned, charmed and threatened people, carried endless boxes around, made tea throughout and been silent when I needed silence most. He accepts that Carrie still walks through life with me. Most of all he makes the future real.

Everyone seems to approve of him, Vanessa, Shona, Alice, even Primrose-Jane. She says he reminds her of Jim when he first came to live with his aunt and uncle. Her opinion means a lot to me now and to my surprise she has contacted me often and helped me enormously with piecing together all the lives and faces in the tin, although there is so much I feel I will never know.

Anna will meet Daniel soon too, because she's coming to London with Jacob in a few months' time, 'If only to remind myself of all the reasons I ran off in the first place,' she says. Because I really want to see her, and also because it gives me a deadline on the house, I begged her to stay here. It means I must get a good chunk of the work done by then. With the promised help of Daniel and Alice it should be fine. Perhaps Anna and Jacob will help when they arrive. Mum and Dad have signed over the deeds to be shared between us, and I'm not sure whether that's because they can't face thinking about what needs to be done or because they want us to work together. I suspect they are drawing back but it doesn't matter. It will be good to have this with Anna, something to bring us closer. I have her box of photographs here for her and I am ready to talk. I'm preparing a tin of my own, too, for the future. It's full of all the things we've let slide— photographs and memories from my parents' house, Jim's pamphlets, Nan's boxes of images and drawings by me and Carrie.

Imagine these tall, elegant rooms with light streaming through them again, warmed with people. Vanessa can stay here when she's finished putting her mum's home in order in Manchester. Alice and Florence can drink tea in the garden, help me choose the colours and fabrics that will suit the house. They are working with me on the book of Nan's photographs and their eye for historic detail is invaluable. Shona and David will come for dinner, with me and Daniel, when he's here. He wants to paint a room in Evie's favourite pink, to make her feel welcome when she's able to stay at weekends. For once I'm not scared of what's next. Because I know now that the end of life is when you stop living, and you can choose when that will be.

Acknowledgements

This book has been several years in the making and I am grateful to many individuals for their encouragement and forbearance. Most of all my family—to my sons, Ben and Ted, for their unswerving faith in me; and my husband, Matt, for sparking the first idea with his Uncle Jim's tin and for his patience and love. Although all the characters in these pages are works of fiction, the inspiration for Jim was Matt's Great Uncle Jim, whose tin full of news clippings and photographs has remained a family mystery.

The friendship of many wonderful women has sustained and encouraged me, for this book in particular my first reader, Becky King, and my constant reminder of the importance of words and stories, Lisette Abrahams.

I would like to acknowledge the kindness and generosity of author Tracey Iceton, who mentored me through the completion of the final drafts with wisdom and understanding. Huge thanks also to the wonderful team at Cinnamon Press who make the difficult parts of publication a pleasure and who are always a joy to work with.

Also by Jody Cooksley

The Glass House

What is a life without Art and Beauty?

Not one that Julia chooses to live. And so she searches the world for both, discovering happiness through the lens of a camera.

A fictional account of pioneer photographer, Julia Margaret Cameron, and her extraordinary quest to find her own creative voice, The Glass House brings an exceptional photographer to life.

9 781788 649438